PATH OF THE PIÑON

RON KING AND LINDA KING

Illustrations by Timothy Montain King

Color Edition

Sift Solutions   Lake Vallecito, Colorado

This edition was prepared for publication by
Ghost River Images
5350 East Fourth Street
Tucson, Arizona 85711
www.ghostriverimages.com

To communicate with the author
contact us at
info@siftsolutions.com

Cover design by R. L. King

COLOR EDITION
ISBN: 978-1-7372718-0-2

Library of Congress Control Number: 2021914005

Published in the United States of America

August, 2021

A print version of this book containing B&W images is also available with ISBN 978-1-7372718-3-3.

And a Kindle ebook version with ISBN 978-1-7372718-1-9, as well as an Epub version with ISBN 978-1-7372718-2-6 are also available, both with color images.

Dedicated to Woof who walked many of the same
trails and felt the beauty and ferocity of Mountain
under a large table rock at an early age.

PROLOG

New Mexico has been a well-known magnet for mystery and for blending the curious with the commonplace. Ancients were attracted and found it a welcoming location to settle and leave their obscurities. It drew artists like Georgia O'Keefe following the legendary light, Spanish conquistadors like Coronado searched for the fabled seven cities of gold, and Billy the Kid and Jesse James were attracted to the lawlessness. Scientists gathered, exposing secrets of the atom and harnessing magical and deadly energies. Radio astronomy dishes were assembled and searched the universe for signs of intelligent alien life. And not to be forgotten, the most famous UFO crash site in the world at Roswell was also recorded in the Land of Enchantment.

But the commonplace is a good place to start. One of my grandparents, Pete, was a sheepherder. Successful sheepherders had no need for bulky muscles, social skills, rudimentary education or basic language abilities, yet few could do the job. It was an art to control range sheep single handedly without the aid of fencing or corrals. A good herder had to constantly guard against predators like mountain lions, eagles, bobcats, wild dogs, wolves, coyotes, bears and humans. They had to keep their herds moving to fresh water and good grazing without dogging their sheep by overuse of their canine helpers.

Although the right clothing, equipment and experience could help the young herders withstand the physical elements, nothing would prepare them for the lonesome desolation many experienced. They were often struck with "sagebrush fever" and were soon reduced to shy quivering personalities. Many found the use of alcohol or drugs a relief. Some did not.

Generally through history when a herder left the corrals for the open range with his sheep the controlling powers were natural. However after the turn of the 20th century in the Southwest, human follies followed them along as well.

Control was the major issue in the Southwest Territories after the Mexican American War ended in 1848. More than fifty years later the people, rangeland, and old Spanish Land Grants were still up for grabs. There were those politically connected in Washington DC who took advantage of the situation until statehood.

In the early twentieth century there were the cowboys and homesteaders, Indians or indigenous natives from both sides of the border, Mexican poor or pawns (peons), Anglo and Mexican politicians, the Catholic Church wanting to keep control of the schools, German spies, Spanish Nobles, rich U.S. businessmen and land barons or those who wanted to be, and guerillas who would ride freely with familiar names like Francis "Poncho" Villa. Some of the fiercest fighting Indian tribes were under great pressure to relinquish lands. Under future statehood, there was to be yet another set of circumstances. At one point some said the US should start another war with Mexico and let the Mexicans win, forcing them to retake the entire mess.

The politically well-connected were dealing the cards at the power poker game. Life expectancy in the southwest was noticeably decreasing.

Book I

Reality Doesn't Bend to Our Beliefs.

<u>DISCLAIMER</u>

Check your beliefs here before turning the page. No one sees reality without looking, outside the mind. Information contained herein is not intended to keep you alive when living in Nature's domain. Any efforts to connect or communicate with Universe, Mountain, Tree, or follow the breadcrumbs in Forest are done at your own risk.

"When we try to pick out anything by itself, we find it hitched to everything else in the Universe." John Muir

Chapter 1 - Early 1900's Aztec, New Mexico Territory

He had seen the Wolfboy Pete, but only from a distance. The priest in his unabashed manner, gazed on the nimble wild boy.

Pete was eye candy for those lucky enough to glimpse the poetic agility of the untamed soul.

The teen stole a peek at the well-known priest, far too fast for the ordinary eye. Using senses without mind-chattering words the Wolfboy wondered, *is this man to be avoided?*

Pete and the priest were each at the top of their game, but in different domains. Each had a distinctly different mystique. Animals were charmed when Pete looked their way. Peasants lit up in the presence of Father Greggory.

Father Greggory, known as Padre to most, was unable to catch, let alone maintain the attention of Pete. It grated on his pride. He knew he couldn't reach for the Wolfboy's hand as he would an ordinary parishioner, and expect the return of all fingers.

Padre was a young good-looking priest barely to his twenty sixth year. He was better than six feet two inches in height with a well-defined jaw and soft brown eyes. He enjoyed physical games exhibiting his athletic physique. His dark brown wavy hair was shoulder length and the perfect frame for his eyes. He oversaw the orphanage and school and was taking over pastoring the church in Aztec in the New Mexico Territory in the early 1900's. He was upwardly mobile, had more ego and ambition than a small town church could contain, with an extremely competitive nature.

He developed a youth cross country team challenging other towns in competitions. He had two boys thought to be the fastest in the distance runs in the Territory and maybe in the States. *Could Pete be tamed and trained to run a course?*

• • •

Pete was on the prowl for goodies watching parishioners exiting mass. Padre was greeting and thanking each for attending as they left the church.

The youth slid out of hiding to follow the sweet smell of ginger. Padre swiftly positioned himself on a log upwind of Pete's route, wafting a gingerbread cookie in the air.

The good Padre had planned the entire incident and knew most of all not to crowd. Sharp green eyes blending with the leaves focused on the cookie, then Padre. *This man makes traps and games.* Pete turned and trotted away. Father Greggory sat patiently waiting, waving the cookie like a white flag of surrender. The smell of ginger, honey, and molasses would not leave the teen's nose alone.

Nearby brush provided adequate cover should the wary teen decide to approach unnoticed. *Be patient and let the sugar do your bidding. Let the young one gain confidence.*

A quick moving hand snatched the cookie, leaving Padre with nothing but air between two fingers. Pete twisted out of a nearby bush and waved the cookie in one hand while pointing to it with the other. Padre returned an accommodating nod.

He saw Pete as a young male with fairytale majesty. He had an interest in young teen males and their newly-established puberty. He stayed in self-denial about it and kept their company never having taken advantage of any young teen. But there were those who would use his fascination in teen males against him if given the chance.

• • •

After several more gingerbread meetings, Padre enticed Pete to watch his magic tricks. He played games with Pete as he did with younger children, pulling a coin from behind an ear that had magically disappeared from his hand. He later made it vanish again. He had the youth point to an obvious fist only to show it empty to enthusiastic wild eyes.

Padre was totally immersed in the Wolfboy. He wanted to feel the touch of the wild one. *I won't do anything improper.*

Pete in time came near with a pointing finger to the clenched hand of the priest containing a coin. He moved slightly and bumped the Wolfboy's finger.

With that first contact he let Pete win the game and the coin. *Only a small touch and just the tip of a finger.* The priest continued always giving the Wolfboy control and confidence. *This youth smells like a pinch of piñon wrapped in a wisp of smoke.* Gestures and body language remained their main means of communication and the electricity grew.

When he turned his easygoing earthy eyes toward Pete, the wild green eyes became a pool without a ripple of resistance. Pete held his gaze and raised him a smile, receiving a warm chuckle in return.

• • •

Father Greggory was a man of many gifts. He had obvious people perceptivity. He was academically at the top of his class in theological studies, clinical psychology, languages and child development. His warmth and accepting smile was always a welcome gift. His air of superiority was easily earned because he had never been bested. His ego was bigger than his smile.

Pete had no perception of ego and it came across as uncommon confidence. In the world of town Padre could be trusted to bridge the gaps.

On short walks Pete would lean down and smell the lower bushes and tall grass to "see" what had passed by. Padre's first verbal question "Can you tell me about the scent you smell?" He received a shrug for an answer.

He captivated the imagination of the wild teen with finger games imitating the coyote and raven. A good finger won a skirmish with a bad thumb which brought a throaty giggle. His steady charming manner mixed well with his charisma and good looks.

Eventually they played hide and seek both verbally and physically. Padre would say the word for an object in English and Spanish then hide one half of a sweet-smelling cookie near the object. Pete found them without difficulty with an acute sense of smell. The second half of the cookie was awarded if the word of the object was correctly repeated in both Spanish and English.

It thrilled Padre to see Pete progress under his tutelage. However he soon learned Pete never reiterated a word unless the wily one was to be rewarded. If he didn't have cookie aroma floating from his pocket, Pete wouldn't play the game his way. Ever. Sometimes Pete would imitate a jay or squirrel instead of repeating the sounds of words. It was obvious to Padre the wild teen would not easily bend to his rules.

• • •

Pete took Padre to a favorite place outside of town. It was a well-hidden old cliff cave dwelling with artifacts scattered about. The only entry was with a ladder. The teen was captivated with the essence of the Ancients in this place. Pete made hand motions about four feet above the ground as if it was a smoothing motion to take the wrinkles out of an invisible bedspread. In unnerving gravelly tones the words "whouden" and "lost" were repeated several times. *This man likes words. He'll be pleased.*

Padre's ego grew two sizes with Pete's invitation showing him a favorite place. He did have a strong academic interest in the archeology and the natural setting. His ear was tuned to the eerie sounds outside made by the breeze while he closely examined old pot chards. However he had no connection to the energy left by the Lost at Whouden.

Pete took his response as positive and pleasing. The day brought something new for Padre to experience.

Padre could sense the spiritual connection in Pete to this place and was put off by it. It was a sin to his mind. Unsurprisingly Padre preferred the devout Biblical experience. He wanted Pete to be attracted to him, Christ and scripture. He'd work on the order later.

Seldom was Pete mistaken on how to interpret body language. This time was the exception. Maybe the odd breezes blowing in Wolfboy's innards when around this man were the cause.

Where the teen had come from there were no majestic mountains. There were many new things to drench a ravenous curiosity in this part of the country including this man of robes and odd aromas.

Body language and the presence exhibited by all things were closely watched and felt by Pete. There were obvious differences in a wolf's mood with his ears back or pointing forward. In the same way there were dissimilar energies connected with cloud constructions and movement. Mountain's formation and posture against the sky were also important. The dark wet cloud could be worn like a robe by Mountain in a ceremonial way. When this happened it was best the passerby heed the importance.

• • •

Experience was key to Pete and was dominant. To Pete, Padre's religion was like rules to a game. Something they both could choose to play, or not.

Padre used words or language as in the Bible and they were central. He would give sermons in a church built by people. He convinced people of the existence of the Creator or God and made them believers in his way of thinking. Teachings like the Trinity for example all stemmed from words and required scholarly perceptions and beliefs. Pete's teachings came from more earthly beginnings.

Due to the way Pete was raised, Pete's survival depended heavily upon being acutely aware and outside the mind's distracting fears, babbling and beliefs. Pete lost the connection to the Creator and Universe when near humans, their beliefs and edifices. Humans built structures whether it be houses, churches or organizations that literally shut out natural creation. Roofs block sun and stars, walls the fresh breezes.

Near the end of Padre's visit to the ancient dwelling Pete got a faraway gaze, made hand gestures overhead, twisting one arm around another like a snake around a pole and squeezed. Then the teen reached down and picked up Padre's cross embedded in the dirt floor and handed it to him. Padre touched his chest where the cross had been. *Must have been a coincidence.* Pete was happy to have baffled Padre. It was a return volley for his confusing coin. But to Padre's large ego, it was perplexing the teen had fooled him.

• • •

Padre tried to communicate the Bible to Pete. The young teen could tell by his manner and body language it was important so stayed with his every word and gesture.

The focused attention gave him hope Pete could understand. There were often hand signals and silences mixed with words to further the conversation. His attempt fell short of his goals.

First Pete thought God would hand out evil which made no sense. God as the Creator would be the glue holding everything together. Evil was something contrary to order and the living organism, Universe.

Next the good priest tried to explain why one should not kill a fellow human regardless of the circumstances. His reasoning was humans were not capable of making such decisions on good and evil and that should be left to God. Good would eventually win out over the long run.

To Pete, that left the wicked or evil ones to do the choosing, killing and breeding over the near term leaving only them to populate the earth. If the good people didn't band together many would be lost in the struggle over the short run. Definitely not to the advantage of Universe.

• • •

"Pete, please come out and run on our cross country team." He made motions like running in place. Pete ran in place with a large grin. *This is STUPID.*

Seeing Pete's reaction he continued. "You make sure no one is ahead of you at the finish line."

Pete gave a negative shrug of disinterest. "For no thing?"

"Yes."

"No law?"

"No, for fun. Does it sound like fun?"

"No."

"No?"

"Pete like wind. Get sheep."

"You feel wind running, yes. And this is the same as getting sheep. Except they are not sheep, they are like you. Maybe even better."

"Me?"

"Maybe faster."

A doubting competitive shake of the head was thrown back at Padre. There may not be racing anytime soon but Padre saw what might motivate Pete.

• • •

Both Padre and Pete would try to catch the other off guard in friendly rivalry. No one was better at a physical game of quick reactions than Pete. The adolescent had the heart of a warrior. Placing his palms on top of the teen's *… There is nothing improper touching hands in this game of quick hands…* he tried to remove either before getting the backs of his hands slapped. He never won a game.

When Pete's hands were on top, Padre continued his losing streak by always missing as Pete's hands moved out of his reach before he could curl his hands over to make the strike. *I do like the warmth I feel from those hands.* When he was given an advantage of a head start, he couldn't win that way either. When he tried to cheat and hit before the game was to start, he remained the loser. All good fun for Pete and captivating for the competitive Padre.

Some of Pete's boundless abilities in the physical world were disquieting. Birds came under Pete's direction to land on Padre's finger. The teen could predict a gust of wind before it shook the trees. At the least it appeared that way. *Of course these are tricks as I know tricks. My coins were hidden between my fingers. I will add these tricks to my list to one day learn, once we can communicate better in words.*

• • •

After a couple weeks Padre finally won a game but at great cost. Pete promised a gift of a newly carved cross if Padre could win a game of sneaking up unnoticed. Pete waited for his arrival ready to spring from a clump of greenery. The smell of his scented cassock close to a half mile away provided plenty of time for Pete to pee.

Unknown to Pete, Father Greggory had placed his incense-spiced cassock on a bush. He had taken a bath and done laundry, all without soap, thereby leaving no soap aroma. The wind was strong and gusty making hearing nearly impossible. He took even more care to approach from downwind. Thus he caught Pete with her pants down.

He gasped and stood dumbfounded, mouth open. *What? Pete is NOT a boy. A GIRL.* As the facts soaked in he lowered himself to his knees upset at the discovery. Pete gave him a pat on the head which was out of character for her but she could feel his emotional turmoil. She added words that would surely help this man who seemed to like them so much, "itsa no thing, nada".

He avoided eye contact. Clearly not confident body language. How could the all-knowing Padre not accept a natural event like peeing? All quite distressing to Pete.

Padre saw Pete upset putting him more on the defensive. It was a tipping point in their relationship. Nothing had prepared either for the sudden changes.

He hadn't realized how attracted he was to the young teen male. *But her?* The images and feelings from the other teens came rushing back and they were boys. His denial was front and center.

Clearly a sign from God. He could not remember any person challenging him as she did. *She is a youngster. Maybe it wasn't God but the Devil who did this to me. Maybe her trick with the bird or wind or knowing when I would move my hand before I did was dark magic and the Devil's doing.* His mind was clear he could stay in control with adequate prayer. *But are there enough prayers and hours in the day?*

Pete was a lost soul, then a young vibrant sensual savage teen. The fairy-tale creature was bewitching in an exhilarating way. In reality she had not changed. He had. A murky muddle weighed on him constantly. He was the cat chasing its tail never knowing it was firmly attached. To him.

• • •

The loss of control in any relationship was totally new to the young Padre. He saw his reflection in a reality mirror held up by Pete and it was not a pretty sight. The irrationality was bewildering. Padre had a shadow or dark side he did not want to acknowledge, and it therefore ruled him.

A day passed, then two. Padre's thoughts raged on. The age difference was not unheard of at the time but he had his vows. *Why do I have these feelings? Be gone!* It became more difficult to retain the objectivity necessary for his position. Pete's physical feminine lure did not pass but bit into him more. It was the classical battle of good and evil.

Pete had a blissful feeling and was not prone to overthinking anything. Because of her childhood experiences she could purely experience without judgments or thought. Therefore she too was blindsided.

The Church at the time was in the process of accepting women as an equal but not all had the belief suffrage was a good idea. This made the gender more vulnerable and less equal under Padre's evolving beliefs.

He dizzily spun around; beautiful and wild, male and female, angelic, sinful then demonic, followed quickly by his conscientious pursuit of his duties as a spiritual leader.

The attraction had his mind twisting like a dust devil in his daily duties. Around and around, tighter and tighter, faster and faster the doors opened and shut. *What insanity.*

• • •

There was to be a music festival in town. *I will find Pete and invite her. Town is my domain. Here she will respect me and my position as others do.* Padre could not locate her and no one had seen her. *I might see Pete at the festival anyway.*

Musicians came with varying talents from the surrounding area. Most of the performers were singing and playing with high energy and rhythm.

• • •

Pete watched and felt the lively tunes from her typical vantage point around groups of people; hiding and by herself. She saw Padre looking for something. She paid him no mind. Late in the evening as the mood softened, she listened to a fascinating melody driving her with an uncontrollable fancy.

A solo guitarist put music in the air as entrancing as a butterfly's flight. She came from the shadows to Padre's side and sampled his hand with the same touch the music was giving her. She let his hand slide then danced around him in the evening air. She moved with natural perfection and smelled as wild as she was. She had never felt the unwavering attention he was showering on her. It was unlike any experience she had ever had. It was enchanting for them both. When the last light note drifted into the night air, she followed it like a shadow.

• • •

Parishioners saw his duties falter. Pete was taking their spiritual leader's attention from them. A few parishioners showed jealousy.

Pete viewed her own beauty through the eyes of the town's people. It wasn't her reflection in a still pond made of light. It was a likeness of their thinking. All quite different from what she received from the natural realm.

There was no question Father Greggory was now possessed by Pete the girl. The attraction became steadfast. He was like the drunk confronted with a light pole. He couldn't put it behind him.

He had all the psychological training to manipulate her and not the other way around …*unless she had the help of the Devil.* He wavered between seeing her a sexy wench, part savage, part goddess, to a demon. *Why didn't I see her lovely feminine smile in the beginning? Unless it was a demon.*

• • •

With his loss of control and bearings he became antagonistic towards her. She intruded on his dreams verifying his obsession about her demonic powers. *Maybe if she wed, the evil demon possessing her might lose his grip. What confusion the she devil is causing me.*

Father Greggory left all his training behind. He clearly pushed her away as he had no control over what she was doing to him. He told Pete she shouldn't be defensive or feel singled out as he treated all the same. She easily saw the lie and it cut deeper. *This man is made of crumpled leaves.*

He acted out his hostility. He confronted Pete about her source of demonic power. Pete's answer was a simple question. "God no goot on demons?"

That's it of course. I will exorcise Pete's demon. I need to get Pete's permission and she practically gave it to me with her question. God is good at getting rid of demons. His Bishop would clear the exorcism. Pete was well known for her peculiar powers.

As he waited for the Bishop's review, he increased his prayer frequency. It helped as he expected. Father Greggory's questions were relentless, along with his prayers. *My God, have You forsaken Me? Was not Jesus questioning his faith on the cross? Or is she sent to help me? Surely if I have faith, all will work out well. Have I hurt a lovely natural magical girl with these thoughts of demons? Do these demons originate from my fears or are they indeed as real as the Devil himself? Please God, give me a sign.*

He would not forsake his vows. He knew normal powers of the flesh were consuming. But the pressures took their toll. *This control she has over me could not possibly be normal.*

• • •

Padre had more on his plate than working with Pete. He was upwardly mobile and politically motivated in his behind the scenes activities. He wanted to control all the education in all the parishes. Before Pete had entered his life turning him on his head he saw a path unfolding giving him the power to use his God-given talents.

He fantasized himself the governing power behind the weak minded American politicians. He saw they wanted the prestige and the corrupt money inherent in the existing politics of children and education. Padre wanted complete autonomy over the schools, the souls and the purse. And if he did the bidding of the DA, he would be given the keys.

Chapter 2 – District Attorney Wagner

District Attorney Wagner had friends in high places which was the source of his power. Blind men saw the DA as shady and he didn't care. It wasn't slyness and cunning but sheer power and control through his political connections that brought his wealth and position. His expertise was pressure and he took full advantage.

The DA elbowed his way to the top without strengthening or contributing to those around him. His main skill was intimidation causing pain and suffering along his way.

He was the biggest braggart in the New Mexico Territory hoping no one would notice the man behind the lies. As long as he could stay hidden from his insipid self he loved every minute he got in front of the public mirror.

• • •

The DA walked down the center of Main Street in Aztec waving to people like a one-man parade. He seldom came to this small northern town in the Territory until recently when legal issues with an old Spanish Land Grant forced him here.

To his left were a few children playing. Ahead of the DA was one of his German Shepard guard dogs. In front of the dog were two bodyguards swinging their heads ready for anything. One of the small children ran toward the DA and the bodyguard straight-armed the crying child to keep the path clear. The mother was quick to whisk the youngster out of the way.

The DA had red hair and a bloodshot flat face like a squashed toad. His eyes dangled like tiny black buttons close to the bridge of his nose giving him a disturbed appearance. He was a mouth breather which kept his full lips puffing. His midsection draped over his shoes as did the length of his cigar. His self-importance hung in the air as he passed by.

His bodyguards wore long black riding coats split up the back. The tails of their coats would whirl out in the wind like dervishes as they twisted around to watch for ever-present dangers. The DA would point, and the bodyguards would bring it or chase it, as need required.

District Attorney Wagner made a show of his donations to charity such as the local Catholic orphanage. They were as self-serving as his dervishes.

At the end of town and his parade the DA made a motion with his two hands, fingers interlaced out from of his overhanging belly. One of the dervishes had a saddle horse ready and by his side before the DA could pull his hands apart. The bodyguard boosted him up and put his feet in the stirrups. The DA waved a final goodbye to nobody in particular and rode out of town.

• • •

Pete was at the focal point of many a tale. Due to her wild manner and wearing furs a wolf came to mind. Thus the tag Wolfboy had been attached. Some saw her pointing to the heavens and made the connection to alien beings giving her special powers. Some stories originated from people the DA tended to believe. With the right supervision the DA could sell Pete or the Wolfboy's abilities to the highest bidder.

He took notice of Padre's interest in the lad and the teen's weakness for Padre. The DA had pushed Padre to manage Pete which intensified the pressure on the relationship. Padre had to regain the upper hand somehow.

Another issue Padre might prove useful was the DA's takeover of an old Spanish Land Grant. The sheriff had turned squeamish about kicking the owner off the prettiest and most productive rancho in the Territory. The Rancho had been in the owner's family for nearly three hundred years. He'd deal with the sheriff in good time but for now he was looking for alternatives that might include Padre in case the sheriff took too long.

The DA would pressure Padre and lean on Padre's Bishop to do the same. Padre, being young, inexperienced, and upwardly mobile in the Church, would become frazzled. Perfect. The Rancho and Pete would be in his pocket one way or another.

• • •

The smell of cronyism from Anglos in Washington DC permeated the air in the New Mexico Territory. All knew it wouldn't last forever, yet it lingered. The Church control of the schools for example, could only be held permanently if either the land was returned to Mexico or possibly through statehood. Statehood could allow Church control through private individuals favorable to Church ideology on schoolboards but it may not be permanent, nor would it happen any time soon.

In the interim DA Wagner was looking the other way as schools by law were to be free of religious control in the Territory. Public funds could be used to pay Catholic teachers but not Catholic schools. However he had legal flexibility in the timetable the Church schools were to be closed. He allowed the schools to remain under Church control as long as Padre fell into line.

If the sheriff wanted to keep his job he had to toe the line with District Attorney Wagner. DA Wagner knew to stay in good stead with the Surveyor General in the Territory as well as a few well-placed senators in Washington DC. They in turn had to play nice with some other unnamed but powerful people known to some as powerbrokers up in a cloud somewhere. These powerbrokers didn't have titles or notoriety. But all knew water ran downhill from those same clouds. And those not involved with the making or enforcing of the laws such as the local Madam, got the worst of it.

• • •

Padre felt the burden of his recent realizations with Pete from morning until night. Add to that the escalating pressures from both District Attorney Wagner and his Bishop concerning the politics of control in the schools, and he lost all equilibrium.

Padre was to also help the District Attorney, the Surveyor General and several senators in their takeover of the old Spanish Land Grant in the northern part of the New Mexico Territory. The Rancho had more than 44000 acres, twenty three outbuildings and a river running through it with all water rights. Grazing rights existed on many hundreds of thousands of acres to the upper slopes of the Continental Divide.

Prior to the auction and sale, notification was done in a legal manner but not in such a way the rightful owner would be well advised of his rights. The documents had been approved by cronies in Washington DC. The winning bidder was Southwest Ranches, Inc. a company with 70% of the stock controlled by the District Attorney Wagner and the remaining stock owned by his cronies who aided in the theft. The DA had spent but a few pennies per acre after deducting his legal fees from the price.

Physical possession was the remaining sticking point. Descendants had lived on the Rancho for hundreds of years. If the DA couldn't get the old owners off before statehood, those squatters as he called them, would get their day in court. A state court instead of his friends in the Federal Court system. Victory by a court's decision was more certain when the court was controlled by him or his cronies in DC. Since the DA was spending enough time in the little town to be sure he could finalize the transfer, he thought it prudent to set up a small office in the local courthouse.

• • •

Now it was a matter of pressuring the sheriff to enforce the law. So far the sheriff was dragging his feet for several reasons. First, the DA had a personality that was repulsive to all who knew him. A second and more persuasive legal argument was the sheriff knew the federal courts were being pressured by the cronies in DC who put their fingers on the scales of justice when approving the procedures and documents. A third reason was Señor Perez, who controlled the old Land Grant, was the architype of what the law is here to protect. Lastly the sheriff knew that good men would be killed on both sides if he went out and tried throwing the old owner off his land.

The DA's court-approved documents were disgusting to any lawman who believed in the sanctity and fairness of the legal system. If Washington DC could put fingers on the scales of justice when approving the DA's documents, the sheriff felt justified and compelled to tip the scales back in the direction of Señor Perez.

• • •

Señor Perez, or Señor as he was called, was steadfastly in control of the old Spanish Land Grant even with trying circumstances. First there was the strange disappearance of his son and daughter-in-law two years earlier. His wife had died from what appeared to be natural causes. Then one of the top hands in his cattle operation had been killed by Indians. Last year his grandson, Juan, had gotten into Chinese opiates and alcohol. All attempts thus far had failed to free Juan including putting him up the mountain as a sheepherder far from any source of drugs. He continually slid further from his duties and the ranching business.

• • •

The DA's condescending tone pressuring Padre squawked in the priest's ears. "Padre we need some help. We both know people would be better off with the schools run by the Church but I can't look the other way forever. Do you understand what I am saying?"

Padre only gave a nod in response while Jeremiah 12:1 rang in his ears. *Wherefore doth the way of the wicked prosper?*

The issue of the wicked escaping for a time unscathed has often been raised. Most recently by Pete.

Chapter 3 – Path of the Piñon

Pete became jumbled and physically ill with all the human clutter surrounding her. Padre's sudden reversal was the pack that broke the donkey's back. She tried to leave but couldn't go far from town without feeling nausea and confusion. She saw him around town which was both a blessing and a curse.

Again Padre tried to convince Pete this should all be dismissed. She should focus on running a race on his cross country team and being in his flock. "Pete you have nothing to worry about. I have no special feelings for you other than what I have for all of my flock. I think we can be the best of friends, you'll see."

Pete gave a wag of her head while turning. Padre grabbed for her arm. Her knife was out and against his wrist before his fingers made contact. Her blade had spoken drawing a trickle of blood. *You think on this.*

Without knowing it rationally, she had a school girl's crush on someone who shoved her callously away. She had not realized she was only another sheep in his flock. She a sheepherder after all.

• • •

She had not been raised on fairy tales and princes. Her true love was freedom and beauty within nature. She had no idea of the powers she wielded nor did she consciously want such influence. It was a genetic response at a cellular level of being attracted to this man. She had a giddy feeling in her gut and she responded to it. It was akin to freedom. And yet the repercussions were quite different.

She could read flora and fauna without any doubts. These two leggeds were not like either. She sought healing within nature after being pushed outside. Again.

• • •

Pete sensed the riddles in the way trees communicated. On a walk in an assembly of piñon and a few oak south of town she felt *go and leave the trees but never leave the forest.*

She turned and waited. There was nothing. Nothing always spoke loudly to Pete. Her five senses shut down for a few moments and she opened every pore for more. A dominant knurly piñon easily engaged her.

The piñon stood for the others with roots mingled underground. They gave energy and nutrients to their guide tree through a maze of complex root systems as a beehive might feed the queen. The piñon in turn returned life to the hive. The remaining trees faded as Pete and the piñon connected.

The knurly piñon did not give pause as these things used no time.

Pete measured the riddle but not in words. A place she had never been

was pulling her. It was high in the mountains above the tree line. An image crossed her senses. *Deeper into the mountains and further away from people I will go. Where trees are sparse above timberline, and plentiful below. Nearby flowers will keep me company. Mountain will be my ally to filter and cleanse, far and away, high in the Rockies.*

Pete was accustomed to these natures. They were completely void of human thought, emotions and personality.

The prominent piñon pine took something from her. She felt it leave. And then nothingness.

The void lasted three days but she had no sense of this time. During these changes she ate a few piñon nuts and drank plenty of fresh water without remembering anything until she felt a rejuvenation filling her neglected consciousness.

A revitalized spirt was returned. *My naturalness is ready.* It did however bring with it a caveat from Piñon. She was to accept more human interaction and not run from it. There were those who needed her abilities and natures. *More? Ok, if I must. I will follow your path and join with any in need on the way.* She gave thanks and felt humility.

She would recognize the place on Mountain by her naturalness. Mountain would reconnect her to Universe. Mountain was a special part of earth having been pushed up by forces larger than the earth itself. Wellbeing would touch her. She was to make herself an earth bed in Mountain by digging a channel of length and width accommodating her size. She was then to fill the trench by lying down and dragging the leaves and materials back over herself.

Piñon knew best how to use Mountain and the earth as they worked together. Piñon trees were well connected to the soil on many levels and always left the earth better for having lived in it. A night in her mountain womb would complete Piñon's work.

The giddy feeling she had while with Padre severed her attachment to Universe. She had done and felt inane dumb things. A lesson learned.

Padre may have had a similar experience but made no admission to her if it were true. Her path was chosen by Piñon with the necessary intention.

Chapter 4 - Pete's Reflections Written Years Later From Her Memory of the Times

I had been tortured by Padre. Actually I allowed the torture because I liked it in the beginning. I dove in the honey and never mind the bees. The attraction snuck up like a cougar. I felt alive and dizzy at the same time.

It was ridiculous considering a priest had rules. I know today. They were insider rules so I'm not sure they would have meant much if I did know at the time. Sex never entered my mind but a lot of other stuff did. Always in the mind. Good place to add and subtract but not much good for anything else. I learned this from Mountain.

I wanted to touch him. What inviting deep brown eyes. Eventually I read stories about Cinderella and the prince. For a short time I liked being human and not just watching them from my perch.

Padre had a way. I was hooked. Like a fish wiggling on a line. I wanted to get away and be pulled in, both at the same time. I loved it. I loved loving it. What a wonderful sickness. Universe was reduced to only me and those feelings. But it was dangerous disconnecting from reality the way my life was then.

I got all messed up. It was tough to swallow like an old rabbit. I chewed and chewed then one day I had to swallow the truth.

The more I denied the facts the more I had to go into my head and leave reality outside. Eventually I understood. I missed the truth. I missed the connection to reality and the natural Universe to the extent it wiggled its way back where it belonged.

My naturalness won regardless of what I thought. I was human. Two arms, two legs and hair on my body instead of scales or feathers. I had to accept the truth to be free. Which by the way, is the hardest part for me and being human.

I think love is real and I'm glad we get to have it. But my feelings needed to be supervised when around two leggeds. What I had was not love but a bowl of good-looking fruit. I now expect these emotions from time to time and enjoy them like licking an ice cream cone. Know it's going to melt and not last forever no matter what the storybooks say. Take what you get when you get it. Easy.

• • •

Those first weeks after leaving Karl's ranch I traveled far and fast. I felt the earth spinning beneath my feet and the wind in my face. I couldn't get enough of the freedom and choices laid out before me. At the top of every hill and around each bend there were always more unknowns. Universe stretched in all directions.

My skin would open up like petals and fill with sun and freedom. This flowing energy fed my naturalness which made me more connected to Earth. I never tired of the life of travel and the challenges of finding a good camp and gathering food. I found other things that also grabbed me.

I avoided people for a while as they seemed to spoil both the freedom and the landscape. It was before I knew many words so I didn't have a way of relating to those who did look inviting.

It should have been easy being with my own kind, but it was not.

Chapter 5 – Journey from Karl's Ranch

The first day Pete was away from Karl's ranch was early March. It would take nearly three months before she met Padre in Aztec. Her teachings would continue as they had for many years but now they came from Universe instead of Selina.

On the third day she was greeted by the sun dawning on new land and a promise she didn't have to travel this trail again except by choice.

It was then Pete's liberation hit her core. Her body was filled with the primordial music produced when unconditional freedom is first experienced. She was free as the breeze in the trees. She had a sense of weightlessness her insides couldn't contain.

Flight was something she often copied with her body language. She stretched her arms out when she saw a bird or butterfly and flew in spirit with those who could defy gravity. And for the first time in her life Pete felt as though she could fly.

Early the third afternoon Pete slowed to a walk. She found a small stream. A female mallard left her some space. Trout were feeding. Sage grouse, rabbit, firewood, building materials for a camp all were close by.

She touched her bare foot into the cool creek water. She got down in a push up position and touched her lips to the surface. She was comfortable here, far from Karl's ranch. She would take time to get a good meal and well-deserved bath.

She collected a few sticks of firewood and found a plant she recognized. She dug the root out of the ground with one of the sticks of firewood. She crushed the root between two rocks leaving two small pulverized pieces of root.

Pete walked to a pool formed by a large rock jutting into the creek. She stripped then scrubbed her underclothes with the root. She rinsed her clothes and put them on a nearby rock.

She took the remaining piece of root and rubbed it into her hair and over her body. She leaned back in the pool letting the stream rinse away the day. She grabbed her clothes and drip dried on her way back to camp.

• • •

Pete's ranch life gave her the realism animals were food or otherwise for the benefit of man. It also gave her a great respect for animals because without them survival would be far more difficult.

Both flora and fauna need water, food and air blurring the distinction between them. Plants didn't roam the barnyard but they were quick to bloom in good times and pass their will to live on to their seed. She noticed plants would happily feed upon dead animals as they became part of the soil, as naturally as the animals fed upon plants.

• • •

As she finished her meal of grouse eggs and trout given up by a friendly stream, she noticed a spider in its nest rolling up its latest victim in its web. At that exact moment a wasp flew at the spider and knocked the spider from the web. The wasp quickly pounced and immobilized its prey. The image of predator becoming prey was not new to her but always hit close to home.

She went to the stream, picked some herbs, and put them in the bowl. A bee gathering pollen lifted off a yellow flower drawing her attention. She stopped and turned, tilting her head, nose high. She inhaled deeply sniffing the air.

There was a sweet smell beckoning. She left the creek weaving a little to the left, and back then to the right up a scent cone toward an old tree stump.

A few bees buzzed near the

old stump. She studied them a moment while they entered and exited a crack. She left only to return a short time later with some green stems smoldering from her fire. She smoked the outside of the hive by holding them near the crack in the stump setting off an alarm to the bees inside. They began to exit in a hurry, each busily carrying something. She stuck the smoking stems gently in the hive.

She withdrew the sticks, put her hand carefully into the hive taking care not to crush any bees, and pulled out a large handful of honeycomb. She lightly picked off a few honeybees. She took her first measured taste and let the sweetness soak into her tongue. Feeling great appreciation for the bees and their skills, she nodded at the hive and held her honeycomb high to show the sky and earth.

Pete traded labor in exchange for the honey. She built a better shelter from wind and weather for the beehive entrance with flat rocks found nearby. She took care to leave plenty of honey for those who had done the work and were more deserving.

She returned to the small fire with her bowl half full of water, herbs and honey. She vigorously licked her honey-soaked hand. She had two sticks flattened on the ends by whittling with her knife. She picked up three stones from the fire and placed them in her bowl to heat her tea.

A doe poked her head around a nearby bush to find Pete watching her in return. Pete made a little mew noise, the doe pulled back, and Pete gave a gravelly laugh. She took a sip of sweet tea.

After tea, Pete put on her coyote furs. The sky had changed its tune a little. She went to her sleeping area above the creek where she had already made her evening bed of dry leaves and grasses. She threw her knife and stuck it in the ground.

She lay down and squirmed her body burrowing and nearly disappearing in the leaves and rubble. She gazed up at the early evening stars with her knife visible and easily accessible by her head.

A bat dove and darted away. The evening noises of a screech owl looking for dinner and a frog croaking to a mate brought a grin. She snuggled down further and let sleep overtake her.

• • •

She had a quick breakfast of left-over dinner from the evening before. Raven was always ready to show her the day's direction and a greeting from the first rays of Sun. Pete jogged a rhythmic curving pattern with her purse strapped to her side. She stopped occasionally to reconnoiter but never to catch her breath.

She made five miles per hour with her traveling jog when terrain permitted. By midday she had generally gone about thirty miles and the heat would push her to look for shade and a good site for evening camp. The location would generally allow washing the day's sweat and dust away which meant she often would navigate near streams whether they were in accordance to Raven's instructions or not.

• • •

Open fields gave many opportunities to find small game. There was an abundance of food as winter's cold edge had passed. Her sling always carried as a headband made it easy to take game like rabbits, frogs or her favorite evening meal, grouse. After taking a rabbit she paused to give thanks.

She motioned her arm in a commanding fashion and the sky filled with a wave of monarch butterflies. They swirled around her and Pete with her entourage continued on together.

The spring runoff meant swollen creeks and rivers on occasion. She knew snowmelt waters could cause her body to stiffen or inhibit swimming altogether. She sometimes had to travel for miles before she found a safe place to cross to avoid hypothermia. This meant taking bridges and the possibility of meeting more people.

Cleanliness, food gathering, and setting up a good sheltered bed were always a priority. Bathing would keep her sleeping furs clean of the day's dirt. She had an old habit of brushing and picking her teeth with a crushed green twig before going to bed to round out her day's routine.

She had learned from Selina drinking water could be a source of sickness if not clean. It was more of a challenge to locate good drinking water with spring runoff. She would walk upstream a hundred yards to see if there was any loading or pollution from dead animals, beaver habitat, farm animals or humans. She sought crystal clear water with no source of contamination that had tumbled and bubbled for at least a hundred yards through sunlight and gravel.

Pete avoided camping too close to creeks or drainages as they were often followed by humans. Her fellow man was not as accustomed to navigating as she was without some definitive path. They often used these water trails to find their way and return without getting lost. Sleeping next to creeks was also generally avoided as they could swell and flood her bedding overnight.

Other things to avoid were starving mosquitoes, horse flies, deer flies, yellow jackets, storm drainages filling quickly with rain runoff, dead snags known as widow makers crushing those beneath them should they fall, and fresh signs of kill from large predators like bears, wolves or cougar. In general, poisonous snakes were not a problem as she avoided their habitats of good cover and warm places in the evenings near rocks. Later in the year however the snakes would be more active.

Firewood, small game and edible plants were more easily located along the drainages. She would pull what she needed from the creeks nearby and make a camp further uphill whether she saw signs of humans or not. Creek banks had bushes and grasses for making shelters, weaving mats and bedding. Creeks had fish or game attracted to the water. Lastly when in earshot they were good for Pete's inner self with their gurgling sounds and close connection to the origin of life.

When the elevation increased, the trees sucked up the sun's warmth like straws and the night air taught Pete to make her bedding warmer. This night dry rotting logs and dry moss made good insulation between her and the cooler night. By using a digging stick fashioned from a branch or bush she'd hollow out a trench within the dry rotting log and pile it on top of herself leaving only her head above ground level. Dry moss was also used to insulate and served as mosquito netting if placed over and around her head.

There were times when she had to accept the imperfect camp. But in general this was unlikely by starting to look early and avoiding situations not right with Universe. All of this prioritization was not done from a list or logically. It was a part of her natural connection.

• • •

She enjoyed the art displayed in nature. She would see pictures in rocks as she did the mobile of clouds in the sky. She carved the outline of a camp robber on a tree limb that finally brought a smile to her face.

She enjoyed rhythm and music wherever she encountered it. From water dripping, trees shushing, to the birds and four leggeds delivering their calls and songs.

Music was the first thing bringing her a little closer to human kind. A sound particularly taking her fancy was a banjo picker playing on his porch. He combined both rhythm and a catchy tune. She was careful as usual not to be seen by the player at least in the beginning. Soon she lost herself in the alluring music and pranced down the hill toward the banjo picker.

Her dance was without equal to anything he had ever seen. His music was unlike anything she had ever heard or felt. Playing on the natural stage in front of him was an interpretation of his music having the happy energy, beauty and passion without the benefit of professional choreography. He hooted at the young fur clad teen. He stomped and clogged with his eyes not wanting to miss a moment of what unfolded before him. She jumped lightly from one foot to the other and twisted from hands to feet.

When it came to an end she turned and gave thanks to the man with a nod of her head. And with a hop and a touch of her heels she was gone.

• • •

Pete was always up early and anxious to meet her day. Her skin was generally pink where it showed on her arms, face and lower legs those early spring mornings. Her breath was easily visible in the crisp early air as she jogged. One day melted into the next and her routine was set.

• • •

Pete crossed a river dragging her purse strapped to the top of a float made of smaller sticks and cattail reeds. Not long after the river crossing Pete saw a particularly odd trail or road with no use that she could see. A wagon or horseless carriage would not do well on it. There was no advantage to a horse either. There were two hard smooth metal borders that enclosed the bumpy road base. There was also a strange smell like a blacksmith's shop.

She had decided to jog nearby to keep an eye on the peculiar roadway. That afternoon she made a camp on a small hill between the river she crossed and the strange bumpy road. It wasn't long and she felt a rumbling and heard an unusual sound from a distance away. She stopped the gathering of firewood to find the source as it might satisfy her growing curiosity of what lived in this area.

A large black horseless contraption belching smoke and making loud clickity clacking sounds passed not far away. Two wagons were attached to it. One contained people easily visible inside. The vehicles had funny little designs on their sides.

The contraption was somehow balancing on the steel streamers bordering or holding the trail together. It had passed her position faster than anything on wheels she had ever seen. As the last vehicle slid by it acted like a curtain opening to reveal in the distance a large blue-grey mountain range dotted with snowcapped peaks.

When she was sure it wasn't coming back anytime soon she went down and touched the steel. She quickly jerked her hand back. She spread her hands apart bringing her ear to the metal. She smiled while she listened. Eavesdropping.

A slow lumbering tortoise about eighteen inches long came to her side.

The track proved to be too large a hurdle for stubby tortoise legs. The tortoise patiently waited. She picked up the dry land creature and crossed the tracks with him. She put him down aiming him away from the tracks. She nodded a goodbye to the tortoise as she had others. She looked to the mountain range and set her course. It must be the Rockies.

Chapter 6 - Mama Bear

Pete's enthusiasm grew with every step of her journey. Each day brought her more assurances and freedom. Her confidence did bring her some problems when it shadowed her awareness. There was a teaching waiting for her.

She was accustomed to not making noise when she traveled. There were many advantages to staying quiet as she moved through the landscape, not the least of which was avoiding human encounters and improving her hunting. Yet there were also disadvantages to a stealthy way of travel.

One morning she came across three young cub bears not long out of their winter den. They each bullied another while they growled and tumbled in play. Pete's sense of blissful freedom mixed with the light-hearted circus performance before her dulled her sense of awareness. She came back from her reverie when she felt the focus of something glaring down.

When two sets of eyes met it was like someone yelled GO in that mama bear's ear. The earth rumbled with 350 pounds of mama not twenty yards up the hill rolling swiftly down at her. A grunt came with every breath the mama exhaled. Pete felt

the fury behind those eyes anchored on her every move. She had agitated a large sow by coming unknowingly between her and her cubs. A bear blunder.

It could have been avoided with a

little extra noise on her travels or keeping her senses open to possible dangers. It was lesson time for Pete.

The bear's annoyance was obvious and no excuse was good enough. Fear and anger spit from her sagging lips and rage from her eyes as she quickly ate up ground toward Pete. Pete wanted to do her no harm with the three cubs still vulnerable but she also instinctively gave no ground to give the bear confidence to chase her down.

The mama bear crashed down at her like a rolling black boulder. The weight of claws and pads on the ground sent a wave up Pete's legs. Two leaning dead snags got in the bear's way. Not for long. The bear did not veer but went straight through them. Pete was next.

When the bear was less than ten feet away Pete grabbed a skinny tree trunk at her side and pulled hard. She reached up for two more handfuls of tree and hauled with all her strength. She dug the inside of her feet into the skinny trunk and pushed up to add more distance between her and the ground. She felt the flimsy tree start to bend as she neared the top.

The bear flew by Pete's perch with all intent on getting between Pete and those cubs. Pete had no more tree left or she would have used it.

Being a black bear and not a grizzly she could have easily climbed Pete's tree…. but she did not. She was content at keeping Pete in the tree and in no position to harm the cubs. Pete looked down and saw the morning breeze brushing the coat on the big mama bear's back. Pete smelled her angry breath from the wimpy tree.

Two cubs had started leaving the area but the third one was curious about the two legged in the tree. The third cub wasn't moving fast enough to suit mama bear. Mama did a quick whirl in the cub's direction and gave him a swat rolling him down the hill. The big sow then turned her attention back on Pete in the tree.

When all three cubs were out of sight and maybe in the next county the mama bear backed slowly away never easing her fixed gaze on the intruder. As Pete breathed some fresh air into her lungs, the irritated mama turned her back on her and followed after her cubs.

Pete realized her error but also knew it would likely happen again when she travelled silently through the woods. She dropped to the ground with a few scratches from branches and one to her pride.

She felt comfortable with the speed of her knife but if she ever had to use it on a charging bear there was a price to be paid. She also accepted the responsibility of raising the cubs if the mother was killed by her hand. Now those cubs could grow up as they should.

Pete's Reflections Written Years Later

I am curious and like discovery but I prefer to watch a mama bear and cub on my terms. Which means I like to see mama before I've upset her. Not afterward when she's running me up a tree like a silly squirrel. It's the same with people. Travel afforded me the space to approach people at my own pace. In the beginning for some reason it felt better to sneak up on them rather than have them come a visiting.

Chapter 7 - Wisdom

As she moved up in elevation she saw damage left by man. Large swaths of forest were leveled leaving only slash and ruts from the log removal. They had harvested timber as she had gathered grouse. Her affinity to trees brought sadness with the sight.

It opened her eyes when she saw natural devastation by fire, pine beetles or avalanche. The larger cycle of death and rebirth had to be realized irrespective of cause. In the blackened dismembered devastation left by lightning-caused forest fires she saw the dark gown of death leaving a trail of renewed space and energy for life. A realization came, spring follows winter.

Life's cycle was like the weather and she lived with it as a constant companion. In those areas where the forests had been struck whether it be by man or natural causes, she found a far greater bounty of life whether it be the little wild berries or the abundance of small game coming to dine as she did. The dark timber in need of clearing or thinning left little light for growth below.

Nothing is ever destroyed without birth or rebirth. If man was too stupid he might perish but Universe with Earth would remain. Humans would be pushed out to make space for something wiser and less harmful.

She saw where a clear-cut logged space had an advantage. It could prove as a firebreak and stop the advancement of forest fires regardless of cause. Man could help Forest and Trees could help Man if they worked together to inhibit runoff from damaging her drinking water in Creek.

These were not Pete's thoughts or ideas. They were more tangible like water and were brought to her by the creeks and rivers and returned to the clouds.

• • •

Pete walked carrying a rabbit in one hand outside her purse. She stopped and put her nose in the air. She backtracked four steps keeping her nose sniffing in the air and turned in a new direction. She weaved back and forth going down the scent cone. A ranch home appeared in the distance. Pete was in Focused Attention as she approached the home. It was a hyperawareness state developed years earlier to address concerning situations and now chocolate cake. Her highly tuned senses were supplemented beyond man's earthly awareness.

A cake with thick chocolate icing sat just inside a kitchen open window. The young teen's left hand reached up to the cake from below.

Pete brought a handful of chocolate cake and frosting down. She licked the chocolate from the back of her hand. Her ecstasy took control of her wits. She lifted the dead rabbit with her right hand up to the kitchen sill completing the trade and slipped away.

• • •

More elevation brought colder nights and the need to wear her heavy furs even though the weather had been good for springtime Rockies. She made thick beds of needles and aspen leaves over a layer of rocks warmed by the afternoon sun and her fires. The early morning chill got her up and started her day's travels.

The snow was receding leaving wildflowers and waterfalls. Every hill brought new wonder on the other side. She resisted stopping in the afternoons wanting to know what was around the next bend. But her realism gene

always won.

The mountains and valleys were stunning but they did give her a closed-in feeling if she never left the steeper drainages in the canyons. She learned to find places on ridges to give an inner feeling of space and freedom.

For someone from the plains, Divide Country was a magical place. But there was something more about the trees and mountains and animals. Something more powerful than she had experienced from the Plains. More welcoming.

A sunrise or sunset was always to her liking with the variety of light.

The distant peaks would open their eyes with a spotlight of morning sun from the east giving her a heady experience of optimism for the day's adventures. The shine from the ice and snowcapped peaks beckoned her forward and made every step a reward some would see as drudgery. By evening the sun on the other side of the Great Divide provided a simple silhouette marking the passing of another wonder-filled day. Not long after the mountains closed their eyes, Pete did the same.

Chapter 8 - Mountain

The higher altitude also brought more difficulty and slower travel for Pete. At one point she had sheer cliffs on both sides. In between was a raging creek and waterfall. It would take ropes, gear and skills she did not possess. The roar was deafening. In the shade was ice from the constant spray and cold temperatures. Her alternative would be to admit defeat, backtrack two days and take a more traveled route used by two leggeds. Her pride pushed her forward.

Raven kept to himself for the most part, leaving Pete to connect and stay aware. However here, he came close to opening his beak. He sat stoically awaiting her decision. If she moved up instead of down he was ready to squawk his piece and call her stupid. He ruffled his feathers against the cold misty air and waited. Pete didn't move up. But she didn't move back down either. And he waited.

She started up again and felt foolishness and pride. She stopped after two strides and tilted her head towards Raven. Raven slanted his shimmery wet head in return which answered her question. After a croak of relief he followed her down.

She went back to choose a different path up and it was more treacherous than the first. It took several hours of fighting Mother Nature for the insight; she was a guest and had no right of free passage. She would wait her time and let her legs lose the ropy rubbery feeling. She wasn't quitting or losing. She was listening to the teacher, Mountain.

Raven's can't smile but he had it written all over his feathered face. *Thank you Mountain.*

• • •

She sought lower elevations keeping to her journey south and west. The challenge once again pulled her upward to take another peek at God's creation looking down. Again she passed by the trees that marked the higher altitudes as she made a final push to make it over the top. Then the trees and vegetation thinned and there was nothing but rock. Scree slides were above her. Unsta-

ble and unsafe to climb. Beyond the scree was a granite cliff towering to the sky. The sun moved behind the cliff and the sky showed the day's high cirrus giving way to storm clouds.

A fallen log about four feet in diameter less than a mile back would be her refuge for the night. She wanted to be sure she wasn't caught part way up if a storm hit.

• • •

She made a lean-to shelter by the log. She piled more fresh green fir and spruce boughs than normal covering her bed with many layers.

Pete sat on a rock by her small fire and finished her tea. If you didn't know how to read a sky you could foretell the weather by Pete's body language. When she expected poor weather, she kept vigilant, constantly looking upward.

She removed several of the large hot rocks from her fire ring and placed them under her lean-to. A couple of flakes gently landed on her as she looked up. She caught them on her tongue. She dressed in her furs and moccasins and put the remaining possessions into her purse. Pete entered her lean-to and closed herself in.

• • •

There was a two-foot blanket of fresh powder and the surface glistened like jewels in the morning sun. The landscape was a smooth undulating cover indicating rocks, logs and bushes underneath to the trained eye. From one of the bumps a sudden movement lifted the snow as Pete pushed branches up from inside her snow cave lean-to.

Pete stood in her furs in the snowy glare and glisten. Snow covered the mountain above except on the cliff's vertical face. She pointed up to the distant granite peak and gave a nod to Mountain. She turned and shook fresh snow from her coyote furs as a dog might.

A hundred yards away a bear came out of its den. The bear shook as Pete had done moments before. They stood acknowledging each other. She turned downhill, slipping and sliding on her smooth-bottomed moccasins, making her descent a game of skill with a thrill in every step.

She had decided she would wander further south and see what the country was like. Sometime after her attempts to impose her will on the impressive 14000 foot mountain range she found the town of South Fork, Colorado. From there she found a road to the summit named Wolf Creek Pass and made it over the top. Elevation at the summit of the manmade road was 10,856 feet.

The number of wagons and men traveling on the muddy road made her a little wary. There were patches of snow remaining but the freight road made the climb child's play to Pete. She left the road at the summit of Wolf Creek Pass to return higher. She wanted to spend the night with Mountain above the traffic on the road below.

She found a shallow cavern made of large boulders with a rock overhang to protect her camp for the evening. Pete sat quietly in her cave in furs, with tea, the fire, and the majestic range as far as eyes could see.

Old smoke marks showed on the walls in the flickering light of her dwindling fire. She was not the first visitor who had used the protected area. Two petroglyphs scratched into the walls showed at least one other had come this way and left a tale of hunting.

• • •

Pete jogged downhill on the western slope off the summit. She went several days before finding a perfect camp where she could stay and rest. She wore her jogging clothes, fur hat, traveling purse and nothing on her feet. Her moccasins were shredded and left as an offering to Mountain.

• • •

Pete had uncanny interaction with the forest creatures in this new beguiling area. The jays and in particular the camp robbers were known for tolerating man and making friends. But the ground squirrels, chipmunks, pine squirrels and the most beautiful squirrel in the area the Kaibab with tasseled ears and flowing whitish-gray tail would dine on crumbs when placed in her outstretched hands. They welcomed her as if they knew she was coming. Some would sit on her shoulders and wait their turn and others would shriek their complaints when they felt left out.

Chapter 9 – A Comfortable Distance

As she traveled the rumors never left her wake. Some labeled Pete as the marauding fur-covered thief. Some made Pete a hero protecting the innocent from their oppressors. The descriptions varied about her weight and height; sometimes standing upright and sometimes loping on all fours. Some had her crawling in shadows or swinging from trees. They all had her wearing or possessing animal skins. Some told of an angelic countenance possessing haunting green eyes and an evocative smile. Others painted a picture of terrifying yellow eyes attached to a wild animal grin containing canines capable of ripping the throat from her victims. Most made up their stories never having seen her.

The bulk of the stories however were about her leaving with hands stuffed with chocolate baked goods. One would have to assume these humans passed the smell test or her chocolate prizes did.

• • •

She jogged through farmland surrounded by piñon, cedar and juniper. She reached the top of a hill and heard noises. She peered over the edge and saw a town below.

There were pedestrians and traffic of all sorts in the distance: horses with and without buggies; buggies with and without horses; men in suits and top hats; and fancy full dresses on some of the ladies. Garbage littered the street and paper blew in the wind which was disappointing but not unexpected with people crammed together.

Her eyes quickly moved to a bicycle weaving in and out of traffic with a horse rearing up when the bike got too close. Her hands shot up over her head with the entertainment. She wiggled her fingers and giggled. When it got to be too much to hold inside she doubled over in laughter. And never made a sound.

Pete saw one of the carriages without a horse making loud pops and puffs of smoke while people scurried out of its way. The horn from the auto sounded like a wounded duck. EONK EONK. Another auto came into view with a horn sounding more like a donkey mixed with grinding metal. HEHAREEAK HEHAREEAK.

Pete eventually made verbal sounds imitating the honking noise to near perfection. Her extremities all bubbled off the energy of the excitement generated. She fit in well with the circus below her.

Pete kept a comfortable distance from large towns or cities as a general practice. But she never missed a chance to look from well-protected vantage points.

Chapter 10 – Women's Suffrage

For the most part after first leaving Karl's ranch Pete left people their part of the landscape and happily took to the remaining. Tiny towns like Aztec could be tolerated if they offered the right incentives.

• • •

Pete saw wagons in the distance with banners attached. They were loaded with women, voices chirping in the breeze. She had little interest in the event. As the band in front of them started to play music it gained more of her attention and she shadowed them.

As the wagons went by she saw clearly the ladies wearing colorful dresses and the most outlandish hats with feathers, beads and crazy shapes. She became more absorbed. The smell of sugary fresh baked goods gathered in her nose in a most provocative way. She suddenly lost all desire to leave until fulfilling the persuasive craving.

There were a few cheers amongst the jeers from male onlookers and the women paid them little attention. There was an obvious tension between these fancy dressed women and many of the men that only showed the ladies their backs. The women were in charge of town this day and the men, by their body language, didn't like it.

Pete stayed to the corners of the buildings like the livery stable. The fancy ladies were undeterred by the occasional egg or vegetable flying their way.

Pete had no desire to leave after witnessing this behavior. She wanted to know the motives without knowing the word. She realized not one woman got angry or raised a voice at the men shouting insults and throwing things in their direction. One man ran from the crowd and ripped a sign off one of the wagons and nothing was done to him. What an odd town this was. Maybe Pete should visit more towns.

At the end of town was a small park and the ladies circled the wagons. They brought out their picnic baskets and blankets and laid out delicious-smelling foods. Freshly-fried chicken, potato salad, cakes (chocolate frosting), pies and cookies all still a little warm to her nose. Her curiosity about these two leggeds continued to grow.

She held out for a short time but saw no harm in approaching these ladies as they certainly wouldn't do her damage when they did nothing to the yelling men of the town. As she advanced a few spoke in low voices to those not facing her. Soon all the ladies turned and the whole group was staring straight at Pete. She didn't want to interrupt anything. However filling her curiosity and a few taste buds made a lot of sense.

"Sit ok?"

"This is for ladies only of the women's suffrage movement."

"What 'womins sfrage moment'?"

"Women, young man, have no right to vote on a national level and in several of the states. Which means we do not have a say in the making of the laws but we must follow those laws. We can be taxed by a government not allowing us any say in those taxes making it unconstitutional taxation without representation. In short we are little more than slaves to the men in this country. We are drawing attention to the fact and are requesting donations from those who think our cause worthy."

The words didn't all make a lot of sense. Mixed with their stubborn resentment and posture against the men of the town she got the gist. These women were also against working like slaves for men. They did not run away from them but stayed to fight them in a passive manner. No man got hit.

She liked the strength of these ladies but saw it was a disadvantage to be perceived a boy. She slowly retreated, never turning her back on the ladies and their picnic. She heard cackles like a henhouse when the coyote is driven off.

When she turned her back to continue her journey she bumped straight into an impressive lady with huge bosoms dressed in red from head to toe including gloves. The small collision showed how distracted she was with the human events around her.

"You look like someone who doesn't spend a lot of time around people. I'd be interested in knowing what you think of all this suffrage business young man?"

Pete gave an indefinite shrug signifying nothing. The lady came at her with a more pointed question. "Do you think women should be given the rights and freedoms of men?"

The next non-committal shrug did not go over well.

"Women, young man, have no right to vote. How about it young man, care to donate what's in your pockets to our cause to make needed changes in the way this country is run?"

Pete could easily relate but had no words scampering from her lips. The painted lady in red softened with a questioning look.

"I mean no disrespect but you aren't a young man, are you?"

Pete shrugged under the strict inspection.

"You can trust me ah, young lady. What is your name?"

"Pete"

"A lady named Pete?"

Pete froze.

"It's ok honey. I wish I could switch back and forth myself sometimes. We have some things in common I'm sure. If you're ever back in these parts, you ask anyone for Madam. Purdinere everyone knows me, one way or another." The fancy lady swung her shoulders and hips as she walked away. Quite a distinctive strut to say the least.

The little town was called Aztec. Pete had cause to come back many times.

• • •

On the same day, hours after Pete's first brush with the women in fancy hats, she was taking a ridge or hogback above the road north of town. She normally stayed off roads but was often in their vicinity watching over them. She heard some screaming from the road below. She couldn't see the source of the commotion but could tell the woman screaming was terrified. She decided to investigate while keeping her distance and found one man holding a naked woman's arm while she was trying to pull away. A second man was sitting on the ground trying to pull his boots off.

Pete sprang from the bushes and slashed the arm holding the screaming woman. His hand and arm went limp gushing blood with the exposed bone and tendons. The man howled in pain and immediately released the woman. He quickly turned toward Pete and tried to grab a gun in his belt with his remaining good right hand. She swiftly exposed the elbow joint as if she was butchering the leg of a lamb. The arm and hand fell limp releasing his pistol.

The man on the ground was now up on his feet with both boots removed. He tried to stand and she severed his suspenders with the next move of her knife making his pants take a trip to his knees. Another hack with her blade separated him from his underwear and revealed an upright stiff member.

She moved only her yellow green eyes and with the vigor they levied, spun him around so his bare ass was between his most cherished parts and her knife. He turned and stepped from his pants all in one motion. He had no doubt what her knife would do next. He was only two steps behind the man with limp bloody arms.

The two men put their energy into whimpering and not looking back. If Pete had been a cat she would have been flicking the tip of her tail.

Turning to the stunned victim she tossed her some clothes found lying on the ground nearby. Not a word was spoken between the two while the lady put her torn dress over her tousled hair and then started looking for shoes.

Pete saw wagon tracks and followed in their direction. She retrieved the lady's buggy and purse on the ground close by. The lady was rifling the pants pockets lost by the man who had left in a hurry. She held up several gold coins and approached Pete.

The lady held the coins out to Pete but Pete didn't make a move. "I saw you at the suffrage rally."

Pete shrugged.

"I want to give you a reward. This could have had a worse ending. Thank you and please take this." She dropped a few coins on the ground and stepped back sensing Pete was cautious around humans.

The woman appealed to Pete to take the coins but Pete remained unmoving. The lady reached for her purse now in Pete's hands. Pete held it out to her.

After receiving the purse the lady dug inside and pulled out a small card. She purposely placed the card under the coins on the ground and got aboard her buggy. She nodded at Pete and slapped the reins on the rump of the horse.

Mrs. Frances P. Harding

Colorado School of Mines

Golden, Colorado

Pete picked up the coins and card and since they were small found room in her purse. She wasn't sure she would find room enough to keep them permanently but gave a nod for now.

Of course when the tale was told in the Territory it grew and was quickly attached to the stories from before about the Wolfboy.

The lady relayed the story to Sheriff Curry in Aztec. She was well-connected and she was a good friend to the wife of the Secretary of the Interior Ethan Hitchcock.

So the tale grew like Pinocchio's nose about the Wolfboy who used his teeth as well as a knife to humiliate an entire band of outlaws of a score or more. It wasn't long after the encounter with Mrs. Harding that Pete met Padre in Aztec. It was there the human games began, leading to Piñon's Path and the gathering of Essie.

Chapter 11 – Essie

Essie was five feet three inches if she stretched a little. She was a little plump at her best. When Essie was young she suffered burns losing half her nose, her lips and eyebrows, and showed massive scars up both arms and back.

Luckily the burn didn't affect her brain. She was quite proficient academically. She spent a great deal of time reading and improving her mind to the extent some would consider her gifted. Her social skills, if she ever got the occasion to use them, were top notch due to her voracious reading on the subject. When comfortable around people, which wasn't very often, she had a pleasing sense of humor.

What didn't get developed was her coordination and physical confidence. As a result she grew up the brainy clumsy ugly duckling shunned by her peers.

Pete's Reflections Written Years Later

One of the popular games two leggeds play is torture. Their favorite target is each other. If they can find something different about somebody or a group of somebodies they torment them without end.

I saw some big pant boys mistreating a short girl with wrinkled red skin looking like last year's maple leaves. Her face was a crumpled scar with a shock of light-colored hair falling toward her nose. She wavered back and forth when she walked, like a turnip rolling and wobbling sideways. Each foot stepped with no confidence even if the path was smooth and level.

When I saw those bullies, you might say I deferred to my human nature. They were asking for a licking and I needed to work off some nasty.

It wasn't like anger but something that needed doing on Piñon's path to gather her up and assist Universe. The Turnip covered her eyes and I lost about two pounds of nasty. I heard a loud sheep bell in my head and then it was over, my knife was put away, and the bullies were gone.

Essie was not like other humans. Not on the outside, and not on the inside. Through her I saw humans a little differently. That must be why Piñon wanted me to gather her up.

Chapter 12 – Finding Pete

Essie's Diary

Today I met Pete. It was the best of days, it was the worst of days.

I was being tormented by three teen bullies outside Aztec in the New Mexico Territory. The two smaller boys were a head taller than I was. The largest was a bulky oaf like all the Morales clan holding his baggy pants up with suspenders. All three were walking backward in front of me poking me with pine needles. I had my journal over my face to protect against the pests. My bright yellow dress was splotched with mud balls thrown by the three. All were spitting and snickering as I started to cry through my book.

"Come on … show us your ugly face. You ashamed of it?"

"Now she has to cry. What a baby."

"You think you're so smart because you know books. Smart your way out of this little miss stinky face."

"You're so ugly you have to sneak up on a glass of water."

I peeked between my fingers and saw a funny hat on top a wild feral looking kid in peculiar clothes on his haunches in the middle of the road. He moved with a lion's grace yet had a relaxed lighthearted look. He had a gingerbread cookie man securely held in his teeth. A wide smile appeared behind the cookie as the kid positioned a long stick horizontally about knee high to the shorter bullies. When the stick struck the back of their legs as they continued to walk backward they all lost their balance at the same time. The strange kid quickly stood pulling their feet upward, finishing what had already been started. All three bullies flipped backward and hit the ground hard.

When they raised their heads they saw nothing but knife tasting the air in front of their noses. Behind the blade, and the cookie, was the same wild grin I had seen moments earlier. When Morales, the largest boy, opened his mouth it was filled with dirt and his ear was notched like a farm animal. Blood spirted and fear replaced the laughs on their faces. My stomach retched but it was all over by then.

The young teen took a bite out of the cookie and spit orders sprinkled with crumbs. "Shoes off." And shoes came flying off.

"Shirts off." All three showed nothing but skin above the waist.

"Pants off." They glanced at each other. All three gulped down their pride and hurriedly complied.

"Go go", pointing back toward Aztec. None of the three ever looked back. The big bully held his left ear oozing blood down his arm. All three hobbled barefoot in their underwear down the rough road. The boy in front of me with his funny fur hat chewed the last of his cookie.

I didn't want to pull my hands down from my face for two reasons. First there was my looks. Second, somewhere on the ground was an ear wedge.

• • •

My protector was taller than I was by about five inches. His clothing was different: short pants of soft tanned leather barely below the knees, no shoes, a frivolous rabbit fur hat and a large purse strapped several ways around his body. He was thin, had fairly short brown hair, sinewy muscles and was years younger than I. But the most striking difference was his face; a wild wary look, green eyes darting and nose sampling the air with nostrils flared. He had dispatched my persecutors like Sir Lancelot without breaking a sweat.

This teen must be the Wolfboy I had heard tales about. He was curious about my face in the beginning, but not like others. He came close and watched my mouth forming and firing words. It must have sounded something like: "Name'sEssie. Mybrother couldn'tpronounce Stephanie andit cameout Essie andthenamestuck."

He was totally focused on my mouth and drew closer examining the source of the noise. "Thank you forwhatyoudid but youcould seriouslyhurtsomeone-usingaknifelike thatandgetinto bigtrouble."

He came even closer and touched my mouth gently with a finger until I quieted or at least slowed my speech. I was beginning to get the problem wasn't my looks. I had a slight tendency to talk a lot and rapidly which I finally understood was the issue taking his attention. OK Diary, I never shut up. "I … know … it … isn't … pretty … but … its … the … only … face … I've … got. A … pot … of … boiling … bear … fat … spilled … on … me … when … I … was … a … baby."

His head tilted at my words. I continued articulating in a slow and deliberate manner. "Thank you for your help. What is your name?"

He nodded and stared at me. He left a large blank space in the conversation. I wanted to know a little more about this kid thus I tried to keep him engaged. I continued my slow speech pattern. "You don't talk much. Where do you live?"

He stopped. Again I spoke slowly. "You're so ugly you have to sneak up on a glass of water." His lips leaked a little smirk. "I can tell by your smile you understand some things. Why don't you want to tell me your name? Is it a real bad name?"

He shrugged a negative shrug then a wag of his head for 'no'.

"I live at the orphanage as both my parents abandoned me after the burn accident. The orphanage lets me stay on if I tutor the malcontents kicked out of Padre's school. Nasty work teaching expelled students and keeping control. I hate it but it's a roof over my head. I would do anything to get outside of those walls. I could exchange teaching you how to read and write in English correctly for learning to live off the land and be free."

His bare dirty callused foot gave a swift sweeping motion clearing needles and twigs leaving bare ground. It was clear there was not a single solitary grain of civilized sand between those toes. Then his dirty foot with flexible toes picked up a pile of little twigs and put them to one side of the cleared area. He dropped a rock a few feet from the twigs on the other side.

He spoke in a silky gravelly voice and always pigeon English. "Insiders … bullies…two-leggeds," pointing first to the twigs with a dirty toe.

A beetle entered the cleared area and walked toward the pile of little twigs.

While the beetle continued toward the pile of twigs he threw his knife and it stuck blade first near the rock. The same dirty big toe pointed to the knife.

"Pete."

"Your name is Pete?"

He frowned and pointed again to the beetle with his toe.

The beetle just short of the pile of sticks hesitated. It inspected the pile of twigs with its feelers and then turned in the opposite direction without coaxing or touching. The beetle continued toward his knife and the rock. It was like the beetle knew to inspect the two choices. Pete squatted and pointed to the beetle with his finger as it stopped at the rock.

"Bug choose. Outsider. Easy."

We had already started communicating. I knew his name. Pete. I knew the bullies were insiders. I knew Pete and the beetle were outsiders. I was being told to choose and I already had made the choice.

Yes Diary, he was comparing me to a bug but no one is perfect. My choice was outsider, 'easy'. Socially I already was an outsider anyway. Everything after the decision to leave the orphanage was not 'easy'. My life had not been an easy one and the encounter with the bullies was the last straw on the camel's back. I didn't feel safe and knew I had to make a change. I had no idea at the time the enormity of the choice.

• • •

Pete had me put on boy's pants, shirt and shoes and abandon my dirty torn dress and sweater. I looked real funny with pant legs rolled up far enough to keep them out of the way of my feet. I did a practice lap across the road and back. I puffed a little but I was psyched. This was going to be the rest of my life. He swept the road with one of the long needled pine branches. He had erased our tracks and maybe cleared the road of the piece of ear. Interesting.

We packed up the remaining clothes and stuffed them inside the large fat boy's shirt. Pete took the suspenders and wound the clothing bundle including coats and pants into a pack I carried. We left soon after with Pete carrying his staff and large purse. Ahead of Pete was a huge raven. Glossy iridescent black feathers and a thick wide beak. He must have had a wingspan of nearly five feet. He would fly in a direction and then wait for us to follow, one wing slightly drooping while waiting with a haughty attitude. Almost like we weren't going fast enough to suit his highness.

Chapter 13 - Survival

Essie's Diary

Following behind Pete were more of Pete's rescues, two fawns still in spots. I brought up the rear carrying the clothing pack making a pitiful wheezing sound. The noise didn't draw any concern from my leader.

I was not accustomed to being a pack animal but I didn't want to complain. The long and the short of it was I couldn't keep up. I fell numerous times as I got tired and it didn't take long for my legs to feel like rubber. I found it easier to fall than to get back up. I knew I had to keep up or be left behind. Therefore I feel the need to write in detail, Diary, about our life and survival in case he leaves me stranded.

• • •

I don't want to make this sound sensational Diary, but Pete was not human. Once he stood pointing up ahead. "What am I to look at?"

He stood steady, continuing to point. After ten seconds a cougar came bounding over a hill and stopped suddenly within one stride. It collected its kinetic energy, glanced at us over a shoulder, and then uncoiled in a single bound in a different direction. It left more like a bird flying than a mammal. Scary and exhilarating.

Pete was interested in imitating the cat's motion as he had to wait for me anyway. He leapt, stopped on a dime, and then turned in a graceful pirouette. Then exploded in a different direction. It was an incredible sight; first he knew somehow what was about to happen with the cougar appearing, second the cougar's display of athletic ability to stop a thirty mile an hour run and collect energy in one stride, and lastly watching Pete practice the same motion but using two legs to do it.

• • •

We were not on any road or trail but traveling cross country with no way to tell our whereabouts. I knew we were going up in elevation. You don't have to be a pioneer type to know up from down Diary.

Pete would zig and zag, first one way and then another, while I would walk the straightest line I could, making my overall journey shorter. Pete had three speeds; gone, fast, or sitting absolutely still, eyes scanning like a bird of prey.

Pete was always over some hill jumping a bush or something. He'd climb trees or rocks to survey the upcoming terrain or where we had been. Sometimes it meant food, sometimes we changed directions for our way up the mountain. The fawns would at least wait for me to catch up before they would zig and zag after Pete. I was continually worried because without Pete, I would be trail meat for the next wild carnivore. In a way I felt good about what I was doing. I was protecting the young deer. A predator always catches the slowest in the herd.

Pete sprang out of nowhere when I thought he was at least a mile ahead. He put a hand to my mouth. It was then I realized I was prattling on about my lot in life and he needed quiet. He used his ears as well as his sense of smell and sight to know the surroundings and everything in it. Under the circumstances, I reluctantly consented.

I looked ahead and saw an open meadow. There was no sign of humans. "I wish I could be like you and never feel afraid. I am totally lost and if you run off I would be bear food…"

He made a motion with his hand like it was talking at me. He shook a no at me. I got the message. I was talking yet again and he needed quiet. Pete made a shushing sound "Shusheshsh" near a large tree on the edge of the meadow. He turned to me and put both hands over his own mouth. He made a point of an exaggerated tiptoeing by the tree.

When under the tree the wind gave a little gust and I heard the exact same sound Pete had uttered. "Shusheshsh". The tree was clearly a shushing tree. I got out of there as fast as my thick little legs could throttle.

• • •

We traveled for three days without spending more than a single night in any of our camps. This put maybe fifteen to twenty miles between us, the town, and those bullies. Eventually we made it up close to the Continental Divide about ninety miles from Aztec but that took more than a month. I lost all track of time except looking back at my notes in my journal.

The weather was good and our camps were simple and primitive. We ate what Pete carried plus some finger food plants he gathered along the way. I slept comfortably in bully clothes. As I write this I realize I was extremely tired and I would have slept soundly stark naked on a pile of rocks.

I learned why Pete hadn't cut my pant legs shorter. I could roll them down over my feet at night for more warmth and keep mosquitoes away from my ankles.

Our meals were meager and I felt myself wasting away. Skinny is the result of too little food and too much exercise. Not what I was born to be. I learned why Pete made the big deal about choosing when we first met. It was my choice.

When we first started I was reluctant to eat something new. After the first day I could eat tree stumps. If they were poisonous it would put me out of my misery. I didn't die.

• • •

As we went up in elevation I saw more meadows and fir with fewer tall pine. We slowed our pace and became more relaxed in our travels. Pete made fewer trips behind to check our trail for people or predators.

Pete stopped by a little creek exiting an open meadow. I started to talk again. "Aren't you ever afraid out here alone?"

Pete shook his head. "Teachings."

"What's teachings?"

Pete started moving his hands mimicking talking with thumb and fingers again. Then he put his hand to his ear. "Firetime talk talk talk. No goot now."

• • •

Later in the afternoon we took more time and set up our first respectable camp. I was shown by actions, not words, how to stack dry branches by a fire ring. Pete had made the ring by piling six inch rocks two deep in a small circle.

He took my arm and hauled me toward some dry fallen branches. He held them out motioning for me to take them. Then he took my arm and dragged me back to the fire ring. He pushed the branches down with me attached until they touched the ground. Then he unwound my fingers forcing me to let go. He pointed back to get more branches by nodding and coaxing with a shooing motion.

Next I was to build a shelter with bedding. I brought soft bedding materials starting first with thin flexible branches giving some cushion from the sharp granite and pointy rocks close to a fallen log. Next came pine boughs and last soft grasses and dry leaves. When done, I stacked branches thick with needles over the log completing the lean-to shelter. All in all it was about fourteen feet in length. Plenty of room for us and our packs to stay dry. After he showed me the order of making the bed and shelter, he left.

With a bedroom this luxurious it was no surprise we shared it with some other little creatures. Indeed the first good bed in three days and we had little rodents as bedmates. Funny little mousey fellows that wouldn't be content without scurrying hither and yon making their needed noisy work a full night affair.

• • •

When he returned he had two grouse breasts, two large mushrooms and a

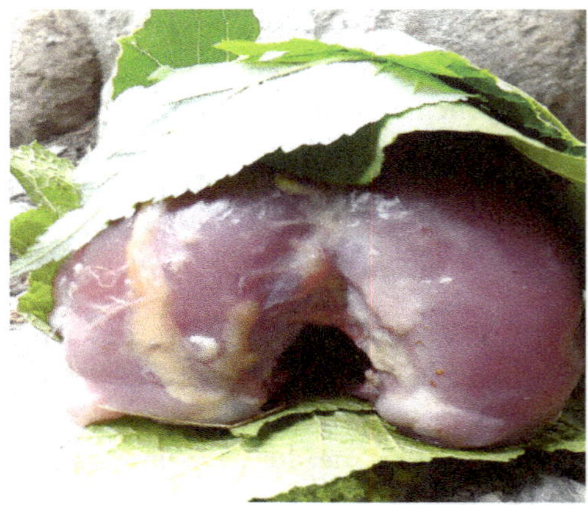

bunch of herbs and wild onions. He wrapped each breast with herbs and onions and then with leaves. Another bundle of leaves surrounded the mushrooms and tubers. He buried them all under coals in the fire ring.

When I was done with my chores I looked for Pete. He had small flames going in the fire ring and was down by the creek near a deep pool about a hundred feet away. Raven appeared to guard the bathing pool strutting back and forth. Pete disrobed at the edge of the pool and stepped into the creek. Not a care or a concern for what I might think. Completely free. What a blessing.

I didn't want to look but I couldn't help myself Diary. Honest. I wandered down toward him. From the rear he showed sinewy muscles from calves to shoulders. Muscles rippled through his back. He displayed smooth beautiful olive skin and moved with absolute grace. I worried a little about rape but knew I definitely needed a bath. I decided to take the plunge when Pete was done and hope for the best.

Pete was the exact opposite of me; lanky wild beauty, perfect skin, illiterate, ill-mannered and proud of it. And then I saw what I could not believe. It was somewhere between complete envy and disappointment. I wasn't sure it was appropriate for me to be traveling with a boy. And, I was not.

"My oh my, boy Pete is girl Pete with skin I would kill for." I didn't realize it but I actually spoke the words. It was little more than a whisper but when I did, she looked up. I looked down at my burned skin on my arm. When I looked up she was splashing, turning and scrubbing in the snowmelt creek water like an otter. Snowmelt I might add is cold Diary. It wasn't long and Pete was getting out of the stream. She gave her hair a ringing out and a shake. Stark naked she wandered down the stream to drip dry in the sun. God what a lean tanned machine. Yes Diary, it is called envy.

The two rescued fawns played in the creek a little below our bathing pool where it was shallower. All three were equally at home in the icy stream relaxed without a care. Wild and magnificent to see.

And then it was my turn. I entered the deeper pool Pete used above the fawns. However for me it was cold to the point of pain. If Pete could do it with a smile, surely I could do it without screaming. I was wrong.

It had to be a form of meditation or some yoga trick. She could force her mind and body by a will I didn't have. I knew someday I would smell awful if I didn't bathe. I would eventually reek to the extent buzzards would circle. I made a simple choice. Nothing lasts forever; pain, life, nothing.

I entered more slowly this time. That was worse. I tried it again and this time I went all in to my chin with one big splash. I got a little dizzy, then numb. The numbing gave me a reprieve. I feared blacking out and drowning. My fear was for nothing. Blacking out would have put an end to it. No end came. I didn't linger but I got the job done, ducking my head to rinse everything head to toe one last time.

Once done and leaving the creek I felt an exhilaration as the sun did its work. The adrenalin rushing and the knowledge it was over was overwhelming. I felt proud. I didn't care if it was one of the deadly sins. Maybe this would be the beginning of a new me. Or maybe not.

• • •

When Pete returned to camp she hardly noticed my presence. Now clothed carrying a few sticks of firewood and wet underclothes hanging from one of her fingers. She deposited the firewood near the fire ring and hung her odd-looking wet underwear on a nearby bush.

Pete had whittled a 12-inch stick and balanced it on a nearby rock. As she walked by the stick, she gave it a little touch and started it moving like a teeter-totter timer. Maybe I'll learn someday what that's for Diary? Not.

There was a pile of fresh green aspen leaves on a flat rock. The rocked served as our table and was about four feet in height. We each took a handful of the leaves and spread them in front of us making a covering over the table rock.

Pete reached down into the fire ring with sticks making tongs in each hand and pushed burning coals aside. I watched intently as I had built up a good appetite for dinner over the last few days. Yes Diary, I needed to lose a couple of pounds. That part of my life was over. Today I feasted.

Pete removed the food from the coals wrapped in blackened leaves steaming. She peeled the darkened leaves with the sticks exposing hot green leaves and then our dinner inside.

She put our dinner on the leaves in front of each of us. Then we ate standing around the flat rock with our hands. No complaints by me. This was worth the three day wait. Who needs utensils?

"I'm famished."

"Fam … ished?" Pete delivered quite deliberately.

"Famished … very hungry"

I rubbed my stomach. Pete nodded. Pete made hand gestures of talking (fingers against the thumb) then motioned to the sun trail through the sky and shook her head no. Then she placed her hand to her ear.

"Talk talk no goot. No talk talk."

I got the drift. "You don't talk a lot but you eat well." The feast was too good to ruin with talking anyway. I learned another important lesson on survival. *Never talk when you can eat.*

I hesitated eating the mushroom. I knew the stories about how deadly some can be. It had a large stem and a spongy bottom instead of veins. Not like any mushroom I had ever seen.

My hesitation didn't take long. It had a firm but not crunchy texture. Not a strong smell or fungus taste.

We took a walk around to see if anything was out of place or needing tending to before darkness. She looked for marks or signs of trouble like bear tracks in the dirt or their fresh scratches on tree trunks. We found tracks near the creek but nothing that bothered her. I think she knew the bear was leaving or tracks were not fresh. I need to find out why Diary.

When done we washed up at the creek with sand and water that cut the food from our hands and faces.

• • •

"Did you get lost and become a feral kid?"

"No lost. Fare.. all ?"

"Something returned to an untamed state that was once domesticated."

"Much words 'Un ..tamed' 'domesha..' da da da."

I will have to cut my word usage down. "Sorry. What's it like when you kill something and eat it?"

"Eat or no eat."

"I don't kill, I eat what you kill."

Pete pointed at me abruptly. "kill greens."

"Yes, I kill plants I guess. When you put it that way I don't want to eat at all."

Pete laughed and pointed again at me then rubbed her stomach, "get fam … ished… bye n bye."

"Yes, I guess so. Ever gone to school?"

Pete wagged her head no.

"Why not?"

"Sheepherder." Pointing to herself with great respect.

"Where are your sheep, sheepherder?"

"Ah ya eh ehh." She shook her head no. *Romulus and Remus were shepherds so maybe there is a connection to being suckled by a wolf.*

"Are you from around here Pete?"

Wiggled her head no.

"Do you travel alone?"

Nod.

"Not afraid?"

She shook a no at me.

"Bet you want to know what I'm thinking?"

Pete shook another no at me which ended the conversation unceremoniously.

Chapter 14 - Turnip

Pete's Reflections Written Years Later

I never called Essie the name Turnip out loud. Turnip the tuber wasn't meant to be derogatory but simply descriptive of Essie in those days before she gained confidence and trimmed her softness. It was the picture I had of her walking and talking and I go by pictures.

Turnip made me smile. If you ever sat and watched the personality of a turnip you'd know what I mean. Turnip was different on the outside than I was but not so different on the inside. I didn't notice it for a while. Life takes time.

Her outside had short heavy legs that couldn't keep up. She wasn't built for speed but more for sitting and teaching. She could remember words from a book. Whole pages of words.

Sometimes I wanted to carry her to show how it feels to not fight earth but be free like the breeze on it. To be anywhere doing anything and have it be home. She would someday crave to be free after tasting the first little lick. She would get there. I needed patience. It must have been another lesson sent from Piñon on his path.

She did have a most annoying trait. She would talk and ask questions when she got a little nervous. And she was always a little nervous. Nobody learns with their mouth open. Not sure about the physics of the mouth but open the food hole and it shuts down everything else. Mainly connecting to Universe. If she opened her confidence and senses like ears and eyes, the answers would appear.

I started connecting to Turnip which helped me learn how to connect to people. I never thought about connecting to people before. It also showed me in words what I do when I connect. I connect first with all my senses: hands, ears, smell, and eyes. My taster is connected to smell so maybe that also. Then connect with legs and feet without shoes solidly into the earth. Then something else pushes through I have no words for yet.

When Turnip's racket broke my connections and link to Universe I needed to be more careful. Things passing by did not fit together without the connection and my naturalness was broken. It was the same when I was around Padre.

Not only physical pieces, but every "thing". Everything as in energies, colors, empty spaces, every "thing" whether eyes can see it or ears can hear it.

My memory was poor in the beginning. Remembering words or names was difficult. I didn't have to know a name as long as I could fit the piece into the proper place in Universe. Then I could use that piece of the puzzle regardless of what it was called.

Sometimes there were apparent dead ends. A space at the end of a branch where nothing fit. I paid special attention to these places for missing pieces.

I respected Turnip because she had determination and was willing to take a risk. She also had her genius. All hanging out for anyone who cared to look.

I wanted her to lead on our trails to get the feel of freedom and choice. I would go off and hide and wait, ready to follow her lead. She would stumble, fall or go around in circles. Her genius wasn't leading.

Chapter 15 - Teaching Pete

Essie's Diary

I noticed I was talking slower. Not less mind you Diary but with a more measured cadence. I'm not sure if it was better for Pete's learning and communicating or if it was the result of living in the mountains. They were having an effect on me that is difficult to put into words. The result was the same either way.

"How old are you Pete?"

She shrugged and grabbed a fly out of the air with a quick move of her hand. 'Clop'

Pointing at me "talk talk."

"Do I look bad to you? Does my talk sound funny to you?" Pete shook her head no.

"They call me ugly names like 'noface' or 'mushmouth' because I can't pronounce words well with tight skin on my face and no lips."

She shook her head no again and looked straight at me appraising something.

"You have no problem looking straight at me. It's actually quite a pleasant experience for a change. I don't always know what you are thinking however."

Shrug.

"I really like your voice."

"Clop." She grabbed another fly.

"The low gravely sound of your voice is quite engaging. I like it a lot. Too bad you don't like to learn more words and show off your voice more often."

A long pause and looking nowhere in the distance. *So much for psychology.*

• • •

"Are you afraid of people Pete?"

Pete shook her head for no.

"You avoid people..."

After a long pause, "Aaa void?"

"Do you try to stay away from people?"

Shrug. She didn't appear to understand 'try'. She was full of nothing but 'do'. I rephrased.

"You did not avoid me and those bullies and you could have. Why?"

"Two leggeds no goot. You (pointing) aaa-void."

I shrugged a Pete shrug and we laughed. It felt real good for a change.

Pointing at me again, "run away in dress, look down down down."

"Yes, I guess I do. And I get angry knowing I must live inside this shriveled skin and others do not. It's not fair."

"Not fair?"

"Things aren't the same for all."

"No, no fair in …" and she gave a large wave of her hands outstretched for the world or Universe.

"Are you saying there is no fairness in the world?"

Nod

• • •

"Pete, let's play a word game."

"Word gae..me?"

"Yes, game.. ga-me is something fun."

"Game… same grouse, deer, elk?"

"Yes, it is the same word. Sometimes the same word stands for more than one thing."

"Stupid. One word .. one thing. Stupid."

"Are you stupid, a stupid human?"

In an unsure manner she put her thumb and forefinger together to show only a tiny little bit stupid human, maybe.

"Ok Pete, what's this?" I pointed to my front tooth.

Shrug

"Tooth. Ok, what is this?"

"Flower."

"Yes, but what kind?"

"Rose flower."

"Tooth, flower.. rose flower. Yes!"

Nod. Pete grabbed a gingerbread cookie from her strap-on purse and broke it in half. She took the half cookie and bit both corners. She pointed at the remaining shape.

"Word." And she pointed at me.

"Mushroom"

"Yes!"

Learning had to go two ways. I guess she wanted me to observe and then give her a word as she had to do. I never knew for sure about Pete.

• • •

Pete began her desperate search for knowing every word for everything she could find. At first they were all objects she could point at. "Word… Word" came the commands. Later it was emotions or concepts she would mime or show by the art work of her hand gestures. She feigned anger, sadness, being lost and there was no end to her endurance. It turned to obsession but I matched her intensity word by word, resolve with resolve.

I enjoyed being the teacher but discovery always went two ways.

Chapter 16 - Together

The two had character delivered up in shovelfuls. From the beginning they were good for each other. Life had touched them both similarly at a young age; both had been burned in their own way. Each were making headway turning curses into blessings.

The two were given outward beauty by birth. Essie would have been a real nuisance to many a boyfriend if life had dealt a different hand. Her blue eyes still sparkled in the right circumstances. Essie had a natural charm as obvious as a bonfire on a cold blustery night whenever she decided to let it fly. And Pete could bring it out.

Pete had an angular striking beauty with boyish short chopped hair not far from getting in her way. Her movements were graceful, her voice unbelievably silky, her eyes were haunting when not flitting or angered, the chiseled features of her face unforgettable, and her lips were never far from giving away a smile. Her attractiveness was enhanced by a lack of flamboyance and an abundance of unpredictability. More like the wolf rather than the peacock. Most encounters with people were brief and full of an energy distracting those close at hand. She had a volatile manner and a knife with the same demeanor.

Pete never had a true friend with two legs and was never subjected to typical social pressures. She likewise had never experienced loneliness without humans as she was intrigued and connected to every 'thing' on the planet. It put her miles ahead of those concerned about what the other person thought. She was not self-conscious in the slightest. Her reflection in a pond went wanting for attention. She was attracted to the fish.

There were more times than not Pete needed to be alone with Universe. And the constant talk was then avoided to complete the needed connectivity.

Essie got teachings she could utilize if she stayed wild. Pete learned lessons she could apply if she cared to join human society. At this stage neither of them had confidence they could actually make it in the other's world. All of which brought the question to Essie's mind "Why did Pete allow me to join her?" A question Essie would continually ask herself in those early days as she

had no knowledge of Pete's commitment to Piñon.

They stayed around the first good camp for several days. There was plenty of game easy to take if Pete made herself a bow. Good hardwood was needed then proper seasoning which would take time. She had seen twelve bucks (two fists full of fingers plus two fingers) still in velvet. A lot of velvety horns.

Chapter 17 - Learning

Essie's Diary

This was a relaxing day compared to the first few. We finished cleaning up and returned to camp to put things in order by dusk. Darkness would have made the job more difficult without torches. We packed loose items back in Pete's purse and put the purse under the lean-to. We gathered more dry leaves and a little moss, stuffing it all under the lean-to next to the log. I presumed my soft materials were not adequate.

Clouds were accumulating and she kept looking to the sky. We were ready if it should rain I suspected.

We sat by the fire and brewed tea. Pete first put herbs and creek water into our only tightly woven bowl. Next she took three little hot rocks from the fire with green wood tongs and placed them in the bowl. As the tea brewed Pete worked on a weaving project of tightly woven grasses. The mood changed and Pete relaxed her rules on talk talk.

"You have some magical way with animals. How did you get the magic?"

After a long pause, " 'ma..gic' word hide much."

That blew dust in my face. I wasn't sure what she meant.

"Do you mean I use the word magic to cover up things I don't know?"

After a long pause, Pete nodded. I moved on.

"Do you ever feel bad or evil when you kill to eat?" I was grappling constantly with killing or starving.

It was difficult for me to not fill the emptiness with talk those first weeks but I learned. I had to. If I wanted an answer, give Pete the space in which to answer. Eventually, nearly an eternity by my standards, she shook her head no to my question. First she rubbed her stomach and said "no bad evil".

Next her hand imitated something on her arm with her index finger eating or probing. Apparently a mosquito with its proboscis. Then Pete imitated something catching and eating the mosquito with her other hand. Next she placed her flat hand on a rock and pretended it was quite hot by making a sizzling sound. Pete took her hands and motioned a large half circle stretching from sunrise and sunset. She brought her hands together at her waist, interlaced her fingers, pulled her palms up, and wiggled her 'happy fingers' with a large smile while talking.

"Bug eat Pete, fish eat bug, Pete eat fish. All … one … happy… <u>fam.. ished</u>. Easy. Goot?"

"Yes, good I guess. But mosquitoes make a terrible first impression. I hate their loud vulgar whine before I serve them me for lunch."

"You eat fat fish, get happy."

I continued to speak deliberately and slowly which is not easy for me. "Good Pete. I understand and thank you for the explanation. You've already learned the word 'famished'. You know the word 'fire'? Here is the word written using letters of the alphabet."

I reached down and picked up a stick. I smoothed the dirt with my shoe and scratched the letters in the dirt then pronounced the word.

"F" "I" "R" "E" "Fire."

Pete shook her head no.

"What do you mean, no. No what?"

Pete pointed at the word written in the dirt.

"… No hot. No … no cook. No fire."

Pete reached out and tried to warm her hands over the word "fire" scratched in the dirt. Pete shrugged the obvious and shook her head negatively. "No goot!" She put her hand over our evening fire as it was dying down and gave a smile and a nod.

It took me by surprise like many things from Pete.

Pete inspected the little bowl she had been weaving, wrinkling her brow about something. She worked on it a little more and finally gave it her ap-

proval. She bent down and picked several little wild strawberries growing around sunwarmed rocks to protect them from the chilly night air. They were no larger than the tip of my little finger. I hadn't even noticed them until she started picking.

She handed the bowl to me with the strawberries. I grabbed one and let it melt in my mouth. It had more fragrance and flavor than any I had ever had.

I made a big deal about it. I gave her a lot of praise about the craftsmanship and finding wild berries and she ignored me completely. Turning, she started whittling on another stick. After a few moments of being left alone she asked about a word she wanted to know. "What … talk talk Yeha Yeha" She made noises mimicking a Stellar Jay perfectly.

"Chatter"

Pete nodded.

"Chatter no goot. No chatter teaching, do teaching."

I remember chortling at the accusation of being a chatterer and she got the word from me.

"Why did we sneak past the big tree on the edge of the meadow a few days back?" My first priority was to learn how to survive on my own and this question kept nagging at me. Maybe it was important to my survival.

Pete tilted her head not understanding.

"Why did we have to shush or be quiet when we went by the big tree on the edge of the meadow our first day after leaving Aztec?

Pete put her finger to my lips.

"No talk tree. Shusheshsh." Pete mimicked the shushing sound again.

When she produced the sound she became more like the tree. The oddest thing. She didn't grow bark but she still became more like the tree. Or maybe better said she blended into the sound and it was difficult to see her as I normally did. She blended is the best I can put it.

I was not going to get questions answered about the shush tree. I also needed to pay more attention on how she got her food and prepared it but the perplexing got my attention as long as I was well fed.

There is an absence of collecting and cooking techniques thus far in here Diary. But here is a story about gathering that left me wondering.

• • •

I cherished my original bowl made by Pete filled with wild strawberries. About two weeks after receiving it she took the bowl away from me and handed me another woven basket full of wild raspberries.

When I asked her if I could have my bowl back she shook her head. "No, here", pointing to the ground. Maybe every bowl has a life expectancy or I wasn't supposed to get attached to things. So much to learn.

Another lesson was when she showed me how to start a fire and keep it going after a rain. What kind of wood, where to get the wood, how to make the fire or coals for a good source of heat for cooking or warmth.

She started by grabbing my hand and pulling me to a spruce tree. She moved her hands at a distance to have me remember the tree shape and color. She pointed to fir and aspen and compared them by looking closely. She crawled under the heavy low branches of the spruce as I stood outside waiting for the next part of my lesson. She came out and took my hand and pulled me down inside the thick low hanging branches. They could easily shed all the rain and snow. It was perfectly dry inside the spruce branches even on a wet day. An excellent place to find good fire starter wood.

Useful but mundane compared to the mystery surrounding the shush tree. My mind had a tendency to wander and she often had to bring me back to the more important subjects like food, warmth and shelter.

She broke a small spruce twig off and handed it to me. She broke another for herself. She snapped it and it broke easily. She had me snap mine. She took another and held it next to her ear. She snapped it. I held mine next to my ear and snapped it. Dry, and easily broken. *Snap.* That crisp feel as it broke meant it was prime fire building material. Not green with life.

She took another stem. It was limber and had some moisture in it. It wouldn't break, it wasn't dry and it would not be good for starting a fire. But good if we wanted to make some smoke to flavor our meat or build a bed.

We found other types of wood and different sizes and each had its purpose in the upcoming event. Size and type of wood were all important factors. Larger wood would last longer once lit. We took the armload of wood we gathered and laid it next to a little fire ring made of rocks. She treated the pieces of wood as she would a forest creature. She would smile at each and place it carefully on the little pile of small spruce kindling making a teepee type structure about eight inches in diameter. Then she leaned a few more slightly longer and larger pieces against the teepee.

She struck a match, stuck it inside the structure and lit the small pieces inside. I had to ask but knew I shouldn't. "Did you make the matches?"

An exasperated shake of her head and I got one word. "Trade."

Then back to business. Flames were quick to take over the little pile of sticks. In a few minutes she added a few more pieces of larger branches and we had a good fire. None of this needed words except for my senseless curiosity about matches.

Words and questions were frowned upon. Doing and attention to detail was useful in her classroom. And like all classrooms some of the minds would wander off and needed to be brought back to the learning at hand.

My nearsighted vision wasn't good except for reading letters on a page when my nose was touching it. Eventually I learned my difficulty with vision was not eyesight as much as a lack of attention or closer to the point, not actually looking.

How things looked, smelled, felt, and were heard were essential to Pete's teaching. Around this time she started pulling her own eyelid back with a thumb and forefinger forcing her eye more open. It was an embellished way of getting me to 'look' and not think I was looking.

"Nothing here," Pete said putting a finger to her temple. I guess the point was why would I go there to look for real things? Open my eyes. Because at that time I was still convinced in my arrogance I did have 'reason' to use my mind. Color me silly Diary.

Chapter 18 – Dining Companion

Essie's Diary

Pete had little respect for humans. She was not afraid of people but would prefer to avoid them as she would a cloud bursting rain. Unless she saw some benefit in their company such as trading for matches or sweet baking, no need to go out of her way to associate with her own kind. I wondered if she knew they were her own kind in the beginning.

I kept copious notes to refer to if needed, always writing the day's events around the campfire. I didn't get many questions answered in the beginning. In retrospect, I don't think I was ready for most answers anyway.

• • •

I'd heard stories about her running with wolves but they were only stories to my way of thinking. There was no doubt she had abilities alien to the normal human. Another example came about around the campfire one evening.

According to her story that had more hand motions than words, a coyote wanted to know what she was doing living like one of them. He was wary as was Pete. Blending well with the bushes in the beginning he felt safer and ready for a hasty retreat.

Eventually they started

knowing each other and conversing in a relaxed manner. Not like human chatting but more connected and being one with each other. They shared some 'naturalness' together.

Coyote wanted Pete to watch something. Pete gave a courteous nod. Coyote went out and stood by a rodent burrow. After a short time a rodent stuck his head out. Coyote grabbed it by the head and killed it.

He flipped it up in the air and caught it again mid torso. The coyote "knew" which hole and when it was coming up.

In return Pete cooked the meal. Coyote was interested in the use of fire. The meal took two hours to prepare and Pete kept Coyote occupied and interested the entire time. Pete said if you don't keep a coyote interested, they wander off. I found the same was true for Pete.

Pete's story continued. First the fire, then the coals, then burying the rodent in leaves to steam and tenderize. All the time each was learning the ways of the other.

Coyote explained the catching of the whistle pig. First Coyote saw the whistle pig go down a hole. Next he put the network of tunnels interconnecting underground into puzzle pieces fitting neatly into Universe. They only fit in one way with the rodent coming out of the designated hole. Coyote knew which hole before the rodent knew. Then it was history.

I'd seen Pete point to things before they happened like the cougar bounding ahead of us. I suppose this is how she likely did it. No Diary, she would neither confirm nor deny it.

He was an animal of short attention span. Pete could relate quite well. Good predators were always on the lookout for a meal which kept their focus shifting. Once the prey was seen, nothing could interfere with the link to their next meal.

By the end of the story both Pete and Coyote had learned. There were good people and good coyotes but not all were good. Evil does exist. Neither tried to get advantage over the other. They simply learned what Universe had to offer from differing perspectives. Somehow all without words.

Pete "gave" the story as best she could to give me the feel of connecting I guessed. I got it was as true as the moon above by her manner. To this day I do believe it was. She'd prefer I didn't believe anything.

When I asked her if she could trust her dinner companion if he ran out of rodents she said, "If all goot, you went to Creator." Not sure I got it but maybe she meant nothing was perfect in this world of ours. Like nothing was fair.

"You tell the story like some coyotes are good and some are not. You know the difference?" I had no doubt she would kill some coyotes faster than I'd take the life of a mosquito but she didn't appear to lump all coyotes together.

"Easy. Some coyotes goot. Some no goot."

I saw the difference once I looked. In fact it started being 'easy' as she would say. I asked her, "Is it easier to see evil in coyotes than people?" I was starting to think that was true.

"Coyote easy. Two leggeds, no."

"People hide their tracks better?"

Pete nodded and shrugged in what I would call short two letter gestures. I wasn't sure she understood and it looked like she was

trying to brush me off the topic.

I drew out her name in a questioning way, "P e e e te?"

"Quack?"

"Quack! What kind of talk is that?"

"Duck talk. Says 'what?'"

"Never mind." Maybe you had to be there Diary to hear her perfect imitation of a duck 'quack'. Then she pronounced in English the words 'duck talk' with the tones of a duck all while keeping the look and straight face of a duck.

• • •

The following evening I questioned Pete again about her story of dining with Coyote. I questioned it as a scientist might. Not doubting her veracity but to be sure I got it straight. The long and short of it was it got under her skin and she thought she needed to prove it. It was one of many times things happened around Pete I could not explain. Her story wasn't reasonable with everything I knew. At least I could not explain it to anyone and not be locked up.

Pete walked out into a clearing and made a loud long coyote howl. She waited and did it again. By the third call a coyote came to the clearing where she was standing. He held a rodent in his mouth.

Pete cleaned it, cooked it and offered me a hind leg. She broke off a front leg and sucked the meat from it. She returned the cooked rodent to her coyote friend missing the two legs. He bowed his chest to the ground reaching his front paws toward her and trotted off.

I stood there with the hind quarter in my hand and she glared at me. *Now disbelieve silly Essie,* was the look covering her face. She shook her head at me and trotted after the coyote. I know it's true. I saw it. Reality doesn't care what you believe Diary. But the belief that anything is possible may be a door to reality.

• • •

We were walking not saying a word and Pete stopped, tilted her head and said, "You stop here". I stopped and waited and she started jogging away. I yelled, "Hey, how long do you want me to wait here?" I thought she may be trying to get rid of me.

"I go, you stay. I go there." She pointed to a faraway flat top hill with a white dot of a cloud over the center of it.

"For how long?"

She returned, pointed at me, pointed at the ground, put her palms down on the ground, and said, "You stop here."

"Until next week? How long?"

Totally left me standing there not knowing whether she would be gone for the day or a month. She came back before dusk. Scary.

• • •

Pete made a statement today I took as me needing to be right or wanting to know all answers. "You no look goot SE if you no can answer." Then finished up with a grin, "Pete look goot all ways."

• • •

I was both terrified and exhilarated during this time. I knew something was happening and my life was changing. In a moment of despair I cut the cord tethering me to shore. There was no doubt I was adrift in this new natural current called life with Pete. I could not blame anyone, or give credit to anyone, but myself.

I had no clue as to what or where it would all end. The object of this lesson was I was harder to kill than I thought. Which started down the path again of, why think?

Chapter 19 - Boundaries

Pete's Reflections Written Years Later

Essie did not give up easily. No matter how I swatted away each question she came back with more. She had many fears of the outside. Fear made everything harder for both of us. She also believed words and thoughts as if they were the real thing.

Words are finite boxes adding limits to everything. The mind prefers barriers and has trouble without them. People ponder the chicken and the egg without getting anyplace. Essie taught me to use words whether I liked it or not.

She told me not to mix tenses when I write. But I am going to anyway because what used to be true still sometimes is true.

Nature is unbounded. Life is cyclical and has no boundaries. My mind won't visualize infinity. But the concept is easy if I connect to Universe. Every step has a step behind it and a step in front of it.

Time is not numbers on a clock but is change. Sun moves across the sky only to rise again the following day. The clock is human's best attempt at displaying change, imitating nature and reality.

• • •

Essie had to get her mind out of the way and words were limiting her progress. Humans make words to define things they think they know. Which leads to the question of how can the mind grow to understand what it doesn't know?

I'm doing this with words. For the last time, please don't believe them. If it leads you to something you can experience, that's another matter. There are many contests when I am around people. No matter if I mix tenses or not.

Chapter 20 - Expanding Universe

Essie's Diary

I was in pathetic physical shape those first weeks traveling with Pete after the bully incident. It was painful and slow slogging. At the start she would push me but never more than I could do. Each day she extended the boundaries a little more. Each day I begrudgingly got a little stronger.

Pete whittled me a staff or walking stick. I had to spend many hours with the fool thing. I could understand the need for a tool to help me walk, but she also wanted me to become a gladiator.

Pete was in the creek doing what she did best. Showing off. She put on an exhibition to illustrate the value of working with the staff; how it could keep me from sliding on the slippery rocks in the creek especially if the current was strong. It would support and balance my body. I was on the bank doing what I do best; asking questions.

Pete got out of the creek and walked up to me. We were eyeball to eyeball on the creek bank. She put her palm over my lipless mouth for at least ten seconds and then removed it.

"Am I to learn without quest….?" And Pete quickly returned her palm to my mouth like a lid on a jar. Again. After more than a minute she slowly lowered her hand to see if my mouth was still running. As I took a short breath to start up again, she quickly replaced her hand and patiently waited. Yet again. What she lacked in vocabulary was more than surpassed by her resolve.

When I realized I was not going to be given due process to state my case I stopped trying. She placed my hands on the staff signaling for me to swing it. I swung it. I guessed at the time I was to learn how to kill a rabbit or grouse with it which I had no intention of ever doing. She could do the killing and I would do the eating. A symbiotic relationship made in heaven.

Pete took back the staff. She spread her legs in a sturdy looking position, one leg slightly ahead of the other balanced on the balls of her feet for stability and power. Then she put both hands on the staff and made several quick moves with arms and hips showing a balance of speed, grace and power. It was natural to Pete to connect the staff to the earth through her legs, torso and arms. Pete handed it back to me.

Of course I had questions but could I ask them? No, of course not. Pete once again approached me and started to put her fingers to my mouth. I took a quick step back and placed my own hand over my mouth. Pete, satisfied she was the victor and I the vanquished, nodded in acknowledgment and continued with the lesson.

She grabbed a scrawny branch from the ground and hit my staff and looked away as if too bored to continue the fight. I stood there and took it. Pete got a fierce warlike look on her face and made a lunge at me striking my arm with her little branch.

"Ooh, you hurt me!" I lunged back at her with the staff and she easily side-stepped my return blow.

"Hold still and fight you coward! Why do you choose a smaller worthless stick?"

Pete pointed to herself with a gruff tough look to show the size of the fight within. Someone of her stature didn't need much of a weapon.

"Easy, Pete hit, not stick."

Pete let me get close again and I broke Pete's rotten tiny stick. Pete illustrated her recent schooling from me by exaggerating the pronunciation of "good" instead of "goot".

"Really really good?"

Pete gave a quick shrug of her shoulders with indifference. We laughed and I chased after her with my staff. I was no match for her speed even when she was back peddling and I was running full speed ahead. Pete's agility and fighting ability were more instinctive than learned. She could never teach anyone to be at her skill level, let alone me.

• • •

I saw no purpose for all this pretend fighting as it wouldn't teach me how to gather and prepare food, shelter and clothing. I wondered for a brief instant if maybe I was supposed to accost bullies and take their clothes and send them naked down the road. No, not even Pete would consider the proposition reasonable.

One day in a fit of frustration I let out a small teeny tiny whimper in desperation as Pete easily dodged my attempts to hit her. Pete gave a whimpering sound of a child crying as she turned and walked off.

"Hehewhuhu Whehewhuhu Huu"

"If I don't like it here I can always go off by myself and be a picnic lunch for the bears. Without your knife and violence you are … you are… chicken liver."

I continued to yell even louder as Pete pranced off. I prefer my troubles to be taken more seriously. "That's why you have to be a loner with a total vocabulary of six one syllable words. Ever wonder why people don't like you? NO COMPASSION."

Pete went from a prancing self-assured athlete to a likely imitation of me. She became quite unsure footed as if she were walking on rolling round rocks. I could almost see the ground was full of unseen hands grabbing at her ankles.

Suddenly she doubled over and rolled to the ground writhing holding her stomach.

I was panicked. I couldn't get there fast enough. I bent down on all fours and stared into Pete's beautiful tanned olive skinned face.

"Are you hurt? Are you sick? OH, please don't die. No, not way out here anyway."

Pete's eyes blinked, then opened. "Essie chatter chatter ... chick..hen liver, no com... passion hurts Pete. Bad Essie."

Pete let a little smile crinkle from her gorgeous lips followed by a low gravelly giggle. I experienced the full impact of her stupid sense of humor. She got up and took a deep breath to help compose herself after her funny joke. There was no one there to appreciate the joke except Pete. But appreciate she did.

· · ·

She enjoyed natural art but was not opposed to reforming the natural elements she encountered. She generally would disrupt her sculptures before leaving, but not always.

· · ·

In the first day or two after Pete's confrontation with the bullies she was distant. In retrospect, it could have been a result of her relationship with Father Greggory. Possibly the detachment was an aftermath of her healing process and exchange with the trees. After a few weeks her cheeks were developing smile lines.

Pete had traveled nearly 900 miles in less than three months before we met. Something had kept her moving until recently. Her travels had taken her from a remote little farm on the prairies of South Dakota to Colorado and the Continental Divide.

I knew I shouldn't ask but I wondered if she was considering staying the winter in one of these little camps we set up.

"Do you ever plan things Pete or do you wing it by the seat of your pants?"

Shrug.

"Maybe a better question is how do we prepare for winter? Will we bury ourselves and hibernate or what teachings will prepare me for winters?"

"Look. Not with eyes. Universe chattering chattering."

"Are you saying to me 'watch and listen' is your plan? To survive winter you want me to watch and listen to Universe? In what language?" Pete turned and walked away. "You're not concerned I take it?"

. . .

She patiently took her time finding a new camp except those few days after the bullies. It was generally well protected from view and not easy to stumble upon accidently. There were times she chose a form of protection like a large rock overhang or under spruce limbs when weather looked threatening. However it was seldom as the weather was pretty good.

Her cooking area was not around her sleeping area. This would keep any hungry four leggeds away from our sleeping area which would be safest for all concerned.

. . .

She would wander off on occasion without any warning or reason I could decipher. Then just as mysteriously she'd stroll back into camp as if I weren't there. Yet she was quite attentive as long as I didn't try to express my needs verbally by chattering or whining. She would see or sense these desires and do something to accommodate them. I started using this sense of hers to better advantage. Sometimes.

There were times she would sit and study some living thing without moving for hours. She was in their world. She was part of the mountains, water and sky. During these introspective times I had a realization my scars were the boundaries of my world.

I could expand my universe by simply allowing it to grow. It was my choice.

. . .

Days we didn't travel there was more time for "teachings". I got more than I gave. One time I wanted to show my appreciation and I made a large blunder. I reached out and touched her. She, with astonishing reflexes, recoiled.

I got it. I had gone way over the line. I had been accepted and did something unexpected. She exuded something that might have come from the wildest critter in the mountains. I gave Pete plenty of room until she was willing to break the personal space boundary.

Chapter 21 – What is Reality

Essie's Diary

We were high in the Rockies at a place surrounded by curtains of towering granite cliffs. Below our camp was a crystal mountain lake with several long flat boulders jutting out into deep blue water. Fish in the early morning and evening would jump or roll from the water to catch flying insects and reenter with a "plop". I was learning to pay more attention. If I could determine what the insects looked like I may have a good bait if I could find bird feathers of similar color and tie them to a hook with a similar shape. Somehow.

• • •

Pete sat by herself using both hands to twist clockwise and counter clockwise on a smooth green branch about three quarters inch in diameter and sixteen inches in length. It was the start of a flute. She peeled about an inch of bark from one end. Then she tapped the peeled end on a rock and the outer bark slowly came loose from the white wood in the center. The bark became a hollow tube.

She put it down as I was standing there watching. Pete motioned for me to sit next to her by placing her left hand palm down on the log. Pete then put her right hand on the log on the other side and a little owl landed close by her hand. Bird-E was no larger than a clenched fist.

Pete faced me and peered into my eyes. I couldn't stand the silence for long and she knew it.

"I'm not sure what ……"

Pete took my index finger and softly put it to my mouth. This time with a great deal of gentleness. A monarch butterfly landed on my shoulder at the same time. It didn't flit like most monarchs but rather it floated in slow motion. Its striped plump little body hung down and looked more like a fairy with monarch wings. It made me feel a little self-conscious about my chatter. Clearly my mouth needed to be still. The monarch lifted off my shoulder and took

my desire to talk with it. It fluttered first up, then down, then away.

Bird-E flitted to the ground to get a better view of the action. Pete picked up a spruce cone near Bird-E. She touched my index finger to the cone and a drip of thick pitch stretched from the cone to my finger as she pulled the cone away.

Pete gently put my finger under my nose and the pungent smell registered a sharpness on my brain. She then brought my finger to her nose and I knew she was sensing exactly what I was experiencing.

Pete bent down again and picked up an orange chanterelle mushroom. She put it under my nose to get the subtle orange fragrance. Pete pulled it under her nose and received the same mild scent. Bird-E watched all from the ground.

A sheer granite cliff with crevasses full of old snow running more than a thousand feet in the air towered behind the little lake.

A large piece of granite near the top broke free and made a series of crashes and echoes. Reverberations filled the air like the smells from moments before. Everything blended in a surreal manner and exited like the butterfly.

I heard a beckoning eerie sound echoing from the lake. I glanced to my side where Pete once sat and the space was vacant. I got up from the log and tilted my head in an attempt to locate the source. Bird-E became my guide and flew to a nearby bush. I moved toward the little owl, and it moved again in the direction of the pothole lake. I followed with my staff.

I located the source. It was Pete and she was on the large flat rock protruding into the lake. The tiny owl was standing on the rock near Pete. Pete channeled the mountain air through the bark flute sending a current calling to all things. A trout surfaced. It made a wake that traveled out in an otherwise calm lake.

Music went from the flute and Mountain returned an echo accompanying the melody. The harmony gave me a spiraling chill. Light from the sun became muted and a ruby haze filled the area emanating from foliage, fur and feather alike.

Pete pointed a raised finger to a velvety ruby image of a mountain lion coming like a slow wisp of smoke from around the bushes. The eyes of the cougar were florescent yellow. It had a fluid motion, stopping for a moment with a swirl of soft crimson light from the movement of its tail. Nothing was

overlooked by those eyes. My insides sank to a cavernous deep.

A camp robber came down and sat with us on the log and added a few staccato comical notes to the musical score unfolding. I could see the color was in each short little breath of the jay. It dissipated quickly.

Pete put the flute again to her lips. My heart was opened and free when the haunting notes transported me to beyond the world of sight and sound. I must have had a giddy grin plastered across my face. A breeze brought harmony to Pete's melody through an instrument of distant boulders. This was the place where rainbows were stored. Everything before now was a myth. Society, time, philosophy, and even myself.

A voice came from somewhere beyond. *I would know I had chosen well if I could hear a whistle without a breath.* I had chosen well? Chosen what? Chosen to come with Pete? And …

And with my questions the enchantment was wiped out with an abrupt crash of silence. I waited. Nothing. I ached for the reverie to continue. It did not. I had lost it.

• • •

Later after supper Pete brewed berry tea and handed the cup to me. I took a sip and returned the cup realizing she was sharing. Pete smiled and we sat watching the rays of sunlight disperse the ruby haze.

The monarch returned and landed on our near empty cup. Pete gave a nod of thanks to the little yellow fairy on the rim. We got up and walked up a hill. My staff was now my walking stick. It was coming alive and a part of me.

• • •

Pete took the staff softly from my hand a distance uphill away from the lake. She started digging a narrow trench with the staff by softening the earth perpendicular to a downed log. Bird-E landed on the log and watched. We used our hands to remove the soft earth and then she softened more.

Pete had assembled fresh-cut boughs, sticks, dry grass, needles, leaves and extra bully clothes nearby. She handed me the bully clothes and motioned without a word to put on extra layers of clothing. They were to be my sleeping furs. Pete put boughs and then needles and leaves in the trench. Pete laid down face up and nestled in the nest packing, rearranging it for a comfortable bed. She got up and motioned for me to get in. I laid back and looked up. Not at Pete but at the face of my caregiver. Mountain.

Pete picked a blue columbine flower and offered it to me. I reached up with both hands and she put the flower between my palms. I gently folded my hands together encapsulating the flower stem just below the blossom. It was a different feel; not stem or flower, but life. I had never felt life. Pete lightly pushed my hands back to my chest by directing the flower to take me.

And it did.

Pete placed the staff beside me in the trench and under my right arm. She made the gesture of her two palms together as if she had a treasure within her hands.

Pete covered my body with more leaves and dry grass keeping my head uncovered and above

ground level. It was quite comfortable and a warm feeling swept through me. When Pete was done, she placed a thin layer of dirt on top the dry grass. I felt a second tranquil serene wave radiating into my body to stay the evening.

Pete put branches, sticks and boughs cantilevered over the log protecting my head like an umbrella. It permitted a view of the oncoming night sky toward the horizon but would protect me from weather should it be necessary.

Pete raised a burning stick and a radiant jewel shown in the night about ten feet from me. The one jewel became two in the dark, then back to one. For certain the glowing spots were a reflection of the light emanating from the burning stick but changing from one to two and moving in all directions was pleasantly perplexing. The glowing jewels jumped like a rabbit back and forth nearly touching the ground then up several feet and hovering, then back down. Sometimes as one, sometimes as two, both in perfect unison that no fireflies could emulate.

The connected glowing objects soared up in front of me and then hesitated putting on a show just for me. The glowing eyes were off again through the boughs and bounced along a foot or two off the ground for many yards at a time. I think Pete was as taken with the flitting embers as I was. In a blink, they were gone.

Pete raised a finger and traced a path across the night heavens. Following it was a shooting star leaving a momentary trail.

• • •

My attention was trapped by the vastness of our universe which in turn was connected to Universe. Pete was connected to every part. She reached down and stroked my scared and sunburned face. She looked deep into my being with her green-eyed gaze and it felt like she scoured my insides. I was floating, leaving myself behind. It was obvious in a strange way without knowing, Pete was leaving to build her own earth bed. I didn't feel alone.

• • •

I saw jewels on the needles from stars in the sky.

The moon clung to a branch and might drop where I lie.

• • •

Clouds moved in and covered the night sky. They glowed and produced a light show with lightning bouncing back and forth between them. Then a large flash and Mountain grumbled. Not in discomfort but displaying some measure of patience with an old rival. I was in good hands.

Rain started dripping but I was well protected under my shelter. Before long the storm moved on clearing the stage for stars again. I felt a peaceful slumber washing over my body.

• • •

It was barely dawn and visibility was more shadow than light. The sky had a dark grey hue as I stood on the same echo rock Pete stood on the afternoon before. I was still dressed in layers of bully clothes watching the lake appear from the darkness. A few twigs fell from my hair in the cool morning air. A wolf's howl in the far off distance brought promise for the day. I was compelled to return the call and I heard my tones in wonder.

I knew I was with Earth or Mountain or something primal. My mind tried pulling me away from the most comfortable feeling I had ever had. I quickly gave it up as I was at choice. When I did, my thoughts became an illusion no longer needing my attention. I was not a pile of ugly scarred skin. Something else was soaking in wordlessly.

I let fly another cry, not an imitation of the howling wolf, but what was inside me needing airing. It frightened me, it enlivened me, and it connected me. It was everything, and it was an absence of all things.

A high-pitched repetitive three note tune let the creature know he was not alone. Pete approached with her flute in hand and we, along with the distant howling wolf, gave the morning its due.

Nature was playing a song not just a tune without words. Lake enveloped and cleansed me. Mountain wrapped me in his cover. I looked up and there in front of me was a robin. I knew absolutely it was a robin. She stared straight at me with a look of, *Take a good look human.*

Her colored plumage was beautiful but unlike others of its kind. She was red white and blue with a white star on a blue background printed clearly on her forehead.

My mind interjected it might be the Fourth of July. I thanked my mind and went back to her. A place of my choosing.

She was all alone. The hair on my body prickled and my skin tingled.

I knelt by Lake and saw my image in front of the reflection of a beautiful shimmering magnificent Mountain. Mountain saw me as I saw Mountain and Robin.

• • •

We were definitely connected to everything else. We stood in silence and for the first time it felt good. Really good. I sensed my body as lighter. My internal voice sounded smoother and less wanting.

"As long as I don't try too hard, I get a glimpse of this little crumb called Essie fitting perfectly well into this big cake called Universe. And this small speck is not made of bone and damaged skin. I am spirit and nothing done to my body changes that."

Pete dropped her head and nodded dejectedly at my need to express everything in words. A fish cruised by leaving a small wake in Lake as it worked its way from shore. Pete left the same way.

• • •

Bird-E had me fooled for a while but I think I glimpsed what could have been the bird behind shining eyes produced with the glowing ember from Pete's burning stick. To this day I feel there were tricks involved particularly with the ruby haze and cougar. I never could figure them out.

I didn't ask Pete about any of this. I wouldn't dare to bring whys or hows into the world that had no words, let alone questions.

As I write this Diary an idea crosses my mind. I saw things I couldn't explain. I believed some, didn't believe others. This could have stopped me from seeing what was. What a cosmic joke if I choose to believe or disbelieve in a fact like gravity. Just a thought. I won't believe anything.

Chapter 22 - Sheep

Essie's Diary

A week later we were camped under a huge rock, held up by other enormous granite boulders forming a tabletop. After a big midday meal of trout under our natural shelter overhang it began with a bang.

The sky opened suddenly and made a beaded curtain of rain and hail outside our rock shelter too dense to see through. The noise of the shower falling was loud enough to drown out some of the rumbles of thunder.

Pete had a peaceful calm come over her with the rumbling from the sky as if she was secure in the arms of the almighty. I saw her look to the sky and give a thank you smile. Just a quick glance but I was starting to look. And see.

· · ·

Pete gave a struggling attempt at a new vocabulary word. "The sky has … eh ah pers eh ah perspir… ation?"

I had to smile at her progress. She fought words like I did my walking stick. I knew words were not her thing and her mistake was not meant as a joke.

"That's good Pete. Pre cip i ta tion is rain or water from the sky. Per spir a tion is sweat or water from the skin. Both will keep our skin moist or wet."

"Easy, I kill pers pir ation. No use."

"Oh no please Pete. 'Perspiration' is a wonderful word … for sweat when we are hot. It's perfect you have made the interesting connection between the two words. It is poetry to interchange the two words like you did. It opened my eyes to another way of looking at rain. I enjoy your creative use of language."

Pete nodded with understanding.

"What happens if you try to live with insiders?"

"Insiders and dresses no fit Pete." Her sentence was punctuated by a flash of lightening and a crack followed by a rumble of thunder. *Maybe the daughter of Zeus?*

"Insiders don't fit?"

"Insiders sick."

"There's no doubt about the bullies having a sickness."

The afternoon shower let up as quickly as it had started leaving a chilling coolness and a perfect full rainbow. The large boulders released some of their warmth gathered from the morning sun. The perfect ending.

• • •

I wish I could have extracted more stories and teachings in those early days when she was nothing but natural. I tried on several occasions to have her explain some things further. It would always get an answer like, "No. Words no good on Raven." I wanted to get more information on Raven but "No". And she would stop talking altogether.

In the beginning it was difficult to know if 'words no good' was a short-coming of hers because of a lack of vocabulary or of mine for a lack of understanding of her extraordinary world.

At some point I realized why she could not or would not explain some things. Once you "know" you don't need an explanation. If you don't "know" already, no words can rectify it. Two legged's minds and language hadn't developed to the extent of Universe. This concept she knew inherently without being able to describe it better than "No".

• • •

As always Pete wore her purse and zig zagged ahead of me. I walked with bully clothes slung over my shoulder still tied by suspenders. I remember sauntering with more confidence and steadiness in my legs. It felt like something was loosening its grip. I was in the beginning throes of getting unstuck. No, I would never be like Pete. No one could be. Most humans were not made to return to Eden.

As we traveled downhill I watched for wildlife and possible herbs for tea. We remained above timberline picking our way around rock outcrops. Pete would sail over the bushes and I'd find a way around them.

We were on one of several large sloping plateau meadows about a mile across and several miles in length. It gradually sloped to the southeast and in

the direction we traveled. We passed a monument or cairn made of stacked rocks at least nine feet in height made by sheepherders. These were some of the navigational tools used by sheepherders.

On either side of the landscape, the terrain fell off into green forests and then to rivers thousands of feet below.

Wild flowers lit up the expanse before us, irrigated with narrow brooks from the afternoon thundershowers. Lichen on the rocks also added to the various bright colors.

Ahead there were two herds of sheep about a mile apart. The first herd was considerably smaller than the second. Faint sounds of bells CLANK CLANG and sheep BAH BAH BAH were in the distance.

"What do you think?"

"Easy, no think."

Of course.

• • •

We continued down the sloping meadow. The little brooks crisscrossing the ground became more prevalent as we got to better pasture and closer to the sheep.

Long before we reached the sheep, the sheepdogs set off an alarm by barking. One sheepdog rapidly and aggressively approached us and all my newly-found confidence evaporated.

"Peeeeeeete."

Pete stepped in front of me, bent in a ready position, and gave a quick head fake stopping the sheepdog in its tracks.

The dog remained frozen and stern-faced. Pete gave off a similar look. The dog gave a tiny wiggle of its bobbed tail. Pete tilted her head slightly and the wag of the stubby tail became more pronounced. Pete showed the dog the back of her hand and allowed the dog to smell it. Then the dog went around Pete frisking her with his nose, sticking it where it didn't belong.

When done the dog approached me with the same intent. I tightened and inched backward.

"Stop, he smell for evil."

"What does that mean 'he smell for evil'. I don't have evil or anything that smells like it. If you don't learn to talk better I'm dog food."

"Funny S. E. Now Shusheshsh".

There's that shushing sound again. Pete made the same gesture she made the day she built my earth bed. Her palms came together as if holding the columbine flower.

I took a deep breath and attempted to relax. The dog completed his examination of me in an ill-mannered way with his nose between my legs. He then took a few steps back allowing us to pass. His eyes never left Pete's. We walked toward the sheepherder's camp ushered in by the dog.

Pete looked over the area in Focused Attention as we approached. There were two young men in front of us. One young man slept on his back with a straw hat partially shading his eyes. He remained oblivious to our approach. The raising and lowering of his chest showed him to be soundly sleeping.

Sitting beside him was a second kid whittling. He stared at Pete with wide eyes for a full minute then looked down when he glanced at me. A nice looking guy really. His air was that of a scared deer once he was caught eyeballing Pete. He was about Pete's age, maybe fourteen or so, with his best feature being large gold flecked brown eyes. He had a lanky build, curly brown hair and sensual lips. Too bad he got up and left to watch the new people from afar.

I thought a warm hello would be a good way to get things started off on the right foot but no. Neither of those two guys uttered a word. One slept and the other ran off.

The thin fellow didn't twitch an eyelash or dare a second glance. He sat nearly thirty yards away throwing his knife up and having it come back down sticking in the dirt each time. It was some version of solitary mumbletypeg which is a stupid game boy's play with their pocket knives. Not even my disfigured face could draw him from it. Quite unusual.

When it was clear there would be no harmonious discourse I started to talk to fill the uncomfortable gap. I yelled at the distant kid and he ignored me. The sleeping young man remained oblivious to my efforts as well.

Pete delicately touched Mr. Sleepy Guy in the ribs with a dirty toe. With no result, she touched him again a little harder with the side of her callused foot. Then without any more warning she flipped his hat off his face with her foot and he raised his head with considerable effort. I would guess him to be older than Pete but likely younger than I, maybe in his early twenties. He was considerably larger than Pete and quite soft looking with fat cheeks and no muscle tone whatsoever. He spoke sleepily.

"What you want?"

"Nothin yagot."

Pete left shaking her head. I remained behind staring at the groggy sheepherder when I felt Pete's grip clamping down on my arm. I reluctantly marched beside her looking behind me.

"What is the problem with you? You were as rude as those two, tipping the hat off the sleeping sheepherder."

"Ru u de? No sheepherder. He sleeps."

I had nothing else to say. If 'rude' didn't say it to her, nothing would. But I had plenty to talk to myself about. I continued at full speed ahead with my line of chatter knowing it would drive her crazy. I ended with a small summary for her benefit.

"You wander like a deer without caring to know where you are. You have no time to talk to anyone on this long journey to … to nowhere."

In the distance there was the larger herd of sheep up a gently sloping side hill. We walked past a little lake toward a camp with a wagon and a wisp of smoke from a dying fire.

Chapter 23 - Ernesto

Essie's Diary

The BA BA BA ing and the neck bells CLAG CLAG DING made welcoming music. Something caught Pete's eye as she bounded a brook. She bent and picked it up giving it a shake. CLINK CLINK. It was a rusty sheep bell from years back.

As we approached the larger herd the sheepdogs set off an alarm but none approached. Pete walked toward a clearing and a sheepherder's wagon. A man sat on a rock with his lunch looking in her direction.

Pete approached in Focused Attention. The man was in his late thirties or early forties with a sturdy stocky build. He removed his floppy medium-brimmed work hat as we advanced. He was balding. A bright colored neckerchief was around his neck. His dark twinkling eyes were a perfect backdrop for his winning feature; his smile, which was missing a fair number of teeth.

Pete did not return a smile. She warily scanned the area and the man in front of her, ears alert, nostrils flaring. The Sheepherder spoke first having no reaction to my scared face or Pete's wariness. He used English first then Spanish as he was figuring us out.

"Not many come our way strangers."

Pete gave an acknowledging nod. Pete cautiously handed the man the little bell she found moments earlier.

"Thank you. My name is Ernesto… and yours?"

"Pete."

"Good to meet you Pete. *Mi casa es su casa.*"

Ernesto swung both hands to show the wide-open spaces of his home could be our home as well. It did show some degree of humor. When he laughed, it was the laugh of a considerably larger man. Pete remained serious and pointed at me with her thumb.

"*Se llama S… E.*"

Ernesto smiled at the thumb flipped at me from her side. *She spoke Spanish and I only taught her English?* I was instantly distracted by Ernesto's eyes. He looked unwaveringly into mine and spoke in English.

"My pleasure Essie. I see few willing to brave the great outdoors. Virtually none with so few belongings up here on the face of God. Even those with feathers or four feet find it difficult. Could you spend the evening? Maybe share a story and a meal with a humble sheepherder?"

I turned to Pete with my disfigured mouth opened in disbelief with his poetic flowery words. "Pete?"

Pete continued on alert in Focused Attention. Raven flew in behind Ernesto I thought unnoticed by him. The large bird looked more confident for some reason and stood taller than his normal two feet in height.

Ernesto mimed Pete's demeanor. Head tilted, nose to the wind catching any possible scent for danger. I saw what Ernesto was doing. Pete didn't get the imitation.

Ernesto smoothly changed his mime to me. He walked waggling his head and shoulders pretending to carry a walking stick and a pack on his back. Pete gave a slight smile under the twinkle in her eyes.

Ernesto continued with his act not knowing the bird was behind him imitating his actions. He went down on his haunches but this time walked with the unmistakable stiff-legged swagger and right arm slightly down like the wing of Raven. Raven couldn't keep his eyes off Ernesto.

Ernesto brought his arm up and then let it down, like Raven was doing at that moment behind him. They both tilted their heads. After a few strutting steps Ernesto hopped on two legs straight at Pete on his haunches.

He angled his head stretching his neck toward Pete's purse. Ernesto lowered his arms, now wings, even further in a gesture of begging while extending his head and neck toward her. Pete opened her purse and flipped a small piece of dried food at his face. He caught it in his mouth and made the exaggerated motion of a bird gulping.

Ernesto rolled over backward in delight and returned to his feet from a handstand. It was obvious Pete had not known such human antics. Pete turned to me in an animated manner, "Raven!?!"

I nodded. Pete dropped her Focused Attention with his stunt and gave her consent. "We camp."

"We are most pleased, Mountain Court Jester, to accept your kind offer. We shall return by early evening."

Ernesto winked at me. What a wink that was. I melted. Ok Diary, I melt easily. I'm cheap chocolate.

• • •

Our camp was down a gentle hill from the central plateau near a stream. Good drainage to help keep the mosquitoes at bay but not gone unfortunately. Like all connoisseurs of fine cuisine they would travel miles to dine at my eatery. Our firewood consisted of small dried branches neatly stacked next to a fire ring.

Pete started our conversation which was a little unusual. "Essie, sheep good."

"You miss the old life? You want Ernesto to have good feelings about you? It's called a good first impression. I think you can handle that, 'easy', as you say."

"Yes, Wolfboy chocolate stealing gone."

We finished our camp setup. She hung clothes by two tethers well-protected from weather close to the trunk of a spruce. There they were out of view and also protected from rain.

With our hair a little wet and some clothes drying on bushes we left our camp for Ernesto's.

• • •

A fire did its job on three iron pots off to the edge of the fire ring. As we entered he spoke. "I'm checking on sheep for the evening. Care to join me?"

Pete nodded.

"You two go talk sheep. Shall I look after supper and stir the pots?" Ernesto nodded a thank you and left with Pete. Oh what a charming man.

And it did smell good every time I raised a lid for a little stir. The spoon needed to be licked often to be sure the bottom wasn't burning. Ok, Diary, licked may not have been the perfect word. Maybe slurped.

• • •

When they returned I was waiting patiently hoping Ernesto wouldn't see the missing stew. We normally ate earlier in the day hence I was thinking about food. Lots of food. My stirring increased my appetite.

There were benches, seats and tables made of logs and large flat rocks not far from the fire, as his fire was small. The cooking area looked similar to what Pete and I often used.

"I am happy you could join me. I hope Lamb stew is alright? Please take a seat anywhere."

"Perfect. I'm famished."

Pete grinned at the word but it registered nothing on the face of Ernesto. Pete took a seat directly in the smoke and not too close to the fire. I sat out of the trail of smoke. Ernesto grabbed a bowl and dished stew from a pot next to the fire and handed it with a spoon to Pete. He did the same for me, then took a bowl for himself.

He passed a pot with warmed tortillas. Pete took three and I took one and glanced at Pete in disgust. Ernesto took three tortillas for himself.

"Mind if I join you in the smoke away from mosquitoes in their hour of hunger? They are bad this year with all the wet pasture."

Pete nodded. Ernesto sat on the log but not close to Pete allowing the smoke in the gentle breeze to do its work. I shooed mosquitoes on the other side. We all ate heartily, including the mosquitoes. I hadn't realized it but Pete had always chosen campsites nearly free of mosquitoes. Here, where wet pasture was necessary, there was little choice. The numerous seats around the fire provided the right environment regardless which way the winds blew with or without campfire smoke. I didn't have the experience yet on where to sit when being eaten.

A little later Ernesto removed a lid from a fry pan far from the heat of the fire and exposed its content. "Pan dulces? They won't be any good tomorrow."

Before Pete could give her nod the sweet bun dropped on her plate. Ernesto poured more tea and a coyote howled in the background. HARK HARK YIP YIP WEHOWEE YIP YIP YIP WEHOWEE "A coyote gathering the pack. Doesn't sound lonely."

Pete's mouth full of sweet roll nodded a grunt in agreement.

After swallowing first and as politely as I could to keep up the conversation, "Do you talk to the animals? How do you know it's not lonely?"

Ernesto answered with toothless grin. "Well yes I talk to them, but seldom do they listen. Gathering sounds differ from a lonely bitch. There are yips in the gathering and then maybe a howl often used for hunger or feeding. It is more staccato and can be used by more than one to collect the pack and promote their common consent. The lonely sounds are howls, more like longing for a loved one, with notes held longer covering more octaves performed legato."

Pete had a stunned expression on her face with the music exchange. The music talk was way over her head. I held up the conversation. "You know music as well as mime, tend a million sheep and cook delightfully under these primitive conditions."

"I know nothing but I play at all things. My music does drive the bears away. I wish it could do the same to mosquitoes. Do you play an instrument?"

Ernesto looked at me and I gave a noncommittal Pete shrug.

"Do you dance?"

I shook my head no.

He looked at Pete and she gave a non-committal shrug duplicating my own. Ernesto mimed our shrugs.

"Is that a yes or a no shrug? Never mind. Feet do not lie."

We all pitched in. Dogs were fed, dishes done, and we stacked more firewood near the fire in the dwindling light. Plenty for the evening and a morning fire.

Ernesto went inside his wagon and brought out a violin and a mandolin.

He held both instruments up within my reach. I took the mandolin. "Maybe I can find a couple of strings I like on this thing."

Ernesto sat and did a little tuning on the fiddle. Then a few quick strokes struck the air with lively music. His eyes and hands both danced to the rhythm as if he was listening and not playing. Fire licked the air keeping time along with Pete's callused feet dancing in the dirt.

I chimed in on the twelve string mandolin. A beautiful instrument. Ernesto motioned with his head and body for Pete to rise. She did but not at first request. It was the music that eventually overcame her inertia.

Ernesto put the bow to strings and started a second tune. As he did he stared at Pete with a rhythmic bounce in his body. Pete started uncontrollably with her feet. Then both legs bounced. She tried her best to sit on them but they won. They squirmed out from under her. She launched herself up and let go a smile, not at Ernesto I was happy to see, but in complete appreciation of the music.

Ernesto's music and simultaneous dance was full of life, matching his personality. Bird-E came from nowhere and took a seat in a stunted nearly dead spruce tree. He tilted his head first one way and then the other watching the show. It's not believable to me it's the same bird I saw the night of my earth bed. *Oh please little owl, don't go just yet. I have many questions.*

As the tune became more mellow, Pete swayed in the music; graceful and spontaneous. Each cell of her body guided the adjoining one with no self-consciousness whatsoever. Her hips and arms absorbed the music as it moved up her body. She became a limber tree being stroked by a magical breeze. When the music ended, Ernesto bowed at Pete holding his eyes on hers as tears stained his cheeks. She turned a graceful half turn pirouette leaving the firelight. It was instinctive and classic Pete. She had never seen a pirouette I feel certain. Yet, that was the perfect finish.

• • •

I started a more subdued tune on the mandolin. Pete returned, got a cup of water, and watched my fingers make the music. At the end of my piece, Ernesto blurted to Pete across the campfire.

"Why do you dress in boys clothes?"

"Pants, no dress."

"Eh, yes Pete. But why do you wear boy's clothes?"

"Easy, boys wear boy's clothes."

"If you are a boy …I am an onion."

Pete gave a startled look and a grin that said, *game on.*

"Boys don't walk far to pee and boys definitely don't dance like that."

Pete grinned at Ernesto. "You smarter than looks."

"Pete!" but Pete was unfazed with my scolding.

"Oh Little Bird. She only knows truth, not like us. We live in a make-believe world of what is not. Think of the power she has. I bet she has paid dearly for her gifts."

Ernesto went on. "Here's a question Pete. What are you looking for in a husband?"

"Not looking."

"OK, why not?"

"No why."

"If you were interested, what would you be looking for?"

"Man no talk."

Ernesto piped up, "Sounds like Ed."

"Ed?"

"He's the guy you might have met today with Juan who didn't talk a lot."

"No husband. No babies, no clean house, no wash clothes. No. No."

Ernesto got things back on track. "Now that you think I'm smarter than I look, why do you wear boy's clothes?"

Night sounds filtered through our crackling little fire. Ernesto spoke softly again, this time turning towards me. "We are at the bottom of the food chain out here. Bears, coyotes, mountain lions are faster than us with more cunning. But she belongs out here. Timeless and knowing like this mountain, the raven, and the night sky." Pausing for a moment for a thought. "Do you know her story? Her beginnings?"

I gave him my best shriveled smile and an unknowing glance. Ernesto smiled as I began to play again. He gained Pete's attention. "A pot of beans is smarter than I look. Why do you hide in boys clothes?"

Pete looked away distractedly.

"Easy, want man work."

"What a waste of beauty. The way I was raised was to see beautiful women cared for and protected by their husbands. You should both be in a kitchen giving your husbands many babies."

Pete got agitated with these words. "Sheepherder spits sheepshit." Then out came the more important to her. "You Raven?" Pete imitated Raven with wing down on her haunches.

"I have watched this bird many times in recent years. He has come and watched me is more like it. You know this bird in camp today?"

Pete nodded a little questioningly.

Maybe she'll lighten up on me for my questions.

"You think it's the same bird... your Raven?"

Pete nodded. "I know Raven." Emphasizing the word 'know'. I tilted my head in wonder. It would be difficult in the world I know for the same bird to be in two places a thousand miles apart nearly every day.

"Does this bird have other distinguishing traits or marks?"

A nod came from Pete then "Bad wing no two feathers."

"Yes, the raven visiting me has had two feathers missing recently and they are now half grown back in."

Ernesto directed his next statement to me. "You may think I am crazy with a head stuffed full of voodoo but there are things I can't explain. This bird Raven has often visited me over the last two years. I asked the bird to explain himself in as many ways as I knew. I started with words in Spanish then English knowing words were not likely going to do it. Then I asked by gestures and mimes."

I was into it. "Show us how you would ask if not in words."

Ernesto shrugged with head tilted and a questioning look. He pointed his palms up and tilted his head the other way. When done he took both hands and swept the sky overhead arms extended. Then he continued in words. "The only answer I got was 'patience'. May have lost a little in translation but that was the gist. I waited. And here you are."

"How did Raven deliver the answer 'patience'?"

"It was actually a little comical. He walked around in a little circle slowly several times with his head and both wings drooping."

After a short pause he continued. "I was raised Catholic and went to a Catholic school. I'm not sure a good Catholic would consider Raven was given special powers from God or Raven was a demon sent from Satin as our culture often characterizes the bird."

Ernesto had given me some ideas. "Pete has collected me and given me help. A raven helped Noah when he returned to the ark and gave witness land was near. Are Raven and Pete sent to help me and possibly you as well?"

Ernesto tilted his head and I gave him the time he needed. I saw wheels turning. "Ravens were given a special place in the Bible by the number of times they are mentioned. In one place the Bible implies they drive their young from the nest at an early age. Are we to kick our young from the nest and let them fend for themselves?"

"Maybe that fits somehow with your question on Pete's beginnings. I too was raised Catholic in the orphanage in Aztec Ernesto. You are blending the worlds of Catholicism, nature, and the spiritual through Raven. My understanding is this is not accepted by the Church."

Ernesto looked into my eyes resolutely. "Then we both went to grade school in Aztec. We may know some of the same people but let's go to the more interesting first. I was never any good in school and I am mostly self-taught as I love to read. Many things are teachers if I keep my eyes open to the possibilities. To have two birds of the same breed and size with a droopy wing following both of us and not have two birds here now stretches the imagination. In order to see I must keep only one belief: everything is possible even if it seems a little crazy to my five senses."

It sounded to me like Ernesto was saying the same thing Pete mimed many times when she used her fingers to open her eyes wider. We should accept all things and not let our beliefs close our eyes.

More evening noises filled the gaps in the conversation. Pete blurted in the clear crisp evening air. "Raven have demon?"

Ernesto turned to Pete. "Maybe you should ask Raven your questions in your way. I know it's not an easy thing but something tells me you will know how."

Ernesto had more on the subject of help. "We have needed help for a long time. Señor Perez has many legal problems with the American government and the Rancho, and losing his son. … and I have many problems with his grandson, Juan. A few good cowboys can generally be found but good sheepherders are another breed. You met Juan and Ed on your way down the mountain?"

I nodded yes and Pete was slow to stay with the conversation. She was off somewhere maybe connecting to angels, demons, or Raven.

Raven came swooping into camp. He strutted up to Ernesto with right wing down and did a little begging with his mouth open. Ernesto gave the bird a morsel and Raven came over by Pete near the smoke, but not in it. He had different body language around Pete. No begging permitted I guess. Raven was clearly comfortable in his relationship with both Pete and Ernesto. This was peculiar but around Pete nothing should be labeled.

Ernesto took his time then picked up the conversation again about Juan. "Juan is the one either sleeping or eating. Ed's quiet and shy because he's self-conscious about his stuttering. I hate to see him put pressure on himself trying to string two words together in less than five minutes."

Pete showed signs of coming back to the conversation and a small recognition of what was said. "Juan does little to help with the sheep but his grandpa Señor Perez es El Patrón. We have spoiled Juan. Ed could be of great help if he wasn't afraid of talking to me."

Pete looked at Ernesto, taking in the many words. *Little help?*

Ernesto picked up the look in Pete's eyes and answered as if Pete had spoken. "Juan is less help than he used to be. He's had some problems with drugs. Every year he gets a little more useless." And after a long pause, "You showed on our walk you know sheep and I could use a hand up here. What do you two say?"

Pete shrugged and wagged her head pondering the idea. I looked at Pete to see her decision. It didn't come.

"Tomorrow when you are ready we will pay Juan and Ed a visit and you can make up your mind?"

Pete gave a tentative look. I nodded knowing she would take more time. Ernesto put a few sticks on the fire keeping the social setting alive, mountain style.

I was wholly impressed with this man and his knowledge and compassion for the world around him. I felt I could say or ask anything.

"Do you have eyes for Pete?"

"You do have a way of inserting a question. I have eyes for Pete like I do a shooting star or a young colt kicking up his heels on spring grass. I don't want a romantic encounter with these delights. But I would be crazy to not look at what God has provided in any form of splendor. And to turn my head from beauty is like giving God and his creations a kick in the teeth."

"I need to know what you think Ernesto…the truth. I know I'm not pretty but am I too ugly to be around normal people?"

Ernesto feigned disappointment. He grabbed his heart as if I had thrown a dagger into his chest. I got it.

"Oh, no Ernesto. It's a compliment. You are way better than normal people. I can never attract a husband as fine as you. But can I hope for even a plain average guy?"

Pete gave an incredulous glance.

"I'm serious Pete. I might want to attract a guy someday and this face can scare the hair off a bear. To make matters worse I don't have any place to smear lip rouge or eye makeup. You know how those dumb boys go for that stuff."

Ernesto mimed another shot with the dumb boy comment.

I continued toward Pete. "Don't you want to fall in love?"

"Love?"

"Yes, the achy feeling inside you can't make go away?"

I rubbed my ribcage with a pained look on my shriveled face and Pete confidently gave her reply.

"Oh, easy. Bad much-rooms".

"No Pete! Don't you want to have babies some day?"

Pete gave a shiver of complete revulsion.

"If I had more than these slits in my forehead you could see me rolling my eyes right now."

Ernesto shook his head in an exaggerated mime of a dog shaking his head to help rearrange the ideas to make sense. Ernesto mimed falling in love... worshiping at my feet.

"I would be happy to put you at the head of a long line of beautiful women … if you return tomorrow evening and play some more."

"Ok, ok… enough. As if I could count on your outsider opinion anyway."

"Outsider?"

"It's a long story."

"How about another cup of tea and a bedtime story Essie?"

"Sounds good to me. It's been a long day."

I curled up to Ernesto's side and got a good whiff of armpit.

"Maybe tomorrow is bath day Ernesto?"

Ernesto gave a big sigh. "I would take more baths but the water here is painfully cold and it hurts me way down to my liver. But anyway… once upon a time there was this slightly crazy Spanish Knight called Don Quixote of La Mancha who had a trusted squire named Sancho Panza,…."

I settled in this strange wonderful talented man's arms. I looked across to Pete who was already engrossed in the old classic and closed my eyes… while holding my nose. The Tortoise and the Hare was the night cap.

Chapter 24 - Five Bears

Early the next morning Pete ran into Ernesto's camp hollering. Ernesto peered out of his sheepherder's wagon, sleep still in his eyes.

"Ernesto, quick quickly. SE drowns. Quickly!"

Ernesto still in his long johns hobbled while trying to pull on boots. Obviously not built to run, he now tried to keep up with Pete hobbled by untied boots. Pete turned and encouraged Ernesto by waving hysterically. She could easily walk backward and stay ahead of him.

"Ernesto, quicklier."

Pete overlooked the little lake as the puffing Ernesto came up from behind her. Pete pointed down at a large rock touching the edge of the lake.

"S.E. down there. You go quick!"

Ernesto moved as rapidly as possible to a pile of clothes on the rock jutting into a deep place in the lake. Pete yelled down.

"Jump in. Jump in. Quicklier."

Ernesto pulled off his boots and splashed into the water. It was over his head at that spot.

"Yee AHHAA, hace <u>frío</u>!"

Ernesto swam out. He spun around while treading water with head up. He stuck his head down under for a better look. Still no sign. "Nada" he yelled. He held up a hand and shook his head to show Pete he found nothing. He found Essie standing beside Pete.

Essie mimed taking a bath by scrubbing under her arms. Pete slung a piece of squashed soap root at his head forcing him to duck below the surface again. He came up, found the root and scrubbed himself clothes and all. Ernesto's chattering teeth kept his grumbling unintelligible, until he came out and found a flat rock warmed by the sun. He yelled at the top of his voice, "Whoever said cleanliness is next to Godliness never put their little toe in that lake."

• • •

Ernesto came out of his wagon dressed with hat and colorful clean neckerchief around his neck. Pete poured tea and offered Ernesto the cup as a peace offering as if it were her camp.

"Now that wasn't bad was it?" Essie said a little apprehensively.

"It's like hitting myself over the head with a rock. It feels sooo good when I stop. The bathing can kill you up here."

"I can definitely agree but once every couple of months may be worth the risk."

Pete raised her nose and pointed it at Ernesto, acknowledging his new fragrance. He gave a forgiving smile now the chore was behind him.

• • •

The visit up to Juan and Ed was delayed. The day of Ernesto's bath quieted down and was followed by an easy meal before dusk. Cleanup of dishes had started in the wagon when the dogs sounded the alarm.

Five bears had run swiftly into the herd and cut out a bunch of ewes more than 400 yards away. The balance of the herd was scattering in all directions. Three brave dogs chased bears and fated sheep. The remaining dogs helped Ernesto to control the frightened herd now moving both uphill and down.

The bears were pushing about twenty head of sheep ahead of them and the dogs would soon overtake and stop them. However three dogs against five packed bears would only lose dogs.

Pete grabbed the lead rope of the horse tied to the wagon and flew aboard in one smooth easy motion. She took out after the lot of them; bears, dogs and sheep. She had no saddle or bridle just the lead. One of the younger dogs named Jorge left Ernesto and ran after Pete barking with all the excitement. Ernesto may have sent Jorge to help. There was too much confusion to know.

Pete controlled the horse by her knees on his ribs and the lead rope leaning or pulling against the horse's neck. She stuck on the horse and became a part of the animal as if she was part of his mane flowing with every stride.

She had only the two knives on her belt and her sling around her head where it always was. Horse and rider were gliding easily in one fluid motion as they ate up valuable ground toward the marauding bears.

The horse was fine until the last fifty yards but the sight and scent of bears was starting to stiffen his stride. Pete tightened her grip with her legs while grabbing a fist full of mane at the withers. When she nudged him forward he stiffened more but she stuck tighter to him than the patch on her britches. She was having none of it.

She got to within twenty yards and slid off the horse while the horse was still galloping. Her legs were moving to catch the ground in flight. She was weightless as she landed and moved across the ground like a gust of wind. No one but Mountain had the time to appreciate the daring athletic moves of the young teen.

Moments after her dismount her horse veered from the action out of harm's way. The animal put his head down and bucked twice kicking high into the air to free himself of the phantom Pete no longer on his back.

The bears were now stopped at their first lamb kill. She ran at the bears and dogs until she was less than five yards away. The dogs were putting up a terrific battle but were in constant danger of being opened up by the slash of bear claws. Normally several dogs would surround one bear and keep him spinning on his rear until help could arrive. In this case they were clearly outnumbered.

Pete picked up a stone and the sling made its first direct hit on the largest black bear of 400 plus pounds. It did little more than anger the bear but definitely got his attention. She put in a larger stone this time knowing it might daze him but never kill him. The second stone found it mark and the bear came straight after her. The second hit caused no more damage than the first.

Bears can't run long distances at full speed but for thirty yards they are quick. They can easily outrun a human but Pete wasn't ready to leave. Pete stood her ground unflinching. The aggravated bear made his charge. She pulled her skinning knife while waiting for the collision.

As the bear made ready to hit her she made a last second move to the side as three inch claws at the end of a powerful paw swung by her belly. The momentum of the heavy bear in a straight line kept him from moving laterally as rapidly as Pete. As the bear went by her she reached down and got her knife blade just under his drooping slobbering jaw. His hide was tough. Her blade sharp.

He continued for more than ten yards past her position when he rolled to a stop and whirled to look her in the eye. She heard a bark from Jorge behind her and looked over her shoulder to see a second bear coming at her. Jorge came at the second bear from the side and dodged the first paw by leaping over it. He ran behind the bear lunging and attacking his back side to put him on his rear. The bear spun keeping weight on his rear and made every attempt to kill the little pest Jorge. However the brave dog kept just ahead of his paws and claws. The bear was twirling like a slow top on his rump with front paws held high swinging at air.

Pete swung back to the first angry bear as he got his bearings. As it sunk into his thick skull she was still standing, he rolled forward off his haunches to make another charge but this time obviously under more control. He would not miss her again. He approached in a more methodical manner twisting his head making a thunderous growl.

She cocked her head to listen to Jorge keeping the other bear occupied behind her. Pete replaced her knife and bent down for another heavier rock. She placed it in the pouch of the sling and with a quick overhand motion the rock was heading for the first bear's head while he was moving toward her. It hit the side of his head as he turned which was likely the most vulnerable part.

It had the desired result. He stopped dazed and had to gather himself wondering what was happening. He slowly fell to one side then lost all control of his balance and fell to the ground.

The stone had not knocked him down but had slowed him enough to let the knife wound under his jaw finally do its job. He had bled out and there was now not enough blood flow to the brain to keep the huge bear functioning.

She turned and saw the second bear stationary except for his head that would track her trusty sidekick as he ran around behind the bear barking. As the bear got close to finally putting claws on Jorge, the dog jumped back in the opposite direction. The bear's attention was on Jorge making spectacular leaps and agile moves which was confounding him.

Pete slipped behind the huge bear shadowing his top-like moves. She reached around the bear's neck with her skinning knife below his lower jaw and gave a slashing motion as she moved swiftly backward. The bear's attention never left the dog until he fell over with dying gasping heaves.

She called Jorge to her side and he unwillingly obeyed but not until she flashed him two critical green eyes. Jorge was not done with the intruder even though the bear didn't move anymore. And now there were three.

The remaining three bears were kept busy by the three herding dogs. The dogs had them bunched together but since their backs were to one another the bears had the advantage over the fast moving dogs. One dog went sprawling with a yelp and a tumble to one side only to leap back into the fray. Another dog was hit by a flying paw pad but only nicked by one of the claws.

Pete didn't want the dogs to be exposed to the danger any more than necessary but she also didn't want to take the dogs attention from their task at hand. Any order may turn their heads or attention and cause them harm.

She put Jorge on whoa and gave him one last glare. He'd done his share.

Pete moved in front of one of the bears and stood behind the dog keeping the bear's full attention. Her target was eight paces in front of her and above the level of dog's head. Her silent weapon was launched and sunk deep into the bear's neck. Her throwing knife did the needed damage. First he started to wobble and then fell to one side with the knife stuck deep in his throat.

Jorge could no longer stand it and he roared past Pete with ears trailing knowing not to make eye contact with his boss. There were now four dogs and two bears in the fight but the bears were able to protect each other's backs. She silently motioned Jorge to her side raising her arm up then pointing emphatically to the ground by her side. He reluctantly came.

She pointed at the downed bear and her throwing knife protruding from his throat. She gave the command to fetch the knife. The dog looked at the bear and incredulously looked back into her eyes. The bear was too large to drag back to her. Again she pointed to the knife and pulled her skinning knife from her belt. Pointed at it. He whirled back to the bear. She would have used her skinning knife as a throwing knife but it would have left her unarmed to face the last bear.

He waited his turn to retrieve the throwing knife between other barking dogs. Jorge shot in but didn't have a firm grip before he tried to return. He left without withdrawing the knife. He had to go back. His second attempt was successful after a firm grip and some heavy tugging. He delivered the throwing knife back into her hands.

As Pete turned to take the knife from Jorge's mouth she saw from the corner of her eye the two remaining bears starting their charge toward her. She had both knives out now one in each hand with her focus clearly on the impending danger when two quick shots rang out.

One bear tore up turf as he hit the ground and the other roared spit as the bullet struck his side three feet from her waiting knife. With a quick leap the rolling bear passed beneath her.

Pete turned to Ernesto to give him praise for his timely accurate shooting. A wide seldom-seen smile of appreciation flashed in his direction. Ernesto was down on knees and elbows quite low to the ground with head tucked between his shoulders. He stretched his neck out and cocked his head in her direction. He moved slowly like the lowly tortoise, just one limb at a time.

Ernesto pointed his now tortoise-like beak made by puckering his face in her direction. His face then took on an apology for interrupting her quest of fighting dragons and windmills. With the raise of one eyebrow he turned to the main herd and his day job.

"Slow Sancho tortoise?"

"I had to finish my beans and do your dishes hijo."

As he left with a swagger in his step she saw more of the previous night's story unfolding. His name was no longer Ernesto, but her beloved and trusted Sancho who was supporting her folly. She changed her demeanor with a nonchalant innocent smile as if nothing had happened and turned to skin the first and largest bear she had killed. She tapped the bears belly in a gentle gesture of thankfulness and started the process. Her horse was nowhere in sight having his fill of the scent of bear. He left her the wearisome process of getting the heavy wet hide back to camp.

The dogs had gotten the remaining herd under control with the bears no longer a problem. Pete, in no hurry to hear more from Ernesto, had gone back to salvage what she could from the bears. Jorge was both curious and leery of the motionless bears. His adrenalin was not leaving anytime soon.

Pete took time out and gave Jorge a wordless talking to, ending it with a gentle pat on the head. He had done a good job except for his returning to the fight breaking her whoa command. *This should never happen again Jorje,* but she was pleased with his contributions and bravery in battle. She wagged a disciplining finger in his direction.

Ernesto and Pete knew they had more than their share of luck losing only one of their herd and no dogs killed. The one herding dog had an injury not easy to heal but he would.

All settled down later that evening. Ernesto said, "It is unusual for bears to pack-up like wolves or coyotes and when they do they are exceptionally dangerous." Then he gave Pete a gentle scolding with his admonishing finger as she had done to Jorge. His finger however was accompanied with a light hearted Ernesto Sancho smile and thankfully no pat on her head.

"I haunt you Ernesto Sancho?" Pointing to sky.

"Something like that." After a caring pause and a grin, "I have a couple questions Pete. Did you know that horse had never been ridden?"

Pete nodded apologetically.

"How'd you know?"

"His back hair long and talks."

"How did you know you could ride him then?"

Pete and Ernesto would be good friends. Pete would do it again if the need arose and Ernesto knew it. Ernesto wouldn't change what was. He was smart enough to know he couldn't. And what little he had time to see that day of Pete's abilities would not be easily forgotten. Pete put up three fingers. "Three questions Sancho."

Pete sat attentively with nothing more than a nod to answer Ernesto's grin while she gave Jorge a well-deserved ear massage.

Chapter 25 - Sheepherder Pete

Ernesto was back to his smiling self with never another word or gesture about the bath or bears. He led Pete into Juan's camp. Ernesto hollered at Juan who sleepily came out of his tent.

"Juan. Juan. These sheep can't watch themselves. I have decided to get you some help. This is Pete. Pete does not work for you. Understood?"

Juan shook his head and stumbled back inside his tent.

"Take a good look Pete and let me know what you see. We will talk later." Ernesto turned back down the slope to his herd.

Pete took a walk around the herd. She sampled the water and pulled some browse and grass. She inspected coyote scat, dismembered dead lamb bones, and ewe carcasses pulled away from the herd by the predators. When she walked into the herd they did not scatter. They allowed her to approach and run her hands over their bodies, in their ears, and peer in their mouths.

Pete returned a couple of hours later to Ernesto's camp and found him watching after his sheep.

"What did you see?"

"Easy. Move sheep more and kill coyotes. Water before evening bedding. Good clean wool."

"How many ewes?"

Pete flashed fingers on both hands signaling counting by tens while Ernesto gave his verbal sum.

"Ten tens of 10 fingers plus two 10's plus six. 1026"

Pete nodded.

"Five ewes short. Lambs?"

Pete used her fingers as before flashing numbers.

"Ten tens of 10 fingers plus four 10's plus four. 1044. Short twelve lambs. Eehoo that is worse than my last count. You do know your way around sheep. I know Señor Perez will treat you right but he won't like what I have to tell him about his grandson. Will you stay? I will get you pay when we get down the hill and back to the Rancho."

Pete looked straight at Ernesto and gave him a slight wiggle of her head, no more than the thickness of a fingernail. Ernesto gave a big smile. Nothing would get past either of these two outsiders.

· · ·

Essie's Diary

It brought tears to my eyes to watch the rapport grow between Pete and Ernesto. Trust would flow between those two.

I started doing more herb gathering and cooking freeing Pete to spend more time with the sheep. The result was I was alone more and had time to gather questions. And an odd thing happened. I also had more time to 'see' answers for myself.

· · ·

I mimed Pete's nodding and shrugging making fun of her gestures. "You shouldn't be cluttering your vocabulary with all the shrugs and nods. Pete I am serious. I want to know more than a bobbing head can tell me. You are learning enough words to actually communicate something more than a grunt."

"Easy. Insiders make com-pli-cations. Two leggeds make words and walls… make com-pli-cations."

"Nice word, 'complications'. And yes, true. Civilization has its problems. But words can show us things we can't see with our eyes."

Pete jerked her head up in defiance of the statement. "Pete no see? Pete see with eyes shut. Easy."

"Like love and all of written history? You can never see both sides of a tree at the same time."

"Many many words and sayimnothings. You talk old history. I make new history. Words no fight. No cook food. I walk and see all sides of every thing."

"You learn words while I learn to thrash your wild ass, let's try that."

I grabbed my staff and chased Pete with the darn thing. Pete scooped up a small branch on the dead run.

"Have you got 'whack' any idea what a waif like me goes through? 'whack whack' This face should have perks like 'whack' people feeling sorry for me… 'whack'. This face should get me out of a lot of trouble. 'whack' But I never get into trouble making it a total waste!"

Pete beamed as I fought better.

"Do you feel 'whack' sorry for me Pete?"

"No, you big sorry without me." Pete had a wide grin. Lots more wide grins lately I noted. Not sure if she saw humor in the way I was fighting or her choice of words.

"D. H. Lawrence 'whack' said 'I never saw a wild thing sorry for itself' 'whack' I guess you would not understand what 'sorry' is."

Pete pulled back in wonderment of what I said and I gave her a good one 'whack'. Pete howled with pain and her own stupidity.

"Owoo ... cheat... no fair. No fight and chatter ...no non.. sent aheh D H Lore... Ants."

I ran at her with stick raised forcing Pete to defend herself in earnest.

"Easy ... easy. 'whack' You like hornets. 'whack'"

"'I want you to learn a decent vocabulary. <u>VO</u> 'whack' <u>CAB</u> 'whack' <u>U</u>'whack' <u>LAR</u> 'whack' <u>EEE</u> 'whack''whack'.'"

I lowered my stick and continued. "You can see what happened to me... it's written all over my face. But I want to know more about what happened to you. You sit like a frog on a log croaking and bobbing your head. I cannot understand frogs."

"Croaoaok" came a perfect frog imitation with a lovely wide smile again and a cackling accompanying it.

It was around this time Pete starting losing her extreme wariness and started letting her guard down. Not always and not completely but after taking stock of the situation she'd relax a little.

I'll always think it was Ernesto who broke through the ice. He was perfect; funny, energetic, an outsider, a communicator extraordinaire, jack of all trades, never threatening, and totally honest with her. The end result was she started communicating at a higher level and in more depth. Diary you may start getting answers instead of questions.

Chapter 26 – Doin Nothin

Pete was watching her herd when Ernesto arrived unexpectedly. Pete didn't turn but recognized his presence. "Ernesto Sancho."

"Yes Pete. I wish I knew how you do that."

Pete turned and smiled. Ernesto repaid the greeting in a similar fashion.

"Do you think you could handle a few more head up here until next week when we leave for the Rancho? Pasture's a little thin below."

Pete gave a positive nod.

"I'll drive them up in a few hours. You keep an eye out and bring them together?"

Pete gave a second nod.

"Now where's my darling Little Bird?"

After a short pause Pete tilted her head at the drainage to the west. Ernesto gave a wiggle of his head and proceeded in the direction given.

• • •

Ernesto, Juan and Ed with two dogs brought in 400 pair of ewes and lambs to Pete's herd. Juan sulked the entire time. Pete adeptly gathered the sheep into one larger herd and settled them down. Ernesto waved goodbye and the three left Pete to her herd.

A short time later a menacing presence gathered behind Pete. Pete put her nose in the air and went to Focused Attention.

Pete amplified the sound of grass and boots and recognized Juan's approach. Juan bent down and grabbed a rock and readied to throw it at Pete.

"What Juan."

Juan surprised, stammered, "I ain't doin nothin."

"Don't do nothin here Juan."

Juan turned and dropped the rock making a clear THUD.

Pete gave a nod.

• • •

The nights were cold and clearly fall was in the air. Frost lingered un-

til mid-morning at the upper altitudes above timber line. The little brooks that irrigated the upper pastures were showing ice on the surface until mid-morning. The colorful aspen leaves now the same deep shade of gold as the rising moon were playing their clattering rhythms and danced all a-twitter with the slightest breeze.

Ed wandered out to where Pete was viewing her herd and sat on his haunches beside her. They both said nothing and were comfortable doing so. He looked over at her and she glanced toward him almost simultaneously.

He stuck his chin toward the herd with raised eyebrows. Pete pointed toward him with a single finger. He gave a confirming gesture. She raised up from her cross-legged position on the ground smoothly giving the appearance of defying gravity. She trotted off allowing him to take a watch. It said many words for Pete to trust him with her sheep.

Chapter 27 – Cloudless Thunder

Essie's Diary

It was a beautiful fall day and Pete headed off to the side of the large meadow of sheep. I ran to catch up. Ok Diary, waddled.

When I arrived by her side she was walking in the forest downhill off the edge of the plateau pasture. She stopped and cocked her head. She motioned to hold me up and pointed to her feet. She felt something. She focused her sight ahead and slightly downhill.

I started hearing something, like distant drums. It wasn't long and she pointed to the north. I started hearing crashing that accompanied the rhythm of the ground thumping, drawing nearer.

As the pounding approached the intensity of vibrations increased. I knew better than to speak or ask her anything. She was focused. Her nose lifted and pulled in air. As she tasted its qualities she had a smile come to her face.

The hammering became easily felt. Before I saw anything she put me behind a large spruce stump and gave me a hand signal to stay put. No words. She then ran down fifty yards and in the direction of the oncoming attraction.

I could hear the sound of bushes cracking, mews and squeals of distant communications. Deadfall and rocks were being struck by a thousand clubs each setting loose vibrations with every blow.

When I saw the elk burst through cover, over and down the hill toward her, I couldn't believe it. Hundreds more cows and calves fanned out across the forest moments afterward. The side hill was erupting with running elk moving in a large migration to the lower grazing lands to the south. They didn't bound like dear but trotted like horses. When I gathered my wits I realized Pete was running alongside them in her easy athletic way catching the wave of herd energy and touching those near her. She greeted and hooted at them. They gave her little notice. She could easily run at their migrating speed and did until totally out of sight.

Neither the four leggeds nor Pete were showing any signs of fear or fatigue.

I couldn't help but wonder what would happen if she were to fall amidst the thrashing hooves. Silly thought. This was Pete in her element. As secure as the trees and stars. To take her out of it would be criminal.

It was a thrill and a privilege to get the ringside seat I had. I didn't dare move if I was so inclined. They were dodging and brushing by the tree stump I was safely behind. I had no one to talk to but myself. And for once I was better occupied with the real world. I could reach out and touch those close at hand as they trotted by. I was swept into the moment. The fur was thick and coarse and they paid me no heed. This was Pete's world.

The smell of bull elk was strong. Different from cattle. Several came by easily weighing over a thousand pounds each with huge antlers towering five feet above their heads. The odor was as profound as the hoofs hammering.

There were at least five hundred head. Two thousand hooves like sledge-hammers in rolling unison. We were lucky to live in these mountains and the rent was free. I was thankful for the opportunity to share in the spirit of this day. Yes Diary, happy for the choice I had made to join Pete. Pete may not agree but it was worth every frustrating moment she had to bear.

I couldn't help but worry what would happen if this land were ever over-run with people and their houses or regulations terminating the use of these pastures and forests. The warm feeling of sheep bells and ba bahing would be lost to the history books.

Chapter 28 – Down the Hill

Essie's Diary

Pete had readied her sheep and brought them down the west side of the plateau making it look easy. When her sheep were near Ernesto's herd, they blended like two creeks into a river. Ernesto gave a wave to Ed on horseback.

With the help of two dogs, Ed herded sheep on the east side of the plateau keeping all the sheep moving together toward the south and lower elevations. The ba bahing and clang of bells filled the mountains with warm gratitude and appreciation. Pete turned 360 degrees and raised both arms high overhead in a salute to Mountain and a good bye and bye until they met again.

Juan and I rode in the wagon with Ernesto. Juan generally sulked or slept during the day in the wagon and sat up at night feeding the campfire long after we'd gone to our beds.

Ernesto moved the wagon down the mountain avoiding obstacles in quick succession: large trees, bog holes, rock outcrops, deadfall and blow-downs.

• • •

The tall mountains were far behind. It had snowed up the hill the previous evening. It was smart of Ernesto to leave. It would become extremely inhospitable at our summer sheep camp.

After a few days we were out of the fir and spruce trees, and heading to pine, piñon and scrub oak. In a week we were back to more level ground with some being irrigated.

The roads made traveling easier below but it didn't make the job any easier with the sheep. It was a challenge to keep the sheep together when traffic from wagons and the noisy horseless carriages wanted to get through the large herd. It also made Pete uneasy as she came closer to humanity.

The air was considerably warmer particularly in the mornings with the elevation drop. The country opened up more with fewer and shorter trees.

A handsome farm boy mended fence with his shirt off showing a

good physique. He stopped his work and watched Pete do her magic on the sheep. If I were her I would have worked less with the sheep and more with the hunk watching. But I digress.

He removed his hat and wiped his brow. His hair was similar to Pete's hair length and color. I watched Pete from my perch on the wagon. She showed a quick double take using only her eyes. Not noticeable if you didn't know Pete.

Me, I gave that boy the attention he deserved; a long, lingering meandering look. Whew, what a body attached to that gorgeous face.

Good pasture was harder to find the last couple of days forcing them to push the sheep right along toward the ranch. When they got close Señor Perez knew about it. He was there to wave a welcome. Señor Perez had a weathered kind face with calm eyes missing nothing. He stood smiling on the hill overseeing the end of the drive.

The last one hundred yards the sheep passed between two fences forming a chute tapering so no more than one or two could squeeze through at a time. Two sheep counters were hard at work as the sheep passed in front of them at the narrowest point. The corrals filled with thousands of sheep.

Juan had traded places with Ed the last morning to drive the herd to the corrals. He was on the near side of the herd with two dogs to keep the herd moving and the stragglers from turning back. A few thousand head of sheep can be a handful.

Señor Perez turned to the far ridge. Three dogs came over the ridge and sat neatly in a row. They were about five yards apart as if to observe but not bother the sheep. Sheep ambled calmly over the hill toward the ranch, past the dogs and on toward the counters near the chute as if by magic.

When the last of the sheep had trailed toward the chute leaving sixty yards vacant on the side hill, the three dogs remained motionless like sentries. It appeared the sheep had herded themselves home. Señor Perez had a questioning look as he stared at the dogs. Sitting. In a row. At attention.

Pete made her entrance by trotting over the ridge on foot weaving back and forth as if pushed by unseen forces first a little to the right, then to the left. She backed up, jogging in place and collected imaginary stragglers with the shooing motion of her hands now more than a hundred yards behind the herd. She was hamming it up. Pete style.

Pete took a large leap in the air and touched her feet together. As she landed she gawked at the magnificent sight before her. There was a huge spread of cattle with many sections under pasture, several outbuildings, corrals and a bunkhouse. The other direction was a large ranch house with an enormous barn and several more outbuildings and barns. Everything was in magnificent repair and the pastures showed plenty of lush green irrigated pasture even for this time of year.

Pete passed the three sedentary dogs. She turned and jogged in place motioning for them to spread out behind her by pointing with both hands. They quickly fell into place forming a semicircle behind her as if she may need herding even if the sheep did not.

She tried to escape from the team of heelers, first one side and then the other, keeping them engaged and away from her sheep. She knew a work dog had to work and she provided them the challenge. The dogs nipped at her heels as if she were a straggler. The last of the sheep continued in a calm manner toward the ranch corrals and paid no attention to the shenanigans behind them. Ed had jumped from the wagon and whittled his way toward the sheep, the last to be counted.

• • •

Ernesto and I unloaded gear from the wagon as Señor Perez approached still smiling at what he had seen. Ernesto and Señor Perez shook hands and spoke English in front of me.

"You look fit Ernesto. The old wagon got you and … and some helpers down the mountain?"

"That mountain, the wagon and my body are always a challenge. And I do have stories to tell you and some I may not believe myself. But first allow me to introduce Essie. Essie, Señor Perez. She and Pete have proven invaluable."

Señor Perez held my eyes with his.

"Pleased to meet your acquaintance Essie."

"The pleasure is all mine Señor Perez. I have heard much about you and your fine ranch."

"Thank you Essie. I would like to talk more later when things settle down. In the meantime I hope you will accept our humble hospitality. Please make yourself at home while I catch up with Ernesto."

Señor Perez and Ernesto spoke Spanish as they walked from the wagon. "Digame Ernesto, que …"

I was joined by Pete soon after. "Did you see the boehunkus with his shirt off leaning on his shovel on the way in?"

Pete shrugged.

"And I suppose you didn't get that funny girly feeling flitting around inside you?"

Pete shook with a grimace.

"I'd love to clean you up, smear lip rouge and paint on your face and drop you in a slinky dress with a slit up the side. Maybe some fancy shoes. Then stand back and watch the fireworks."

"Beauty tricks? SHOEss? Understand <u>NO</u> word? No girly feeling. I rip out by roots."

"Ok Mr. Grumpy Pants."

Chapter 29 – Señor and the Rancho

Ernesto had seen government surveyors on his way in and was anxious to know what exactly the situation was. He tilted his head toward the surveyors. Señor Perez was always even-tempered and spoke Spanish when he could.

"It's part of the Surveyor General's disposition."

"Are they still trying to steal the Rancho?"

"I'm standing on it now and I'm not leaving. Maybe they need to figure out what they want first."

Ernesto sighed.

"I've never seen anything like that boy Pete. Where's he from?"

"He's not a he, he's a she. She prefers to be a he to avoid women's work. And when we have time someday I have a story about that kid and five bears. She's not real talkative but real useful up the hill."

"More useful than Juan?"

"I hate to say this but Juan does more harm than good once he's out of your sight. He had big losses before Pete showed up. And you saw how she can handle anything with fur on four legs."

A grey cloud settled over Señor Perez but he went on. "Did you see any sign of drug use?"

"No, none at all. After you had me check and clean out every square inch of the wagon, I felt we were on the right path."

"Do you think part of his reluctance to work is left over from his drug use around here?"

"Maybe but I'm no expert. Something made big changes all of a sudden. I wondered often what his source was and how he got started."

Señor nodded. His pause was to ponder the same question. "Is Pete looking to stay on this winter?"

"If you were to ask, maybe yes."

"I guess we could put the girls out in my son's old cabin. Do you think they can get along ok out by themselves?"

Ernesto nodded and grinned. "When they found me at 12000 feet they were alone and doing well. Probably better than I was with a wagonload of equipment. Pete is made of scrub oak and rocks. And you saw how she moved. Not like any human I have ever seen. But I have one warning Señor. She's wild and free and I fear if one of the hands gets out of line, she may butcher him faster than I'd kill a coyote. I know it sounds exaggerated but it's not."

"Hmm. Do you know about schooling? Sister Primly has given up on Juan's schooling."

"Pete is learning now from Essie about school things probably for the first time. I don't think she's seen a book yet. As far as I can tell, Pete was raised by weeds that didn't talk much."

• • •

Essie's Diary

The day after arrival

Ernesto and Señor Perez talked alone on the porch. We stood about one hundred feet away knowing all this had something to do with us. Pete wore rawhide and I had on bully's clothes. There were a lot of farm noises and smells, like chickens and cows and pigs drifting through the area. Pete's eyes never stopped darting and her nose was like a butterfly on the wind. The wary look had returned.

Ernesto left and Señor Perez waved at Pete and me to join him on the porch. I walked up the steps and Señor Perez pointed to a seat nearby. Pete stayed put.

Señor Perez raised his right hand over the porch rail and his fingers slowly beckoned for Pete to approach. Pete acknowledged his signal by dropping her head and walking to the rail near his hand. She put her hand on the railing and swung over like a gymnast, clearing the rail and never getting close to the steps. Pete sat on her haunches off to the side of Señor Perez looking out from the porch as if her participation in the discussion was not required.

Señor Perez looked at Pete for a moment and then turned to me with a warm grin. "Ernesto had an idea that may work for you, Pete, and Juan. I would like you to school Juan and Pete if she cares to join your class through the winter. I will pay you $10 per month plus room and board. If you are successful with Juan, I will include a bonus of $2 for each passing grade he earns in his subjects."

"What about Pete's grades?"

Pete stiffened.

"Pete's gender will remain a secret if you wish but school is less important for her. We have … fewer expectations for women."

Pete's eyes darted and showed confusion.

"Señor Perez, with all due respect, suffrage is taking over this country. If Pete doesn't have what it takes because she is short-sighted, lazy or stupid, so be it. But please give her the same opportunity to pursue excellence as Juan. The competition may even prove helpful to Juan and give us a better result."

Señor hesitated, and raised an eyebrow. "I like your idea of challenging Juan. But if Juan doesn't pass his tests next spring, you get paid nothing extra for either."

"Fair enough. But if I can teach them both successfully this winter I will want more than $2 per subject passed for each."

A small grin gathered momentum across his face. He was not offended in the slightest and liked the boldness and horse trading.

"Ohhh?"

I had gained confidence around Pete so I continued. "Yes, since there is great risk of failure in this enterprise there should be a greater reward for achievement. If I am successful I should get $3 for each subject passed for each student. If I fail, which is a distinct possibility considering Juan's apathy and Pete's wildness, you keep all my pay including the $10 per month."

"You Essie are a natural born negotiator. You have a deal if you allow me to drop in and watch from time to time."

"I encourage you to drop by as you like. I would also appreciate any background you can give me on Juan."

He nodded in appreciation of my take-charge attitude. Señor Perez looked over his shoulder to Pete behind him. "Pete." Pete nodded, raised her chin, but didn't move.

Señor Perez spoke in nearly a whisper. "Pete?"

Pete turned and bounced on her haunches closer. Señor Perez continued in his soft manner and enunciated slowly and clearly.

"You put on quite a show yesterday with the sheep and dogs. I'll pay you $10 per month plus room and board starting last month. Your winter duties will be ranch work, maybe spending some time on the winter range, going for supplies if needed and attending Essie's school with Juan. You'll have to buy common work clothes because when you go to town you represent this ranch which means you will conduct yourself …. as best you can. Interested?"

Señor Perez waited for Pete's approval which took some time to appear. His patience prevailed. Pete gave a miniscule wag of her head.

"Then it's agreed?"

After Pete gave a more affirmative nod, Señor turned to me.

"Teaching Pete and Juan, and helping out where you can shall be your winter duties. It might mean you will conduct classes out on the winter range or wherever you can work it in with their duties. Tests will be given in town at our schoolhouse to judge their progress and your bonus."

Pete and I nodded in agreement. Señor Perez stood up from his chair with a smile on his face and called for some tea to be brought out on the porch.

His housekeeper came out moments later.

• • •

The chime of a fine china cup nestled in its saucer. Pete had never seen beautiful china and nearly spilled her tea while holding it up to look at the bottom. She lapped the couple of drips before they fell from the cup.

She ran her fingers over the light fragile glazed pottery showing a colorful floral pattern with gold trim around the edge on each piece. An aroma came off the freshly-poured orange spiced tea giving her nose a treat that mixed well with the beautiful china. Lastly the taste was every bit as good as the smell. She swallowed slowly and allowed it to linger before she let it slip down her throat.

I was most uncomfortable knowing poverty can always afford good manners. Señor Perez however never flinched, stiffened or gave any indication anything was amiss as he pushed the plate of cookies a little closer to Pete.

Pete downed them all. Be still Diary. It gets worse.

She poured herself more tea to save Señor Perez the trouble. When the pot was nearly empty Pete turned it over and shook it to get the last drop. She stuck her hand down the inside and licked her fingers. Next came the milk. Without using the cups provided she tilted up the pitcher and gulped it all down without hesitation or breath.

Pete was not uncomfortable in the least. She was feeling at home now and felt no danger or intimidation. I on the other hand was reaching new lows in this social setting. If we weren't fired we'd be treated like raccoons that broke into the kitchen.

• • •

I never spoke a single word about the tea, milk and cookie incident. One of the few times in my life I could do without. I thought the firing would speak for itself. But it never happened. Pete got invited back a couple of days later without the rest of us. Just her and Señor. Go figure.

• • •

There was a lot to do the first couple weeks after returning from summer pastures up the hill. Inspecting, culling, sorting and in general looking over the entire flock. There were also meticulous inspections and upkeep of gates and fencing. It was all exciting to Pete watching

Señor Perez's operation. Time for school was limited which was fine with Pete.

Over the short term I needed to tend to our new living quarters. It was an old abandoned cabin of Señor's son with a huge fireplace. It had plenty of daylight through the partially chinked walls so I had hopes Pete might consider living inside. Not.

It had been months since I walked on a flat level floor. It actually felt odd to my legs. I'd died and gone to heaven.

Chapter 30 – A Second Dose of Madam

Essie's Diary

The first day of class wasn't class at all. It was a necessary trip to town to get materials for the ranch and classroom, along with a grocery run.

• • •

We left in a wagon for town with Ernesto at the reins. Both Pete and I were dressed in bully clothes, as we had no other appropriate things to wear at the time. It was quite a distance to town and after maybe a mile Pete slipped off her shoes and wiggled her toes. You could hear each digit complaining about the incarceration. Two minutes later she jumped down from the wagon.

At first she ran alongside but it wasn't long before she was off in the distance doing whatever Pete does. Ernesto was thoroughly entertained.

• • •

By the time the wagon got to the little school house Pete was jogging close by us. As I hopped down enthusiastically, Pete soared up in the wagon and sat there.

When I turned to wait for Ernesto I saw him with the same strained face Pete wore. He set the brake, got down, paced back and forth and then reluctantly came toward me.

Pete flew down and patrolled around the wagon. Twice. She took a deep breath, pulled her bully hat as if it were a helmet, and trudged toward us. She had the wildest look on her face I had ever seen. She stopped short of us and waited.

Ernesto and I entered to renew our past with Sister Primly who had taught us both through her career. More recently I taught those she had kicked out of her classroom at the orphanage, such as the bullies. Ernesto and I had our age difference and neither of us spent much time in town, thus our paths had never crossed until we met up the mountain.

I turned and hoped to see Pete coming through the door. Instead I saw her peeking through the window with her hands shielding the light allowing her to see inside.

• • •

I got along quite well with Sister Primly as we spoke the same language; books and education. Sister Primly was a proper speaking, grey-haired wiry lady that was aging well. She left us to get some books from a coatroom in the rear of the one-room school house. The class remained subdued and respectful of the normal quiet rules in a classroom setting. The schoolhouse had a wood stove and stovepipe near the center of the room. Desks were filled with students of different ages.

Sister Primly returned and spoke to a student in the first row. "Randy, will you take these books out and put them in their wagon?"

Randy took the box from Sister Primly and walked out the door. The kids started to rustle and get a little antsy. Sister Primly settled the kids by a single hand gesture. They immediately responded.

Sister Primly spoke quietly and clearly to me. "I know you will have no trouble with the teaching material itself. Your trouble begins and ends with Juan and the young man staring at us through the window."

"Yes ma'am."

"I know Juan should start all over again but they don't make study books aimed at teaching full-grown men. Beginning materials are aimed at holding the interest of the young." Sister Primly looked to Pete at the window with her hands still shading the glare. Turning back she continued. "However large your salary at the ranch it won't be adequate compensation for the job ahead of you. I look forward to seeing your results in the spring."

She turned to Ernesto. "And you … Where there is trouble Ernesto, you are either just ahead of it or trailing close behind. It was that way in school and now several run-ins with the sheriff." Sister Primly took a deep relaxing breath. "If Essie needs anything besides a whip and cattle prod which I expect Señor Perez to contribute, please let me know immediately."

Sister Primly pointed to the door at the back of the room while looking at Ernesto. Ernesto, head down, turned for the door. I was two steps ahead of him pretending not to hear what I heard.

• • •

There was a Women's Suffrage rally with parade on Main Street. The local Madam, quite the character in our little town, was brightly-dressed in red, head to toe. A Suffrage banner was immediately behind her. Our wagon brought up the rear like a caboose.

Ernesto drove the wagon through town with people jeering and cheering.

Pete was in Focused Attention and clearly uncomfortable in this setting. We passed Father Greggory. Ernesto took a long look at Padre and gave a nod. Pete stiffened at the sight of the priest. Nothing more.

As we went by the sheriff, Pete's nose sampled the air. She might have possibly heard what Sister Primly said about Ernesto and the sheriff or she was picking up on something else about the man behind the badge.

We pulled up in front of the general store. A few people walked the boardwalk. I remained in the wagon with my box of books from Sister Primly. Ernesto and the store keep carried out boxes of goods to the wagon while Pete secured the load and tarped it.

Ernesto introduced the storekeeper to Pete. "This is Pete. She may be in alone sometimes but Señor Perez will pay the bill."

"Sure thing Ernesto."

The town Madam walked by with a distinctive walk; right shoulder right leg exaggerated. You couldn't miss her and by the look she didn't want you to. The Madam had similar height and build to Pete with the exception of her bustline being considerable where Pete could easily pass for a boy. The Madam raised her eyebrows at Ernesto who was just standing there. Ernesto gave a toothless smile in return. "Señora."

"Good afternoon Ernesto. I see you have two helpers today to help keep your pants up."

Ernesto nodded, embarrassed. I found the exchange interesting because this was a side of Ernesto I had not seen. The Madam gave me a wink. "Do come by my hotel if you are ever in need of anything."

Pete had a definite interest in the Madam. They had met before somehow. There was no doubt this woman exuded confidence and a special kind of energy. And then, without warning, someone pulled the lid off Pete's mouth. Words came flowing out like water from indoor plumbing.

"You take rich man?"

"We meet again. It's been a time since you bumped into me at the picnic. No, no rich husband. I don't want a husband."

"Me too. Why fancy dresses?" And with this I started fidgeting. Ernesto turned from the wagon and walked up the boardwalk. I thought at the time he might walk home without us.

"I'm a working woman."

"What work?"

I interjected, "Pete!"

"It's ok. I service men, Pete."

" 'Service' word? You wash clothes, feed, mop?"

"No, we entertain them which also includes taking care of their sexual needs for money."

"We?"

"'We' is me and my girls. There are way too many men wanting our services for only one of us to handle. Besides, I'm getting a little old for that end of the business."

I could feel the color entering my scared skin. I turned to follow Ernesto but immediately spun again making it a full circle. I'd have to suck it up and hear this out.

"You have money for babies?"

"Oh No, I should hope not."

"Men pay money and no cleaning or have babies?"

"Sometimes we give a freebee but most men have to pay."

"Freebee?"

"It means it's on the house, no charge, no money, our services are free."

"You breed, and no babies. Man no want kids for work?"

"No, they don't come to me for offspring. I am despised for a lot of things in this town but that's not one of them. People don't appreciate my stand on women's suffrage or my brothel. Some people complain I entice wives away from their 'natural duties' forcing their husbands to come to me to fill the void."

"Men don't want cleaning or babies, just fun breeding?"

"My, you do have a way with words. Yes, fun breeding, as you put it."

"You goot breeder I bettcha."

"Practice. Lots of practice." And she strutted up the boardwalk as Ernesto returned to the wagon.

Ernesto tipped his hat and swung back onto the wagon without another word, now way past embarrassed. The quiet boomed from Ernesto's seat as he grabbed the reins and released the brake.

Ernesto fell a long way today. Sister Primly said things Ernesto might prefer to forget. But the Madam had pulled the covers off in front of Pete and me. He was not equipped to handle this kind of thing any more than I was.

Pete and the Madam hit it off extremely well. They were perfectly happy in their own skins and lives. They could care less what people thought. It gave them both a freedom I envied.

Over the last month I was convinced Ernesto was a magician and master of his domain. Now he knew I could see the magic left off at the edge of the mountains. It would take us some time to get it sorted out.

The Madam continued strolling by the storefronts as we left town. Pete's eyes unwaveringly followed the Madam. I must admit, mine did too.

• • •

As we were leaving town Padre was standing on the boardwalk with a large grin. He looked pretty good if you asked me but I think any hunk with big brown eyes looks good. Anyway he boomed as we went by. "Hello Pete, we've missed you around town."

He got a shrug and her eyes locked on the road out of town.

Chapter 31 – Essie's School

Essie's Diary

We set up a classroom in a corner of one of the old sheep barns a few days later. I had a small chalk board, a large table and four chairs. Maybe Ed would get curious or we'd have a visit from Señor.

I wanted to force Pete and Juan at the same table. I intended to work on Juan first as I had a start on Pete up the mountain. I didn't want Juan vegetating or sleeping.

I could see Pete keeping him engaged in a head to head battle, one way or another. I was pretty sure whose head would be the hardest. In the beginning I didn't see it as an academic contest. This would be brute force, mano a mano.

Pete wore boy's clothes purchased in town except for her bare feet. I wore a dress purchased at the same time. Pete and Juan showed no interest in learning. Juan slept with head dangling toward the back of his chair. Pete stared outside through the open door. Longingly. I walked over to Pete and tapped her on the shoulder.

"Pete. Hey Pete?"

I finally got her attention back indoors. "Why not help me be the teacher here."

"No teaching Robin for nests."

"I'm not teaching nest building."

"What teaching?"

"Things I know and you and Juan don't."

Pete shrugged her non-committal shrug.

"Pete, what do you want for keeping Juan awake?"

"Outside."

I pondered this first staring at Pete, then at Juan. "Ok, I will get you out of here today if you can make Juan pay attention. But you cannot take his pants. It's embarrassing when you do that. And you can <u>NOT</u> hurt him ......
too much. Seriously Pete, if there is any permanent damage I... I know Señor

Perez will not put up with an ear-marked grandson. We'll be out in the cold this winter."

Pete nodded and grinned at the challenge.

"Pete, hear me on this. <u>COLD IS BAD</u>."

Pete imitated her favorite stellar jay again. "Yeha Yeha… You go now."

I left the barn and closed the door allowing them to work things out. Outside I kept my back to the door trying to eavesdrop. I heard rustling noises first. Then there were sounds of Pete under pressure, stressed and yowling. I was worried at what I had done.

Then Juan's voice, "It's time you get respect you little…" followed by more crashing sounds increasing in volume. There was a short shrieking gasp and then, nothing but quiet for a full minute. Then some quiet voices passed back and forth. I left the door and wandered around in a short circle. Pete opened the door, stuck her head out, and gave a bird chirp sound with a nod to return.

The whole thing maybe took ten minutes. I went inside to survey the damages. Two chairs were overturned. Both their faces had scratches and red marks. Hay and dirt filled their hair. I immediately went to Juan's ears. They were dirty and red but both were intact. *Thank you God.*

Pete looked pretty good considering Juan outweighed her by fifty pounds. Moving slowly down Juan's torso I saw a six inch cut in his pants above his crotch exposing his underwear. I saw no blood but I wouldn't have been surprised to find a wet spot.

Pete glared at Juan. "Word time Juan."

"I'm sorry Miss Essie. I'll stay awake and pay attention."

"Nice Juan. I never considered for a moment you wouldn't." I handed Juan a paper with three drawings of an apple, house and dog. "Write something about each drawing in English. This will help me learn what you know and what you don't. When you are done write the entire alphabet at the bottom of the paper."

Juan gave an unimpressive nod and Pete spit quickly in his direction, "Juan!"

"Ok, yes, yes. I would like to learn every day and I will be happy to write the alphabet Miss Essie."

I handed him a pencil and motioned Pete to go outside. I had anticipated the need for a couple of walking sticks if Pete ever wanted to go outside and learn. It didn't take long. I gave Pete the short branch and I retained the longer more effective weapon. We were outside, which fulfilled my promise to get Pete out of the classroom.

"We are fighting. Say it."

"We fight!"

"We <u>are</u> figh…<u>ting</u>. Say it."

I struck once for each syllable.

"We are figh… ting!"

Pete struck once for each syllable.

"We are fighting with sticks. Say it."

"We are fighting with sticks!"

"We are fighting to the death!"

Pete smiled and I did the same. We saw Juan come to the open door to watch. We both charged at him swinging our weapons wildly.

"We are fight ing Juan."

"Yes!"

After chasing Juan back inside we returned outside. Standing there at a distance Señor Perez and Ernesto looked on. They glanced at each other then back toward me. They each shook their heads, grinned in unison, and left. *Whatever works.*

• • •

A few days later Pete did the same exercise Juan had done with the three drawings of an apple, house and dog. "Tell me something about each drawing," was my only directive. I knew what she knew about the alphabet hence I didn't push it. As it turns out this little exercise was the key that partially opened the door. It helped me understand her thinking processes along with details I could follow up on to get the full picture of her early life. But no time soon.

When she was done I took Pete over to a world globe Señor Perez donated to my class. I reached down and pointed to a place. "Do you know what this is?" Pete gave a smirk as if to say no, and who cares.

I looked into her eyes as she attempted to read mine. I spun the globe and reached down with my finger and pointed to a place. "Here is this Rancho." It gave new meaning to the world. It put everything together in three dimensional space. She was visibly taken with the big picture forming under her hand as she touched the Continental Divide. She saw the Pacific Ocean designated by the large blue area west of California. She had heard of the great body of water and could not grasp why it didn't pour off our earth. Her mind raced. Good.

She was using her mind and not her "natural" way. "Any time you would like to ask questions or talk about the world globe, I am here." She stared at the globe as I left her with her thoughts.

• • •

Pete picked up an eighth grade science book with interesting pictures and started asking questions. I started reading what was under the pictures. She wanted to learn to read. Everything.

She was quick to learn the alphabet and the phonetic sounds they made to form words. Next I had her into a primary book about Dick and Jane. Pete put the book down and picked up the eighth grade book. She took her index finger and pointed at the book. Then glared at me. The challenge for me in the beginning was getting Pete to pick up the stupid book about Jane and get the basics. Pete wanted to choose the books. I had to keep up. Same as in her world.

. . .

I did little more than wave at Ernesto over the next month. Pete took the wagon into town once a week and I went with her sometimes. She'd tell me about Ernesto and things they'd talk about. She said Ernesto would ask about me and how things were going in class.

I didn't think his checkered past in school or with the law would bother him very much. He may even take pride in it. I could tell he was embarrassed about the Madam thing the way he walked away from the wagon that day in town. Maybe it had something to do with her remark about "us helping to keep his pants up".

. . .

Señor Perez was curious about Pete's history but always mindful she was not an ordinary teen. Probably no teen was ordinary, but some were more or less ordinary than others.

Señor learned all things in Pete's world belonged to Pete which included the space around her. He saw Pete as wild and skittish. Señor would have to wait with a great deal of patience to get any closer. And that man had patience.

As for Juan, he had been stuck. He knew he was far behind and thought there was no way to catch up. Why try. Pete gave him good reason. Now we had to wait and see.

Chapter 32 – Padre's Strategy

"Yes, I've given it some considerable thought Mr. District Attorney but as of yet, have only a sketchy plan."

"Well let's have it Padre."

"Señor is a good Catholic. Pete could well have a spell over Señor Perez making him difficult to deal with. He has been weakened by the disappearance of his son, daughter-in-law, and foreman. Now his grandson is not well." *You may have a hand in all of this.* "Señor believes in the power of exorcism and has more than once been amazed at Pete's powers. I will use the excuse of an exorcism to clear the Rancho of nearly all but a few ranch hands for daily chores. It will make it easy to simply ride in and take physical possession with no casualties on either side."

"And is it true that you can do an exorcism on a place like the Rancho?"

Without answering the question directly the priest gave some Biblical trivia and continued. "My first step is to gain Pete's complete confidence. This might entail having her run in a long foot race. She would undoubtedly win. Afterwards I hope to have an exorcism of the demons possessing her. Señor has never seen an exorcism. It could likely rock him off center to see the power. If I can get all these things lined up I may get him to clear the Rancho enough to give you the opportunity you need."

"And you think you are qualified to perform the ritual?"

"Maybe not as qualified as I would like but I think in this case it had better be someone familiar with Pete and the Rancho."

"Quite a plan Padre and quite a lot of hoping, thinking, and might this and that. Don't take long Padre." Padre bit his lip and held his tongue.

"Last chance Padre, or I'll have to make some changes to our schools as well. I will have to follow the law and close down the Church's control. I can't give you cover on your history with teens either. I'll need to look more fully into the complaints about you. Do I make myself clear?"

"Yes, I definitely see the importance. But pushing Señor too hard and fast could spoil the results."

"Don't take long or I'll take the reins myself. Clear?"

"Perfectly."

"And Padre there is always a possibility this Territory may one day return to its original owners which would give the Church complete control over the schools again indefinitely."

"What are you saying?"

"I'm saying that war is never out of the question and next time Mexico might pick up all the marbles. Particularly if they have outside help."

Padre was happy to leave the DA and had no desire to follow up the "outside help" remark to lengthen the conversation. He never liked the DA or his power-wielding ways. He knew his plan would likely take at the least several months but didn't want to let that cat out of the bag.

• • •

The DA was not a stupid man. He could see the delays necessary for Padre's plan and the various outcomes were not all to his advantage. He had to get the Rancho prior to New Mexico statehood or else he would lose his advantage in the courts. Therefore he was going to use Padre's exorcism plan as a backup. He already had an iron in the fire that should eliminate the problem.

• • •

Padre needed the Bishop's consent for the exorcism. This was the easiest part of the plan. The Bishop wanted to stay on good terms with the District Attorney and his DC cronies until statehood. Statehood would give the power to the locals who could eventually control the ballot box and the Church's position with the schools one way or another. Because of separation of church and state it might need to be done through local school boards. Padre's plan could possibly eliminate the bloodshed which would occur if the DA took the Rancho by force.

• • •

The difficult part was to get Pete to agree to do the exorcism. Padre knew better than to approach Pete at this juncture. He asked Essie to broach the topic and get tentative approval. He could verify Pete's desire to have the exorcism at a later date.

• • •

"If you agree Señor I'd like to dispel the idea she has demonic or supernatural evil powers."

"Anyone who's been around her knows she's not evil. I must admit though she can do things no other human can."

"Sure, I don't see Pete as evil either. But I don't want people pointing a finger at her and yelling 'witch'."

"Me neither Padre. If you need my permission you have it but I won't tell Pete she has to do the exorcism."

"Sure thing Señor. I wouldn't expect that. Afterward we can exorcise anything remaining here. If all lines up do you think you'll be able to leave with immediate family and as many hands as you can spare for a week? You'll need to leave a skeleton crew to do needed daily chores of course. Do you have any place you'd like to visit?"

"No, not right off," Señor said hesitantly.

"Maybe you could take some needed time off?"

"We might do a little fishing up north. It's been quite some time since I've had stars as company."

Padre knew he could pull it off. He also knew Sampson or someone like him would love to kill a few good hands particularly knowing the DA would protect them. This way the lives of innocent people could be spared. His conscience was cleared along with his path.

Chapter 33 – Pete's Arrow

Ernesto had picked up mail the previous week from town and delivered it to the Rancho. One piece took Señor by surprise as it was from the Recorder's Office. He opened it right off and found an invitation to review some documents that would show ownership of his Rancho. The wording was vague but clearing the title was mentioned. He thought it might terminate his legal problems. Someone would come out to the Rancho to save him a trip.

• • •

Things slowed even more at the Rancho, but not in schooling. Pete asked for some time off. Pete thought she could do better in school with some rest and relaxation. She had a special place she wanted to visit and would be back in a couple of weeks. Señor didn't like the idea but Pete would be Pete. She told Señor he could keep her pay. He smiled and said she'd earned "poco tiempo" working seven days a week up the mountain. But be careful. He was always worried about a "girl" out there alone. He was giving the wild one a little time to get used to fences.

Sometimes people made decisions contrary to the nature of things or they didn't have any link to "common sense." Señor Perez had common sense. Pete saw it as a connection to Universe.

• • •

A man arrived from town on horseback delivering the long-awaited title information from the Recorder's Office. He slowly got down and took the steps up the front porch. He had a piece a paper in one hand and a pistol on his hip. He knocked twice. Señor's housekeeper came to the door. The delivery man needed Señor's signature.

• • •

Pete was taking the road back to the Rancho after her time off. A horse and wagon were coming out with a horse tied on the rear. The horse pulling the wagon was familiar but not the horse tied to the back. She saw it was one of the Morales brothers at the reigns but never could tell that bunch apart. They all looked alike to her. Large and ugly.

This man was definitely not someone Señor would hire. And he was using a Rancho horse and wagon.

She dropped her hip purse and bow beside the road with a couple of arrows in a quiver ready if she saw some dinner in rabbit's clothing. She waved the driver down and was greeted by the gruff man in too big a hurry. She needed some time and wanted to engage the man while she connected to whatever was going on.

"You seen Señor Perez?"

"He's not here anymore." The statement made no sense to Pete. Pete was sorry she had already dropped the security of her bow.

"Where's Señor Perez?"

"Don't know. He left one day and said I could run the place. Now you run along and don't bother me anymore."

A lot didn't make sense as it spun around. The large bearded dislikeable man telling her to "run along" didn't help. He didn't say he was the new owner and she wasn't sure what 'run the place' meant. But she was doing her best to make a good first impression as Essie had often mentioned.

As he drove by nearly brushing her off the road she saw a bulge under a tarp in the back of the wagon. Whatever was covered looked about the size of a yearling pig or a small man. A *tarp covering a dead pig? Could be taking it to the dead pile but cover it and head away from the ranch?* Pieces weren't fitting.

She grabbed her bow and one arrow and sped after some answers. Essie's words about a first impression kept buzzing around mixed with a lot of curiosity. She sprinted by the wagon. The more she saw in the back of the wagon, the more she knew something was way wrong.

She jumped in front of the wagon and grabbed the horse's bridle with a firm grip of one hand. Bow with arrow alongside in the other. The animal drug her back on her heels for a few yards until the wagon stopped. "I said you get outta here," came the thundering voice from the bearded driver.

Pete swung up on the horse backwards, nocking her arrow and drawing it back all in one swift motion. She pointed the arrow at the man. *Maybe not good first impression.* The man raised his hands to his crumbled hat.

She looked carefully at the cargo under the tarp. She saw boots slipping out from underneath. A pair of tied legs were next squirming to get the tarp to one side. She couldn't tell for sure as the person's head had a bag over it but it could be Señor. He had the right size of legs anyway.

Her eyes dug like two shovels into 'Runalong' as she sat the wagon horse backwards facing him. Her toes were playing like little chipmunks dangling off the side.

Runalong watched Pete's eyes for any weakness. If he pushed her too hard she might let the arrow fly out of fear. He had no doubt she would have a moment of hesitation he could use. He looked again into her scorching green stare.

Pete's left hand aligned the bow with arrow straight at the big man in the wagon. Her right hand had her fingers taut to her cheek.

Pete made a connection between the big man's palms on his hat and her fingers on her bowstring. As his large paw slid slightly from the top of his hat, the bowstring slipped down to the tips of her fingers. Any further and she would lose control. No thinking or emotions.

"Whoa. I thought I told you to run along."

The person wiggled into view. Not one flicker of fear came from behind the arrow. He was looking for dread in her eyes as his hand moved no more than a quarter of an inch.

"First answers. Hands on head. Up up. Señor? Señor Perez?"

Nodding excitedly.

"You. Last warning. Señor Perez this man run ranch?" She wanted complete clarity and no mistakes.

Señor shook a vehement no in the bag.

"You want out Señor Perez?"

An exaggerated nod for yes.

"So I suppose you are going to believe this old fart and not me?"

"Easy, *Sí.* You make work."

"Why you little son of a.. "

"PSSSTing chud"

He should have believed those green eyes and the deadly arrow aimed at his chest. Pete's bow sang a short song as she sat less than ten feet from the driver.

The arrow pierced the chest of the big man driving the wagon. It separated the ribs slightly to the left of his sternum cutting through heart and lungs. He fell back over the seat, mouth open. Eyes still disbelieving.

Chapter 34 – Talk to the Sheriff

Pete scrambled aboard the wagon throwing her bow in back and removed the bag and gag from Señor. Next she cut the old man's hands free with a single swift swipe. He was slow to realize what was happening and Pete was moving faster than his mind could track.

"Feed, water?"

"*Sí*. Pero neccessito encontrar Sheriff?" Mixing Spanish and English with all the stress.

Pete repeated with some hesitation. "Sheriff?"

"Yes, yes. We should talk to the sheriff and make you a hero."

"No, no talk. No need."

"No, you are a hero. We need to see the sheriff. I want you to be safe from the law and not run from it."

"Señor, no good talk sheriff, maybe you talk? OK?"

"Yes, as you wish. We'll get this matter settled with the sheriff this afternoon. He may need to come out to the ranch."

• • •

Señor had been through an ordeal. A large bearded man had come into his ranch house and killed his housekeeper. Then he tortured Señor Perez until he revealed where he kept his cash. He knew this was his death ride. The big bearded man only wanted Señor's money to make it look like robbery or he would have left him dead in the house with his housekeeper. His main purpose was to remove Señor from the Rancho. Señor in a dazed manner relayed the story as best he knew.

Pete turned the wagon around toward the Rancho. Señor made her stop. He wanted to see the sheriff sooner rather than later. After a short conversation Pete turned the wagon back towards town, leaving Runalong beside the road.

• • •

The sheriff took only a quick statement in town seeing Señor had been through enough for one day. He wanted Pete to take Señor home.

• • •

The sheriff in a wagon went ahead of Pete and Señor back to the Rancho. He was there to pick up the bodies and view the scene. He was gone before Señor and Pete returned. He'd return in a few days to give the old man some time to recover. Then find out more from Pete. The scene told him most of what he needed to know.

• • •

Pete was ready to make her beeline out of town when Señor requested a stop at the general store for supplies. With his housekeeper gone he was hoping Pete and Essie could help out a little until some other arrangements could be made. He was a man Piñon would easily have chosen for her to help along her path. She would have aided this man in any case.

"Could you help out around the Rancho for a few days Pete? I know it's not one of your favorite things to be indoors. Essie may be able to help as well."

"O k."

"Maybe it would be easier if we stop by the store and you can buy anything you would like to fix. I eat anything."

"O k. Not good with this."

"I know Pete. But let's make it fun."

"O k."

Pete took Señor Perez home and watched after him. The ordeal did not mix well with his age.

• • •

Pete had no skills with the food she knew Señor Perez liked but she did her best. She asked him to help give her ideas and he did. As Señor made progress, he realized this was an opportunity to know Pete a little better.

Hot red or green chili was not to Pete's tastes but he seemed to thrive on it. She ate her share however of the beans and chorizo sausage. It was a spicy meat and went well with eggs or beans and pan bread she made for him.

Señor exuded old world manners and charm. New sensations for Pete. Their time together would benefit both.

The Rancho was not just a shelter or roof. It had a past she could feel. Not unlike the dwellings and petroglyphs she had experienced in her world. Señor was a living descendent of the actual history she was feeling.

It was not the first time she had been inside. However now she could connect and feel things during his naps. Señor could sense she was getting more than an eyeful of fancy decorating. There were paintings on the walls she wanted to know about. They were about the history of the Rancho. The talk brought more of the insider's world to Pete's eyes. She sensed the history and effort of the hands working the old leather and wood furniture.

During the first evening after Señor Perez had fallen asleep Pete snuck quietly out to be with the sheep dog Jorge to properly guard the house…. under the stars. She had too much roof over her head for that day.

• • •

Señor Perez was a tough wiry type unaccustomed to allowing setbacks. He was a fighter but the fight had been taken out of him.

In the beginning he planned to have Essie spell Pete with the house duties. However Essie was distraught over the killing of the housekeeper and the realization of how cruel life could be beyond the confines of her shriveled skin. The killing went way beyond Pete's killing for food. One was evil, the other was a necessary part of Universe. Señor was also enjoying Pete's company persuading him to leave Essie alone and to her grieving.

For the first two days Pete fed and took care of Señor Perez making herself always available. After she had shoveled plenty of food into him she shamed him into showing her his ranch on his buckboard. He was bruised from his beating but the outdoors would do him good. Her manner of nursing included tough love.

"You know this ranch better than I do Pete."

"You have more. This g o o d."

"You want me to get out of the house and get fresh air."

"Easy, you smart boss."

Could anyone not love this girl?

• • •

"Please what you see?" Pete pointed to a creek.

"I see where my father first took me fishing. I see where my son and I had a bad argument. He was a young teen and knew everything. I miss him so."

"Sorry, so sorry Señor. Thank you to give what you know. Hill over there Essie's cabin. Has sadness and, and fuerte. I like it."

"Yes, sorrow and strength. There is a long history to that hill. Men have died there fighting for this Rancho."

"Thank you Señor. This is gift."

"Me also. You fight like a hardened gunfighter and now you are a nurse. Thank you for making me do this."

She drove the wagon back to his ranch house as she could see his strength waning. She sensed his will to fight was beginning to sprout.

• • •

There were wall hangings, pictures and figurines with considerable history but no functionality whatsoever. Intriguing to Pete was the looking glass on the wall. She was struck with the two legged behind the glass. She gave a small curl to her lips until the newness wore off.

The tale told around the territory of the killing of the outlaw fugitive was not attributed to Wolfboy but the ranch hand Pete. The new stories about Pete were a little stretched as they were with Wolfboy but none had the slightest effect on Pete. She was happiest when left alone. By humans.

• • •

District Attorney Wagner wasn't happy with the outcome of his number one plan for the takeover of the Rancho. The younger Morales had botched it and failure did have its consequences. The DA was glad Pete was a good shot. No loose ends to connect the DA even remotely. He was also pleased Padre still had his exorcism plan in the works.

• • •

Four days after the carnage out at the ranch Sheriff Jim Curry returned. He wanted to satisfy himself and get the remaining facts. When he rode up on his horse Pete was standing there waiting for him to dismount.

"How you doin Pete?"

"Doin ok."

"I've still got to ask you a couple more questions about what happened if that's alright? We don't like vigilantes or folks taking the law into their own hands. Ok to ask you some questions or do you want an attorney?"

"OK. Easy. You ask."

"A man was killed by your hand, is that correct?"

"My arrow go through him."

"This is nothing to be smart-mouthed about Pete. You could be in serious troubles here." After a short pause he started again. "Did he at any time reach for his gun or make any sudden or threatening movements?"

"Yes, warning warnings. He moved hand. I was first. He was not." Señor walked out on the porch.

"Have you ever killed before Pete?"

Señor spoke up, "Sherriff she's not getting into any trouble over this. I wouldn't be alive if it weren't for her."

"I gotta ask these questions Señor Perez. Now let us be. We'll be done soon. You ever do any killing before?"

"Sure, many times."

"Yes? I checked and didn't find any record of anyone matching your description around these parts involved in killings. Where'd you do this killing and did you ever do any jail time for it?"

"I kill every week. Need food. Never go to jail. You got good food in jail?"

"You are not taking this seriously Pete. And you had better not get in any more trouble while I'm the sheriff in these parts. You've never killed any humans before?"

"No."

"Tell me how you learned to shoot a bow like that?"

"Practice and no husband."

"Ok Pete. But I can't imagine any man worth his salt keeping you for a wife. I was worried you might be a little upset about the killing but you seem almost happy about it. Are you?"

Señor couldn't take any more, "Sheriff that's enough."

Pete went right on, seeing Señor didn't need to get upset any more than he already had been. "No, not happy."

"I can't find you on any wanted posters which means I got some good news. There was a reward for the guy you killed and it should be in my office in a few months. He's the brother of Sampson the older Morales. You do know the older Morales won't look kindly on you. Better keep your head down. Ok?"

"Not sure with money or head down. I talk to Señor."

"Good, you do that. But I have one more question Pete. Sorry to have riled you two but it needed to be done. A more important question needs to be asked. Why do you think the younger Morales tried to abduct Señor Perez and not just steal and run?"

Pete shrugged a no idea reply.

Señor broke in. "It's not hard to put a good guess together Sheriff. There has been years of them trying to steal the Rancho and not succeeding."

"Who is 'them' Señor Perez?"

"Check whoever got the winning bid Sheriff."

"Are you accusing the District Attorney and his partners Señor Perez?"

"The boot fits Sheriff."

. "Those are mighty powerful people you are accusing. I'd need a lot of proof and maybe even then it might be hard to get a court not controlled by them."

"I know Sheriff and with their positions they could have your badge by sundown and you pushing up daises by morning. But it's the only thing that makes sense. If the real motive was robbery the younger Morales would have shot me quick and taken far more. No, that bunch from Washington wanted no body and no way of telling what happened. Their timing was perfect except for my housekeeper and Pete here. I feel extremely bad for my housekeeper's family."

"Run that by me again. Why not shoot you and leave you on the Rancho?"

"The people in this territory would be up in arms if I was shot dead and the DA took over. Too many would question it because everyone knows who would be behind a killing like that. You need proof. These people use common sense. No, the safest way was to kidnap me and leave some doubt as to who did what and why."

"Pete did he say anything to you about kidnapping or taking Señor Perez?"

"No. He said he take over. No sense."

"Yes Pete, little sense. I intend to go out and have a talk with the Morales family. And again Pete, I'm sorry if I ruffled a few of your feathers today but you did kill a man and it's my job."

• • •

Originally Señor didn't think the old abandoned cabin Essie and Pete were living in was fitting. He thought it improper to have ladies out where ranch hands might be dropping by unannounced. As it turned out with the death of the younger Morales, there was little doubt the amorous cowboys wanted anything to do with the ranch hand Pete.

"Are you sure Pete the little cabin is ok? It is run down and far off the beaten path."

"It's very, um, unpeckable. Thank you."

She had an 'on-off' switch. He could ask her to do anything around the ranch and it was 'on'. But where and how she slept or took time off was not his choice. Her switch went to 'off'.

In the end Señor knew Pete would be a handful but he did love that handful. After what she'd done to save his bacon and what Essie was doing with Juan, they were a gift from God.

• • •

The sheriff wanted to be sure things were settled in the Morales family. Sampson was a concern. He had been a hired thug and might take offense at someone killing his brother. The sheriff also wanted to get a motive for the younger brother's actions. He went out to have a visit with Sampson and his mother.

Sampson stood by his mother on the porch. As always he was wearing a huge faded blue pair of overalls hanging off him like a tent. They left no sign of knowing soap and water. The buckles on the shoulder straps were both rusted. He wore a floppy brimmed hat drooping down each side toward his ears. His mother barely reached his waist. As might be expected there were tears easily flowing from La Señora.

"Señora I wanted to let you know how sorry we are for your loss. Nothing is worse than a mother losing her youngest."

Through the sobs she managed to nod her head. "Gracias."

Sampson was close by and seemed unmoved by the event. "Is everything ok out here Sampson?"

"Sure, we knew that brother of mine was going to get his head shot off one day. It came as a shock a skinny girl got him. But if she didn't break no laws or nothing…. We know my brother was always getting hisself into trouble. Guess I'll let it go."

"Well I'm glad you're taking it that way Sampson. He was involved in a kidnapping for sure and according to witnesses he would have likely hung for the crimes he had already committed if I'd a caught up to him first."

"Sure am sorry Sheriff but I didn't know he was back in town."

"I'm not here to get you for harboring a fugitive. Just following up on a few other things."

"Wouldn't lie to you Sheriff. I'm a little surprised a young gal with a bow could do that kind of damage. But I'd rather see him dead from an arrow than squirming at the end of a rope."

"Thanks for being straight with me Sampson and if I can make things easier somehow with your mom, please let me know."

"I'll do that. And Sheriff the kid that killed him?"

"Yes"

"You know she might have been the one that took a piece of my nephew's ear off?"

"No, I didn't know anything about it. You want me to look into it?"

"You do what suits you. Might be best if she doesn't show up and make nice around here to explain nothing. There's a limit you know?"

"Sure Sampson. I understand. One other thing. Have you got any idea as to why your brother was out at the Perez Ranch?"

He gave a shake of his head.

"No idea then as to motive or who might have hired him or if he did it for his own reasons?"

"Nope Sheriff. Like I said we hadn't spoke for a time."

"Ok, thanks Sampson."

Sampson nodded, put his bulky paw on his mom's shoulder. They both turned and never looked back.

• • •

The danger Pete had faced brought home to Señor once again outdoor ranch life was not the place for a girl. She was quick to remind him it was a lone girl who made the tough decisions without the help of men. A second fact she hesitated with, then out it rolled. His housekeeper had been working inside.

"It is difficult for me to put a young girl alone with a herd. It is a man's job and men...."

"Señor Perez, I..I" and she stammered having total respect for this man but not wanting to give an inch on her choice.

"Yes you did Pete," he interposed knowing what she would say. "You took care of a very bad man and this man is grateful. A fact not easily forgotten. But you deserve a better life than to be alone in the wilderness. You deserve to marry, to have a husband and a baby on your hip. Don't you want to wed someday?"

"I busy that day. With freedom. No man gives freedom. I have hands full of me!"

Her choice of words was a delight. "Yes, I think I understand. But if you become one of my sheepherders I might ruin your life to never know holding a child and watching your children someday have their children. You would make an amazing mother."

"I hold these mountains and they hold me. Messy baby's butt not like stars on mountains? Yes?"

"I was born a man. It is different for me."

"Not too late to learn woman's work. If you do ranch, floors and laundry easy."

"Well I.. eh well maybe. I don't know because …..because, I forget.. now who is the boss here?"

"You are boss, Señor. Good boss. You want and I do on this ranch. But my life, I write. I herd sheep when they were bigger than me. No easy for mustang to be saddle horse. And hard on mustang."

Pete could feel the wheels turning. She let them whir. She never was one to let a little silence go to waste.

Señor's words quietly flowed. "I owe you my life. I will not stand in your way again unless there are problems. I enjoy your English and I hope we have many years to practice our English skills together. Comprende?"

"Si, Señor Perez. I have never met any man like you. You have .. you have... I don't know the word but soon I will."

Señor Perez opened his mouth to make one last valiant effort and the words stuck tight. She held all of the cards. He had to laugh at himself. *Old beliefs die hard.* She had the sand to survive the New Mexico Territory without the help of men, even in spite of men.

"I don't want you to take this the wrong way but you shot two arrows. One took a man's life and another has gone through me. I appreciate life even more now I know you. I am grateful to have you here at the ranch. But Pete you must let me win one here. You should collect the reward from the sheriff when it's time. If you would like me to put it in the bank for you I will. We might even start a savings account to one day buy your own sheep. Ok?"

Pete nodded with a little shine in her eyes. Selina had once mentioned Pete owning sheep. Couldn't quite get her arms around owning permanently with money what she already had. Freedom and sheep.

Essie's Diary

After the Pete hero stuff faded away, we finally settled into that first winter. She also left what I called crazy stuff in a different world. Not immediately and not all at once but wild started to fade. Killing another human or taking part of an ear off stopped occurring on a regular basis.

I did miss the surrealistic mind blowing adventures. The ruby-colored yellow-eyed cougar and the earth bed adventure was not of this world. Now it was replaced by the chemistry of those around the Rancho. Pete allowed for a few doors to close that others might open at least for a while. There were fewer attempts by me to question those things behind doors no longer open.

Chapter 35 – Nag Nag Nag

Essie's Diary

I was reading to Pete before school actually started. The practice was continued after the start of class as well. I made sure it was fun. When a book was to Pete's liking she would open her eyes wide and glance back and forth then look to the top of her head. She would lay back on the ground and let the words connect to her experience and soak in.

Pete liked Rudyard Kipling but had difficulty with the vocabulary and phraseology. She would often have me repeat and repeat some passage until it would have some meaning she could grasp. Pete would whirl her hand with finger pointing to the sky to request another repeat of the same passage. When there were words or phrases Pete didn't understand she would take the same hand but let all the fingers fly up and vibrate violently back and forth while expressing a frown on her face which was a request for meaning or translation.

A quote requiring numerous handshakes and twirls were Kipling's words: "Now this is the Law of the Jungle -- as old and as true as the sky; And the Wolf that shall keep it may prosper, but the Wolf that shall break it must die. As the creeper that girdles the tree-trunk the Law runneth forward and back -- For the strength of the Pack is the Wolf, and the strength of the Wolf is the Pack."

And a finger twirled toward the sky again.

• • •

My conversations with Pete were profitable in several ways: she was improving with leaps and bounds picking up vocabulary and sentence structure, she was less frustrated when attempting to express ideas for which no words exist, and our talks gave me a chance to look into her realm.

She remained connected to some things I could not understand. I went there on her terms accepting sometimes when I had no idea what she was communicating. I wished I was learning as quickly as she was.

She hated to admit it but she was enjoying learning and competing with Juan for top honors. The competition was helping Juan as well. The chauvinist hated to be bested by a girl.

• • •

Pete would disappear on days she had 'free'. Free meant she wasn't going to tell me where she went. I have a way of nagging like scratching nails on chalkboard. There were not many ways you could get me to stop unless you included killing. Pete hadn't ruled that out.

During my whining I asked why and she said she couldn't tell me. I repeated my 'why' question on numerous occasions.

The conversations went something like this after her communication improved. "You won't tell me or you can't tell me about where you go and what you do?"

"Both. Now comes 'why' question."

"Yes, Pete the mind reader. Why won't you tell me?"

"It's a waste of time and words."

"Make a good attempt and I'll leave you alone."

"How long? Ok. OK, easy. You listen good. Then you think to understand and make beliefs. Belief is not real."

"Listen 'well'. But anyway, you mean I listen ok but afterwards you object to my thinking which is all nonsense?"

"Not personal Essie."

"Of course I take it personally. You're telling me I can't think, so don't believe anything I think."

"No, don't believe things. We all think, same as breathe. We are here to create in real world not believe in imaginary."

"You are frustrating me Pete."

"I tried to avoid but you chose. You chose like bug. You chose to come with me and you chose to use words when I said it doesn't work."

I took a deep breath and persevered. "So why not have beliefs?"

"Have lots. Believe in wind or not. It doesn't care."

"And the point you are making is… ?"

She snapped her fingers in front of my nose. She startled me out of my head and into the real world of her quick moving hand and snapping fingers. *God she was quick.*

"What must I do to go with you on free time?"

"You have empty head of everything believed."

"Would it be a good start if I keep an open mind?"

"Not sure of the 'open mind' thing."

• • •

The nagging did get me somewhere. She finally relented and said she might take me but no talking or asking questions. Obviously. Ever. And secondly, if I did see "naturalness" (her word not mine) I could then talk to her about what I knew and share the vocabulary list. I agreed but I had to wrap a rag around my thumb, stick it in my mouth and sit silently to show I could "do quietness with no whys". Yes, I did it. I had dry raggy mouth, I gagged a lot, but it was worth it. She took me but not before more games like me begging on my knees which produced a gravelly snicker.

Chapter 36 – Thou Shalt Not

Padre had made several attempts to engage Pete with no success. Essie however was easily charmed by the man. "Tell me again how you get Pete to open up and talk to you."

"She says little unless learning or in a classroom setting. You'll get nowhere in areas of her world we find difficult to see or believe. You will hit a wall because she can't discuss, assuming she wants to, a topic we have no words to describe."

Padre asked, "Do you believe the stories about Pete killing the younger Morales?"

"I think we're all capable of killing under certain circumstances but those stories sound a little stretched. I know 'thou shalt not kill' Padre, making you of a different mind. Me, I would kill to protect myself from certain death if I could."

"What if it wasn't self-defense?"

"Like preserving her way of life or another innocent or good person like Señor Perez?"

"Yes, that's a good starting point."

"Pete would defend good against evil. Wouldn't you?"

"I suppose. But I don't think I could kill in that defense if for no other reason than my vows."

"Sure. Many wars have been fought regardless of your vows. To help you see things her way, here's my take. She sees Universe as a large living entity. Universe is good. It can survive and eventually overcome evil but it might take hundreds of years…and good people like Señor Perez would be killed without some help from her."

"Will she ever trust me again?"

Ah, the real question. "I like you too much not to say it. You may have noticed Pete avoids being controlled. You have been controlled by people and have done their bidding. She will not understand that kind of behavior."

Chapter 37 - Whouden

Essie's Diary

The haunting soft sound brought a chill. Pete blew a second soft note from the large round flute she had made from bark. Like a ventriloquist's voice, the breathy note returned from nowhere. A similar soft note played by the breeze through the rocks. This time it was not Pete. I got up to follow the music as if I was being called. Pete touched me gently to break the spell and sit me back down.

It felt like I was under a magical influence and she pulled me back from the musical breeze. After being roused from the spell it crashed through my thoughts the place was haunted. *Oh, no believing while here.* A woody fruity euphoric warm fragrance beckoned me to return as the music had done moments before. It had a piney quality like piñon pine. I will have to give some study time to the fragrances of frankincense and myrrh.

I was regaining my wits when I heard Pete continue with her flute as if calling to someone. Then she stopped. We waited. I heard the sound of several footsteps on gravel but saw no one. Pete nodded, got up and we finished the journey to her special place.

She called the place a name sounding like "Whouden" but quite breathy. The pronunciation was like wind whishing through a deep cave with a little echo as it departed. As I have previously stated, she was exceptional at mimicking natural sounds.

This is a summary from Whouden and my time there with Pete. I have the same advice for you that I got. "Don't believe anything including me."

• • •

Be patient Diary and look between the leaves.

I learned more of "the Lost or Ancients" by not studying as I have always done, but by connecting to something. Then I took what I got. Period.

In the beginning I fingered something dear like a piece of clay pot or

tool. I was lucky to have Pete close by even if she never did tell me much. I could sense her connecting. I attempted to do the same.

Pete drew a few lines. It was meant to aid in seeing the Lost. I saw a duck then a rabbit. Pete looked at me curiously. Odd how my mind switched back and forth. Duck Rabbit DUCK RABBIT. I shook my head to clear it. Pete just said, "the Lost" and walked away.

I sat there for a long time, Diary. Finally it came to me that if I was going to contact Pete's world I must clear away and be free of the encroaching influence of words, labels, definitions, and yes, my mind.

If I am what I think, what if I don't think? That's frightening. I felt a rush of heat. I was getting close to the abyss. Nevertheless I had to stay with it. Pete would not spoon feed me with words, and I knew then she shouldn't.

• • •

Without Pete to point the way I would have never seen this cliff cave dwelling or the petroglyphs. It was near the top of a box canyon not easily accessed. Pete told me to stay where I was. I didn't like it but did as I was told. A few minutes later she brought a ladder made from straight branches and rawhide about seven feet tall. She leaned it up against the sheer rock exterior. She went up first and gave me a hand to enter.

A large bolder overhang formed the ceiling of the cave dwelling. Pete was unable to stand up and I had to slump a little to make headroom. Perhaps the Lost were short people, or dirt and sand had blown in over the millennia making less headroom. In either case the floor was soft dirt and could have easily been removed.

Whouden was likely first inhabited more than a thousand years ago. This particular dwelling was comprised of two rooms, one larger than the other. The smaller may have been for storage. The bigger room appeared to have been for shelter and living at least for part of the year.

The open cave had been made into a dwelling with an entry made by stacking flat rocks stuck in mud to form an exterior wall. The mud mortar was protected from weather by the large rock overhang. The front barrier looked

to be about eighteen inches thick leaving the larger room twelve by twenty feet. I would guess Pete hadn't done or repaired the rock work but of course I could not ask.

Pete had placed a recently-tanned skin over the entrance with a gap at the top for smoke to escape. There were black smoke marks on the inside wall and ceiling that could have showed her a good location for the fire ring.

She had stacked firewood before our arrival unless the Lost left her a house warming gift. Remember Diary, I kept 'no mind' with no 'whys'. When the fire was lit the smoke did escape up and out the cave ceiling above the door flap maybe like it had a thousand years before.

There were glyphs etched on the rock walls and some appeared to have some paint or stain; some outside some inside made by chiseling the patina covering the rock surface. I have my doubts as to the origins of some of these.

One glyph appeared to be from an older era much cruder than the others. It looked half human and half plant with a head and one eye at the top then arms. Below that two stems having three fingers or branches, with roots at the bottom. A long-necked animal like a brontosaurus was barely visible and could have been some artistic license from the artist. Or not.

Pete would stop at one glyph and touch little round buttons or circles etched on a tablet. The petroglyph was inside the larger cave room where we camped. She would look at it, look away, and then let her eyes return slowly. It appeared this being was not a human as it had antenna sticking out from its head. The being appeared to be manipulating the device with the buttons.

I had heard stories she was connected to alien creatures

mixed in with the rest of the stories. Someday I may know the truth.

She grabbed her upper right arm with her left hand. "Dream, dreams." She spoke in a distant tone. Apparently she had experienced dreams associated with this glyph. Maybe not.

• • •

I found pieces of old potshards and small dried ears of corn no longer than my index finger on the inside. Pete also used intact pots to drink. They had rounded bottoms obviously not made for a table.

She got a faraway gaze, drank and then raised her drinking vessel in tribute. I assume it was to the potter. She never offered me a drink from one and I didn't ask.

This was vintage Pete. She was in the presence of something I was not. I watched and wanted to connect to something more than shards and architecture. It was not easy to keep my yapper shut, but I had to do it.

I would say she was in the company of the Lost by her movements. I would guess she was connected and feeling the tempo of lives long gone but that's only conjecture. Maybe they weren't long gone.

She did not have the normal Pete energy to her step but moved in a slow disciplined manner. When she touched and used a small old pot, it was an emotional interaction. Like visiting a frail old great grandmother.

Pete was able to feel the life and energy at Whouden. There was something real and palpable going on around Pete. As real as the dirt floor I was standing on.

If Pete was any good at reflecting the Lost they were calmer and more methodical than modern man. They were less cerebral probably without the mind's yammering which maybe allowed them greater awareness of their environment. Maybe they had a great deal of serenity. It leaves our cultures worlds apart and difficult to compare as the old ways would drive modern man off the cliffs. And maybe vice versa.

Eventually, even to me, there was an obvious presence. There was a shifting of something inside my guts pushing and pulling and then elevating up my chest to my throat. There was an ever present rhythm similar to a chant or a distant drum but it was felt, not heard. I'm sure she also was aware of it but probably not at the same level. It showed in her body language. She transitioned to be even more preoccupied and meditative by the second day.

Her darting eyes and her hawk-like stare were both appeased here. She was recharging her batteries and maybe greeting old acquaintances. Neither may be accurate.

Señor Perez was less than enthusiastic about us leaving and it showed with his relief when we returned. He had pride yet concern for his piece of sky "cielo".

Chapter 38 – Two Realities

Essie's Diary

Ernesto came the closest to knowing or at least expressing something about Pete's connection to Raven and nature. He may have even been on a similar wave length if wavelengths exist on 'the other side'. I wanted to pursue the idea with Ernesto before going to Pete.

• • •

"Ernesto, I want to talk about Pete and her abilities."

"Not easy to talk about Little Bird."

"So I gather. But I still want to see if I can write and publish something about it."

"I am sure you can if you could follow the right trail. I think you can do anything."

"Thanks Ernesto, let's have it. You know something about Raven?"

"Only to know I don't know. Yes I have thoughts but I have to dismiss them in this realm."

"Please give me your thoughts then, even if irrelevant on the surface. I can use them if nothing else to keep more aware when I am around Raven or Whouden."

"Ok. First some observations. We know Pete knew Raven long before either of us laid eyes on him. From the beginning the bird didn't seem quite right around me. Not like others of his kind in this dimension anyway."

"And you knew this how?"

"Raven's look or posture. No bird I ever saw would come in and just watch me for any length of time. Sure, he would strut around and steal some of my food like a normal raven. But after the theft he'd fly to a perch and observe me rather than eat. Little things like that."

"You see and sense things that I do not. And this all leads you where?"

"We know the bird spent time with Pete nearly a thousand miles from here until recently. We also know for the last two years Raven spent some time around me most days until we all met. Not every minute but generally an hour or two nearly every day. Physically not possible. At least as far as our minds will accept."

"I know that to be true as I saw the bird most days myself when traveling with Pete."

"You see, that is the problem Little Bird. Each of our minds alone would soon pass this non-reality off. Together we give it more reality making it harder to overlook."

"If you always had a bird around you and I had one around me, there should be two now we are together. However one and one became only one."

"That's what I like about you Little Bird. Quite good at math too."

"Cute Ernesto. But not cute enough. Where are the two birds?"

"Yes, I get it. There could be two birds a lot alike. And then one gets killed just as we meet. Too many coincidences. What other possibilities do you see Little Bird?"

"In the history of the world there was quite a focus on divination. I found it interesting to connect that history to the topic of Raven, Whouden and the Ancients. I originally thought ancient knowledge was generated from mass hysteria. But later I found similar history ran through different cultures over thousands of years. This led me deeper into soothsayers, prophets, seers, oracles, shamans, sorcerers and the like which now leads me back to our discussion today."

"So where are we Little Bird?"

"We clearly see in today's world it's not politically correct in many circles to believe one and one equals one any more than believing in the ancient wisdoms. Maybe best not to mention these beliefs as anything more than voodoo, magic or downright hokum."

"Is hokum a scientific word?"

"No Ernesto. You are still trying to be cute and you don't have to try. Those seers were able to connect humanity with the infinite. It was the backbone of religion and philosophy long before Christ. The seers could interpret nature, from a bird in the sky to a crash of thunder. Only a few however had visionary or prophetic knowledge that brought major differences to civilizations."

"But how does the pagan academic stuff before Christ fit this Raven business?"

"Just a hypothesis Ernesto. Needing proof. Pete may be uniquely suited with her connection to Universe and 'naturalness'. Maybe this is an effort to reestablish a wisdom we could use today. Not meant to replace any religious ideas like Christianity but to make us more aware of things no longer discernable through our senses. Maybe she was chosen by the Ancients or Seers as they could foretell the need in our time. Maybe they even had a hand in her upbringing and settling her down here with you."

"Are you saying we are in the future, now?"

"No, but I am saying Raven traveled without Pete to you over the last couple of years. Raven, or maybe the Ancients who might have been the driving force behind Raven, chose to bring Pete to you. They already knew your world would be advantageous for their project."

"What project?"

"To reunite the Ancients or their knowledge with us as they can tell our future is dim without it. We know from Pete's stories Raven was a guide who showed her direction. Raven watched you over time and maybe deemed you would be a good bridge. You put her right at ease from the first day. Not easy to do with the wild one.

"We also know Pete was surprised when you already knew Raven or a bird coincidently quite similar. It showed she had no knowledge of all this unfolding. We also know she chooses the company of Ancients. Raven may have had a hand not only in bringing her to you but introducing her to Whouden and the Ancients."

"That makes sense but I'm not sure making sense is the way to look at these things Little Bird. But it is all we have. You have not mentioned yourself in all of this. Have you asked Pete why she picked you up along the way?"

"I did. She said it was part of a prophecy by Piñon and a promise. When I asked if she could tell me more she shook her head."

"Doesn't that give you a little more on the side of the argument this was a plan by the Ancients or Raven Little Bird?"

"Maybe, but it is exceedingly vague. It could have been a plan by Piñon alone, or maybe not. I know it came after she had a strange bout with Padre. She is never clear. I need you to shed light which is why I wanted this discussion. Now show me things that either prove or disprove the hypotheses the Ancients are somehow behind all this."

There was a long silence but Essie stayed with it. A little teaching from Pete about silence is golden. "Oh Little Bird, I can see something there in your words but I would prefer to have it soak in a little deeper."

"Glad to hear you're thinking about soaking Ernesto. When done, please give me some proof either way. I also worry building a robust mind in Pete may cover or place a shadow over her natural abilities sought after by Raven or the Ancients." Ernesto looked into my eyes and all the intellectual stuff disappeared.

• • •

Essie's Diary

Nearly a week later.

"Are you done soaking Ernesto? I can't get questions answered from Pete. Let's take trees for example. I feel like I may be expanding reality by adventuring into peripheral awareness. But like peripheral sight, it's not crisp. And when I turn to get a focus, it disappears."

"Peripheral awareness. Hmm. Just suggestions. Pete would know best. Walk among trees that invite you. Don't talk out loud or to yourself and clear your mind of things you think. Be with the tree that attracts you on whatever level you like. Maybe something like when we look at each other. Visit the tree several times and touch the tree as you would a loved one or maybe even a lover. Imagine an entrance and find yourself entering this tree. Don't think about it just enter and feel the life that abounds from below the earth's surface through the trunk to the furthermost leaves. Then go out at night and spend the entire night alone with the tree that grabs you."

"All good but the night thing Ernesto. Not liking that. I get scary things running around inside when it's dark outside. Do you want to accompany me on this little adventure?"

"Sure, but trees a crowd."

"Oh, now a punster."

"You started it with all these words Little Bird."

"Seriously, this tree thing is heavier than I thought."

"It may be heavier than you can think. The tree will want all of you without distraction. I don't blame him."

"You're making my scar tissue wrinkle in on itself while turning a new shade of purple Ernesto."

"Music to my ears."

"Ernesto be serious."

"I am."

"What is it about night that will be useful?"

"Night affects you doesn't it?"

"Well, yes."

"Maybe it affects this tree also. The leaves won't be working with the sun at night which will allow this tree to devote more energy to you. If your mind needs reason we can talk botany, photosynthesis and sap. But won't you then have to wash all that reason stuff away to follow in Pete's footsteps?"

"Ok, I'll work with it Ernesto… but I won't like it."

. . .

Pete proved my mind was the controlling factor in seeing, so maybe my observations are crazy. I still wanted to tie it all together and get it on paper for others to independently analyze under the scientific method.

I asked Pete to give me a map or picture of how to get to Tree, Mountain and Whouden but not in a geographic sense. Maybe I could make a path anyone could follow.

. . .

She took me to a tree. No, not just a tree but THE Tree that would convince any human to never 'think' of trees again in the same way. I looked at the tree. It stared back. Not only with eyes but with an energy that could rip my guts out. Then, when appropriate, respectfully hand them back.

I'm not sure how long it took but I looked over at Pete and she was gone. She knew what I would experience. I was totally unprepared for what I confronted. This was his majesty demanding respect.

My mind was not going to accept what my eyes were seeing and my body was feeling. Similar to Raven but more gravity. I left my mind or as some might say, I went out of my mind.

I got that the other trees around us were in awe. They too knew they were in the presence of greatness or power. King Tree was part of this astonishing creation called Universe.

King Tree had a three hundred pound rock off the ground about four feet that he had grown around. Science states trees grow taller from their top, so explain how he grew around the boulder, picked it up and lifted it four feet off the ground if a tree grows taller from the top. Is science wrong and my studies of botany not valid? Maybe you think Diary, science is wrong? Maybe he grew up with the boulder from the ground? No, don't try to explain any more. I don't want to know about it.

Pete didn't want to hear any more from my mind and I got it. King Tree was a concrete absolute example of things that don't make sense to a mind. No matter how a tree grows his majesty can't do what he did.

If you are seeing a mouth and an eye in King Tree that's your mind trying to make something it might know out of what you don't know. Nothing wrong with it but you are limited by your mind. And what it can comprehend. Too bad.

I knew this was a male tree. No I didn't check. I didn't have the guts to spend the night with King Tree Rock in His Mouth of course and I never did touch him. I didn't dare. But that was a powerful experience. Thankfully he didn't reach down and touch me. One of the first times in my life sex was out of the question.

• • •

A week later I dared to ask Pete about a way of tying it together. She stood, stared and pointed back up the mountain. Probably toward King Tree. What a tyrant.

• • •

If only one person in the world can read and write, it has no value. The value and power of Pete's communi-cation with the Lost or within nature increases exponentially if it can be done or learned by others. Maybe I can fill the gap Diary.

• • •

I never made it overnight in the outdoors by myself. I did feel differ-ently about trees after touching one in a sensual way. I found a tree I was comfortable with and called him Cedar but I felt self-conscious doing it. The name alone gave me a little thrill. There was something that made me feel some-where between a pervert and a lunatic.

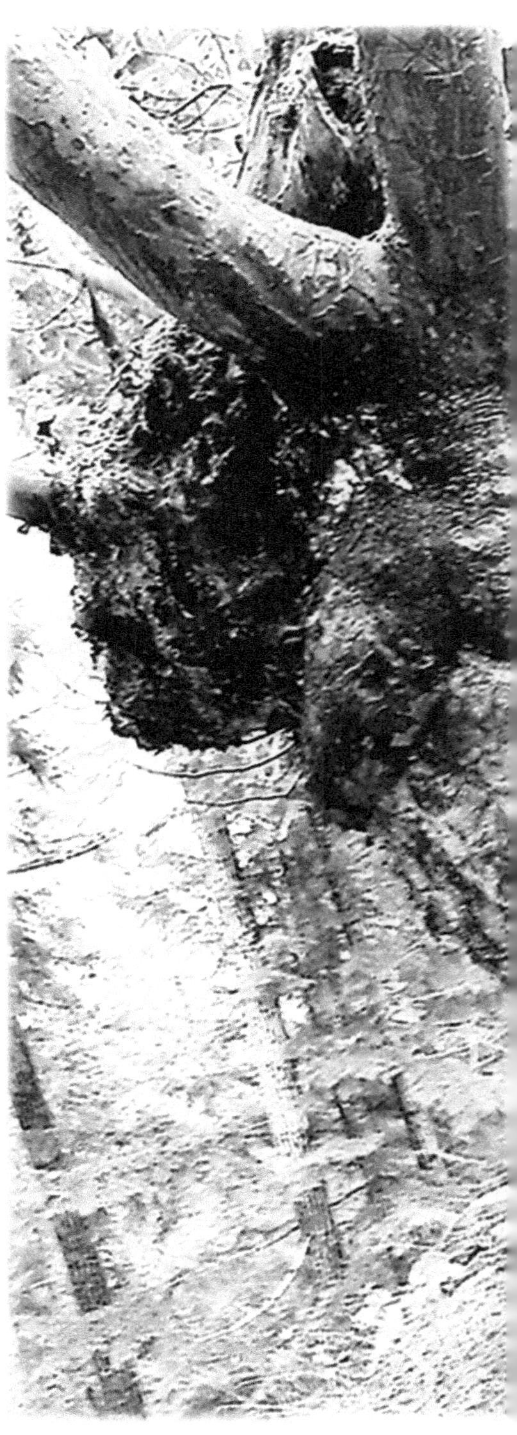

When I asked Ernesto about it he said it made him jealous and envious. He went on and on as you might imagine. He danced around swinging his arms like tree limbs in the wind. The more I yelled for him to stop the more it turned on his antics.

Finally when he calmed himself down, he gave me his answer as to why I felt weird. He said maybe it was my mind's way of keeping control over me (or my 'self') by separating me from things it could not grasp. Those things were a threat to the hold my mind has on me.

I never wanted to discuss it with Pete because she would not want to intellectualize about those things. But I did continue to spend a little free time with Cedar. Once a few hours after dark until it got too creepy. Never had any great epiphanies but the other trees seemed to become more alive. The sounds were louder as night progressed over Cedar and me. My breathing became a dominant part of my consciousness as I sat touching the trunk of that tree. I guess I was fortunate Cedar didn't try any funny stuff.

After Cedar and then returning to Whouden I noticed a little more change. I was getting something more alive connecting everything in Universe like an organism with parts working together. To me the glyph that appeared to be half human and half plant symbolized this connection.

• • •

I was with Cedar one evening and wanted to know what I needed to communicate better with him. I got this answer. *What is it that shows less the more light we put on it?*

My mind immediately kicked in making suggestions. Maybe it's night or darkness. Maybe it could be a lot of things. I let it go. No place for Mind. According to Pete it will come sliding by later. *Be ready to grab it.* Pete said it was like hunting. I would never know exactly what I was going to have for dinner.

The next time I was with Pete I asked her the same question, as nothing had come slithering or sliding by. "What is it that shows less the more light we put on it?"

She whirled straight at my scarred little face. "You chattering at Cedar!"

"Well no, I've spent some time with Cedar and wanted your advice. And it's not your tree."

"My advice. Don't do it." And she turned to leave.

"Wait Pete. I'm serious. Can you help me with a riddle? What is it that shows less the more light I put on it?"

"First you have a question. Then Cedar gives a question that makes the answer to your question easy. Cedar doesn't give questions to many. You must have found Cedar mighty hungry for you. You find out if it's ok for me to help."

"Ok, it sounds like Cedar gives me a riddle to answer... which is like a question. Yes, it's ok to ask you to help. Honest. Gees."

"You got permission?"

"Yes, easy even."

"Easy? You stretch truth like taffy candy. The worst is Cedar turns you and me into dirt and sucks us up the roots."

"Nice Pete, but I still want to know."

"It might make bark out of you to keep you out of the innards."

Ignore the little comments Essie. "What do I need to do to communicate with Cedar?"

"Open up to Cedar like you open a book and learn. This is like saying put one foot in front of the other. Next you go walking yourself. You will not do it exactly like anyone else. You walk with the riddle not talk to me and DEFINITELY don't chatter to Cedar. It will hit you like a branch in the face."

"I thought you said it would come sliding by?"

"I did. Different trees, different days, different ways. And you more likely to aggravate than connect."

"Thanks Pete. You are certainly good at this stuff." Pete stood there looking at me. I repeated again "You are good at this."

"Oh yeh, I'm special." And walked away with a grin.

In summary I would say my efforts to summarize and make available a new way of communicating were failing miserably.

• • •

Pete appeared to do things with light. Different colors like the panther with a ruby haze. Light is directly connected to Sun. Sun shines light everywhere on earth over Mountain and the heavens. In her words, "Light makes the earth and everything on it and around it."

Hard to believe.

She gave a gravelly laugh after my thought, "Good Essie. You got it." Did she get my thought from my body language?

If it is real, it doesn't need to be believed, it just is. It's another way of conserving energy. With the belief system muted a person might have more room or capacity for more important things, like the realities of Universe. And maybe, just maybe, things like Raven and ruby panthers could be more a part of our awareness and not be completely "mindboggling".

Listen, feel and sense. Look for more than meets the eye. Take the ordinary buzzard. Yes, Diary they are here to clean up the carrion. Is that really all there is to it? Vultures are a symbol of death but if we go further, they show us rebirth as part of the life cycle. In that realm they might have more power than we can imagine. They could be caretakers of the soil giving birth to all either directly or indirectly. If we don't look, we can't see.

• • •

She told me I could give her words to cover what she didn't know how to describe. I said the word 'tribalism'. "Here (in Whouden) tribalism still remains after the bodies have long gone from the earth." Pete tilted her head in a manner to encourage me to explain more. Of course I could not.

The more connected I was to Whouden the more relaxed I felt. The more relaxed the greater my ability to link with the energy there. I had never had that sensation before around people. Of course these people were dead, but I digress. In any case it was a gift.

• • •

Pete told me about the time she shared Whouden with Padre. The Lost resisted his presence and let Pete know. He was not considered evil but simply not ready. Padre had wrapped himself too tightly in something Pete had no word for. The results of the 'wrap' were he was shielded and couldn't share or accept. In Pete's words "no gifts". Interpret the two words as you will. I suggested the word 'narcissism'.

Again Pete wanted more on the word 'narcissism' by her body language. I thought it was a lot to lay on her but I continued slowly. "The term 'narcissism' originated from Greek mythology. The Greeks were an extremely old and advanced culture. The young Greek Narcissus saw his own image or his reflection in a pond and fell in love with it. Narcissus was attracted to his own reflection or looks and it consumed him. It took all of his powers.

"Envy comes from narcissism Pete. It was possible Padre had envy of your skills even though he thought them sinful. It may have made him belittle what you had at Whouden. Or not. I know that's a lot to swallow." Pete gave me a nod.

We talked about Padre more and neither of us could point to either good or evil. It was a jumbled personality. Pete asked me if Padre would go back to Whouden.

"Why do you want Padre back at Whouden?"

"The Lost."

"To work on Padre?"

"Maybe."

"They want to fix what ails him?"

"No. Padre is medicine man. They peel layers."

"… but what do they do after, 'peeling'?"

Shrug.

"I have an idea that may interest you. It could get Padre back to Whouden but at some cost to you. The Catholics have a procedure called exorcism. It gets evil or bad spirits called demons out from inside humans. Padre wanted to talk to you but until now I saw no reason to help him. However if you would like to get him back to Whouden, and he thinks you may be possessed or have demons, why not tell him he can do his exorcism but it must be done at Whouden?"

"Demon stuff could be trap."

"Could be a trap, yes. I don't want to tell you it is, or isn't. I don't know. It's an idea to consider and maybe not a good one. I don't see you as having demons hence, what's to lose? And I want to be honest with you. He asked me to talk you into getting this exorcism."

"He fears to ask himself?"

"Afraid may not be the right word but he feels there is a lot of distance on a lot of different levels between you. That being the case he feels the mere fact of him asking would get a 'no'. But he thinks if I were to ask, maybe you would at least consider the possibility."

"Smells like fear, looks like fear, and walks like Padre."

"I can see your point Pete."

I felt honored to be let into Pete's world.

Chapter 39 – Don't Inscrupulate

Essie's Diary

"Do you like praise or flattery Pete?"

"You don't make this easy Essie."

"And you don't make my learning 'easy' either. Look how far you have come. You are now starting to understand subtle differences. Do you like praise or flattery?"

"I like the real thing. Praise is real and when you give me praise I like it even if I ignore it. When you give me flattery it … it is because you want something."

• • •

Pete's curiosity was a driving force with anything she did and the world of ideas and words was no exception. Her vocabulary was quickly being flooded but words often missed the mark. To Pete words made stick figures instead of a fully-detailed portrait of everything her senses could accumulate.

Abstractions in words were fleeting and rare and philosophical concepts like "knowing what you don't know" were nonexistent and torturous for her in the beginning. She was intellectually challenged to remember things after her upbringing with Karl and Selina. She did however have a great capacity to tie everything together. Sometimes I could ask her a question and she could come up with a correct answer not in the book.

Pete displayed no hesitation nor was she ill at ease with showing what she didn't know making her progress incredibly swift. Sometimes Pete's questions were extremely confronting as she expected her teacher to have the same feelings she had. Practically none.

She had no qualms about asking me questions. She would never let go of a question until it was answered to her satisfaction. Her difficulty was hearing. She couldn't always hear my questions.

Pete learned words like she learned the use of her sling. She was a little intense at times to the point of frustration but not to the point of being self-defeating. Her mentor Grubby had taught her the fundamental element of success; never give up.

Pete made up a word if I didn't have one. Never mind if the rest of us didn't know it. She was proud of herself when she had a word I didn't.

• • •

One day I was looking over her shoulder at her writing. She placed her hand on top of her paper and said, "Don't inscrupulate until I'm done." I knew exactly what she meant. It wasn't in the dictionary. Yet. I slinked away rather than telling her it was a teacher's job to 'inscrupulate'. I'm not sure why this word struck my funny bone, but it did.

• • •

There was a cottonwood tree not far from our classroom. It had blown over recently and still had the green leaves attached to prove it. She looked at it several times as she passed. Then on an impulse sat on the trunk while listening to the creek in the background. She heard the music of drips and gurgling sounds and heard a rhythm she liked. Do do de duble duble de do do de de duble duble de do do de was often repeated.

She carefully inspected the tree trunk and started chopping the tree with an ax made from a sharpened creek stone tied by rawhide to a heavy branch. She cut a section of the tree about fourteen inches in diameter and eighteen inches in length. She removed the section of cottonwood. She worked on it when she had the time.

She smoothed the outer axed edges, removed the bark and then started gouging out the interior of the tree leaving the outer portion about one inch thick. As she went down into the center it became more difficult. She put red hot coals inside to assist her in removing the charred wood and ashes easily. About halfway through the center of the trunk she turned it over and repeated the process starting at the other end. When she was done she looked through the hollowed-out piece of log.

She had two small pieces of soaking deer rawhide and stretched them over both sides of the log. She pulled and stretched then tied them with wet rawhide strands to keep them stretched. As the rawhide dried it drew up and got tighter.

The following week she took her rabbit skin hat and cottonwood drum and went back to where the cottonwood tree had originally fallen. She sat and listened to the creek, birds and squirrels and do do de duble duble de do do de de duble duble de do do de. She put the drum between her knees and sat absorbed in the rhythm and the natural notes. She touched one of the dried stretched skins making a barely perceptible sound. She stirred it slightly with her hand and touched it again with a scrape and tap but this time a little louder. Che tump… che tump. Her spirit had left the here and now and helped the cottonwood have a last word with his friends.

• • •

I was outside the hay barn when I overheard a conversation between Pete and Ernesto. Ok, lighten up Diary, I was skulking around snooping and looking through a crack in the siding.

Pete pitched hay down from the loft to sheep below. Ernesto spread the hay allowing all the sheep to get their fill. Pete swung down from the upper loft on a rope, and did it with a loud "Oweee".

"You always know where the fun is Pete. Are boys not fun?"

"Boys are fun for some things. You are fun."

"But you don't want a husband?"

"Two leggeds are not geese."

"Ahhh…Yes, and what difference does that make?"

"Goose chooses a companion, ah ah mate, for life."

Ernesto's face clearly didn't see that one coming. "Ah, yes. I sometimes forget." Pete grabbed a fly from the air with a single stab, 'clop'. She opened her palm and the fly stayed there unfazed. She gently blew on him and he flew off.

"I've seen you do that dozens of times and never miss. How do you catch'em every time?"

"Most two leggeds see the fly and move where it's been. I see where it's going."

When Ernesto got his legs back he continued. "I guess I understand, but, but… I don't really. Is Essie enjoying teaching?"

Pete shook her head no. "She's much ah eh … 'honorary'".

Ernesto got the point and took it in with a wrinkle in the corner of his mouth.

"Essie is the most beautiful and warm person I have ever known. She's got a beauty my heart misses." He pulled at his overalls.

Oh, be still my soaring heart even though he's not a goose. I continued listening pressing my ear to the point of getting splinters in it.

Pete ran at the rope and used her momentum to swing way up off the floor back towards the loft.

"How's the studies coming? Juan doing well?"

"He's beinhaven I like to call it. Essie allows me to make words sometimes. We don't like waiting for smarter. It's like watching wool grow."

Ernesto grew another large grin as it sunk in. "Do you think your talk with Juan did him some good?"

"Words not good with that boy."

"Your knife speaks words Juan understands."

Ernesto took a finger as if it were a knife and cut across his pants above the crotch. Then it was Pete's turn to give a gravelly giggle.

"Town tomorrow?"

Pete nodded.

"Do you think Essie's going?"

Another nod came from Pete.

• • •

The ride into town was pretty quiet. I didn't want to push Ernesto any. However I did want to get past the embarrassment with Madam or whatever was making him shy away. We exchanged pleasantries and remarked on the scenery. I hated it.

In town Pete packed the wagon while Ernesto and I carried goods from The General Store. I exited the store with a long-handled broom when I spied the Madam a block away. I had a few questions that needed answering. I strolled toward the Madam with the broom still in hand.

Ernesto brought out his last box and helped Pete secure and tarp the load. There was no way Ernesto was going to get tangled up with the Madam again so he waited at the wagon. Unfortunately the Madam was walking back with me toward the wagon, and Ernesto. The tension rose as we got closer.

I was carrying the broom upside down like a walking stick while talking to the Madam. Three men approached us from the side. One was the sheriff. I learned later the other was District Attorney Wagner, a big wheel in the territory. Tagging along with them was the deputy.

The sheriff's finger pointed straight at the Madam and jabbed her in the chest, backing her up. "I've told you about our streets" he bellowed.

The deputy watching the sheriff imitated him by jabbing me with his finger pushing me backwards. The deputy who was clearly an inept idiot was feeling mighty important.

"Look you ugly little freak. You should watch the company you keep." I regained control from the deputy's push backward, grabbed the broom as if it were my staff in the power position, and struck the deputy's legs below the knees putting him sprawling.

Mr. Wagner with rifle in hand stood blocking Ernesto who had run to my rescue. Ok, maybe not to my rescue but I like to think it was. Anyway, Ernesto arrived grinning and checked to see if I was alright. Then he turned to the sheriff. Mr. Wagner put the barrel of his rifle between Ernesto and the sheriff. The deputy remained on the ground moaning like some baby and rubbing his shin. *Thank you God.*

Mr. Wagner was the first to speak. "Let us handle this. Attack a peace officer and you are always wrong in the eyes of the law." The dervishes were already at his side.

"She attacked me with that broom," the deputy was quick to point out from the ground.

The sheriff gave a scowling reply to his deputy. "Deputy, you should be ashamed of letting her of all people get the best of you."

"Well those squatters work for Perez and they shouldn't even be in the territory."

The sheriff was all for putting us in jail and got riled with Ernesto. I was totally proud of myself. It sure did feel good not to be the one in the dirt. I didn't have time to think. I just did it.

I knew Sheriff Curry had it in for Ernesto from several run-ins. It appeared those feelings went both ways. I also knew the sheriff was aggravated with the manipulation of the law by the DA and his cronies and was getting a great deal of pressure from the DA to eject Señor from his old Spanish Land Grant. The sheriff did not step in thus far even if it meant his job. Maybe his life.

Today it boiled over. The sheriff was a foot taller and a hundred pounds heavier and Ernesto wanted a piece of that lawman. Hard to believe the sheepherder doing impressions in his camp in the mountains was the same guy ready to kill the hulky sheriff.

The Madam and I were pushing Ernesto back toward the wagon. The sheriff was looking for trouble and was hoping Ernesto would start it. Ernesto wouldn't let it go. "You know the law as written protects the Perez rancho."

The sheriff stood tall, hands on his gun belt glaring. The deputy yelled from his position sitting in the dirt. "You're talking about old laws. The old laws weren't even written in English. Juan will never take title to the land and the recorder will see to it."

Ernesto was a gentleman around ladies. He didn't use full force to get back in the sheriff's face. But I could tell he had the power to do it if he wanted to. *My hero.*

We walked towards the wagon with Pete already at the reins just like she knew I wanted to be with Ernesto. Like many times before in the wilderness, she knew what was to happen and was prepared.

Ernesto looked into my eyes with tears in his own. "I can't believe what my Little Bird did."

I melted. It was all worth it all of a sudden. All those weeks training with Pete. We stayed quiet in each other's arms until Pete spoke up over her shoulder. "What new law?"

"You have the ears of a wolf Pete," was Ernesto's reply.

"What new law," she repeated. "What law, what is the recor dur?"

"The recorder is the American government man who keeps the history of the land in his book. But his book is new with only new records and new words in English. It doesn't have the Old Spanish Land Grants with the words in Spanish."

Pete understood all too well. Ernesto's answer was enough to keep her quiet while I got the full story in the back of the wagon.

"The old records are kept in Spain and were never given to the recorder here. They were of course in Spanish which made them suspect in any case. Those in Washington DC with the power and always wanting more were English-speaking. They didn't live in the nearly all Spanish-speaking territory nor did they want to. The recorder and sheriff do what the surveyor general and his cronies like Wagner tell them to do if they want to keep their jobs. It's a corrupt system. This is a rare circumstance the sheriff hasn't followed the DA's obvious requests and forcefully pushed Señor from his Rancho."

"Not a pretty picture Ernesto."

"No, it's not. We let our public servants gain too much power. We have no one to blame but ourselves."

• • •

I was starting to see why Pete had the right idea. Those in power made laws, regulations, or used fear and bullying to benefit themselves at the expense of taxpayers paying their salaries. Stay outside or above this system and take what you want.

Pete chose freedom, chocolate, and assisting Universe to unfold as it should. The wolf weeded out the weak and made the elk herd stronger. The DA was leaving the human herd weaker and only benefiting himself.

We were now living in a society Jefferson warned about. I would be including this in my 'teachings' to Juan and Pete in the classroom.

Chapter 40 – Everything Lives and Dies

Essie's Diary

Christmas and the famous Jesus was talked about in class. I started the conversation with a question. "What made him famous?"

"You ask the dumbest questions Miss Essie."

"Pete, He died for our sins."

"You must have had pretty bad sins if it killed him."

"We all sin Pete. No mortal is perfect." I thought she was joking or at least I hoped so. She had no idea people had boundaries where there was no joking. I didn't want to preach, but give information when and where I could. I saw this conversation would need to wait for a time. I needed to convey to her it's not something we joke about especially in light of Padre thinking she was a witch or had demons.

• • •

It snowed some that winter. I took them out and built a snowman on Christmas Day. Pete stood back and watched the whole process. When I was done Pete made only one comment. "Essie, he only stands there."

Coyotes were always around but seldom heard midday. With Pete's words about the snowman they set up a chorus of clatter. Pete smiled, glanced quickly in the direction of the sound, and said no more. Take it for what it's worth Diary.

• • •

We all had presents. Colorful scarfs, rabbit fur hats and carved staffs were at our sides. Pete and Juan may have had conflicting ideas on religion. Therefore I left scripture to take a beating and did nothing to engage either on the subject. What came was what came.

Pete had no trouble relating to God, the Creator. "All this stuff had to come from somewhere," whirling her arms around. "If God created all Universe it would be easy to create a son who had the power to heal." Padre had laid the ground work for Jesus which was a blessing in itself.

Juan had a different take but it never rolled out of his mouth after he heard Pete's philosophy. He was raised Catholic and saw himself above the teachings like most teachings he obtained from his unsuccessful schooling. After Pete shared from her connection to Universe he stayed wide awake and focused, attempting to grasp what she had said. A good sign.

• • •

Tacked to the barn wall were the two papers from many months back. First Juan's (his name was at the top) with "APBLE", "HOWSE" and "DOG" written under each drawing and the alphabet had missing letters at the bottom of the page.

Next paper had no name at the top. There were no words or letters anywhere on the page.

Pictures were more closely connected to her thought processes than were words at the time. The apple had a tree drawn beyond it and the apple hung from it. It was drawn in the correct perspective.

A little girl with short hair was drawn next to a dog looking toward a house with a tree. The house had nothing drawn near it. Between the house and the dog she drew a fence with vertical posts and horizontal rails. She said the dog's name was Grubby. After that, I learned about Karl, Selina, Caroline, and Whitey.

• • •

I read to Juan and Pete from a letter Thomas Jefferson wrote in 1787 to his friend William Smith. Jefferson justified fighting against one's own government to keep liberty and freedom. Jefferson wrote: *"The tree of liberty must be refreshed from time to time with the blood of patriots & tyrants. It is its natural manure."*

Pete never learned to raise her hand to ask permission and this time was no exception. "Why study these fancy words of dead people?"

"Because history repeats itself. Look how Mr. Wagner and his tyrant cronies take money belonging to orphans and seize land worked by others for hundreds of years. As Jefferson said 'Those who hammer their guns into plowshares will plow for those who do not.' We can learn from this history."

"Insiders spit words like bees that make bad honey. What are lies made from?" Something had just set Pete off.

Pete opened her mouth and stuck out her tongue and pointed to it. Juan laughed at her antics.

"I'm not sure I understand you Pete but ..."

"'But'! That's a little word between something good and something bad. Yes you understand 'but'. Fire word cooks no food. Honey word has no taste, and, and And.. Tree of liberty had no fight. Guns have fight. Words will never help Señor. You spit words that change nothing on this Rancho. His son was killed and it don't look good to me." The pressure Pete had been harboring about Señor and the Rancho just boiled over.

"Doesn't, but…"

"Yes, Miss Essie. Why learn about dead people and their old words."

"A good question Juan."

"Don't let it go to your head Juan."

"Nothing's going to my head Pete!"

"No kidding." Pete smiled proudly. *Whacked his stupid ass.*

"Play nice you two. I see you don't mind using words to fight."

I quickly diverted their attention, "Pete what's a vegetarian?"

"Easy, a bad hunter."

"How do you recognize people and their intention?"

"By the reflection on their face."

"Amazing Pete. Quickly I went on before we heard about Juan's face. "Eight times seven and add four to it, anyone?"

"Sixty" they say in unison.

"Pete, can you spell the word 'invade' and use it in a sentence?"

"I N V A D E Invade. I let the sun invade my body." I loved the way she saw words and made them work for her.

"Pete what would you call a person who threatens you?"

"Stupid."

"Yes Pete. In this case Juan says you threatened him with your knife to do his lessons. True?"

Pete shook her head sweetly and innocently. She was exaggerating what she saw other two leggeds do with their acting in a singsong voice. "That's not true Miss Essie. I did not threaten Juan with my knife. I actually cut his pants nearly stopping his breeding."

"Miss Essie the truth is I think next time Pete will cut deeper. I think Pete is a danger to society."

"Miss Essie I don't care what he thinks. I have no control over what Juan thinks. I doubt he has any control over what he thinks. And he shouldn't be too worried about society as much as the things in his pants."

"Enough. What makes a good hunter Pete?"

"Good hunters are easily .. eh, easily disturbed."

"Yes, I got it. Maybe even easily distracted would be a good way to describe it."

"Yes, you would not make a good hunter because you stay on one thing and don't move from it. You won't see something move out of the corner of your eyes if you are looking at a book or listening to words in your head. You would likely starve most days because of this focalizing."

• • •

I well remember the day Pete got hit right between the eyes with word images.

I was showing her photos of birds. She immediately recognized the peregrine falcon with wings and talons outstretched diving for prey. She closed her eyes and her body swayed as if using the air herself.

I read from the book under the photo while she sat drifting in the breeze: "The proud peregrine is so majestic. If you can't watch death, you can't watch the peregrine. It deals death swiftly."

She fell back off her bale of hay on the barn floor and cried. Tears filled her eye sockets and streamed down her cheeks. When they stopped a small grin started that migrated across her face to a big smile. Then words spilled out and the tears started again. "Thank you Essie."

• • •

Although Pete had an interest in the wolf's social life and predation, nothing surpassed the peregrine. The following day she pinned a sketch of the peregrine to the wall of the classroom.

However, more importantly to me, she placed another sketch beside it of our sheep barn classroom and surrounding landscape. It had the bird's perspective a thousand feet overhead. Maybe she was in better contact with the angel within, flying without the constraints inherent in mortals.

• • •

Much later I had a special assignment for Pete. I thought she may balk but that didn't stop me. I wanted her to go find the good-looking farm boy and play nice using language she had been learning. She told me about the conversation and it went something like this.

"What is your name?"

"Fred, why do you ask?"

"What's your favorite food Fred?"

"Fresh homemade pie. Why do you ask?"

"I'm supposed to practice talking to you."

"Practice talking?" After a long pause, "Ok, I'll bite, what is your name and what is your favorite food?"

"My name is Pete and grouse liver is my favorite food if I don't consider sweet stuff like chocolate frosting."

"Why do you need practice talking?"

"To learn polite conversation."

"Are you going to pay me?"

"No, this is a freebee Fred."

"A freebee?"

"Yes, no charge. The Madam in town gives freebies. I don't pay you money and you don't pay me money. It's only for fun."

I was proud of Pete for strutting up to that hunk Fred. She gave me the basics of what was said before I got there and added, "I don't see the point."

"There is no point. That is the point. It's only a game."

"Stupid game."

• • •

We were making great progress that even surprised my best expectations. I remember this encounter with Pete. We were all dressed in winter coats and Pete-type fur hats. Juan was doing his writing lesson and I was getting Pete to talk more and more about how she saw things.

"Pete tell me about how you see life and nature."

"What do you mean, how I see it?"

"I would like to see what you see but I don't."

"You can't see because … because. Ok, try this. You are too attached to your ways. Life flows in and out of everything. You can't 'see' all this with eyes only. Nobody can. It also comes from emotions you can't see. You feel it more like you would a sunset but it's nothing like a sunset if it's a tree. Or I hope you would feel the sun as it leaves the day behind, but sometimes I wonder. Do you see how frustrating this is? And then add to that some things can be seen but only if you look the right way. It's too complicated and beyond my… my patience."

"Yes, yes. You have said Universe unfolds and you have also said it's cyclical. How can it be cyclical? Unfolding makes changes but they are not cyclical."

"Those are words and not mine but yes that could be close." She grabbed a piece of chalk. She drew a three dimensional counterclockwise spiral. "Unfolding." Then she turned sideways to the blackboard and kept her hand moving. A cyclical motion making a different view, a two dimensional end view, of the same phenomena going counterclockwise. A different way of "seeing" the same thing.

Maybe what she wanted to say but couldn't was there are more dimensions than two or three. From the end the spiral was showing a repetitive cycle. However from the side it moved through space with time… unfolding. After that display I was energized. I grabbed a piece of chalk and put directional arrows on both views and looked at her. She nodded yes.

"And those things to unfold we can't see yet but are there nonetheless?"

"Maybe. And maybe some can see them. Because they know how to look."

"Only a little more Pete, I promise. Rabbits and men live and die. We may feel bad if someone we love dies. Yes?"

"Easy. Everything lives and dies. Mountain cut by rivers bleeds mud, not just men and animals bleed. Do you feel bad if Mountain goes to rivers then ocean? Does this mean a baby plant is exactly alive like a baby human? No. Plants don't bite or poop in their pants."

"Mind candy Pete. Do you see life in a rock like you do in a tree whispering on a hillside?"

"Walls and words keep insiders away from the real world."

"Go on."

"What?" Pete grinned now playing mind games with me.

"Write me a paper about rocks."

"What?"

"Stop it Pete."

"Do I get to go early?"

Then I gave her a dose of my game playing, a coy shrug.

"Do you promise?"

"Yes, write the paper and you can go early?"

"You don't look like a promising person."

"Yes, I promise… I promise really pretty please promise so…." I wanted her writing more than life.

"Ok, but first I go early, then tomorrow I write."

"You know that one doesn't work Pete."

"Ok then I tell the story today, write it tomorrow?"

"Ok, you drive a hard bargain you horse trader."

"Done. God created Universe and everything is connected and lives. Some things live like animals and trees and other things live like rocks. Rocks live and push back when we squeeze them. A rock's shadow always moves. It can run down a mountain. Rocks breathe in the heat of the sun or fire and blow it into our tea or earth beds. The reason why a rock's life is different from a chipmunk's is a rock can't be killed in the same way. Both eventually change into something different. And this is where you want more talk and I walk out."

Pete got up and I launched into my questions. "What about when a rock…."

"Hey you slave owner. You promised!"

"Yes, but I didn't say when."

Pete flashed anger and squinted daggers at the insider double-talk. I could feel myself squirming and Pete read my body language as easily as I read a newspaper. Pete danced out with a wiggle in her rear giving me what for.

Chapter 41 – Ernesto the Teacher

As spring approached the tempo around the ranch increased. Pete was the go-to for anything sheep. Her speed and knowledge around the pregnant ewes was better than a veterinarian. She had a touch exposing trouble before it happened. She'd put her hands on the animal, roll her eyes back as if she was reading a chart on the top of her head, then go to work.

Sometimes she was able to save the young lamb but had to dispatch the ewe and sometimes she could save the ewe without the lamb. When she lost them both she would pause for a moment and take a deep breath.

Time and again Señor Perez wanted to learn more from Pete about her knowledge. She would shrug and make light of it as if she was too humble to speak more. When pressed however, she could not explain what she knew or how she knew it.

Señor Perez after failing miserably wanted Ernesto to learn about Pete's knowledge. He knew Pete could tolerate Ernesto better than others. If Ernesto did learn anything he too was unable to put it into words. The best he could come up with was her hands were smarter than most people's heads.

Ernesto told Señor Perez the owner being close may hinder Pete's abilities and be a distraction. Señor Perez would not accept defeat easily therefore keeping his watch from afar. Sure enough he saw Pete's attention went from sheep to him when he was present. Even at a distance.

• • •

Essie's Diary

On several of my trips to town I ran into Padre. It felt more like Padre ran into me. He knew I liked him and trusted I would do his bidding.

"Hello Essie."

"Hello Padre. All going well at the orphanage and school?"

"Yes, all is fine. You look like a little sun has kissed each cheek." He always gave me the opportunity to give him some information on Pete.

"Thanks Padre, I feel great and more confident than ever before. It has something to do with Pete but it's hard to put my finger on it."

Always he finished with his patented smile that cut the heart of many a lady, even though his backward collar made him off limits.

• • •

Pete would not be limited to learning words when she got a taste of interesting humans who used them. Father Greggory held the key to people, or at least most humans, by being able to manipulate them. That wouldn't mow much grass with Pete ever again but she had an increased interest in watching him operate as she might want to learn his people skills.

Pete had not been able to judge Padre correctly because she misread his body language, or maybe was confused by his intentions and abilities. She came to me for my take.

I told her Padre was gifted academically with psychology and people skills. This allowed him to misdirect or deflect what truth she might have been able to receive from his communications comprised of body language and words.

When I was speaking to Pete about Padre she was absorbing something else with her 7th sense. Maybe it was her 8th. I lost count. She said I told her with my body language Padre would physically charm any lady, which would also be disruptive to an innocent girl like herself. Pete got it and put it all together not by what I said but what she picked up by some girly wiggle I must have had.

She nodded and gave her thanks and approval. I took it for what it was worth. I wasn't the teacher of a dumb student. I had a student requiring more of her teacher.

• • •

She saw contradictions in all my words like too many cooks spoil the pudding (as she remembered) and yet many hands made the work light. "What a waste of time to have all those words that cancel each other out." She saw it her way and I thought it mine.

• • •

One day I got up quite sick and it got worse when I walked to the sheep shed classroom. Pete was waiting outside and when she saw me she said, "You look awful. I don't think you should teach today."

"But ha can't do that Pete," through a stuffed nose. "My job is too important."

"You think this earth is going into an 'orbituary' if you let us off one day? You think history is more important than your life?"

"You mean do ha think this earth is going out of its orbit or do you mean the earth is going to die and need an obituary?"

"Neither will happen if you go back to bed and no school." If you liked humor, you loved Pete.

• • •

The first yearend tests all went without a hitch. Of course I worried and fretted but my students pulled through like the champs they were. I think both pretended they didn't care in order to take the pressure off. The excitement came after they found out they both passed and they both did well.

We had more great adventures and I don't want to cut them short but after Pete threw knives at a bear four times her size everything else was anticlimactic. She was submerging herself within a potful of insiders that may have given her the same thrills. At times I felt bad about it in case she lost her old abilities. But what do I know.

Through the following winter Pete read everything she could get her hands on around the ranch like Ernesto did. There were always chores to be done of course but the pace was slow and allowed her many hours of reading during the winter months. When she had questions of Ernesto he was quick to give a meaningful answer and sometimes he'd even spend pay on getting her a book that would give her an answer in depth. He never came right out with the answers but led her to them which made him the true teacher.

If she wanted the answers spoon fed he did his best mime. One of them was pretending he didn't know the answer but was willing to look. He faked something flying and would duck with its near miss. He wasn't sure what it was. Maybe it was a figment of his imagination and his eyes would open wide. It was clear he hoped it wouldn't happen again. When it did he pulled imaginary fruit from the imaginary tree floating by. He stuffed the fruit in his mouth chewing slowly and swallowed sticking his neck out to show he barely could get it down his gullet. Oh God, I love that man.

Chapter 42 – Exorcism

After Essie asked Pete about an exorcism, Pete went silent for a couple of days. Then she returned to Essie with abrupt confronting behavior. "What exactly are these demon things? Do they look like maggots? Why do you think I should get rid of them? Are they bad and evil or only considered bad by insiders?" Her eyes never left Essie's at the end of the barrage.

"I am not the one to explain demons. As far as I can see you don't have demons and it's Padre who has issues. Maybe you should talk to Padre. I know you two have a strained relationship but you are no longer that Wolfboy you once were. You have evolved. Maybe Padre has also. Of course you might think he has changed for the worse but there is only one way to find out."

Pete felt excitement with the encounter of the Lost versus Padre at Whouden. She saw the exorcism in itself as a nonstarter because as far as she could tell she didn't have anything to exorcise. That being said, she also had nothing to lose for the same reason. Padre's large dollop of charisma added sugar to the cake if she could get a handle on the hunk of a priest and have him meet her halfway.

• • •

"Padre, I want answers before I do this exorcism thing. Why not come directly to me? Why run to Essie?"

"I am not proud of the way I acted and that may have tainted my confidence. You are right. I should talk directly to you."

"I'm not proud of your actions either. That's a good start. I admit I didn't do well also but it was my first time with the relationship thing. I have an excuse. Are you using this exorcism as a scheme to get even or control me for something I might have done to you when we first met?"

"No Pete. The exorcism will not put anything into you to control you or get even for anything. It can only remove all possibilities of you having demons so people around here will stop speculating. So far at least the idea of having an exorcism is starting to work. We dropped into another level and are willing to be more upfront and truthful. From now on if I have a question or you have concerns about anything on any topic we should talk openly, honestly, and directly to each other. Thank you for your part in getting this started."

"What do you want from me if I do this worming?"

"Pete, first and foremost I want you comfortable with the entire process. You need to get all your questions answered. Although you didn't ask, demons are nothing like worms."

"Where do we do this?"

"Where would you like?"

"At Whouden. That place of Ancients I took you to."

His faced dropped about a foot but not for long. "An interesting choice and a bit unusual. I would have to do some extra preparations but that is not impossible. Anything else?"

"Can I invite others?"

"Yes, they have to be respectful of the process but I'm sure anyone you invite should work. I would like to know who in advance that I might talk to them about what is expected."

"Our relationship is not good. You know that's why you ran to Essie. I don't want you on some tall horse looking down at me anymore. That uppity stuff won't hunt Padre."

"I understand and I have no reason to be haughty with you as you well know. This process should be good for both of us."

Pete and Padre had several more discussions. Pete got a little uppity but Padre handled it.

• • •

Essie's Diary

Padre wanted a controlled environment and I could ask my questions in advance. "Have you and Pete decided upon a day?"

"Yes, Essie, we start Good Friday."

"Is there any special reason why you chose that day?"

"Yes, it works best for both Pete and me. She has the weekend off and I am to be away Easter week and allow Father Timothy full rein as it may be his last Easter in the church."

"What should I do?"

"Just follow my directions. Be sure you bring at least one other person. Someone strong. Maybe Ernesto as I trust he's a God-fearing man and will respect the process. Oh, and please fast the day of the exorcism. I invited Señor but he thought the location would be a little difficult for him physically. I agreed."

"What should I expect?"

"Expect the unexpected. I may ask you to hold Pete down for example."

"Does it ever hurt?"

"I'd rather not predict or have any preexisting conditions on the exorcism. If there is some pain it will not likely be remembered."

"Does it take long?"

"It takes as long as it takes."

I could only hope he knew more than he let on. He did give me explicit instructions which gave me some confidence. Padre wanted Pete recently bathed and wearing loose fitting clothes like a nightgown. Good luck on the nightie.

He didn't want me or Ernesto to interfere, no matter what we saw. I had enough training from Pete about keeping my mouth shut but this was more. He wanted my complete support and prayers for what was about to happen. I imagined something like a séance. I didn't think Padre was going to dress up like a fortune teller but I could see the potential of an extraordinary escapade. And when I put Pete in the mix, there was little doubt.

• • •

I talked to Ernesto about making it a foursome and explained the situation. It was going to be a learning experience and give us an opportunity to see Pete and Padre in a new way… maybe. He couldn't be himself which meant it was not going to be what he might call fun. He had an academic interest in the ritual to be performed the same as Padre had a similar interest in the Lost. Yes, he was a God-fearing man but maybe not in the way Padre was. He agreed to attend if for no other reason than to support Pete.

• • •

When I asked Señor if Ernesto and I could take a few days off he said in his soft-spoken manner it would have to be at a time when we could be spared. I gave him the day it was to start and it gave him pause. I could tell he flashed on Good Friday and Easter Weekend but then went to possible conflicts. He quickly came back to our conversation with a smile. "Be sure to let me know if I can be of any assistance." He asked no questions and made no other comments.

He was a devoutly religious man although he seldom made it to church. He read the Bible each Sunday and would often walk alone in the early Sunday mornings with his thoughts and his Bible. He had a religious alter in his home and was known to be in prayer Sunday mornings before his walks. I wondered what was going on behind his calm knowing eyes.

• • •

On the weekend of the exorcism Pete, Ernesto and I were to meet Padre at Whouden on Good Friday before noon. Pete wanted to go alone which meant when we got there Pete, or the Lost, had already chosen the area for the exorcism. The area selected was inside the large room Pete had shown me long ago.

• • •

Pete was dressed in loose fitting skins sitting on a perch watching Padre in his black robe struggling to unload his packhorse and carry his burden up the ladder. No big smiles and easy going manner from either Padre or Pete.

When Padre finished taking what was needed up the ladder he was a dirty dusty mess. He showed signs of injuries including scrapes and bruises on his hands. He kept his pious manner throughout and then left the large cave room.

During this time Pete had gone up the ladder and laid down on her mat, hands across her abdomen, knife strapped to her side, and eyes wide open. Her energy was palpable when Ernesto and I went up the ladder and found our mats. Pete had taken down the skin across the entrance.

All was tranquil except for a light breeze easily perusing around the rocks at the entrance. Padre broke the calm by his flashy entrance, with clean cassock flowing. "Welcome" came his voice reverberating against the walls of the cave like he was talking to people in the far reaches of a huge cathedral. He lit his incense burner.

• • •

It started simply enough with prayer and asking God's help with what was about to happen. We prayed for each other and for what was to take place.

Pete remained a little stiff and in Focused Attention. I don't know if Padre knew about Focused Attention but it was obvious to Ernesto and me. She was not afraid by any means but not letting her guard down either.

Padre bent low to her and removed her knife extremely cautiously. The tension in the room increased dramatically as the knife was gently placed beside her but not touching her. He paused again at the sight of it as he stood, then moved on.

He took each of us individually and made the sign of the cross on us using holy water. Then he sprinkled everyone, including himself again with holy water. Afterward he knelt and prayed to Saints and started reading from Psalms.

There was a short time of silence as Padre knelt in prayer. When done he boomed a startling message giving commands to the "unclean spirit" and any of the accompanying minions attacking Pete. He threatened the spirit with all the power God holds. The demon was told to give up his hold on Pete, by some sign to reveal his name, time of departure, and to follow Padre's instructions exactly. Lastly he commanded the demon spirit to harm no one present at the exorcism.

None of this was anything like what I had anticipated. It was demanding, not requesting, with a shouting ferocity. I looked to Ernesto and he was riveted.

Padre took Ernesto emotionally by the seat of his pants and threw him into the proceedings. Nothing was boring for Ernesto.

Padre was only getting warmed up. Latin prayers started and with them shadows. A single small cloud moved across the sky casting a portentous grey gloom lasting not more than a minute. A guarded look washed over Pete's face, even after the return of the sun.

Her expression was wiped away by a dark shadow of swooping wings through the cave entrance. The incense mixed with the fatless flying figure and made an ominous presence across the room. The two together painted the ancient cave with three dimensional art work. The tension mounted as the shadow and the bird became one.

Raven made his entrance landing softly next to Pete. Like Padre he wore black and carried an undeniable presence. With Raven's arrival came a wary expression on Padre's face. With the bird's iridescent appearance the room was swept with the distinctive fruity piñon fragrance I had smelled on my first visit to the cave dwelling. Once again a euphoric feeling washed over me with the sweet aroma.

Padre spoke to Raven and commanded the bird not to distract. "I know exactly why you are here. You have been summoned by demons. It will not help the harbinger of evil. Demons be gone! Be gone! Be gone! In the name of the Father, the Son and the Holy Ghost." Padre walked back and forth in front of Pete.

Raven bounced on Pete's chest and looked into her face. Then the bird slowly turned and glared at Padre with beak open and tongue slightly out giving him what looked like a sneer. Raven stepped down from Pete and gave a good mime of Padre standing tall strutting back and forth. The bird made a few guttural sounds and squawks sounding like Latin words sprayed through the croaking throat of a raven. "unus uniksum EX aanus".

Padre sent Raven away again and with that command, Raven swaggered away from Pete. Not in any hurry mind you but took a couple of steps, then turned and waited. A deep sound came forth. "Croak Croak!" Padre returned to the tasks at hand.

I looked at Ernesto and he had a most electrifying expression on his face with the surrealistic drama unfolding. He knew this bird and it was no accident. I returned to the stage in front of us.

Pete sat up slightly and when she did Raven drooped his other wing. He mimed Padre again. The two drooping wings looked like his black robe flowing to the ground while walking back and forth in front of Pete. Pete's entertained expression showed none of this was her doing. The Focused Attention was replaced with pure appreciation for the bird and the humor.

Padre stood tall and was yelling, making his head stick out by stretching his neck. Raven turned and gave it right back to Padre yelling more Latin sounds as the large black bird stretched its head bobbing in and out.

The breeze outside increased in strength. It set loose some odd sounds akin to choir voices with a definite cadence. It had to be the wind but never have I heard anything imitating the voices of humans as well. The windy vocal sounds gained volume and increased in tempo with every repetition. First there was a single voice, then another making a duet. Back to the single voice then the accompaniment of an entire choir. There wasn't music from the choir but more like chanting. Of course it was the wind. I think.

Padre continued with his exorcism prayers followed by Our Fathers, Hail Marys, the Apostles' Creed and others. I had to let go as the room energy intensified.

The proceedings became a blur at that point. The prayers and incantations threatened the demons within Pete with a repetitive rhythm. When Raven came back and tried to interfere Padre yelled at the bird.

Padre had become more animated and agitated. It was the same man that had a couple of hours before lugged loads of things up the ladder in a diligent manner.

He started again with the Hail Marys and they came fast and hard, like a kettle drum beating the words out. Waves of vocal noises from the wind came rushing around the corner bouncing off the walls of the cave room. They were in competition with the Hail Mary's and the two became dueling voices. One against many. The vibration from the voices gained mass and felt like pillows pounding on my sides.

Raven had started swaying and staggering. He paused unmoving for several seconds then fell over in a fit of flapping wings. It was then Ernesto started shaking his head as if this all had a dizzying affect. He was to be there as a guest to pray and give support to the proceedings. *Hold yourself back Ernesto. Please don't mime Raven now. Please!*

When the bird fell over on his side it heaved and coughed and made puking sounds. Nothing was coughed up but it looked like it might happen any moment. Padre didn't stop but looked over to the bird with an all-knowing look. Raven got up, turned and looked at Padre as if to say, beat that if you can. "Yaminuas wakinus"

Maybe it was Raven who had collected a demon. He's always been a little odd. The motion of wispy smoke was alive. It may have come from the incense burner but it appeared to be in competition with the incense burner. The smoky stuff encapsulated the incense burner and what it was producing. It controlled the incense smoke and made it oddly inaccessible. The little statue of the Virgin Mary was not affected by the alien swirling of smoke but everything else was, as it had taken the room by force.

Lastly the body of smoke spun around Padre changing his color like the ruby haze changed the cougar. But this time it was more golden. It never touched him but isolated him from us. Over and over from his hypnotized trance he delivered like a hammer the Hail Marys to himself rather than to Pete. The choir of voices were now accompanying Padre instead of competing with him. His words became slurred making them unintelligible as the cadence slowed.

Finally Padre fell to all fours. He barked something like a dog. He made a terrible face and a horrendous gut wrenching sound deep from within. He stopped and rolled to the ground convulsing. He opened his mouth and appeared to be laying an egg through his lips. It was a white amorphous glob like he was puking up his stomach while his respiration rate increased dramatically.

I started to go over to see if he was alright and Ernesto grabbed my arm and shook his head slightly. *I was not to interfere.* Padre lay unconscious, eyes rolled back and eyelids fluttering.

The glob might have been alive when it first came out but no more. Whatever it was had now rolled in the dirt and was motionless. This took on a new perspective way beyond the price of admission. And it wasn't over yet.

Raven jumped on Padre and flapped and pounded again and again. Up and down. I couldn't tell if the bird was mad at Padre or was helping to revive him. Again and again Raven jumped as if either pushing something out or kneading something in. Or both.

The smoke gathered itself, swept around the room and eddied outside brooming out the heavy emotions and drama.

Pete showed some of her normal color as the natural noises from outside broke the new day. Difficult to believe an entire afternoon and evening had passed. Obviously Pete was no worse for the wear with her part, whatever that part might have been.

Pete gave up her mat to Padre and Ernesto. Ernesto was on the floor with Padre. Padre's eyes finally rolled back from under his eyelids. He was not conscious but relaxed and breathing normally. There was nothing else to be done. We would wait this out with Padre. I would hate to try to explain anything to a doctor if one did come out.

Pete went outside, stretched, and greeted a great new day. It was all about Pete and not about Pete.

Chapter 43 – Afterwards

Essie's Diary

"Did you feel anything a little strange during this?"

"You are joking Little Bird, right? Every rock within ten miles had to feel something more than strange. It felt like I was gathered comfortably into a strong river's current after which I was trashed down the whitewater of life."

"Yes, something similar here. What is your knowledge of Exorcisms on birds or animals?"

"I don't remember the Church considering animals to have demons but maybe I'm wrong on that. You see I missed several days of Catechism when I was a kid. And you?"

"I don't remember anything on the topic either. Did you smell that sweet warm piney smell? I had smelled it before with Pete on my first visit to Whouden."

"Yes. It replaced the incense fragrance from the room somehow."

Pete gave a solitary single shrug and left early. She had already made her position known on other occasions. To her we were scrubbing our experience of the realities. No thank you.

Ernesto and I built a fire. Padre's condition remained stable and unchanged. His breathing was even and he rested comfortably the following day and night.

Easter Sunday I awoke midmorning to find Ernesto holding Padre's head. I got them both some water. Ernesto had a blank happy look licking his dry lips. Padre's confused look wavered, then settled to gratitude.

• • •

I tried again to clear the confusion. "What do you think Ernesto?"

"I don't. Mainly because my equipment isn't capable. The exorcism was … what it was."

I noticed my mind's yammer after Ernesto remark… and Pete's preaching. I didn't want the yap anymore. I needed peace. Don't do the mind thing and make it something it isn't. The glyph on the wall with those little button things looked like the future to my mind. Now it looked like a glyph with knobs or buttons. Then I let the buttons be.

Clearly Padre, or his dark side that he did not want to acknowledge, had some kind of a confrontation. It left him with a blank look when he wasn't napping. So I let Padre be as well.

• • •

As for me and absorbing Whouden and the Lost, Universe, Raven or whatever, it fades. The exorcism was too much. I had to let it go and let the exorcism be as well. I am a comfort junkie. If I want more I have to take risks, and the abyss is a formidable threat.

As a parting gift I finally got the riddle from Cedar in answer to my question of what I needed to communicate better with him. *What is it that shows less the more light I put on it?* I had hidden from myself like my shadow hides at noon. The answer was simple. Little 'me'. To communicate with Cedar, I had to first know me.

Chapter 44 – Dumb Teacher

Essie's Diary

Pete and Padre would speak on occasion when Pete did a gopher trip to town. Only a few words of greeting in the beginning but eventually a new relationship developed. It doesn't mean it was all good, just different.

Padre was now dealing with his dark side and had some control over his ego. Her humorous tongue was sharper than her knife and she was relentless pressing her advantage. If a rumbling from the past with Padre would erupt, it wouldn't last long.

Pete and Padre were now on an equal footing in some arenas anyway. It allowed for a real relationship, not one of fancies and fantasies. There was no sign of anything romantic which was best for all concerned on all kinds of levels. They were two remarkably talented humans coming from different worlds making a connection that could benefit both.

• • •

My class went on as if nothing had happened. Juan stared at Pete while Pete read Henry David Thoreau. Without looking up Pete spoke in a low voice to Juan.

"What are you staring at Juan?"

"I think you are more civilized than you used to be and I'm wondering if you want to go on a picnic or something?"

Pete stifled a smile. "What would we do Juan, talk about my civilization?"

"No I was thinking we should try being nicer to each other."

"You want to go far away somewhere and be alone with me and a box of food with chocolate cake?"

Juan nodded his approval.

"And my knife?"

I crinkled my wrinkled face and saw a similar look on Juan's. I stepped rapidly into the fray. "Am I interrupting something important?"

"I was telling Juan, I don't think these books work on him. As for me, my head has too many words lately. I think it could explode. Maybe we should do some exorcisms on words instead of more reading."

. . .

Ed came to visit class three times and never for very long. He might have had other duties I don't know. I wanted to teach him how to read and write to make a difference in his life. What I didn't want to do during the process was to make him talk. If he spoke, or made the attempt, it would be because he chose to. No pressure. After his first visit I slept on the question of how to teach a kid without having him utter a word. No reading out loud or answering questions. So I decided to ask Pete.

The answer was simple; Pete style. "Make a rule no talking in class. Everyone had to point, write or draw what they could, or go outside and let Universe answer questions."

When he came the second time he pointed to outside when a question arose. Both he and Pete left arm in arm, laughing. I guess I got my answer. When you have a dumb teacher take advantage of the situation.

Chapter 45 – Jealousy

Essie worried Pete had eyes for Ernesto. Pete had even used the words "I do love that guy." Then she concerned herself with Ernesto's feelings for Pete.

"Little Bird you have no equal."

"I know I shouldn't be possessive Ernesto but I've been through a long drought. My whole life. Maybe it's crazy but I see you admiring Pete."

"Of course I do. I know you do too. You worry about these things. You distort your insides. It would be healthier to trust and have the confidence any man is fortunate to have you. Pete is marvelous, yes, but she doesn't have your maturity and skills. And most importantly, she is not you. If I am stupid and push you out of my life for someone less than half my age, three times my speed and not attracted to me romantically you should be happy to get rid of someone so senseless."

"You assume my jealousy is logical. And of course it makes me even more undesirable but I am an addict. You are my fix. I can't stop or even consider losing my connection. I hate all this and I hate myself for doing it."

"Then I will give you plenty of space to work it out. I am glad you are able to come and talk about it. It is why there is no one else like you on this planet."

"And other planets?"

• • •

"Pete maybe you can help with something. I want to keep Ernesto not just in my life but as a father to my children."

"So keep him. He's a good choice if you want to change stinky diapers and mend socks. He might even help with the smelly chores."

"But every time he looks at anything other than me I feel him sliding away."

"You mean if he looks at me or a ewe or a pretty rock you get jealous?"

"Yes, exactly."

"So you think he has wandering eyes?"

"Well, yes. He's a man."

"And what have you got against Cedar being the father of your children?"

"PETE!"

"I never thought Cedar had wandering eyes so it was an honest question. Back to your problem. Not only does a wife have to clean poop out of diapers but she also has to worry she may not get any more poopy diapers."

"Yes, ok. Let's say you are correct."

"You have fear Ernesto is not the perfect one as he may wander off?"

"Yes. Yes."

"So you want to put him in a cage?"

"No. Don't be foolish. He would hate me for doing that."

"So you know this will drive Ernesto off and you are the cause of him wandering off."

"Yes."

"And you feel panic like getting lost because you have to have Ernesto. Without him you are nothing. Just a slimy worthless woman human thing?"

"Yes, and move on from the unfunny demeaning questions please. Give me answers."

"OK, you can't love what you need. You just need it. Take your stomach for example. You need it and you need it filled all the time."

"Pete!!"

"No, wait. I'm on a roll here. Do you need him or love him?"

"Both."

"No, can't do that with choice. Choose. You try loving what you need like your stomach. Do you love your stomach? Truly?"

"Ok, ok. I get it. What would you do?"

"Enjoy diapers and Ernesto and the whole mess. In my case if I ever caught myself being jealous, which is not possible to ever catch me at anything, but if I did, I would not worry. I hate worry more than poopy diapers."

And off Pete pranced. If she could whistle a happy tune about herself, she would have. Just to make her exit a little more fun.

Chapter 46 - Pete's Early Lessons

Boys
Essie wants me to write about boys. She wants this lesson because she likes boys. Boys don't interest me. Boys with dazzle cover my insides with silly stuff. I try to ignore it until it goes away. I tell her I am not interested in her advice about boys either. It is wasted time to talk to her sometimes.

Sex
People come from sex. No sex, no people. People make a big deal and rules about sex. The word has three letters. That's all there is to it.

Evil
Universe helps naturalness and hinders evil. Evil is eventually trapped and eliminated but not immediately. There are two reasons to kill. Food and evil.

Killing
I hunt and trap. I kill some food before I eat it. Other food while I eat it. Everybody kills sometime when they eat. Chew seeds and nuts, and they don't ever grow. Chew a weed, put it in the ground, and it turns yellow with death. Cut the head off lettuce and it dies.

Writing
Writing is about what we have in our mind, not the real stuff. Turning mind things into words is easy. Dog, apple, house. Turning a word into something real is not. I don't know how to turn words into a real dog. The word has no fur and you don't pat a word. There is a word "smell" and I can put it together with "wet" and "dog" but I still don't get the same thing as when I sleep next to a wet dog.

House
Being outside all the time is good. Not everyone likes the outside. Living

in a house wears it out. It has to be kept clean. Food gathering gets further and further away because you eat everything close. The roof shades the stars and sun. The walls keep out wildness. I am connected to wildness like bark is to a tree. I don't live without it. If you want to be part of the real world, stay away from the inside of houses.

Me

My name is Pete. I was a baby once which means I know I'm not perfect. In the beginning of me there wasn't much and I don't remember anyway. But babies learn.

My two first friends were Grubby and Raven. I loved Grubby. Grubby had to die. Some of me misses Grub's body but I know his body hurt and had to go.

Raven is a teacher like Grubby. He is harder to love and he doesn't like patting.

Boys Again

Essie wants me to write about boys again. She didn't like what I wrote the first time but will not fess up. The real purpose is to keep me from writing foolish things about her which I will do anyway. Boy crazy isn't good. Since it goes away eventually by itself I see no reason to give up freedom to get boys in my life. If it were like hunger I would have to pay more attention. In case you don't get what I mean, hunger doesn't go away until you do something about it.

• • •

Pete's Later Writing

Ed

I liked Ed. He was easy to talk to because we didn't talk. Actually we couldn't with words.

For example, one day I was watching the herd and I sensed his coming but I said nothing. He tried to say my name behind me so he wouldn't startle me. He knows not to sneak up on people. But what he said came out like "Pe pe pe pt pt pt" and he kept it up until I went over and put my fingers over his mouth. I couldn't think of anything else I could do to make the misery stop. He sounded like one of the horseless buggies pt pt pt pt.

He was real nice about what I did. Essie says it was rude when I did it to her but Ed seemed to like it. The afraid look in his face started to wash away like dirt in a stream and the pt pt pt pt stopped. We stared at each other and that was nice. He stroked my hand to show appreciation. Nobody had to talk. We were both floating down the same river. Before it stopped it was like a smooth ride that gently bubbled into a rabbit hole.

Ed motioned for me to sit beside him by patting the ground. I sat close because we were having a connection happening. We sat for quite some time and then I saw his eyes tracing something near him in the grass. He reached down and let a little mouse run up his arm. Anyway, he did a good job with the little guy making him feel right at home on his arm. It was his way of saying I made him feel better when I stuck my fingers over his mouth.

I wanted Ed to know I could understand what he was showing me. I motioned for the mouse to come over to me. He came a running and bounded right up my arm to my shoulder. I mean the mouse of course. It made me think the little mouse was more than a onetime thing.

That mouse needed a name. He first became Mouse. Mouse had a way with us so I pinched off a little columbine and he took it by the stem and ran back to Ed. The flower was fatter than Mouse but Mouse was longer. Ed put his hand on the ground and Mouse ran up his arm. He stopped and Ed admired the columbine and the little runner. Then Mouse dropped the columbine in his hand and went back to his shoulder to whisper something about me I suspect.

Around Ed I could say anything and he liked it. I told Ed the little Mouse was not a mouse but a rare snufflemousakiss because he liked to snuffle on Ed. Ed could never say much because he stumbled over his words so badly. But Ed was gaining confidence except with words which was good for me as well. I tried to get him to say the word snufflemousakiss. He laughed himself into a silly fit as he had trouble saying Pete. He could imagine what he would sound like spitting out snufflemousakiss. I told him for the sake of all we should keep the name Mouse.

Ed had a good sense of humor which is important. If a stutterer can't laugh at himself he'll have a miserable life.

Well, anyway, that is how two people should connect.

Padre

When I first saw Padre I could tell he was different. Not only because he dressed funny but because he could see and know things I knew but he saw them inside out. He knew how to make lots of fun which is important.

He never demanded. He was too clever for that. He never wanted to know about things I didn't want to talk about. He knew what was inside me or made me think so. I would often catch myself talking to him like Raven and like Raven we didn't use many words.

Sometimes he knew what I wanted before I knew. He stayed far enough back I wanted to touch and smell him. He listened until I learned what I needed. He also made me feel I was a large part of his life.

Padre talked about the Madam. He told me "Madam coaxes women away from their husbands and then makes a good business with those husbands." I said "Padre you put fear in people if they don't come to Church and give you money." He did not talk for a while which made me feel good. But there were times I didn't talk for a time either. It made me feel good to have his teachings.

An example was when he taught me something from the Bible. It was Psalm 121. It was about me lifting my eyes to Mountain. Which was obvious. He didn't make a lot of words but the silence between the words said a lot.

Later I learned words so I could write this. He said help I received from Mountain didn't come directly from Mountain but from the Lord Jesus, the Maker of all heaven and earth. And it was the Lord who would not let my foot slip on Mountain. When I was in the hands of Mountain, I was in His hands.

And I wanted to know how that was true. When I saw Mountain in the distance, it was Mountain that guided me no matter where I was. Mountain was made of rock and was solid between my feet even on the steepest slope. It never weakened to leave me unprotected. If I did not respect Mountain and keep humility, it would break me. When I was at the top of Mountain my insides soared.

He said, "It's easy to see why you give so much acknowledgement to Mountain but I hope you see why I give more credit to the Creator." I had to shake my head no.

"A basket holds your load and you might give credit to the basket. Before you created the basket it was nothing but grass unable to carry. It was you the maker who was responsible for the creation and all it could do, along with God of course, who created the grass and you. And what you felt when at the top of Mountain? It was God who ascends above and beyond Mountain. You were getting a little closer to the Creator." My turn to let it soak in while I stayed quiet.

• • •

It was powerful sometimes around Padre. "You were like bait in a trap Padre. But like the cheese one day you were eaten. Take my hand Padre."

"I think you were sent to do just that Pete." His strong beautiful hand reached for mine. We were both connected again. Relationship with humans is the hardest thing to do.

Cross Country

Several years had passed since my first meeting with Padre and his wanting me to race. Madam thought I should run on Padre's cross country team to show men what a girl can do. The race I entered was to select the five fastest in the territory. Fifteen boys plus me came for the event. The first five across the finish line would make the team. The first four would run in the scheduled meets with the fifth being an alternate.

The race would be twelve miles long. The fifteen boys had a tour of the course the day before I got to town. I would have to keep up with the group to know the way. There were to be flags set to keep everyone on course which would help guide me.

It was meaningless running in a big circle around Aztec. It would have been better to start in Aztec, New Mexico, and end up in Durango, Colorado. Eventually we did run cross country.

I was curious what it would be like to have other people beside me. It was interesting to feel the competition of humans.

Animals race and play for fun and to keep in shape for hunting. They sometimes play tag and if the one behind can catch the one in front they change sides. Wolves and coyotes also play tag, tug of war, or just wrestle and slap each other around.

People got more into racing. They used their eyes when they got ready to compete. They sized each other up. It took their naturalness away from running. If I wasn't careful I did the same. Competition was fun because winning was fun but staying light during competition kept the bad away. I liked running with nature and Universe. We were one.

Padre was the official starter. He had us line up on a line, fired a gun and we were running.

After Padre started us there was a lot of bunching and pushing to get in the lead. I saw no reason to do that as it was a foot race, not a fight. I stayed behind and let them burn energy. As they started to weaken it was easy to pass the last in the line. As the next few dropped back the same happened.

After five miles there were four of us in the race at the front. We were all on Padre's team. The two in the lead were built to run. They had long legs and lean muscles. They had the most confidence. Behind them was a heavier-built kid. He had no form but plenty of stubbornness. He would churn the dirt and never let up. All were a great help to me as I stayed behind allowing them to show the way.

They were experienced at racing. I was not. It was fun in an odd way to see who could win a perfectly meaningless race. Two legged competition was contagious.

I waited until the last mile marked by a green flag. They were ahead of me but I could feel they were not going to let up or give up. They were not like the others I had already passed.

I went up beside the heavy kid and he tried harder but his legs would not do his will. His legs tied up and he lost speed the more he tried.

The front two noticed me because they increased their pace. Which made me step a little harder which made them press a little more. Now I was beginning to understand what the last hour was all about. It came down to winning. Winners have fun. Losers go home.

I knew I could go faster. It was just a matter of when I let go of the reins. They showed signs of straining. Their muscles gave off little bits of tension and their confidence was missing. But they might have a good finish left in them. Better than mine. I had no idea. Padre called the last part of the race 'the sprint'. I thought I had better pass them and get some distance they could not overtake if their sprint was faster than mine.

All three of us pushed our muscles and my legs began to feel heavy. I had a will and a way and the other two runners only had will. I felt a calm come over me and I drifted to a lighter place where I could ride the flow.

Their feet sounded heavy behind me. I floated above the ground. My feet barely touched as they pushed me forward.

I learned later I won the race when I ran through a red ribbon. But I kept running until the rest of them finally stopped chasing me. It did feel good not to be one of the losers.

Ernesto smiled like he knew what I felt. Padre was beaming. Señor and the Madam were also there. Señor's smile was less than a beam but said more to this sheepherder. Madam had a smirk saying we girls just whupped those guys. Yes, winning is fun, but it is nothing like running free.

My Last Race

I was on a team. My team was me and the two I ran with the month before near the finish line. Our team score was kept to see which team could get the most points. The winning runner got four points for his team, second looser in line got three points for his team and third got two. The team who got the most points was the winning team.

When I arrived there were a lot of people mainly at the starting line but also spread out along the way. The distance was about the same as the first race. This race however didn't have such steep a hills.

A man with a speaker thing announced who was competing. When they introduced me as the only girl in the race the people all turned their back to me. It was all together and all at once. It was planned.

They didn't want a girl to beat their boys. I didn't understand during the race but Madam explained it later. She liked more than anything else in life to watch me run those boys into the ground. She knew competition.

Anyway the race was easily won by our team as we took first second and third but it came as a surprise to me how it ended.

We were ahead of the rest of the pack by a long way nearing the end and we all looked at each other and ran in a line making us all the winners at the end. We all knew what to do without a plan. It was fun to be part of that team.

It was what Essie called comradery. I decided it was my last race but I was not sorry I had done it. I hoped Padre wasn't disappointed as I know he sure does want to win everything every time. But my two teammates were the best and would do it without me tagging along.

Chapter 47 – Bank

Pete was eventually convinced by Señor Perez to collect her reward from Sheriff Curry for the wanted man she killed. Señor saw the opportunity to bring her a little closer to the twentieth century by visiting the bank.

"I like the idea of buying a ranch someday. But I don't see why you think a bank is a good hiding place. Every human on earth knows money is in there."

"Yes Pete, they know. That is why there are often armed guards in and around banks."

"But they still get robbed, right?"

"Sometimes, yes. But not as often as you might think. You only hear about the ones that get robbed. The papers and people make you think it's common when it's not."

"Ok, but it seems to me if I go bury money somewhere it has no chance of getting robbed. Even if there are no armed guards."

"You have a point Pete. What I will do is if your money is ever stolen from the bank I'll cover your loss. That's how sure I am your money is safe. OK?"

"OK, let's go put the money in the bank."

"Yes, it will be fun. First I'd want to escort you to the sheriff's office to pick up the reward then introduce you to the bank manager and open a new account."

"Is it ok if Essie goes too?"

"Sure, the more the better."

• • •

Essie's Diary

Señor had a lot of influence on Pete. It wasn't words with him it was presence. Señor was marinated in class.

Señor had it all planned of course to allow Pete to see how the other half dressed and conducted themselves in a bank. Pete didn't wear a dress for the occasion but she slipped on some moccasins just before going into the sheriff's office as well as the bank. Señor had his hand on the front door of the bank and Pete hopped on one foot while putting a moccasin on the other.

"Hello Señor." Looking at Pete. "I don't believe I've had the pleasure?" Pete stared straight back at the man.

"Hello, I'm here to see where my money goes in your bank if that's alright?"

"Yes ma'am it is perfectly alright. Please step this way."

Señor was already grinning at what was sure to unfold. Life had its challenges with Pete but there were times it was all worth it.

"Can you show me where my money will go?" We all followed the manager to the vault. It was already open. The manager ushered us through the large steel door. Pete looked all around and measured the thickness of the door with her hands. Then gave it a rap with her knuckles. Nodded approval.

"Are you going to mix my money up with all this other stuff?"

"Yes but you will get a little book that says your money is safe in here."

A scruffy-looking man entered and went to the teller window out front. Pete whispered to the manager. "That man doesn't look like the kind my money should be mixed with."

"He's one of our most prominent ranchers. I will personally vouch for his character."

Pete spied some cookies on a little table over in the corner. "Can I come back and visit?"

"As often as you like."

"Gingerbread is my favorite. Taking two if that's ok."

"Pete!"

"He said I could come back. Just saving a trip."

Chapter 48 – Tracking Pete

President Theodore Roosevelt, 26th president of the United States from 1901 to 1909 made great strides with the help of the naturalist John Muir in setting up National Parks. Muir was nicknamed both "Wilderness Prophet," and "Citizen of the Universe". John Muir and President Roosevelt had stayed relatively close after Teddy left office due to this tie.

Roosevelt was wholly at home in the world of power and politics and was known as "a steam engine in trousers". Roosevelt had always been drawn to nature and was an avid hunter. Muir had an ability to turn the wonders of nature into a glorious spiritual experience unequalled by others save maybe Thoreau or Emerson. When people of power in the establishment wanted to drain the water from the great Yosemite Valley to quench the thirst of San Francisco, John and Teddy were an unbeatable team.

As might be expected their mutual respect didn't come easy at all times. Teddy was a forceful man not allowing timidity in his presence. He was literally a bull in a china closet and was proud of the nickname. Muir was far more peaceful and spiritual and could be easily drowned in Teddy's world but saw little alternative.

It had come to the attention of President Roosevelt with a letter forwarded to him by the Acting Secretary of the Department of the Interior, Mr. John Woodruff, there might be a Wolfboy roaming in the New Mexico Territory upwards into southern Colorado. Teddy subsequently wrote Muir asking if he had any knowledge on the subject.

Muir was quick to write back and confess he had never found any direct scientific evidence of such a creature. He had however heard many stories and it would definitely be within his realm of interest. He would, therefore, be willing to make himself available and travel to wherever he was needed and explore any evidence should the President need a trusted representative.

· · ·

The stories of Wolfboy were dwindling. The exception came to the sheriff in the form of a reward poster offering a reward for anyone who knew the whereabouts of a wild boy, also known as Wolfboy. A reward was offered by one Mrs. Harding.

$$\bullet \ \bullet \ \bullet$$

WESTERN UNION

MR. JOHN MUIR
WESTERN UNION OFFICE
MARTINEZ CALIFORNIA

I HAVE POSSIBLE INFORMATION REGARDING WOLFBOY STOP CONTACT SHERIFF JIM CURRY OF SAN JUAN COUNTY NEW MEXICO TERRITORY IN AZTEC STOP

THEODORE ROOSEVELT
WESTERN UNION OFFICE
RICHMOND VIRGINIA

$$\bullet \ \bullet \ \bullet$$

WESTERN UNION

SHERIFF JIM CURRY
WESTERN UNION
SAN JUAN COUNTY AZTEC
NEW MEXICO TERRITORY

WHAT INFORMATION DO YOU HAVE ON WOLFBOY STOP DO YOU HOLD WOLFBOY IN CUSTODY STOP

JOHN MUIR
WESTERN UNION OFFICE
MARTINEZ CALIFORNIA

$$\bullet \ \bullet \ \bullet$$

WESTERN UNION

JOHN MUIR
WESTERN UNION OFFICE
MARINEZ CALIFORNIA

WOLFBOY MAY BE A WILD KID GONE FERAL STOP KID HAS DONE
NOTHING WRONG THEREFORE NOT IN CUSTODY STOP BRING
WALKING SHOES IF YOU WANT TO LOCATE KID STOP

SHERIFF JIM CURRY
WESTERN UNION OFFICE
AZTEC NEW MEXICO TERRITORY

• • •

WESTERN UNION

SHERIFF JIM CURRY
WESTERN UNION OFFICE
AZTEC NEW MEXICO TERRITORY

I ARRIVE FRIDAY AUGUST 12 ON STAGE STOP
REGARDS STOP

JOHN MUIR
WESTERN UNION OFFICE
MARINEZ CALIFORNIA

Chapter 49 – John Muir

Some time had passed from Mrs. Harding's initial report of her encounter with Wolfboy but Roosevelt's curiosity was engaged. Roosevelt had specifically asked if Muir could keep the trip secret to eliminate the chance of having this creature hunted to extinction.

John Muir had traveled by train and then by coach. He was fairly certain the trip was a wild goose chase but he felt the need to be thorough in his work for the ex-President. It would be interesting in any event to travel new country. The exact area had previously escaped his notice. He was sure he could work in some natural pleasures along with the scheduled business for the President.

• • •

John Muir arrived in Aztec and was met by Sheriff Jim Curry along with half the town. Not only did he have fame in his own right but he was the emissary of the famous Teddy Roosevelt of the Rough Riders.

Muir was taken aback by the banners flying and horns blowing as he arrived. He had pictured this assignment as a fairly quiet mission in the out-of-the-way southwestern tiny town. He hoped the focus of the trip was still a secret but he was having doubts.

John used his long trip as an excuse to be shown to his room that had been reserved in advance. But his wade through the pushing and back-slapping crowd went too slowly for his liking. He thanked those nearest him as best he could for their kindness and asked the sheriff if they could spend a few quiet moments.

The sheriff was not about to let the moment disappear without utilizing it. Although he was unable to get Muir to address the crowd, the sheriff was not bashful at all. The sheriff was soon taking the attention away from Muir knowing it never hurts to let the people know about his close friendship with the likes of John Muir and Teddy Roosevelt. Muir took the political maneuvering of Sheriff Curry in stride.

• • •

The next morning Muir and the sheriff were off early in the sheriff's wagon. Muir was relieved to find their departure had not been revealed to townspeople and the true purpose of the trip remained confidential.

Muir learned early on of Pete's gender. It had been explained to him the wolf boy was a wolf girl. He had an upsetting dream of finding a young teen perched on a limb treed by the good people of Aztec trying to shake her loose to the ground.

John was peppering the sheriff about where they were going when the white bearded Muir suddenly stopped mid-sentence and hollered "STOP" as if a bank were being robbed.

Muir pointed to a nearby ten foot high tree. Even before the wagon had come to a stop the elderly lanky lean mountain man had bounced to the ground and was excited about the treasure he had found.

He started picking some sample foliage from the knurled twisted New Mexico Juniper tree. He went into great detail with the sheriff about the similarities and differences with the *Juniperus occidentali.*

He then launched into a discussion more with himself. "Some juniper trees are misleadingly given the common name 'cedar,' including *Juniperus virginiana*, the 'red cedar' used widely in cedar drawers and closets. True cedars are those tree species in the genus *Cedrus*, family *Pinaceae*. Both the Cedar and Juniper have many uses and have been used extensively by indigenous people for……"

The sheriff did not want to appear rude but had no desire to understand more about what was considered firewood. This day would be a long one for Sheriff Curry.

• • •

They spent the evening under the stars and were off early again the following morning on a logging road. Midway through the third day he stopped the wagon and pointed up the hill. "Won't be hard to follow the sheep tracks and the kid won't be far from'um".

Muir got down and took his light load of a sack of dry bread and his walking stick. He was off on his adventure leaving Jim Curry shaking his head. Not only did this emissary of the President of the United States not know the country but he had nothing to protect himself from the elements other than a bag of bread.

It was around 9700 feet where Sheriff Curry dropped him off. Muir had a pace he liked to call sauntering but his saunter was soon reduced to a slow meander up the mountain slopes. The new flora and fauna distracted him constantly. The altitude was also a bother. Thin air made it harder for the older gentleman to pull adequate oxygen into his lungs. In his youth he would not have noticed.

It wasn't difficult for Muir to follow the herd driven up the valley two months earlier with the amount of sign left behind.

He, like Pete, had watched the big ponderosa pine give way to the fir and spruce and eventually the more open country above timber line around 11000 feet in this area. What trees did hold on to the crevices in the rocky slopes near the tops of ridges had a shape tortured by the crushing weight of snow in winter during their beginning years. Next in adolescence they did battle with the antlers of deer and elk scraping off velvet preparing for rut. Lastly if they had overcome the early challenges and reached a height of eight to ten feet they became one of the tallest points in the terrain. At that time they were targets used by Thor as grounding rods. The energy bolts plunged from the sky during the afternoon storms in summer. They tested the character and will to live on those shoulder areas of the mountain most vulnerable to the electrically-charged dark clouds passing over.

• • •

After Sheriff Curry dropped Muir off, he happily wound his way down the mountain in his wagon. He should have given the job to his incompetent deputy. He liked the idea of being seen with Muir and helping his career with the townsfolk of Aztec. There were always positives.

• • •

Two of the black-coated DA's dervishes were coming up the road as the sheriff made his way down the mountain. They both tipped their hats and pulled their pistols. The sound of their pistols was muffled by the trees and terrain. The DA needed possession of Señor's Rancho before statehood. Time was wasting away with the sheriff dragging his feet. Neither Jim Curry nor his wagon was ever seen again.

• • •

Muir sat midday in the middle of a wild strawberry patch with a few greens from his morning's saunter and his bag of dry bread. He was known to eat meat as a last resort before starving but he was also known to complain of the noises his stomach made. He once wrote of "wry faces over our fare, looking sheepish in digestive distress amid rumbling, grumbling sounds that might well pass for smothered baas" of sheep.

He was many things in his youth from a shepherd to an inventor. However the written word never came easy even after his many articles and books. Although he loved the freedom and majesty of the great outdoors as Pete did, his early training gave him an intellectual and analytical component. This is not to say he didn't have a physical and emotional response to God's creation at those elevations.

After his lunch he rested to watch a few small white clouds graze the sky. It wasn't long and he was back again attacking the hill with an unimportant pace.

By evening he thought he might be close but wanted to be certain not to walk in on Pete unannounced at that time. He was armed with news that might put him in good stead but the news from Mrs. Harding could wait. At least Muir hoped it would be received as good news.

• • •

The next morning after spending an uneventful evening close to the fire he kept alive through the night, he was up early and eager. He held little faith this "kid" was a wild beast but the walk up the mountain was inspiring to say the least. He was taken by the majesty of mountains in all directions and a few snow-covered peaks even in early August. They beckoned him as they did Pete.

He was looking forward to the opportunity to meet someone who was totally at home in this setting for months at a time. He had questions about Pete's diet and her reaction to the world around her. Always the scientist.

• • •

Around noon Muir saw a huge herd of sheep with no tent or wagon in sight. The dogs standing sentry from several vantage points soon set off the alarm. He continued toward the herd, accustomed to their kind. He had known shepherds in the past who would actually hide when approached by strangers. The longer he walked into the grazing sheep the more he was convinced he wasn't going to find this Wolfboy shepherd. Several times he turned a full circle only to find nothing but sheep, dogs, puffy white clouds, and magnificent mountain terrain.

He walked on, working his way past the 'baa baaing' on the top of a plateau with a gradual incline upwards to granite mountains reaching for the sky. For a quarter of a mile in any direction he could only see one place to sit comfortably which was a flat rock about two feet off the ground. He made one more complete turn not finding a tree or rock large enough to hide a shepherd near the grazing sheep.

He placed his bag of bread and walking stick beside him on the well-positioned rock. He patiently postponed his search while he took in the scenery.

He heard a little crunch noise behind him and turned to see nothing. He slowly turned back scanning the area to once again watch the sheep grazing. He took notice of another tiny grinding noise and turned in the direction of the sound to find a pica where his bag once sat nibbling on a piece of dry bread. Beside the pica was a large raven with drooping wing and an inquisitive eye on Muir.

It took a moment for John to grasp both the bread and the bag containing the bread had vanished except for a crumb in the front paws of the round short-eared tailless animal about five inches in length. The pica was sitting on its hind legs turning the bread and nibbling it down to a smaller morsel, like a little grinding wheel.

Muir sat incredulously staring at the small creature. "You look to me like Ochotona princeps." He was trying to put the name together along with what might have happened to his bag. He looked over to the raven. The raven was looking all around as if he too needed some logic as to what might have happened, miming Muir's body language.

Obviously the little guy still nibbling next to him didn't eat the bag. He heard a second larger crunch behind him. He quickly turned his head and found miles of open space. Frustration was beginning to fill the aging bearded man.

He twisted back slowly a little forlorn-looking. There was a fat pica, leering raven, and his sack of bread on the lap of a fur clad teenager. Pete offered it back with a 'you're welcome' nod. Muir retrieved the bag with diminished content from his young benefactor.

Muir in a slow subdued manner gave a faltering gesture of acceptance. His newly-found helper gave a nod in return with a crumb clinging to the edge of a smile. His peaceful blue eyes met her dancing green ones in a mountain greeting.

Pete immediately noticed his body language was comfortable in the rugged mountain setting. "Eh..thank you. My name is John Muir."

Pete gave a second nod, while chewing her mouthful of dried bread.

"Are you the shepherd of this flock?"

More nods, still chewing.

"The sheriff in Aztec asked me to deliver a message to Pete. Are you Pete?"

Additional nod while swallowing the dry bread without water. "Ya, Pete. Good biscuits" came the answer in a sugary tone.

"I'm glad you like them. I'm fond of them myself. Have another?"

"Easy, good."

"Jerky?" digging into her purse at her side.

"Eh, ah yes, thank you" came the reply wishing not to decline the hospitality but would have preferred the bread.

"What's the message?"

"He says he has an important message he would like to deliver personally."

"Yes, maybe … someday." Pete raised her hand slightly and a coyote sprang over a knoll a quarter mile distant. John turned and noticed the creature running towards them at a lope.

Many things had changed with Pete but she remained fairly uncommunicative when first meeting strangers. She used a lot more words than a few years earlier but it was still difficult to pull the truth from them. "That doesn't look like a sheep dog to me. That coyote work sheep?"

"No, but keeps an eye on me pretty good. Are you John Muir the writer?"

"Yes." Believing now Pete was no species distinct from Homo sapiens he went to work on her history and knowledge. "How did you become proficient at hide and seek? No first please tell me how you learned to speak. I was led to believe you didn't know more than three words."

"First question Mr. Muir is practice in difficult situations. The second is same thing. Practice."

"God has to nearly kill us sometimes, to teach us lessons."

Nod

Muir rose from the rock he was sitting on and placed his hands behind his back wiggling his fingers as he observed the environment. "I see no signs of overgrazing or your sheep tearing up the fragile meadow pastures? As I have written and see sheep advance elsewhere, flowers, vegetation, grass, soil, plenty and poetry vanish."

"Soon there would be no pasture and then no sheepherder."

"But, but it's how sheep graze?"

"It is how we let them graze."

They both sat quietly letting the conversation climb the next hill.

Muir surveyed the landscape. He stood up. He spread his arms wide. "Pete, what do you have to say about setting aside this wild land?"

"What is 'set a side'?"

"Large blocks of land or National Parks having rules keeping men from ruining the land by cutting trees and roads."

"Who makes these rules?"

"Men in the government."

Raven strutted in between the two. He looked first at Pete and gave a low soft croak. Then turned to John and gave him a loud croak and an exaggerated eye to the ground like a robin looking for a worm. The bird waddled in more or less a twenty foot straight line, abruptly returning to his starting point. When done he took a second lap.

"I have never seen any display like that in my life. That raven is surely trying to tell us something."

Nod.

"So this bird and his behavior are not new to you?"

Shake.

"Do you understand his meaning?"

"Easy. He says you will have people walking in your National Parks over the same ground. Over and over."

Raven stepped back and looked directly at Muir and gave a loud croak yet again. He made an exaggerated show of walking in many directions with an inquisitive nature inspecting rocks and plants of all sorts. Then whirled around and flew away only to return and turn summersaults in the air croaking having a delightful time.

Muir shook his head as if trying to shake a fly out of his white beard. "This peculiar raven is a one-bird circus."

Pete was unperturbed. "Now Raven shows us how you and I will not be able to walk through the set aside forests freely. Our eyes can only see those things near the trails that haven't been trampled. Our souls and hearts will be left behind."

"Don't people have the right to visit the wilderness?"

"If you herd masses of people into a wilderness it will change and become trampled by sheeple. No longer wilderness."

"I like your word sheeple. Let's assume for a moment there are no trails or outhouses and less sheeple. Are you suggesting giving man free rein with an ax against the giant old timers like the Sequoia? Big business would cut them all down. Would you not limit what they gather?"

"There, deep into the National Park, some distance from the sheeple, they can gather, hunt and fish to sustain themselves without count taking care to not waste what nature provides. However not with weapons, saws or lures from the cities but with what they make themselves after entering."

"Then how can the natural wonders be appreciated by enough people to make it worthwhile to set the area apart?"

"Their numbers will grow as hearts and souls show through their skins. They have a sickness now, unable to connect to the wonders. The ignorant will be blessed with a new morality. If you provide them an acceptable place they may find a way home to their true beginning. The rules should be to bring nothing but clothes on their back and knife and string in their pockets. And leave with nothing but a lifted spirit."

"So you see these modern men as having a pathological sickness of the mind or soul or both. And I thought we couldn't converse when I got here."

This little volcano had not quite finished. "How do you keep men who have never got their belly wet drinking from a creek from making laws telling us how and where to drink? These insiders will make rules that will limit both you and I our freedoms to explore these places."

"That will never happen in this freedom loving republic."

"Raven said it would happen and I see in your eyes you know one day it could. How do you keep these same men who live indoors and work in cities from making laws about dogs on rope, camping under the stars and picking anything green in the forest?"

Pete was still not finished. "This country was not founded by laws. It was founded by the grace of God and by people with energy to take the risks and face failure. Most laws came after they gathered for the purpose of independence and a constitution. Do we need laws to tell a simple bird to leave before winter?"

"Are you saying those that gathered and allowed slavery at the founding were of a better morality than those of today?"

"Morality changes as history marches and teaches. Those gathered had the hand of God on their shoulders to first unite North and South and the only way to do that was to allow slavery in those early years. The South would not sign any document prohibiting slavery as it would limit their ability to feed themselves." *Thank you Essie.* "As you well know there are higher powers far beyond the comprehension of humans. I know your Christian history."

"Please continue if you have more thoughts."

"My concern is man's interpretation of God's laws. Actually, I have more worries about man's interpretation of man's laws." This brought a broad smile to Muir's lips. "Making it worse, so many of man's laws are regulations never voted upon by Congress."

A nod came from Muir. "I have spent years fighting man's stupidity. I therefore find your arguments difficult to overcome. Your point is well taken. The inefficiency of big government is no satisfactory answer to the gluttony of a big business."

• • •

"I have read many of your written words John Muir."

"What do you think of my writing?"

"I sense a lot of laboring. We both could get away from the books a little sooner if you chose simple words and arrangements."

"Yes, you are right about my laboring with words. Over and over I plow through the same ground. Where have you learned your words?"

"My friend Essie has taught me many words and ideas. Books have done the rest including your writing John Muir."

"I would like to meet your friend Essie someday. Do you think you could arrange that?"

"Nothing is impossible."

Chapter 50 – Tree Riding

Muir was challenged by Pete's abilities. He didn't know how he should classify Pete's skills on the ladder of life. Not a new species by any means but not like any others he'd met either.

• • •

Muir spent several days in the high country with more lively discussions. He also met Ernesto who had come up to check on Pete and bring supplies.

Muir wanted to know more about Pete from a source other than Pete which did not sit well with Ernesto. Ernesto sat like a stone miming a shy sheepherder. Muir would learn from Pete or not at all.

• • •

Muir entertained them on several occasions around the campfire. He was a good storyteller and told of his adventures using a vibrant vocabulary. He described trees so huge a dozen people hand to hand could not surround their circumference at the base. He told of glaciers and crevasses he explored with his brave and faithful dog Stickeen. When he went to the science of glaciers and how they had sculpted the land many thousands of years ago he had their full attention. And then some.

He told them about his "early-rising machine" he had built of wood, springs and electricity. The contraption chucked Muir out of bed at the same time every day, lit a lamp and opened a school book for him to read. After a while the rising machine took that book away and gave Muir another one. This story caused a great deal of commotion.

During Muir's story Raven strutted, flapped, flew, and croaked at top volume. Ernesto had to sit on his hands or become part of the spectacle with Raven. Raven didn't need any help.

Pete laughed uproariously while appraising Muir's abilities. What sort of mind could conceive of such a complicated yet whimsical device that actually worked?

• • •

Muir watched Pete practice with her toys which were also used for hunting. She could use her knife in either hand and was more deadly at 30 yards with her bow than most men were with their handguns.

All of which brought him back to the real reason for his visit. Roosevelt's hypothesis to be tested was Pete had been raised by wolves or something wild. Muir saw little chance of validation but after his interviews with Pete he was assured she did have unusual beginnings.

To prove Roosevelt's hypothesis he must plan an experiment giving consistent results but she would quickly resist any such testing. He tried to get her to race her dog or explain how she had snuck up on him that first day but always to no avail. She would giggle and dance away. She would not be an easy quarry.

• • •

Muir remembered the times he spent during storms at the top of a swaying tree and the exhilaration he felt. He wondered if that wasn't a good place to start with Pete.

"You notice the storm coming Pete?"

"Yes, happens most days up here this time of year."

"I have travelled many miles swaying in the stormy winds at the top of trees. But the old body becomes less sure and is more bound to earth. Have you ever ridden a storm atop a tree?"

"No, can't say as I have. Lightning up here would give added meaning to 'hold on for dear life'."

"To be sure, selecting the right tree is important."

"It does sound like fun to ride a tree."

"That fir tree below is unscratched and is well protected from lightning by these above it."

"So it is and the winds are just beginning to pick up. Mind if I excuse myself?"

"Not at all. I wish I could join you."

Pete saw to it the sheep were well taken care of then went up the seventy foot fir tree. John stood back and waited for the whooping and hollering to start. He wasn't disappointed.

She rode the tree for all it was worth and in thirty minutes she was back on the ground no worse for the wear except for her drenching by the thunder shower. However the event didn't break the ice free of the target of Roosevelt's hypothesis.

• • •

Muir was at home in the mountains and took great care not to disturb the surroundings other than in small ways like picking a leaf or burning a few dry sticks to stay warm. Nature and Pete had a far greater impact than Muir did.

Muir was not part of the whole in the same way Pete was. At least not to the same extent. He was quick to use his bread along with the berry or onion found on Mountain. But he had no interest in the hare or partridge in his diet. Pete received something further beyond both plant and animal life from her connection to the wild, mandatory to sustain her life and soul.

• • •

After the third day Pete and her coyote friend snuck off to find Ernesto. It was also a good excuse to gather the fresh bread she'd been sniffing.

She went to the sheep wagon first and hopped up to where she smelled the new round of sourdough bread. She broke off a large hunk and stuck it in an empty flour bag carried inside her shirt. She saw Muir's supply of dried bread waning the last time he had offered her some.

Ernesto had seen her going to the wagon from his position on a nearby hill. He came down to join her. When Ernesto came into his camp she was sitting on the ground chewing a piece of fresh bread. He smiled knowing she could smell bread that morning the moment the oven door opened.

They acknowledged each other's presence by joining eyes and sharing a nod. She pulled up the bread and smiled in thanks. Neither broached a topic. The issue would appear in a natural way as they both knew it would.

• • •

After a time sitting on the ground Ernesto picked himself up imitating Muir and crouched behind a small bush. He moved slowly stalking something on all fours and it wasn't long before he found his prey. He slowly approached a rectangular rock large enough to sit on with head down ready to pounce should his victim decide to run. But of course his quarry was easily captured as sitting rocks normally are.

He found a small pebble on top the rock seat and started inspecting it with a great deal of enthusiasm. He moved his lips and grunted like Muir did while making quite a spectacle of studying the little nugget.

He took the unimportant little stone and pressed it between his palms like a book mocking Muir's process with samples of leaves and flowers.

Ernesto's eyes shot to Pete and then quickly away as if he didn't want to be caught studying her. Then he turned away quickly, wiggling fingers behind his back.

Pete smiled and nodded from her seat on the ground. She levied herself up effortlessly like a puff of smoke from her cross-legged position. She took Ernesto's thoughts back down the hill not wanting to leave the sheep for any length of time.

• • •

Pete saw she and Ernesto were more an undivided part of nature which didn't make them better, but different than Muir. Muir needed to stay separate in order to be the good observer and document the blessings bestowed from nature. She did not begrudge him being different in the slightest.

He did not let little things like hunger and cold deter him from his quest. She saw he had no blanket, no tent, and no large pack. When his bread was gone he would do without. Pete admired this strength of character and his love of her world.

• • •

The little mime "talk" Pete had with Ernesto gave her a different perspective of Muir. His intentions and focus was on her. This great observer of the natural world was inspecting her as he might a leaf.

The more he observed the less he was shown by Pete. Finally Pete tired of the game and walked straight up to him, planted her feet wide apart and with hands on hips looked him straight in the eyes.

"If you did more respecting and less inspecting you would see I am not a leaf or branch, but a whole tree."

Muir drew back as if slapped. Then his blue eyes twinkled. "Pete, as usual you have directed a shot and hit your mark. The reason you have been under the microscope…"

Pete stopped him right there. "I am not under anything."

"I was not making progress anyway as you are far more than the sum of your parts."

"You are wandering back in the word bushes again John Muir."

"Pete, do you know the stories about Wolfboy?" Pete immediately noticed his change in body language and directed her attention accordingly paying no attention to the words he had just spoken.

"There is a lady, Mrs. Harding, Wolfboy assisted and saved from two scoundrels. She insists Wolfboy is real and has cleverness and quickness worth learning more about. She has made herself known both to me and the President of the United States and she wants to meet Wolfboy again."

"Does she want you to determine if I am a dangerous animal?"

"No, I don't believe that to be the case but Mrs. Harding is quite out of her element and a little intimidated. She saw you as someone who knew and would use violence. She comes from a society that frowns on violence in general but appreciated your protection. She would like to thank you personally."

"Do you mean she wants to come talk and hand me money?"

"I'm not sure exactly what she entertains but she would like to sit down and talk to you."

"Mr. Muir, I enjoy my life the way it is. Too many people in too many ways change my life in ways I don't like."

"Yes, I understand your position all too well as you know after reading some of my works. But what if she were to come to you as I have done and meet around the campfire some evening?"

"That would be ok but I don't want her money."

"Good, then I will tell her of your whereabouts?"

Reluctant *nod.*

"And something else. The President, that is President Roosevelt, also has an interest in you and asked me to find you and report back to him my findings. The stories described you as something other than human but I see the stories were inaccurate. I can also judge people by their canine companions and your coyote friend demonstrates you are a loving considerate person as well. You are far more sophisticated than any of the stories indicate."

"What is this President like?"

"He has been described as 'a bull in a China closet'. Have you ever heard that phrase Pete?"

The green eyes danced. "No, but I understand it."

"Roosevelt says 'the human body has two ends on it. One to create with and one to sit on. Sometimes people get their ends reversed. When this happens they need a kick in the seat of the pants.'"

She gave a giggle. "I would like this President Roosevelt. What does he say about your set-asides?"

"He sees both sides of the issue and I pray he will continue to do so. You are in a commercial enterprise here using natural resources but take extraordinary precautions with them so they are available the following year."

"Here's something else Roosevelt said you will like. It relates to National Parks. 'Order without liberty and liberty without order are equally destructive.'"

"You and President Roosevelt have given me a pleasant headache Mr. John Muir."

• • •

They had one more day. Pete had gained from Muir's scientific approach. She had to learn to confront him as she would anything she found in nature. He would respond fairly but not without prodding.

• • •

He analyzed things in minute factors and would draw pictures and keep records quite tedious in detail. She could not see the purpose until he pointed out slight differences in plants that on the surface appeared similar. She learned of genetics and how traits were passed on from one generation to the other. Essie had taken her through grade school. Now she was entering higher education.

He showed her the back of a leaf and spoke of veins and then reached slowly for her hand. She tensed but allowed him to take her hand by touching her with one of his fingers. He traced the veins on the back of her hand as he had the veins on the leaf and talked of xylem and phloem and arteries and veins and oxygen and carbon dioxide and nutrients and photosynthesis and everything had building blocks called cells.

She knew each plant was a sister in these woods but now she saw, at a detailed analytical level, the structures connecting life. Essie had brought her words and this Mr. Muir gave her science.

"Did you take a lot of time in a library to learn these things John Muir?"

"I went to the University of Wisconsin and took science courses. But the one to open my eyes and heart to the world of science and in particular the study of botany was a classmate, one Milton Griswold. I had an epiphany to the extent my interest remains steadfast to this day."

"What did you learn from Griswold?"

"He tied everything together around this universe. He organized the world of botany for me so I saw things I had always seen yet it was for the first time."

A long pause took them both as Muir was taken back to some reverie and Pete had a lot to digest.

"Were there other kids there?"

"Yes, many other students."

"Essie's school teaches about trees and leaves and animals. Are these all science?"

"Yes, and many more things are covered by science."

"Like what?"

"The sky with all the stars and planets, plants too small to see with your naked eyes, the human body and all its organs, the mind and how it works, magnetism, energy and forces keeping things together and smashing them apart, and…"

"And how do you see things you can't see with a naked eye. In fact what is a naked eye?"

• • •

He heated a bottle, turned it upside down in a plate of water and it sucked the water up as the bottle cooled. He took a leaf, stuck it stem first into a cup with berry juice and water, and the leaf showed berry stains filling its veins.

She learned of lab classes where she could use her knife and cut things up and see inside with a microscope machine made of glass. It would make a tiny hair the size of a tree. Her world took another step further away from her comfort zone and what she called home.

• • •

She was a willing student and they wasted no time finding similar interests.

She "knew" things he could explain in words in academic detail. He in turn was amazed the connections she had made in nature and could not ascertain as to how.

"You give me the idea you know things beyond what I might see under a microscope. Can you give me some idea of your observations of the world around you?"

"It is quite difficult to talk of these. Do you know what I mean?"

"Yes, we are always limited by our vocabulary. But can you convey things you know in some other fashion?"

"Like how Mr. Muir?"

"I see the impasse here but maybe in a simple show and tell manner with limited tell portion."

Pete turned her back to Muir and placed both arms out. Several butterflies landed on her left arm. Bird-E landed on her right wrist. She waited until both were stationary and lifted her arms above her head giving them a lift into the air. She then turned to look at Muir.

"God's amazing grace." Muir's voice trembled. With these words Coyote sat touching the white bearded man's side.

Chapter 51 – Wonders

"If a president of the United States asked you and I to visit some of the National Parks and maybe additional land he would like to save from the logger's saw, would you join me?"

"Probably not. I like the mountains and trees but I think you are suggesting something else."

"Yes, you are right. It would be our job to give the President our opinion as to the merit of each place we visit and be seen with him in some of these places."

"Soon I would have to sit on a hill with my toes wiggling in the dirt. I can't take much humanness."

"I appreciate your honesty and know the feeling all too well. I must say there is something within all of us once awakened that keeps us in nature's custody."

"I don't think you want someone who disagrees with your ideas on making more laws by men who sleep in soft beds and sit on chairs instead of rocks."

"It is exactly for that reason I want you to be a part of this government intervention. I hope I can talk you into traveling with me as my guest to some of these areas where I might get more of your thoughts while you see these wonders. Have you ever traveled by train?"

"No, but I saw one once."

"Have you ever seen the geysers of Yellowstone?"

"No, not even a picture. What's a geysers?"

"Will you allow me to show them to you?"

"How far away are they? I have a job here that needs to be done."

"If I or any President can convince your employer of your usefulness will you consider traveling with me?"

"You bribe me with thrills Mr. Muir. But I am lucky to have a job with Señor Perez so he must agree. And even then, I don't know how much of the crazy life I might swallow."

"Very well Pete. One slow step at a time."

"Here is some sourdough to make your trip down the valley go a little easier."

"Thank you Pete. What a pleasant surprise."

"I owed you a little from that first day we met."

"Shall I talk with the lady you helped and see if she could get you into a science class?" Muir pulled out a card similar to the one Pete had received several years before.

Nod… nod nod nod then *shaking no no.*

"But I thought you would like a science class?"

"No no. Lab class."

Nodding, "Ah yes, my mistake."

• • •

Muir gained a little more information from Pete concerning her work and left down the mountain the following morning. He felt it had been a successful trip on everyone's behalf. He had found and met Pete, President Roosevelt could have his curiosity satisfied, and Pete's world was soon to be expanded beyond her wildest imagination. He laughed to himself when he thought of the phrase *wild imagination.*

He saw Pete was different from others and he would enjoy showing her "his" Yosemite as he had shown the President. He knew her influence of more hands-on experience was needed in the political circus rather than the sway of campaign finance.

He got a glimpse of how she might have snuck up on him. She could enhance perceived sights and sounds and use them to her advantage. *But how?*

Quite an image in his mind seeing book-learned lawyers in a prone position trying to drink out of a creek, ties dangling down like straws. He laughed out loud in the spruce grove as he sauntered down the hill sampling the bread she had shared with him the previous afternoon.

• • •

WESTERN UNION

THEODORE ROOSEVELT
WESTERN UNION OFFICE
RICHMOND VIRGINIA

WOLFBOY NAMED PETE STOP WOLFBOY IS GIRL STOP NOT SURE HOW TO PROCEDE STOP

JOHN MUIR

WESTERN UNION OFFICE
AZTEC NEW MEXICO TERRITORY

• • •

WESTERN UNION

JOHN MUIR
WESTERN UNION OFFICE
AZTEC NEW MEXICO TERRITORY

MAKES ME ALL THE MORE INTERESTED STOP KEEP UP THE
GOOD WORK STOP

THEODORE ROOSEVELT
WESTERN UNION OFFICE
RICHMOND VIRGINIA

Chapter 52 – Decorum

Several months later Señor Perez requested Pete to come see him. He had been sent word from President Roosevelt. Pete's presence along with John Muir's would be greatly appreciated relating to federal lands set aside for wilderness, nature preserves and national parks.

• • •

Señor Perez had little breath remaining. He wanted to make it happen.

He had no knowledge of the sheriff's words to Muir describing her gender. "I have a telegram from Muir requesting your presence with him on a tour of federal lands."

"Yes, set aside lands is what Mr. Muir told me."

"Did you know they wanted you to join them?"

"Yes, but I thought you needed me around here."

"You are an important part of the Rancho Pete but this is important for the country. You are making history. If any president or an important man like John Muir makes a request I would like to cooperate. Maybe you could see your way clear to … also cooperate?"

"Then you want me to go?"

"If you would like to go, I would like to see you go. Yes. Yes. Yes. Now there is the delicate subject of you being a girl."

"Why is this a 'delicate' subject?"

"In this country women are treated differently than men. They are subject to more scrutiny. They don't vote for example in some states."

"You mean I don't count?"

"Well, no. You count a great deal to me. However, there are certain things young ladies need to be wary of such as traveling with men without a companion."

"Why is traveling with men worse than traveling with women? I think whoever made that rule was a man who wanted to leave women home doing laundry."

"It has to do with what is proper like having good manners and upbringing."

"I travel with Ernesto and is he complaining about my manners?"

After gaining some composure Señor continued, "No Pete, Ernesto never complains about anything. Especially you of all people. What I mean to say is young ladies shouldn't travel alone with men without a female traveling companion to keep a sense of propriety."

"I'm not sure what this propriety is all about. Essie talked about it once and it was obvious she had more of it than I did."

"But you do understand there are rules which is a good start for this discussion?"

"Yes, there are rules AND I have no say in making those rules BECAUSE I don't get to vote." She took a deep breath realizing she was getting het up with a man at the top of her list. "Sorry Señor. You didn't make the rule I don't count."

"Well, yes. Moving on. Is it fair to assume you didn't discuss your gender and you acted like a young man when in the presence of Mr. Muir?"

"I acted exactly like me."

"Then it is safe to say you acted less like a young lady and more like a young man." And quickly added before Pete could fire another shot. "And before you get all excited again, there is nothing wrong with acting like a young man. You for example were doing the work of a young man. Therefore Mr. Muir would have no idea you were a young lady and would make no special arrangements to follow the correct decorum."

"I don't know if Mr. Muir knew I was a lady or a man. The subject didn't come up around me or I would have told him the truth. Yes, if there are different rules to be followed if I am a girl instead of a boy, he most likely didn't follow the correct rules. Maybe. At least I hope he didn't. But I am not offended in any way so can we 'move on' as you suggest?"

"Ah, eh, yes. Yes. I would like for him to know the truth, assuming for the moment they don't know your true gender, to avoid misunderstanding or embarrassment."

Pete gave an exacerbated shrug.

"Ok, how about this Pete. You should be correctly chaperoned."

"This 'chaperoned' means I have a supervisor?"

"Well, not exactly but more like a traveling companion that.. ah.. makes for good manners. We are dealing with the President of the United States."

"You are not asking for my say since I have no vote. When I am alone, my vote counts. In fact, it is the only vote that counts."

"Maybe it's not a good idea to bring up voting in these political settings."

Getting wound up again Pete persevered, "Well wouldn't that be awful to persuade the President we should all have a vote and choose to live free under the sky in a land that has declared 'all men are equal' but women are not?"

"Well, eh not exactly but you do know of a young lady that could travel and camp outside when needed. Essie for example."

"No, that won't work at all."

"Why Pete? We could keep your secret well hidden."

"Won't that look a little out of place for Essie? She is a girl after all and since I may appear to be some heathen male I might be putting her together with bad manners. Highly inappropriate if I do say so myself." Pete jabbed her thumb into her chest.

"You do finally have a point. Unfortunately. Maybe that is possible but maybe, just maybe, you can act a little tiny bit like a well-mannered girl to keep a favorable reputation for Essie?" Pete looked at him until he relented and cast his senseless idea of Pete wearing dresses and ribbons out of his mind.

Ernesto would accompany Pete unless there was a last minute uproar due to gender. Señor would have the advantage of Essie around his Rancho since he had not found a suitable replacement for his housekeeper. The President and Mr. Muir would have the possible advantage of Ernesto's abilities to settle Pete down and in the end that may be more important for the success of the trip.

Pete had no idea of the conversation between Muir and the sheriff regarding her gender or she could have made life for Señor simpler. Muir knew he and Pete had already slept under the same blanket of stars but had no intention of sharing the same compartment or room.

Chapter 53 - Feet

Señor Perez was far more eager about Pete's travels than Pete was. To her, climbing over the great Divide without maps, trails or stores of food was an adventure. Taking on five hungry bears with two knives and a sling was exciting. Meeting the public was a bath in a muddy elk wallow.

Pete would be leaving in a month with Muir. Muir had sent telegrams to Señor Perez to help her organize. Señor finally talked Pete into a trip to town to get appropriate clothing.

She could bring her mountain furs but also should have other clothes to keep her from being a spectacle in her meetings with dignitaries. President Roosevelt, should she get the opportunity, would likely prefer to meet her in her hand-tanned skins and natural habitat. However she needed to be prepared for any eventuality.

She could only feel spurned if she bought into their scorn. She had learned at a young age her feelings were her own no matter who said or did what. This naturalness, wherever it came from, gave her freedom. A commodity not for sale in any store.

• • •

The visit to town was a memorable one for Señor Perez. Less so for Pete. It would have been easier to pull a goat through the eye of a needle. She had many excuses starting with she was too busy and ending with a stomachache. The gut ache routine might have fooled Señor except he saw a twinkle in her green eyes that couldn't be contained.

First was the question of a dress. Any affair she might visit requiring a dress would NOT happen. She briefly considered the possibility when she was told the dress would cover her shoes and she could wear shoes of her choice. When presented with the possibility she put her head back to ponder the idea and quickly gave a left and right yanking shake of her head to resume her negativity. She gave a gravelly giggle when seeing the evening wear never having attended any formal affairs. She could picture them being shredded by brush on a stroll down a creek bank.

She couldn't be free with all those petticoats, corsets and things she had no need for to be sure. "Maybe if you put some of this stuff on, Señor Perez, you might feel what I feel."

Señor couldn't contain his laughter. "Maybe Pete, and they would put me in jail."

"Jail is my first choice over shoes and dresses. Maybe, 'you first' is a good idea Señor. I would like to see you with a little lip rouge as well."

Señor Perez had survived several attempts on his life and had fought the best the frontier territory had to offer. He did, however, meet his match this time. He found out what happens when he tried to corner this wild thing.

The second one he blinked at was when she said I'd rather go naked. She started pulling off her leather vest in front of him as if naked was easy compared to what he was suggesting. "Oh wait wait maybe MAYBE you can get used to the attire before making up your mind fully?"

"Maybe?"

• • •

Her feet had a structure showing they had not been imprisoned in shoes. Calluses on the bottom of her feet had the thickness of boot soles. Her feet exhibited a powerful architecture with a high muscular arch giving them more height than the average. They were dexterous, not massive, but displayed strength with their muscle and tendon definition. She would often play with items with her toes, picking them up and turning them over. Her toes were obviously an important part of her and not disinterested little happenings stuck on the ends of her feet like gumdrops. She was a picture of grace and beauty down to and including her toes. But one would have to have a sense for such things.

His last stand was with shoes. Shoes were important to Señor Perez. She wore moccasins in the cold of winter or went barefoot even with ice on the ground. In the summer, it goes without saying. Her trip was going to start early November keeping moccasins a possible part of her wardrobe.

She had several different styles of shoes to try on and none came close to fitting her feet. The ones Pete like best was a brown leather laced up boot with a high square heel, which could not fit her muscular feet. Society had developed a desire for showing narrow feet on ladies which was a sign of breeding and gentility. When it was suggested by the salesman many had removed their little toes to make a better fit Pete turned to Señor. She said in her sweetest gravelly voice, "Have you got a pair in his size?"

She won every battle that day as she saw it about her and not about the Rancho. He enjoyed losing to the dynamic fighter who only sought freedom for herself. And her magnificent toes.

• • •

As Señor and Pete left town they passed the DA and the deputy both standing on the boardwalk huffing and fluffing their feathers. The DA was engrossed in displaying to the deputy, soon to be new sheriff, the power he wielded.

"Deputy, I need to talk to you now, in private."

"When I get the time. I'm a lot busier than I used to be with all this new responsibility. And by the way, it's best if you call me by my new title, Sheriff."

"You're not sheriff anybody yet you little pipsqueak. You're nothing until I say you are. Is that clear?"

"I'm the law now and you'd better treat me with a little more respect."

"I should have gotten rid of them both."

Chapter 54 – How Swift are the Rivers?

Señor Perez had maps out and Pete was engrossed in charting her whereabouts and their first trip to Mesa Verde National Park cliff dwellings. She had seen the globe but never a map this size. She quickly wanted a larger map showing the United States and where was South Dakota? Where was California? Where were the Rockies and the geysers? And how wide and swift were the rivers? And which direction did they flow?

The maps made it all look easy to cover the distances. Her feet brought back the pounding her mind was willing to overlook as her finger traced the distances from maps to globe and back to the maps.

Señor Perez pretended to be tired and asked if she could return the following evening if she had more questions. He thought it might be best not to stack the hay too high in Pete's mind. And Pete returned.

She talked with Señor Perez about the time involvement in travel to Mesa Verde. Then she wanted to get a scale for how long the other trips would be.

He brought out several maps showing railroads and wagon roads that gave them both some answers. He pointed to thick red lines with the words Northern Pacific Railroad. Then touched the map where the geysers were located. This may be the destination of their second adventure on the Burlington RR to Yellowstone.

Then they came back to the map near the Rancho and found the roads connecting to the Atchison, Topeka and Santa Fe Railway where she would be traveling west if she was to see Muir's Yosemite. Yosemite Valley Railroad, YVRR, would get her into Yosemite should she ever travel to California. All without foot travel or connecting to Universe and the real world of wildness.

Señor noticed the changes as thoughts crossed her mind and wanted her to focus on the shorter easier trip fairly close to the Rancho to get her used to modern travel.

"But let's start slowly with the Ancient's old dwellings nearby at Mesa Verde National Park."

"Yes, I see it is close by. Maybe I could meet them there? On foot? It looks less than seventy miles from the Rancho?"

Chapter 55 - Departing

They were to leave the Rancho and travel two days partially by wagon coach and some by train to visit the cliff dwellings of Mesa Verde. Pete's original purpose was to give her perspectives on wilderness. The short itinerary was an attempt to avoid Pete's taking on too much 'society' and to iron out wrinkles such as gender issues. Mesa Verde might also give Muir and the President some insight into her knowledge of the Ancients that had been relayed to the two famous men.

The day of leaving drew near with Señor Perez the most excited. Pete had some trepidation and showed it by spending more time with her coyote friend, Pup. She was sure the trip would be hard on Pup but wasn't sure he would stay put if she left him behind.

Ernesto would also be better off home with Pup and she could trust him to watch after Pup. But for some reason Ernesto was going.

Pete's mind had been filling at an unsustainable pace. She hadn't as yet learned to keep in touch with herself during the process. The first awareness she had of something wrong was when the contents of Universe shook to a frazzle. The stuff in her mind had short circuited the connection. She needed some time to sort through the tackle box in her mind and unravel the hooks and sinkers from the snarled pieces of line. No one saw the need coming except Ernesto. And he was powerless to literally stop the train.

• • •

The stagecoach was boarded and the leaving was left behind.

"Mr. Muir there is something I need to say."

"What is it Pete?"

"What if a name is a trick?"

"Like what kind of a trick?"

"A misleading kind of a trick?"

"Yes, Pete. But I don't understand what your question is."

"You see Mr. Muir my Name is Pete but it is a trick because I am a girl.

But I don't like dresses so most people have no idea it's a trick."

"I have no idea what you are saying or asking if indeed you are asking anything. If it is about your gender, I knew you were a young lady from the beginning. The sheriff told me before his disappearance. I am quite aware of the social mores being violated. Since there is an age difference and you show no discomfort around me or Ernesto, I felt it might work. I will do what I can to accommodate you of course. Feel free to request anything that will make you more comfortable."

"Sure, but I don't need accommodating."

"That's the feeling I had as well Pete."

Chapter 56 – Rules of the Road

Pup needed to bathe but didn't think it necessary any time soon. In general Pup knew when it was time to have a bath the nasty way people did it with horrible smelling soap. He would avoid being seen let alone being caught if possible. When Pup knew it was inevitable he would slither along on his belly pushing his unwilling nose ahead of him away from the nearest soap and water. He knew time was his only ally and it slowly ticked away.

Ernesto was also a little wary of soap and water except if the water was well warmed in a tub. He would mime the belly slither the next time Essie brought up the subject of bathing in the cold water in the high country.

Pete knew Pup would be expected to sit politely in a stagecoach and among other passengers on the train. Pup had no training on good manners and it went against his nature.

Pete tried first to have Pup ride up front with the driver of the coach foreseeing some of the problems but both Pup and the driver didn't get along with the idea. It wasn't long before Pup was trotting along beside the coach but he needed more water than he could quickly find in the dry landscape. Pete had thought to bring some water and it was enough to get her and Pup watered during the occasional stops.

The train was an entirely different matter. The train would start with a jerk, then a bang of metal on metal. Pup would not be contained. But here Pete didn't dare let him loose as he would rather die than lose sight of her. She knew he could keep up but for how long without water and her ability to see to his water was unlikely.

Pup would jump, startled with the first jerk, and then try to escape through the windows. The coyote made the passengers uncomfortable and that was before he started bouncing off the walls. In time he did learn to be a little calmer and only his eyes would fill with dread and fear instead of his entire body. But there was no doubt he was looking forward to his departure from the train.

At a train stop she went off by herself to a watering tank to bathe and go for a swim. The tank was a clay filled pond to hold water when it was needed for the railroad. She stripped and waded in. Pup was happy enough to stand watch for intruders.

It wasn't long before she had gotten out and closed in on Pup to give thanks for his sentry. However she had soap in hand and lifted him in her arms only to return to the center of the watering tank. His eyes spit traitor and his legs would not stop moving but the job was soon done.

• • •

Ernesto couldn't sleep. The noisy whistle was a constant interruption to his naps and dreams of being swallowed by a wild beast.

He tried his hand at keeping Pup calm. He could see both Pup and Pete roiling at being surrounded by the clatter of train and people. Pete would have enough issues keeping herself under control.

In the beginning Pup and Ernesto looked longingly out the same window. No one else would sit by them which helped to some extent. After they had both panted and steamed their window a conductor came by and slid the window down four inches allowing them a little more air. The conductor was clear he was the only one to touch the window.

No further lowering would be allowed by the conductor for the two yet Pete noticed others had their windows completely down. Pete hooted when it finally dawned on her the conductor was protecting Pup and Ernesto from injuries that might occur if they both jumped out the window. The humor and seeing herself in the coyote helped Pete endure the remainder of the trip to Mesa Verde.

Chapter 57 - Humanity

From the beginning Ernesto didn't see Pete changing her lifestyle successfully for the duration of the trip to Mesa Verde, let alone beyond. Maybe someday, but no time soon. Ernesto surveyed Muir as he would a flock of sheep wondering when and where this trip might go wrong.

John Muir and Ernesto were thrown together without a buffer. On the surface they were quite different and were brought together with their common interest, Pete. They had several encounters on stops to get to know each other. It was driving Muir crazy to attempt to view a plant clipping only to have a view of the back of Ernesto's bald head between his eyes and the plant in question.

Ernesto saw no benefit in saving the leaves and flowers any more than he could see this ending well with Pete. There were many millions of leaves and there was nothing special about the ones Muir was saving. It was for this reason he kept inspecting what Muir was collecting.

Pete had told Ernesto of Muir's knowledge of flora and she was interested in learning more about his knowledge of plant medicine. Muir was glad to share his findings and eventually learned to appreciate Ernesto's humor. But Ernesto was an acquired taste for the old bearded man and it didn't come easily.

It wasn't long before Ernesto was bringing his own plant clippings along with local knowledge of soils and subterranean drainage that would be useful to the inquisitive mind of Muir. In turn Muir would gladly share his knowledge of a plant's uses and properties with Ernesto. Ernesto was getting the picture of why Pete was taken with the old man.

• • •

Pete had two days of nothing but people, wagons, trains and more people. There were always boundaries, walls, confinement, rules and humanity pushing in on her. She trudged off into the wind to get air as quickly as possible with every stop.

She had the thought this life was wasted on people only to realize it was people making inventions that made all this fancy travel possible. She then wondered how she had gotten off track when she recognized the voice she was listening to was her own. Yammer. Yammer.

No sooner would she feel the gentle breeze of silence than she would have another thought bringing the chaos of people back inside her head. She was being introduced to this exciting world of doing and trying many new things. But if she wanted to know what was out there waiting for her, she had to give up what was inside; protected and peaceful.

Her first tour was finally nearing its destination of Mesa Verde and the massive ancient cliff dwellings. Her experience with caves, artifacts, glyphs, and Whouden had heightened her interest and helped to put her negative thoughts in the background.

Chapter 58 – Cliff Dwellings

Pete's first views of the dwellings made it clear why the ancients had chosen this way of life. Their elevated positions gave them buffer from the constant dangers of marauding rivals whether they were of the two legged or four legged variety. The ladders that reached many of these dwellings were clearly the only way to have access to the ancients and their stores.

The cliff dwellings were a magnificent sight, architecturally appropriate in the spectacular setting. They were protected under huge massive sandstone overhangs and inset into long narrow caves that would shelter them from the rains and winds that would have melted away the mudding used to form the side and front walls of the dwellings. Some had year around springs in the rear of the caves to provide good water. Inside well preserved were baking ovens still black even after centuries of nonuse. There were other obvious structures as well, including food storage bins and places were "the people" could gather and tell their stories. However Pete could not feel the presence like she could at Whouden.

There were small garden planters outside some of the dwelling areas no doubt for herbs that were used for teas and medicines. Larger plots of land were in nearby areas that could have been utilized for corn crops.

Unfortunately Pete and Muir were not the first people to visit the ruins. It was the intrusion of modern man both looting and building that chased away the life Pete felt at Whouden.

• • •

The afternoon had a find with a special meaning. Pete found an arrowhead worked over a thousand years prior to the cliff dwellers walking these same lands. She felt the concentration on the volcanic glass rock that was brought from many miles distant and then traded to one who could work the material. She sensed the energy of each stroke touching the glass to make the razor sharp cutting edge. She absorbed the history that had been waiting for her since it was lost by a hunter younger than herself.

The boy had missed his shot at a rabbit. His squandered opportunity also cost him a meal and a piece of fur for his new rabbit skin blanket.

Muir watched her intently as she went through the emotions of the young hunter. He could see her thrill, agony and tears but without knowing the source. She gently put it back on the ground where she found it and sprinkled a light dusting of red earth to return it on its journey. What modern man would have seen as a souvenir, she saw as a boy, a soul and a life. She had a way of making the hair on Muir's neck prickle and course down his arms and legs.

• • •

Ernesto sat at a distance watching the whole episode. He knew at that moment what was to happen. He thought it best to leave Pete and Muir to say their goodbyes. His job to accompany Pete to Mesa Verde was done. His trip back to the Rancho would be alone.

• • •

At the end of the day Muir asked Pete if she would like to spend another day and what she thought of the place in general. The answer he expected came quickly and to the point.

"Here I am not a part of the whole but I am a lone survivor. This place revolves around me instead of those who gave it life. Mr. Muir I would like to go back now. I think you understand I am missing fewer people, and my mountains."

"Yes more than most Pete. We can talk of that in a minute but I have a most important question for you. Can you tell me more of this place and how we might improve it? It would prove quite useful to my studies."

"Isn't it too late to save what is already gone Mr. Muir?"

"But don't these magnificent dwellings remain at least in part to give us an idea of what life might have been?"

"They show us buildings that used to be homes. I am happy for that. But a few bones from a skeleton don't let us know the lives. Without the 'will' it is only bones… a graveyard."

"What is this .. 'will' if you can and we have words, and how did 'spirit or 'spirits' miss the mark?"

"You asked the exact same question Essie once asked. 'Was it the 'will' of the Ancients or the spirit of the Ancients?' As best we could determine, 'will' came closest but neither was probably accurate."

Then a pause for both to digest the words. "So if you don't mind I will leave you now. I don't thank people much but I want to thank you."

"My last question I promise. Will you grant me one more?"

"Ok."

"What caused the 'will' to leave and when?"

"I want to give you science but I can't. Modern people's 'will' can drive the ancient 'will' away. 'Will' is fragile and doesn't mix peoples unless a great deal of care is taken. When there is no respect a pollution happens and the old 'will' can't survive it." Another pause and Pete was clearly ready to leave. "These bones are magnificent. They bring a sadness to me."

"Pete you have a gift. Only some can hear because they dare to listen. I'll be happy to escort you back to your Rancho and to Señor Perez."

"No Mr. Muir. You mean no harm but I need to walk my own path now… in here." And she pointed to her chest.

"I can't allow that Pete."

"No, Mr. Muir. In my life, I am the only one to allow. If you could get this big bag back to Señor I will leave now with what I have left inside me."

To Muir the questions she raised were troubling as they had basis. He saw it was important to save what they could but not think for a moment they saved more than what the eye could see.

She watched his wagon leave and she turned with Pup at her side. Her breath was not free and it came and went with a weight she wasn't used to. She and Pup had both survived their culture collisions. One quick look to the bluish purple mountains in the distance gave Pete her bearings. Pup waited for her first step, and then bounded ahead to show he was a leader of the way.

Chapter 59 – Pup's Choice

WESTERN UNION

THEODORE ROOSEVELT
WESTERN UNION OFFICE
RICHMOND VIRGINIA

PETE HAD TOO MUCH MODERN MAN STOP SHE DEPARTED FOR MOUNTAINS AFTER THREE DAYS STOP SHE LEFT ME MORE THAN I CAME WITH STOP

JOHN MUIR
WESTERN UNION OFFICE
AZTEC NEW MEXICO

• • •

WESTERN UNION

JOHN MUIR
WESTERN UNION OFFICE
MARTINEZ CALIFORNIA

ALL EXTREMELY CURIOUS STOP I LOOK FORWARD TO YOUR NEXT VISIT FOR DETAILS STOP SAFE TRAVELS STOP

THEODORE ROOSEVELT
WESTERN UNION OFFICE
RICHMOND VIRGINIA

• • •

Pete didn't want to see anyone. She would get in trouble around Essie's cabin and she didn't want to face Señor Perez and his likely disappointment when she returned without Muir.

Ernesto would know exactly what not to say and give her the space needed. And there was her new home calling itself The Great Divide that would welcome her back.

People were omnivores never thinking there was more to be consumed other than plants and animals. She wanted something else and knew where to find it.

• • •

Señor Perez wanted to alert the deputy, now acting sheriff. Ernesto talked him out of it explaining how little danger Pete was in on her travels as long as she avoided humans which she naturally did. Pete would be in worse danger if the deputy started an all-out manhunt for her. Maybe the deputy as well.

• • •

Señor let out a long lingering breath when he first caught sight of her. She wanted to show him her return to keep him from worry, nothing more. It was more than three days after her belongings were returned by Muir.

• • •

She spent her time out of sight of humans early that winter. She mainly utilized her ancient cave Whouden. It took several months before she could start feeling again the full extent of her naturalness. The gathering of energy to be born again was being stored like the life in the buds on bushes. Spring would happen.

In the beginning she and Pup were a little distant. Maybe Pup knew to leave her alone but he more likely needed to get himself back in touch with life's many dimensions.

But nothing lasts forever and they started working as a team to uncover the fresh game and roots needed for their meals. Sometimes she would start and tend a fire for a few hours to soften the partially frozen ground. Then it could be easily pulled away from the tubers by her digging stick or Pup's rummaging paws.

Once a routine had been established and the energy of connection to those things natural had been restored she found peace again in the yet undiscovered. At the end of the day she and Pup would dance to muted music of their moods. Sometimes she would support his upper body and they danced as partners. They would zig and zag, whirl and twirl, to follow the rhythm only they could hear.

• • •

Pup would often want to give up the play and try pulling his paws away from Pete. Pete would feel the lead of Pup and would fall and giggle entangled in Pup. This would reenergize Pup for another round of comedy. He would stand over Pete growling, snapping and mouthing her, careful never to tear her skin. They were giving to each other and more importantly giving back life-sustaining energy to Universe.

When they were finally done Pup would put a paw on top of her body or leg as if he was the one in charge and the last one standing. The energy had gone full circle.

It was early January with a little snow sticking to the hills. Time had blurred her recent past and what she considered a failed trip for which Señor had supplied ample energy. It felt right to go back to the ranch and be of use where she could. And yes, let Ernesto play his games upon her head. She waited at Whouden until good weather presented itself and started back.

• • •

Pup made his choice and would not go back to the two leggeds with Pete. He learned his place was in the most inhospitable location he could find. Where people were scarce and hopefully nonexistent. Some were made to stay wild. He would be there until she felt the need to join him.

Chapter 60 – Blessed and Different

Pete saw the sheep first, and not long after the dogs were upon her as always. They never treated her as a stranger but always the long lost friend. Their play showed her she was one of them. Their barking excitement and jovial jumping brought Ernesto clapping his hands in a victory type welcome.

"Where have you been Pete and why did you not come back with me?"

"I needed some time and fresh air. Did you finish the trip with Mr. Muir?"

"No, I asked if I could return to the ranch and I think he was happy he didn't have to babysit me anymore. Everything is all ok Pete. No worry about anything. OK?"

"Sure, good. Is Señor Perez ok? Is he at the ranch house?"

"Sure, he worried for a time when you didn't return with Muir. He wanted to go get the deputy acting sheriff to look for you but I told him no need. Nothing out there would want to eat your sorry buzzard hide."

"Thanks Ernesto. I'd hate to think that deputy was trailing me. Is everything ok with you and the sheep?"

"Sure, if we eat, sleep and dance to nature's music, we stay happy."

Pete slapped his shoulder in an uncommon gesture. It didn't go unnoticed by her friend Ernesto. He wondered what she had been up to but it didn't take long for most of his curiosity to disappear. She'd either talk or she wouldn't.

Next she went to the barn to see if her things were as she left them and they were. She dropped her traveling bag in the corner and went to the ranch house door.

Two quick knocks and she would soon see. Señor opened the door and took on the color of joy. She in turn gave a wide smile. Señor stood back from the door and motioned wordlessly to enter.

News of their shortened trip and her desire to return on her own was accepted as Pete's way. She knew she hadn't asked Señor Perez if she could leave for a couple of months. Señor didn't need reasons or excuses. He was glad she didn't offer any.

Señor Perez had assumed responsibility for Pete with the ferocity of a parent. If Pete knew this she would take it as a bridle and bit in her mouth. He did his best that afternoon not to show his relief. He failed.

He walked over to his roll top desk and picked up a card and handed it to her.

Mrs. Frances P. Harding

Colorado School of Mines

Golden, Colorado

She was quick to recognize the card but had no idea why Señor Perez would have the same card she had tucked away. Whoever this lady was, she was everywhere.

"Señor Perez, why does this lady Mrs. Harding follow me?"

"Actually she has a desire to speak with you and I said I would tell you. She has something to talk to you about and thought you may be interested."

"I don't know if I'm interested until I know what it is… of course."

"It never does harm to hear someone out before making up your mind."

"Señor Perez it took me two months to get over the last big idea of visiting National Parks… and I feel bad about it. I don't want to do these insider people things when I am an outsider kind of person."

"Pete, you are blessed and you are different."

"Yes, and if Ernesto was standing here now I would make a remark on what a blessing it is to be different from Ernesto."

"Yes, too bad he missed it."

"Señor Perez her card says Colorado School of Mines. Do you know what that is? Do they have books about holes in the ground?"

"It is the finest teacher's college and college of science we have in the area. Their main emphasis is engineering and mines as they are located in the center of a mining area."

"They teach teachers?"

"Yes, but they are a school of science. Do you know what science is?"

"Yes, yes I am attracted to science. Mr. Muir showed me several things and it was remarkable. Right under my nose all this time."

• • •

"Mrs. Harding I'm sure could tell you far more than I. Would you like me to contact her and let her know of your interest?"

"Señor Perez, I can't make myself go off visiting anymore."

"What if I tell her you will be happy to receive her here?"

"Well… sure. That would be ok. I remember her well enough. She was a bit messed up the last time I saw her but she looks like the kind that cleans up good."

Chapter 61 – Mrs. Harding

The winter went on as most winters do in the southwest with first too little and then too much weather. Spring came a little early and Pete had all but forgotten her commitment to speak with Mrs. Harding.

Upon entering the ranch house Pete was given a letter addressed to Señor Perez but it concerned Pete. Mrs. Harding would be arriving in a week for the sole purpose of talking to Pete. Mrs. Harding had accepted an invitation from Señor Perez to utilize the guest house at the ranch and stay a few days while getting to know Pete.

It was just before lambing and there was always plenty of work to be had. Pete would busy herself to limit her time with Mrs. Harding. Señor Perez was way ahead of the game and made sure Pete's duties were of little importance to the running of the ranch when Mrs. Harding arrived.

• • •

"Mrs. Harding. Please let Ernesto take your bag to your room while you and I chat awhile. I'll have someone get Pete. Can I get you something to eat or drink after your long trip?"

"Something to drink would be delightful. And do you have a place I could freshen up a little?"

"Yes, of course. Right this way and down the hall to your left."

Pete had seen the buckboard coming from town and she had mixed feelings about the new guest. Science is the study of life's unknowns but people should remain mysterious.

• • •

It wasn't long before the short introduction from Señor Perez was completed and Mrs. Harding and Pete were alone in conversation.

Mrs. Harding spoke little of their first meeting with the two marauders as she called them. She looked deeply into Pete's eyes and thanked her with no details. Nothing more.

Mrs. Harding had an interesting easy-going way about her. She was a person of science and psychology. She was an educated woman and worked with the college in Golden in admissions. She also taught one class. But she didn't have the stiffness of Mr. Muir and her speech was more easily understood.

She had curly blond hair cut short and soft blue eyes. Pete was right. She cleaned up well.

Mrs. Harding had corresponded not only with Señor Perez but also Muir and President Roosevelt. She was straightforward with Pete and let her know of the communications. It would be considered a personal favor to the President if something could be done for this "national treasure".

Ex-President Roosevelt in a room full of people could always be heard above the rest. A blustery sort of man having no challenge get the better of him. The President however also knew his limitations. The President would move the mountain to Pete if he couldn't get the job done the other way around.

He was a big game hunter, loved to pounce on people like a gust of wind, and would have gotten nowhere with Pete. He knew if he was to succeed with this hunt he would have to use others better suited with a lighter touch than he possessed.

She made Pete feel comfortable and the guarded nature of Pete's demeanor quickly disappeared. Mrs. Harding was the ultimate mother without mothering. She was forgiving and accepting keeping to the philosophy all things work out as they should.

She took an interest in what Pete did around the ranch. This went well with Pete as they could leave the ranch house and move closer to "outsider" country. She had an interest in Pete's tanning and her skills with the bow as well. She had already seen her prowess with a knife first hand. Mrs. Harding was also curious about Essie and she filed away what she could learn. The subject then turned to science and school.

"Have you ever thought about going to college?"

"I'm not good around a lot of people and words don't come easy. I don't think school is for me. My work is sheep."

"College is not for everybody but it does seem a shame not to take one course and explore the countryside. Do you ever look up a mountain and say, 'No I don't want to know what's up there'?"

"There's been several it took some time to find my way up."

"I bet there has. But you don't say 'I can't'."

"No… I don't like 'I can't'. Makes me less free."

"Right you are. Have you ever been around a college campus?"

"No, I've been around Essie a lot and she went to high school. Is college like high school?"

"Sometimes, but there is more flexibility in courses and the extent to which they might take your mind. You can take one course or pick and choose more of your interests. If you ever want to give it a go I may be able to help with some of the details."

"Details?"

"College tuition, books, room and board."

"What is this room and board?"

"It is where you live and what you eat when you go to college. It is a dorm room with ... ah.. well I see one of those hills coming up. You would prefer to live off campus.. ah.. away from college and come on to campus to take your classes and then leave. Right?"

"Yes"

"Ah.. yes. The main thing is to realize if you have the will, I have the ways. Would it be possible someday for us to spend a few days together camping up the mountain to be around where you are comfortable?

"I guess so. But it's my home. Down here is camping until I can get back where I belong."

"Yes, I see. You clearly belong in the solitude and the power only nature possesses." She had experienced Pete's lethal abilities first hand and now knew it was not an isolated incident. She knew Pete's attacks were in defense of the innocent and neither were premeditated without provocation.

They spoke of many things of interest to Pete. Often their conversations went to the flora and fauna on their walks but also to the mind. Mrs. Harding's expertise in psychology drew out Pete's perceptions making it fertile ground for both. Mrs. Harding had a way of avoiding things when Pete would tense up and let the conversation go in a direction advantageous to Pete. She wasn't sneaking up on Pete or giving Pete that wary feeling.

Pete might be better off with more distance between her and humanity which would limit her in the academic setting at the Colorado School of Mines. However Pete's driving curiosity would benefit her greatly from the interaction with other students and faculty. She also, in turn, had the potential of offering a great deal to others with her unique perspectives.

Pete could easily sense Mrs. Harding was not a tough outdoorsman like Muir but had a hardy risk-taking nature. Unknowingly 'risk-taking' was on the yardstick Pete used to measure people. Less risk was found in a closet but not a lot of freedom to experience Universe.

Mrs. Harding had two days at the ranch and knew it was time to leave. She gave Pete the room she needed. She looked into Pete's eyes again, and they had a few moments together making the trip worth the while, no matter what Pete's decision.

Chapter 62 – Confession

The Church had wanted Padre to enlarge Catholic control through the schools, but the laws after the Mexican American War were in direct opposition. Padre had failed.

New Mexicans for more than sixty years were repeatedly checkmated in their efforts to achieve statehood. This resulted in their land remaining a US territory until 1912, with officials appointed from Washington to skim off the top what they could. Upon that vexation piled others: problems with hostile Indians and outlaws, difficulties involving land, water rights, economics and territorial boundaries. A central issue was the uphill battle for the people to adapt to a new pace and pattern of life with increased competition, one ruled by different traditions.

Persons on the Rio Grande broke into two opposing camps; the supporters of a territorial form of government, and the advocates of immediate statehood. In the main, Anglo-Americans, being in the minority, favored the territorial system to retain their power from Washington. They argued the territory was too Catholic, too Mexican, too Indian, too uneducated, too underpopulated, or too Spanish speaking.

The Hispanic majority tended to lean toward statehood. Once educated to the benefits of putting native New Mexicans into the highest offices they needed to find quality people that would get the job done benefiting the masses instead of a few corrupt politicians, regardless of their race.

• • •

A parent of one of his students warned Padre of a forceful takeover of the Señor's Rancho. The threats were growing in number. The powerful establishment and wealthy politicians were directing their underlings to send thugs to take possession before statehood was finalized to keep the incoming changes of law from clouding their title.

• • •

Something had made a monumental change in Padre: maybe the exorcism ritual, the intervention of the Lost, or Raven jumping up and down on him while he lay unconscious. Maybe just plain old-fashioned conscience through God's will and prayer. Like always, maybe a lot of things but 'whys' don't always find truth.

Padre had a recurring dream. He saw the lambs of Pete at peace surrounding him. He saw Pete smiling at the flock. She then turned to Padre with the same smile. It grabbed his insides and had a profound impact.

• • •

Padre rode out to the Rancho. He found Señor sitting quietly on the porch. "Señor I need to change places with you. Do you mind hearing my confession?"

"Oh? Step into my confessional Padre," and Señor waved his hand to the seat next to him. Padre thoughtfully struggled up the porch steps. "God is always listening, particularly on my verandah Padre."

"There was a plan. The District Attorney Wagner wanted me to use any excuse I could to get you and the top hands off your land for a week allowing them to come in and do what the sheriff wasn't willing to do. This would allow Wagner to get physical possession without alienating half the Territory with killings. They had legal title but the sheriff didn't want to force you off land that had been in your family for centuries. Now he has coincidentally disappeared. Maybe it was the DA's bodyguards clearing the way for someone more helpful."

"Have any proof Padre?"

"Not good enough to be used in court. Also I have been getting threatening notes."

"Did you keep any of those notes?"

"Yes, here they are. They were pinned to young students' coats. You can see they also include you Señor. They want me to feel responsible if you were to die defending your Rancho."

"Why do you tell me this? Won't the DA be your worst nightmare?"

"Yes, he'll be unhappy but it's something I must do."

"He'll make your life miserable. He'll put pressure on the Archbishop to do the same."

"I expect so. But this is your Rancho and your life, hard-fought and won by your family for hundreds of years. I pray this will all resolve itself peaceably and you retain control of your Rancho."

After a thoughtful pause. "Padre I think I am missing something. What power might the DA gain? The DA already has power in this territory and his power comes from Washington, not this Rancho."

"It is only conjecture Señor. I'd be casting stones. But one thing is certain, those who have wealth and power, want more."

"Fair enough Padre. But when you have a couple of stones you'd like to share, please let me know. Until then we'll stay and do the best we can."

"I'll let you know what else I hear."

"Thank you Padre. You will be in my prayers."

Chapter 63 - Defiance

Señor stood on the porch ready to greet those approaching. He asked his hands to let him handle it alone. Not one agreed but were apologetic in their refusals.

Padre walked up the steps of the porch and stood close and in front of Señor's right side for all to see. He had chosen sides or better said changed sides. Pete in her defiant manner soared over the rail and stood beside Padre in front of Señor's left side now clearly blocking any harm that might come his way from that direction. Padre watched her willful neglect of decorum. Essie gripped her staff with stern wrinkled faced and walked straight up in front of Señor on a lower step. She caught hold of some of the energy being passed around. Pete smiled.

There were armed ranch hands and neighbors scattered around the Rancho, under the porch, and in the barn and loft. Among them were Ed, Juan, and Ernesto and many more Señor would not recognize before that day.

Pete spun her knife in the air behind Essie. There was something about that movement that changed things. It made everyone nervous but it also distracted all those involved. And she continued.

Time and time again she spun that razor sharp knife several feet in the air and caught it each time. Never missing. Never concentrating on anything else but the approaching men. She knew where it was going to be without ever looking directly at the flashing steel.

• • •

Essie's Diary

I knew what Pete was doing behind me. I'd seen it a thousand times. This was the first time I'd ever actually heard it however. My worry wasn't the thugs in front of me but the blade whirling behind me. And how close it came to the only good unscarred ear remaining on my head.

• • •

Sampson's men were evenly divided seven on each side of him. They rode past the armed hands and directly in front of the porch. They spread out their horses to each side of Señor. Sampson must have suspected there might be some resistance. He came prepared.

Twelve additional Sampson gunmen walked into position behind those around the barn and corral. They started cocking their rifles to let the ranch hands and neighbors know the gravity of the situation.

The large New Mexican in front of Señor had a wide-lipped Cheshire cat grin. "Look around Señor. When this is done there won't be enough hands to run this place."

Señor did a Pete shrug. Ernesto smiled at the perfect mime. Lots of smiles were being passed around that morning. It wasn't lost on Sampson. Pete spun her knife at least four feet in the air and grabbed it as usual. Never missing a beat. Calm as a warm summer evening. I think both sides wanted her to quit. It took their attention. She did not. I could hear the air move just behind me from the twisting cold steel of her knife. And again.

• • •

Sampson turned to face those same ranch hands around the barn and corrals. The ranch hands were caught, with professional gunman all taking aim at their heads. He waved a finger at them now firmly in control and offering certain death if Señor did not give the order to stand down. He wanted to display how futile it was to continue the fight.

As he waved his finger he noticed a ring of wagons and horses about three hundred yards out coming at the Rancho with a slow steady walking pace. They had encircled the ranch house, corrals and barn. They numbered in the hundreds from ranchers, relatives and friends. And Pete kept spinning her knife.

They stopped within 100 yards forming a tight circle, elbow to elbow. Wagon wheel to wagon wheel. It was clear if Sampson started and won the battle at the ranch house, he and his men would never make it out alive. The area fell still except for a few impatient horses. And Pete's knife.

"Next time it won't be this easy Señor. Law's not with you."

"Looks like the good citizens are, Morales."

Sampson's men moved cautiously back, turned and rode out from the ranch house. When they got to the ring of wagons and horses a hole opened up allowing them to file through. No one fired a shot. Miracles happen.

The rugged people who lived in the Territory had put a stop to the bullying from the DC cronies. They wanted a say in their leadership. They also wondered what this girl named Pete would do. Some came to know what was faster; Sampson's bullet or Pete's knife. Pete stood cold and unfazed when putting her knife back in its sheath. It permeated the air and all who breathed it.

• • •

The retribution from the DA was swift. Padre's role on the porch beside Señor had not gone unnoticed. His leadership of schools in the Territory was rapidly reduced to a classroom teacher for the youngest levels.

Chapter 64 – Edification

Jan 12, 1912, two weeks after the attempted takeover of the Rancho by force, statehood was achieved. The Rancho was now in New Mexico State with lease land into southern Colorado. Local control would rapidly progress. Courts were filling dockets with irregularities of land purchases by the well-connected in DC.

Statehood gave the people a blank slate and the possibility of freedom if they could choose wisely. District Attorney Wagner was running for a New Mexico US Senate seat. It wouldn't be filled for two more months. Padre was working to undermine his candidacy.

Padre didn't want the old caste system under Mexican rule or the existing ways of corruption and subjugation under US or New Mexico State cronyism. After praying on it he saw it as God's plan for him to educate and give confidence to the masses to take control.

If the new voter was given power of the ballot box too soon, it would be an utter failure. Getting the poor motivated to cast an educated ballot when they had enough difficulties feeding their families would not be an easy task. They would be offered lies in exchange for their vote. They weren't ready. Neither was he.

Padre was humbled and challenged by the prospects laid in his lap. He was ready to put his thumb on the scale of learning. He gave workshops on the clout of voting wisely. Freedom would not be free and nonexistent for the majority if they were lazy or apathetic.

• • •

Father Timothy had taken back most of Padre's Church duties and the Church was looking for another young priest to groom. And do what he was told. Padre showed no remorse.

Padre's memory of the exorcism was permanently displaced with calm yet his awareness was crisp. In general he felt as though he was an empty vessel being filled with the realities around him for the first time.

He didn't have the constant color of his mind's ego painting the truth. He had a true sense of the abyss he could not grasp before the exorcism. Maybe this was what Pete experienced naturally. *Stay vigilant.*

Padre would often be seen dressed casually unlike in the past. Sometimes he would disappear from his school duties for several days or even a week at a time leaving it to nuns.

• • •

"I want you to know Pete I'm willing to talk about anything you want. When we met it was a very confusing time and I know now it was a mistake to think you had demons. In your way you helped me through it."

"And you helped me as well Padre. I had human stuff running around inside me and it was the first time. I guess none of us are good at first time things."

"Thanks Pete. I hate to admit it even now but you were a smash hit with me."

"Why do you hate to confess it?"

"It's embarrassing."

"It's embarrassing to be like one of us lowly worms burrowing in the earth?"

"Haven't you ever done something, and learned from it, but don't want to go back and wallow again?"

"No, not really. I prefer to revisit my mistakes. What I hate is doing the same thing again and again when it didn't work the first time. That is what is embarrassing."

"The old term 'learn from your mistakes'?"

"Of course. That's what mistakes are for."

"When I first met you I'd put myself on a pedestal thinking I was the teacher and the holy one. I was the one to hear the confessions. But I clearly held myself first before the Lord. You're my coach when I become separated and lose my connection to Him."

"I'm nobody's coach."

"If not a coach maybe a 'summer's day'?"

"Padre, are you going to recite poetry, to me?"

"A little Shakespeare never hurt anyone. Even you Pete. 'Thou art more lovely and more temperate.'"

"Oh Padre, 'So long as men can breathe or eyes can see
So long lives this and this gives life to thee.'"

"I am always off balance around you Pete. I never know from where you spring. Like now when you spout Shakespeare's sonnet."

"You will always be a summer's breeze to me Padre. You were the first to slide through my leaves. I will keep that little nugget in my locket. And the blubbering that came with it has all been chased away."

• • •

Essie's Diary

No one talked about the battle that didn't happen at the Rancho. It would have sounded like bravado I guess. To me it was all part of the choice I made several years back to join Pete. Some of which gets forgotten if not written on these pages.

• • •

I never got a single word out of Padre about the exorcism. He became a little more like Pete in that regard. Probably for the best but I do have this nose problem and wanting to put it where it doesn't belong.

Pete saw Padre come out of hiding behind his position and church trappings. His manner became more real to Pete. His thinking was two steps ahead of her intellect but maybe she could improve to one day play the game at his level. She was now on an even keel with Padre. But that didn't keep her sharp jibes in her quiver.

Chapter 65 – World War I

The First World War started two years earlier in 1914 in Europe. The United States had stayed neutral. Several times the Germans had wanted the US to take their side and embargo England. The US had not cooperated which resulted in German U Boats sinking US cargo ships along with others of different flags.

It had been nearly patched up when news of German interference closer to home became the rumble from intelligence sources. The Germans were possibly enlisting the aid of the Mexican government to join them.

Federal Marshal McClean had a broad job description. Review and determine if there were coordinated efforts from Mexico or Germany that might intrude on US sovereignty.

• • •

Federal Marshal McClean was making a trip to the northern part of the new State of New Mexico. The marshal was working Aztec, New Mexico, area with a few slim leads. Some of the stories traveled as far north as southern Colorado. No direct evidence Germans had any involvement. Aztec, being near the northern border of New Mexico, seemed too far north for the rumors to pan out but he made the trip nonetheless.

In the beginning it wasn't his top priority. It was common sense to expect trouble, if it came, to emanate solely from the southern border. But this might be what enemies of the US would want him to believe.

• • •

More than one of the townspeople in Aztec sent him out to the Rancho. Pete had grown quite a reputation over the years traveling on foot and knowing every bush and bent blade of grass. It was said she could track a light breeze over solid granite. She would know best about the outlying areas. And rumors.

• • •

Federal Marshal McClean had lost his German wife and unborn son in childbirth several years earlier. He felt best when left alone outside of business hours. Sagebrush was his preferred company.

There was a slim possibility Germany might be attempting to encourage Mexican raiders to cause trouble in the US. The theory was if the US was kept busy with Mexico trying to regain the land lost after the Mexican American War, the US may not be compelled to enter the Great War in Europe.

He was chosen for the job in New Mexico as he had some knowledge of German, English and Spanish. More importantly he had a sense of anything out of its natural place, was tough as nails, and free to travel.

His wife was a German emigrant and his German was learned from her. He grew up in the Territory, knew the temperament of the people and trusted them. When they needed a man to travel and watch for German or Mexican intrusions, his name was at the top of the list.

• • •

When he got to the Rancho, he asked for Pete. He was sent out to a winter pasture where he soon saw signs of sheep and dogs but no sheepherder. Some things didn't change that fast around Pete.

He found human tracks showing five toes and followed the toes. He always considered himself to be a good tracker. *Barefoot sheep herder*, he thought with a smile. Eventually they disappeared over a rock outcrop. Knowing sheepherders were normally a little wary of strangers he sat and rolled a cigarette. He waited for the sheepherder to gather the courage to have a few words. He had no idea of the treat coming his way. With few words.

• • •

Behind him he heard a gravelly tone. He held his hands out to the side as she had gotten the drop on him. "Ok, if I turn and we can have a little chat?"

"Your mouth works from right there."

"Are you Pete?"

"Yep. Who are you?"

"Federal Marshal McClean. I've got a few questions and was told you're the one to ask." He slowly turned, first his head, then his shoulders. In the beginning it was the only way he could catch her shrugs and wags as she was sizing him up. More words eventually came.

Some were in English but most in Spanish. Her suntanned olive skin and short sun bleached brownish hair could pass for more than one ethnic group. He found a person's language and word usage helpful with his detective work. "Have you seen anything peculiar or out of the ordinary anywhere in your travels?" The answer was another wag to go with the many shrugs.

"So you have seen something strange?"

Wag.

• • •

The marshal was a large man with good muscle tone and sun-wrinkled weathered skin. A drooping mustache partially covered a dark shadow of stubble under two steady blue eyes. He was a rugged individualist in personality wearing broad shoulders carrying the weight of losing his wife. He had a simple vocabulary and wasn't the kind to fire rapid questions with his slow deliberate manner. He allowed plenty of time for answers. He would give most an uneasy feeling which was no accident. He looked through them waiting for replies. And signs of lies.

He exuded confidence in his abilities to handle people and rough situations. He was not just another lamb in the herd.

She started with his ID. He showed her a badge and identification of a US Marshal.

"Couldn't I kill a marshal and take that kind of thing?"

"Spose you could." After a pause the marshal had a question in return. "What makes you untrusting?"

"People been disappearing. Government men might be behind it. I never thought sheriffs were going to be there if I needed them. Now I'm afraid they will be."

"I see. The Deputy in Aztec knows me. I spose you can't trust him?"

"Not a chance. What else you got might prove you're on my side and not pond scum?"

"What kind of information?"

"You first."

"I know there is a war coming with Germany."

"That doesn't mean you're on the right side."

"Nope, spose not. Ever notice Pete how the bad guys sound better than the good guys?"

"Come to think of it, yeh. The slippery ones got to be watched real close."

"Well, does it sound like I'm covered in slippery?"

"Nope. Not in the slightest. Doesn't sound like you practice talking at all," and a small smile trickled down the side of Pete's face.

"Does that give us a start on a little trust?"

"You mean cause you can't talk any better than me?"

"Well you talk pretty smooth for someone whose got eyes dancing to every bush in shootin range."

"Do you think I'm a spy?"

"Nope. Just saying I've got to learn to trust you a little myself if this is going to work. Thus far I don't see either of us doing any trusting. Makes me think we've each had a rough time with humans. Maybe we need to start slow."

"I'm not ready to start just yet. Why do you have to trust me?"

"I'm out here alone. Like when you snuck up behind me. I had no idea if you had more than your mouth as a weapon. A lot of people have done things that broke the law and I'm a lawman. Even if I'm not after them, they might think I am. Maybe you did something wrong a few years back and get a little nervous."

Makes sense. "You got other information I might check?" "Well I'm a US Marshal. You can check in Washington, DC if you know people there?" *Slim chance.*

"Do you know Teddy Roosevelt?"

"Ahh, not personally. Do you Pete?"

"No, well barely. I may be able to check."

"Sure, you go ahead. In the meantime maybe we can get a little further along in the trust department. I could be a US Marshal and still be a spy. Maybe what you want to know is if I'm a double agent working for both sides."

"Yes, guess so. Yes, that's probably what I'm working on and don't know how to say it. I like your straightforward way."

"I like your manner as well. You got grit, spit and vinegar from head to toe."

"You got the funniest mustache I ever saw," and out came the gravelly giggle. *No coyote in those big britches.*

And the trust was built one stone at a time.

• • •

However this discourse was nothing like those early days with Essie, Ernesto, or Padre. By this time Pete had become quite proficient with language and could hold her own once started down a trail of words. If she felt like it. But she had found her old ways of watching body language and sensing energy gave her more of what she needed. Character and purpose.

Eventually she promised to lead him to something maybe of interest. The following day she agreed to meet the marshal towards town on a logging road to the old sawmill.

Chapter 66 – Old Mill

She pointed to the road to the mill and the marshal did his own version of nods and shrugs. She brought him closer to the ruts and mule hoofs which his sharp eyes had already started measuring.

Loads that should have been lighter and smaller when leaving the mill were showing deeper ruts, making the tracker scratch his head. Full loads of logs going to the mill should always show the deeper ruts and larger scrapes from mule hooves. The direction of the wagon tracks was shown by the direction of hoof marks. It made a good tracker wonder as to why and what were in some of those loads leaving. No words were needed on the topic of tracking.

It was as easy to read as a first grade reader. He was impressed with her ability to observe and was told in advance of her gender. Her manner, gravelly voice and her sly smile was a ray of light through the wet grey clouds wrapped around his shoulders. The billygoat caught himself wanting more.

This Pete, the new transformed Pete, knew words when it was to her advantage to use them. She could imitate or have a person believe she was one of them. Or she could observe, like the moon, and be as distant.

• • •

The marshal on occasion when interrogating on German intrusion would throw out a few German words to see the reaction. It was a conversation starter at the least to discuss the topic of Germans. The marshal gave Pete a question in German with his best German accent which was no better than his German cooking and on a par with his English. "Sprichst oder verstehst du Deutsch?" Pete noded a simple soft "Ja" but showed a grin at his accent.

The marshal drawled and twanged with the worst pronunciation. Sounded more like a sick animal to Pete's ear. "Wo hast du Deutsch gelernt?"

Pete grinned as it struck her funny. She put the smile down and answered with the perfect accent similar to his deceased wife, "Karl sprach deutsch also musste ich."

Pete could hold her own in Spanish and English as well now which made his wheels start to turn. *Now how in hell is this sheepherder knowing three languages? And one being German at that? No way she's a spy and come right out with perfect German. She sure would be a natural for some undercover work. But that won't happen.*

"Do you speak Chinese?"

"No." A quick shake of her head. "Why do I need Chinese?"

"Oh, no need."

Quite a surprise to the marshal when Pete opened her mouth and out came the perfect German. He was almost happy she didn't know Chinese. That would put her in the suspect category and he'd have to follow up on it. *Unless she could speak Chinese and was a good liar.*

• • •

The marshal said he would like to come back to the Rancho the following day and meet again with Pete and her boss "y su jefe." Pete gave a quizzical look and he chose different words to describe the man in charge, "el hombre a cargo". It was time for Pete to smile at herself. She saw the sheep more her boss but of course he wanted to talk to El Señor. Obviously the man wanted to meet with something other than sheep.

Maybe she could enter the world this man represented. *And hunt.* Definitely more exciting than waiting for spring.

• • •

A meeting was held and questions were asked. Señor wanted his top hands there. No one could offer assistance on Mexicans or German intrusions. The meeting was a flop for Pete as she had great expectations of some kind of excitement. This spy business wasn't all that entertaining.

Federal Marshal McClean revealed he would prefer they keep his visit a secret to make his work easier. Pete saw the reason for the secrecy which was part of the spy business. He left a way to leave him messages via Western Union and went away. No one knew when he might return. He departed with "I'll be in touch and keep me informed if you see something interesting".

• • •

Essie tried to cheer Pete up with spy stories. She wound up telling thrillers that scared herself more than Pete. Pete said over her shoulder as she was heading for her blanket, "This spy game is kinda slow."

• • •

US Marshal McClean visited the ranch for the second time in February of 1917, one month before the US entered WWI. Pete, Essie, Ernesto and Señor were all on the porch when the marshal arrived as scheduled.

He was pleasantly surprised seeing a new face next to a beaming Señor on the porch of the ranch house. She was a pretty young lady in a lacy white blouse, red flower in her hair, and colorful red and white traditional Mexican full rainbow dress.

Her olive skin with mascara and lip rouge shot him a smile that shook him to the end of his boots. The Señorita pulled her vibrant full skirt out to show off all the fancy lace trim and gave a small whirl flowing the dress slightly up and out. She finished with a slight kick with the back of her heel. There he saw familiar dirty wiggly toes he knew well. *Yep, I'm on the right porch.*

When he pulled himself together and got his professional demeanor back he took their full attention. He said what he was about to tell them was to be kept absolutely secret. It was a matter of national security. Pete's ears got hoisted up the flagpole.

German spying focused on Washington DC, Baltimore and New York City. Germany also had a definite interest in utilizing Mexican motivation to gain back land lost in the Mexican American War. The idea of war and German spies were kept from the general public to keep concern to a minimum. The Zimmerman communique was the notable exception to ready the public for war.

Zimmermann, Germany's foreign minister, had sent instructions to the German ambassador in Washington DC to approach the Mexican government with what seemed an extraordinary arrangement: if Mexico was to join any war against America assisting Germany, it would be rewarded with the territories of Arizona, New Mexico, and Texas. This was shocking news to President Wilson. He wanted to know immediately about activity anywhere north of the border involving Mexico or Germany.

Until that moment the War brewing in Europe was far away from their ranch life. No more.

• • •

"I have an idea Marshal. Why don't I get a job inside the places you think might have more information about this war stuff? Maybe I could find out what's going on?"

"I'm not going to put a lovely untrained young lady in harm's way, fancy dress or not."

"You mean if I was a smelly old man you'd toss me right in there?"

"You've got such a delicate manner and know how to string the sweetest-sounding words. No, sorry, you'd need to be properly trained and that takes more time than we have now, unfortunately."

"Do you have the training of a spy?"

"I have some knowledge yes."

"Good, let's not waste any more time. I am your new spy student. You ask Essie. I am a good student."

A deep sigh sucked the oxygen from the porch. Most of it came from Essie. Señor's face said it all. The marshal and Pete were about to meet head on.

"It's more difficult than that. You may be forced to do things you would not normally do."

"So?"

"You could do that?"

"I wouldn't know until you told me what I don't normally do."

"Well yes, you have a point. What if you had to kiss some guy and ten minutes later stick a knife in him?"

"Yeh, that'd be tough until I got to the knife part. Let's face facts. I am going in to get a job, not kiss somebody. In fact I will go in tomorrow and try to charm a job just to see if I can do it. If you don't want me to find employment then don't watch. Things are kind of slow around here this time of year and you'd be doing Señor a favor to get me out of here before I decide to hurt one of his cowboys out of sheer boredom."

"And if you run into a German spy?"

"Things happen."

"Maybe a little preparation, a plan, a disguise even might be considered?"

"Are you going to dress me up?" And she gave another full loop showing off her dress.

"What do you suggest?"

"NO shoes."

• • •

"Can you see the need for a little planning? I'd send you to spy training but they don't take ladies as far as I know."

"You haven't noticed? I'm no lady even if I dress like one."

"Hemm, damned if I do, damned if I don't."

"Don't know what that means."

"Not important now. Ok, we'll see if you have what it takes. I'll give you a few preliminaries and see how you do. Have you ever killed someone?" He already knew about the younger Morales brother and wanted to hear the quality of her lie.

"None of your business." Which took care of watching her possible lie.

"OK, fair enough. Could you if you had to?"

"Sure. If it's them or me, better they learn a lesson. What do you mean 'what it takes'. Don't think you can be nasty and I'll quit."

"Push the thought from your mind Pete. Do I look like that kind of a guy?"

"Ok, we'll see what kind of a guy you are. But you have five days for your teachings then I'm looking for a job."

The marshal knew she would do just that. He'd try to give her some basics on keeping alive. During the process he might be able to talk her out of it. Not.

• • •

The next five days were purely delightful to someone who got bored easily. The marshal hadn't wiped the good morning smile off his face when he got hit with the first question from Pete now dressed in buckskins and moccasins. "You want me to hate you Marshal?" Essie and Ernesto were already walking to morning chores and had to give up the ringside seat. Señor didn't like blood sports.

"Maybe you've thought about it and want to give this spy game up?"

"You wish."

"Then handle it. You will find many things not to your liking."

"Such as?"

"Taking orders."

"Yeh, not to my liking. Is that all spies do is take orders?"

"That's the first thing they learn. Then comes the hard part."

"Ok, start giving me orders and if I don't stick a knife in your gizzard first, I may or may not do your orders."

The marshal picked up a piece of pine. "OK, see that white grub there about an inch long on this pine?"

"Yes, does this part tell you if I am blind?"

"No, it tells me if you are going to eat the grub."

"Get ready for the next part." She picked up the little white worm between her thumb and forefinger and dangled it over her open mouth. She lowered it slowly into her open mouth giving him a good view with no sleight of hand. And dropped it.

"Well don't suck on it, chew it."

She did.

• • •

Pete's Reflections

Next we did a lot of training stuff. We started running but he couldn't keep up so we stopped and did pushups. He showed me what to do and then I did it. Eventually the marshal found something I couldn't do as well as he could. One-armed pushups. I was struggling but getting the job done when he stuck his foot on my back to make me push up more weight. I turned fast then grabbed and twisted his foot with a quick snap. We both snickered over the big lug lying on the ground. And a skinny girl put him there. I saw he could take it as well as dish it out. From then on things went a little easier. Sometimes.

He insisted on some tiny little details and when I didn't see the importance, he'd yell till his neck veins popped out. I had to laugh when he got tense at me. That helped his neck veins some and made him a little nicer to be around.

Chapter 67 – The Natural

He had no authority to take a civilian and turn her into a spy. He didn't have the training either. However, Pete was going to find out what she could whether he gave her a few survival tips or not.

She was a natural, knew the northern part of the state, and spoke German, Spanish and English. She was the most physically active young lady he'd ever met and attractive in a strikingly different way which wouldn't hurt in the spy game either unless attempting to blend in a crowd. If he did this and anything went wrong it would likely cost him his job and what he had left of his sanity. But he continued because Pete continued. He saw it as the only way to help protect her.

"Close your eyes." Pete did.

"Now tell me what I am wearing exactly as to color, type of clothing, everything."

"You have a brown and white button down the front shirt. You have a white sleeveless undershirt. You have on worn blue pants with buttons on your fly. Your socks are dark brown and your underwear needs washing."

"If you were a few years older."

"You wouldn't like me as much and you know it."

"Am I armed?"

"Yes."

"How do you know?"

"I saw a bulge on your back and it smelled like gun oil."

"My God. What do you mean by it smelled?"

"Easy. Stuff enters my nose. It's been recently cleaned and I mean your gun, not my nose. Stinky stuff. I am better suited to stay alive in these parts than you are. And I want you to stay alive. Can I open my eyes now?"

"Sure, open them. I don't think you're ready just yet for this kind of work," stated in a drawled out slow manner hoping he could change the subject before her temper hit. "I'm glad you care about me though and want to see me alive. Are you getting a little sweet on me?"

"No silly, nothing like that. Why, are you?"

"Am I getting sweet on me?"

"You are devious Marshal. You're afraid to answer the question 'Are you sweet on me?'"

"I do admit you are fun and my life hasn't had much of that lately. But I don't go around wearing my heart on my sleeve after my wife Frida died. I just can't do it. I never knew what missing someone was." After a pause and a deep breath he continued in a rambling manner, "Especially with a lady young enough to be my daughter that put me on my backside."

"I am sorry about Frida and I understand. I would like to lift the cloud you carry. So if you change your mind, let me know. There is something about you that attracts me and it's not the droopy mustache. Anyway, I learned the hard way to pay it no heed as it goes away eventually."

"You little she-wolf. You are stuck on me. Do you know the penalty for lying to a US Marshal?"

"Marshal I see no reason to lie about my feelings. I might hide them a little though."

"Well who would have thought? I guess I should have when you were showing off in the fancy Mexican skirt."

They stood staring at each other. He touched her in a friendly way and she felt a zing in the pit of her stomach. She drew back. But not for long.

After that first reaction she wanted to try it again. She touched his hand and then his arm. She pulled him closer. Her hands not able to fully grasp his forearms. He didn't fight it. The slight pressure from her fingers was enough to move his 220 pounds toward her.

"Don't think this girly stuff is going to get me to change my mind about you doing field work. You could get us both in a lot of trouble including dead."

"Perish the thought."

"Then you see it my way and will let professionals handle this?"

"You can forget that thought as well. I'm the one better qualified and you know it. If I can get the information it might save lives not lose them." She squeezed a little harder on his arm and he bent lower. She kissed him. He couldn't resist any longer and kissed her back.

He took a deep breath knowing it would take more than oxygen to resist her charm. With a slow drawl and his eyes looking into hers, "Pete, in a different time and place, maybe. Unfortunately now we have serious matters to deal with. Your life may depend upon it."

"Yours too Marshal."

• • •

"I want you to guess what's going on. You're the one who's been close to this area and noticed things."

"My guess is someone is storing something heavy for later use. Like a squirrel stores cones. The Rancho might be the best place to put it all together if they could get control of the Rancho. Only guessing of course."

"What pieces fall into place with your guess?"

"People missing over the last couple of years. Pressure on Señor to sell his Rancho. Physically attempting to take over the Rancho by force."

"Who was involved?"

"The DA is likely, not doing the dirty work himself of course, but in the bushes."

"How so?"

"Because he was on the paperwork to gain control of the Rancho."

"Others?"

"Sure. Thugs for the muscle and those who gain if they fall into line. Pressure on the Church, Padre, things like that."

"Padre?"

"At first Padre fell into line and did what the DA wanted. Then Padre let Señor know about Sampson's army coming to push Señor off or kill him. Then Padre paid a price."

"I see. He might have access to information but not be part of the ranch takeover?"

Nod, and the conversation went silent while each digested the thoughts. Neither had issues with letting there be some quiet.

Pete continued. "The sheriff disappeared which was strange. Looked like the sheriff didn't do what the DA wanted either. Just one more pointing finger."

"What if you had to hide guns and ammunition and the Rancho wasn't available?"

"Probably hide it in the mountains. Hard to find up there if they know what they're doing."

"Where would that be?"

"There's old mines that might prove a good hiding place and protection. Easy to watch after."

"You know where these mines are?"

"All over the hills," She gave him a large sweep of her hand to the north and Divide Country.

"Yes, maybe so. What about men, military soldiers?"

"The enemies seem pretty comfortable so far. Maybe not coming in from the south or they come in a few at a time without carrying weapons."

"Right under our noses. May be why they are comfortable."

Chapter 68 – Looking for Work

It was Monday morning and Pete was ready to rumble through the front door of the mill. This was the first target business that may know something. The marshal didn't like it but she was going in anyway.

Señor, Essie and Ernesto, like the marshal, all knew it only pushed her harder in the wrong direction if they pushed her in any direction. They all did their best with puckered concerned looks. However threatening the marshal for not finding a way out of the life threatening situation for Pete was fair game.

• • •

It was still an hour before opening time. She hadn't been this animated since five bears. Pete was doing one armed pushups and brushing her teeth concurrently to waste a little time.

• • •

She lost the more articulate Pete and migrated back to few words and sheepherder Pete. "You got work?"

"What can you do?"

"Know trees."

"Most everyone here knows that. Anything else?"

"Good runner."

"I don't know. Do you know the territory well enough to send you out with messages and not get lost?"

"Easy. Don't get lost."

"Do you know any other language other than Spanish?"

"Some English."

"Anything else?"

"No" *Marshal said to keep my German secret.*

• • •

The manager at the mill asked Pete to check back in a week. It was a good opportunity for the marshal to leave and have her out of harm's way.

"Just watch."

Nod.

He was leaving but would check for messages every chance he got on his travels. "Do not, DO NOT do anything and tip our hand that we know anything. Ok?"

Nod

If she found something, she was to send him a telegram. He gave her a paper with his Western Union address and codes if she found something important. The stakeout would keep her busy and out of trouble. He hoped.

• • •

The next two months of winter were more like spring. The high country was short of snow for a change but not time yet to take sheep back up the hill. That would take at least another six weeks or the sheep would tear up the boggy soft fragile high pastures for several years to come.

During that time she kept an eye on the comings and goings around the mill and checked back at the mill twice for work. No work for her yet.

March she saw a rough-looking lady come with a wagon to the mill. She strained to load heavy boxes sealed with yellow tape. Pete followed the lady and saw she had a corral with more than thirty burros. She watched her load the panniers up with the boxes from the mill as well as other items. *Maybe I've found a new place to look for work.*

Chapter 69 – Abandoned Mine

Gretchen Braun was a ruddy-faced stocky muscular German in her early 40's packing burros up and down the mountain. Pete and Gretchen were miles apart generally as the range of mountains went further than eyes could see. However on a few occasions they crossed paths. They had yet to set eyes on each other but both would inspect the other's tracks as mountain people do.

It wouldn't have been easy to talk if they were the talking kind and paths had crossed since the burros were literally tied head to tail on the trail. If Gretchen didn't keep her burros moving they'd likely tangle and she'd have a circus and then a wreck on her hands.

She distinguished herself with her big heavy floppy hat and loose-fitting clothes making her appear even shorter than she was. Maybe it was because Gretchen was short she preferred burros or maybe because they were better at getting around tight places on narrow rocky trails near the mines.

She packed supplies up the mountain to little breakeven mines and took ore back down the mountain to a smelter for $20 per ton. She could get a ton on about fourteen of her burros by packing panniers on each side and a bag filled in the middle.

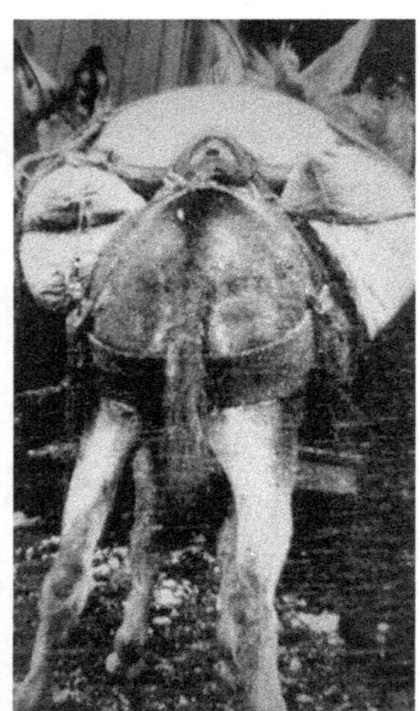

• • •

Pete got a job part time with Gretchen Braun as winter's hold loosened. Gretchen's business was picking up in the general area Pete knew well.

Pete knew the high pasture land better but was aware of the hard rock mining on close-by mountains. Grass didn't grow there but mountains made of granite and quartz veins did well keeping the miners' hopes alive.

Pete was a natural with the burros and had them happy with their daily chores. The panniers were filled with ore coming down the hill from active

mines. Ore to Pete was a fancy name for rocks. They were delivered to a smelter to extract copper and silver.

When Pete returned up the hill she took groceries and equipment destined to be dropped at various locations. Freight was normally delivered to active mines but this time to an abandoned mine. *Abandoned mine?* The heavy boxes with the yellow seal were heavier than if they were filled with rocks. The yellow seal or strap had to be cut to open them. If she cut the seal to learn the contents she had no way of returning it to its original condition.

Pete did what she was told. This trip she unloaded the freight outside an abandoned mine. The directions and rocky trail were not hard to follow. *Maybe the mine is going to reopen? Maybe?* After her delivery she left, secured her burros to avoid a circus, and doubled back to satisfy her curiosity. Within an hour someone was moving her boxes inside the mine. When done he shoveled dirt and rocks back to partially hide the mine entrance. Lastly the worker placed a stick sideways over the entrance. Maybe a sign to see if someone was nosey or a signal of some sort.

When done the mine worker left the area. Pete followed him. He had a small camp nearly a mile away where he could look down and keep an eye on the trail to the mine. She returned to the mine opening.

She went inside knowing there was only one exit. She had no torch or lantern. She used only the light streaming from the entrance. When it ran out she slowly felt in the darkness for vertical mine shafts or manmade treachery. Certain death

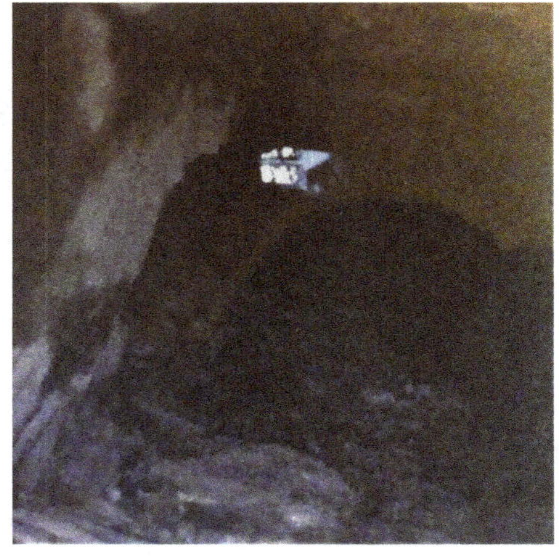

if they found her first.

After nearly seventy yards in she found a stash of hundreds of boxes. She turned and saw something moving across the entrance blocking the light momentarily. She froze. No other movements from outside the entrance.

She left the stacks of boxes and returned toward the light. She  took a deep breath as she approached her only way out. The large brown eyes of a doe greeted her as she peered over the pile of shoveled earth in front of the mine.

Pete thought if munitions were to be moved from the mines they could be more easily moved down the same trails she knew. It would be easier to keep it a secret if there were no longer sheep grazing in the area. If the Rancho had been controlled by the DA and he had the grazing permits to the north he could quietly move the munitions as needed. Things added up if the DA had been successful at taking the Rancho.

• • •

WESTERN UNION

MARSHAL MCCLEAN
UNITED STATES MARSHALS OFFICE
DEPARTMENT OF JUSTICE
WASHINGTON DC

BIRDS ARE FLYING NORTH STOP
PETE

WESTERN UNION OFFICE
AZTEC NEW MEXICO

• • •

It was getting close to lambing hence not much time to waste with the spy business. She checked every chance she got at the Western Union Office in Aztec as did Ernesto. No response.

It bothered her but she was told to only send one telegram to avoid suspicion. She'd follow orders but didn't like it. Two months went by, then three.

Chapter 70 - Weapons

There were only two inspectors outside the ports of entry on the entire Mexico US border. On occasion army patrols worked the borders due to civil unrest in Mexico from Pancho Villa and the likes. However with nearly 2000 miles of border there was little chance of encounters, let alone interdictions, without a great deal of luck.

The most likely way of locating organized smuggling would be from sign left by wagons and the stock needed to pull them. By the time that was found there would be little opportunity to chase down those responsible.

An additional insurance policy might be purchased by bribing the border inspectors should the need arise. There was no necessity.

• • •

An ingenious route was used once to move artillery deep into the US interior. The shipment was delivered to the Port of Galveston, Texas, in an African freighter by African hands. The Germans confiscated the weapons during the first part of the war to end all wars before the US entered in 1917. The daring plan came supported by forged paperwork prepared by the Germans for the shipping. The bureaucracy being what it was, the US Government ended up paying all the bills.

• • •

There were exactly fifty Italian mountain artillery Modello 13s weighing a little over 1000 pounds each and with a shooting range of about four miles. Most importantly they were durable and easily towed by horses or mules over rough terrain. There were a few rounds of dummy ammunition and other antiquated pieces likely thrown in the mix to make a show of training equipment.

Border inspectors were suspicious of weaponry since the Mexican American War. There had been border intrusions more recently from Poncho Villa. Columbus, New Mexico, was heavily damaged by the Villistas who burned several of the town's buildings. Sixty to eighty Villistas were killed along with over a dozen American troops and civilians. Glenn Springs and Boquillas,

Texas, also had problems.

However the Italian Modello 13s were being transported inland far from the border without ammunition or gunnery personnel to man them. Their final destination was a location in the mountains of Colorado at Silverton 500 miles above the southern border. At that distance they would have no value in a border skirmish.

They passed through customs without a hold for more information. The shipment was sent by train running from Galveston, Texas, on the G&RR (Galveston and Red River Railway) eventually through Chama, New Mexico, transferring to the D&RG (Denver and Rio Grande) narrow gauge line to Silverton, north of Durango, Colorado.

There was a Fort Lewis in Durango but it had been turned into a school for Native Americans and was no longer used as a training center for the US Army. It was not the final destination but it was in the general vicinity.

There were no supporting personnel to take their charge when the cannon were offloaded. No one understood all the workings of the US Government but the US Government did pay their bills. The station manager signed for the shipment to get things unloaded and off his rail cars.

There was no one present days later when the artillery left the yard. The depot manager at Silverton Station was happy to see it leave his yard.

• • •

The artillery was moved and stored many miles South and East of the depot. However it was a grueling journey. It was transported in a zigzag fashion through the Upper Vallecito River area down Chicago Basin then over rugged mountain terrain on switchbacks to be stored in an area inhabited by elk, bighorn sheep, deer and bear. It was somewhere in the vicinity of Table Mountain above Cave Basin, a local landmark easily identified by sliding debris down its sheer side. The artillery was well camouflaged within the dark spruce timber below the large open meadows above.

• • •

Those responsible for the smuggling had no chance of being apprehended even if the cargo was seized. The artillery was brought in by foreign vessels using forged papers. If someone caught the "error" there was no one to charge with a crime.

The African ship had no knowledge of the plan and thought they were transporting for the US Government. The daring plan had good reason for success. Everyone was looking for border raids and no one would consider the bold move as plausible. In the end, the weapons went merrily on their way.

• • •

Lighter weapons and additional munitions were carried over the border by Chinese and Mexicans wanting to enter the country. They were willing laborers as they were offered free assistance in entering the greatest country in the world. This time the US Government was not sent the bill.

The US government was looking the other way to keep the free flow of cheap needed labor regardless of what the general public thought of the idea. The plan thus far was working as the US Government was inadvertently allowing the shipments of arms.

Chapter 71 – Silverton

Marshal McClean was heading south to Las Cruces, New Mexico, when he stopped off at the Western Union office in Santa Fe. There he received two forwarded telegrams from his home office; one from Pete sent several weeks earlier with the code "birds are flying north", and another marked urgent.

WESTERN UNION

MARSHAL MCCLEAN
WESTERN UNION OFFICE
SANTA FE NEW MEXICO
URGENT

PROCEED TO SILVERTON COLORADO TRAIN STATION STOP MANAGER VOLKER HAS INFORMATION CONCERNING WEAPONS SHIPMENT STOP

UNITED STATES MARSHALS OFFICE
DEPARTMENT OF JUSTICE
WASHINGTON DC

• • •

The marshal like others felt it was a long shot that weapons would be cached far into northern New Mexico or Colorado. A supply line would need to be set up with a way of protecting it if those weapons were going to be used against the US Army. It definitely was pertinent to follow the lead so he turned around and headed back north.

Marshal McClean proceeded immediately to the Silverton, Colorado,

Station Manger's office to address the urgency of the telegram. His next stop would be see what Pete had found on his way back south.

• • •

"Mr. Volker, I'm Federal Marshal McClean." The marshal handed over his ID and continued in his slow deliberate manner. "I've received this Western Union. What have you got?"

"Marshal, I've been real curious about a shipment of military hardware delivered here last month. We put what we could down in the holding yard under lock and key and what we couldn't secure there was left beyond that area alongside the sidetrack. Within a week all went missing overnight. It was not our responsibility to put it into designated safe hands, but to hold it for pickup, which we did. In over thirty years I've never had a shipment like it and thought it should be brought to the attention of the US Government."

"Have you got the bill of lading?"

"I sure do. I knew that would be first on your list. And it also raised some eyebrows around here."

The Silverton Station Manager handed over everything he had on the artillery delivery. The marshal methodically looked at each line before going to the next. Then his questions started.

"Looks to me all was proper with a shipment of 52 artillery cannons. I see no mention of any other munitions for the cannons in the shipment. Correct?"

"Yes, that's right Marshal. A lot of heavy artillery with no means of causing any problems without the ammunition."

"And what you're questioning with this shipment is why was it to be delivered up here in the middle of mining country instead of to a military base?"

"Yes, along with why there was no one assigned for the pickup and the fact my lock was hammered in the middle of the night. Doesn't quite smell right."

"Mind if I take this paperwork?"

"No, not at all. I have a carbon if I ever have to refer to it. I'd appreciate it if you would get back to me on this as I'm not sure where the screw up might have come from and I'm curious. Ok?"

"Sure. Mind if I ask a couple more questions for my report?"

Volker gave a nod and the continued. "How long did it take you to report this?"

"About five days after they beat my lock off."

"Why five days?"

"I was happy those cannon were gone and I didn't have to do a week of paperwork, the necessary notifications, then a public auction maybe a year from now. But it kept eating on me. I wanted the government to know I wasn't happy about the way they got the cannon out of here."

The marshal gave a nod and a thanks. He'd get back as he learned things…
if indeed he did learn things.

• • •

The fact they were shipped to Silverton was likely an error and he'd leave
it alone if that was all he had itching his insides. The paperwork was not stan-
dard for the military but that might go along with the fact whoever did this
had no idea what they were doing. But add to that they left in the middle of
the night and it made him wonder like it did the station manager. The lock
being bludgeoned off gave him an uneasy feeling.

Each piece had a mule or horse in front pulling the load. The stock with
shoes were likely horses and the smaller hooves unshod were mules. That
brought to mind the organization it would take. Fifty cannons pulled by
stock over rough terrain did boggle the lawman's mind. It all didn't follow a
paperwork error.

He started paperwork attempting to discover some reasonable explanation
and locate possible ammunition in the vicinity for the artillery. Then he hired
a good saddle horse and mule to track the missing artillery. The tracks were
easily found and followed a distance from the station.

Chapter 72 - Neighbor

Pete was disappointed she had not heard anything back from the marshal about her telegram sent several months earlier. However she was home and loving it.

She was on the same plateau where she and Essie had first met Ernesto. Ernesto came up once a month to be sure she had everything she needed and get what he missed from the mountains.

Her needs were the same. Some gingerbread cookies and chocolate cake were always the first to be unpacked. Señor made sure his favorite piece of sky, a term of endearment in Spanish, had plenty of staples. Since Pete supplemented her diet with hunting and gathering, Ernesto had more than enough to stay a few days and leftovers to haul back down the mountain.

"Mind if I stay a few days Pete and eat some of these groceries?"

"Be my guest but it looks like you're getting plenty of feed at the ranch. Those dulces are a killer to your waistline."

She didn't mind him looking things over when he came up. Teasing was to be expected from those you liked. And it flowed as easy as creek water.

He would often tell her to take off for a few days as he could watch her sheep. She did enjoy the freedom and Ernesto was a master at keeping Pete happy. They had a lot in common without the normal human niceties getting in the way.

Within a week he was ready to go back down the hill again and she had the area to herself. The smell of a good man had left with him and it was replaced by a sky full of stars packed tightly, making it hard to find an empty place to ponder.

• • •

Metallic squeaking woke Pete around midnight about a week after Ernesto's last visit. She felt the thudding of mule hooves and horses a few miles distant. Loud clanking and wagon wheels were crunching ground cover and rocks.

These were two legged noises. She had no reason to believe they meant to do mischief. However it wouldn't be long before these people would know she and her herd were near. Her experience was they weren't to be trusted until proven otherwise.

• • •

The moon was nearly full and walking down the slope toward the noises was no challenge. Any insider could have done it as the bright moon on the clear evening was casting shadows. She would have preferred a little cloud cover or sliver of a moon to make herself less visible.

Her eyes absorbed the specs of light in the shadows. The sounds were picked up by her ears, hands and arms acting like antenna. The smells were unmistakable. Metal, wheel grease, draft mules and horses, tack, and man.

She took a seat silently in a shadow behind a downed spruce log making her body part of the tree trunk silhouette. She watched fully absorbed as the activity was curious. She could see a large hollow tube on wheels being unhitched from a mule and then hidden amongst the trees. It was meticulously camouflaged with a cover of netting, then branches with needles and aspen leaves.

It took four men after unhitching to navigate the obstacles and rough terrain for each piece of machinery. She sensed the weight by the two leggeds, their stock struggling, and heavy breathing at high altitude.

She sat for more than four hours until the activity stopped. The men left with the livestock and tack leaving the tubes on wheels. Only one man remained.

She left her hiding place with an uncomfortable feeling. She looked for what tied everything together. Beside two leggeds.

• • •

In the beginning Pete and her neighbor were inquisitive. Neighbor set small little twigs in patterns near and around the equipment and his camp. Pete easily saw the twigs at the unnatural angles and positions. If wind, rain, hail or any four leggeds came around it would cast blame on Pete. *Not very neighborly.*

Neighbor had the advantage of watching from the shadows. Pete persisted in doing the obvious. Neighbor had nothing to worry about now. However when it was time to move the equipment some things might have to change.

Peculiar images went by and caught her by surprise. Universe whispered a song in an ominous voice going down then swinging back up, "bù hǎo, bù hǎo". She had a shiver, but not from cold. At one time she would have grabbed as it past and known more. She let it go.

Pete had her sheep dogs and her own ways of telling if a two legged came a calling. The way the meadow grasses near her camp were bent was a good start but the lingering smell was more trusted. Her neighbor could readily see the sheep dogs. In the beginning he was kept at bay by them. She easily slept with confidence.

• • •

Two days passed with no intrusions on her camp or sheep. On the third day she could smell the breath of a human coming from above not below. Not heavy and only as the breeze shifted and sent a little her way. Most likely the one below had heard or become bored and took a stroll in her direction. She had done the same with him several times.

She got to know him by his smell and manners. He was shy and knew something about snooping. He covered his tracks well. But not his smell. The slightest wisp as the breezes changed direction gave him away. She too realized she was something different in the high country. *Look for what moves and what is out of place.* It was Mountain's first lesson.

The reserved relationship continued. Neither feared the other and both were inquisitive. Neither were the kind to need social contact. Both had a job to do. He could easily define hers.

During the second week he came nearer. Always when she and the dogs were making rounds with the sheep. He must know how many dogs she had or he came ready to silence any dog.

• • •

A large rock was on the windward side of her fire ring. Its purpose was to cut the normal breezes on her fire and some of her eating area.

After eleven days of having the neighbor she found him leaning against the large cooking area rock when she came in from her sheep.

His arms were folded. He was Chinese, dressed in baggy pants and a loose fitting blue silk jacket. It had ties instead of buttons down the front. A floppy short-brimmed hat partially covered his expression. His face had many lines and a wide smile was one of them. He brought a walking stick, kept at his side, and wore no shoes. Pete looked at his toes and then her own.

Pete turned her back on him and walked to the stick she was whittling which was to be a bow. It could be a match to his walking stick although a little shorter.

She sat and pulled her knife and whittled a little more while he watched. She never looked up but sensed his every move.

When he saw her knife come out he thought he knew the ending to this. He had watched for several days as she was well aware. He expected no guns would be used against him at least if he caught her by surprise. But he expected her knife might be in play. And it was.

The man pushed himself lightly away from the windshield rock. He was no longer leaning but was in a ready position about ten feet from where she was now sitting. Pete stayed relaxed but in Focused Attention continuing her whittling. Scrape. Scrape.

Neighbor took one soundless step in her direction and she sheathed her knife without ever looking up. As he started his second she was on her feet in ready position. She looked and took in every aspect of the man in front of her. He tilted his head sizing her demeanor as well. He didn't expect to have this type of confrontation from a sheepherder.

She sensed Neighbor's thoughts. Each gave her a small advantage. She had no thoughts. Nothing to get in the way between her stick and his skull.

His tendons showed many hours of tedious workout. His eyes showed the confidence of practice.

Each noted the knife at the other's side. Neither made them ready. No other weapons were apparent. None needed.

Pete waited. She measured every part of the man; his reach, his staff, his muscle tone, his eyes. Words and mind had no place here. The danger pulled her back from those years of books. But it didn't bring the old friend inside. Something was missing. Something had changed. *Let it go.*

Her neighbor was overly-confident or at least wanted her to think so. No problem accomplishing the task set before him.

Not a hint of fear in either, only a sharp awareness and a focus to better the other. This game had no second place. Pete was first to give a gravelly cackle. Her neighbor was the first to blink.

He tested her speed with a feint to the head with his staff. She showed only half what she had as she blocked his blow. He smiled. She returned it.

He came at her with the intent of sweeping her legs out from under her faking first another blow to her head. Her neighbor squeezed his stick a little too hard letting her know it was show time. He had telegraphed his move. Faster than the streaking peregrine it was over. Her stick jabbed his solar plexus causing a complete spasm to his diaphragm. His next breath would not come easily.

She struck the ground with her bare foot and flew by him while he was still doubled over. She gave him a quick slap midair this time to his head, putting him sprawling. He lost his staff before hitting the ground. She placed her foot on it and the end of her stick on his throat heaving for air.

She motioned him up by a rap to his chin. She pointed the direction he should leave with a flick of her eyes. The motion was not lost on Neighbor.

He made attempts at breathing to get his lungs in working order. He kipped up thrusting his stomach in the air and pulling his legs under him still trying to control his labored breathing.

He was a coordinated athlete to pull that move with his diaphragm still convulsing. He bowed politely from the waist. The politically correct thing would have been for her to do the same. His stick remained under her foot and her eyes ready for more. His stick was now hers as spoils of war. Didn't say much for her manners. Rules don't apply to this sheepherder.

Chapter 73 – Tin Lizzy

El Paso was a major spearhead used by smugglers. Judges, attorneys and federal judicial commissioners were some of the individuals lavishly entertained with gifts including residences complete with servants. Corruption of border officials was a distinct possibility.

But there were other ways to circumvent US Customs and Border Bureau of Immigration at border crossings. Chinese laborers or coolies would get off a couple of stops before entry away from any depot. They were organized to avoid what little border security there was and enter the country illegally. They would often trade labor for their passage by doing work for several weeks bringing contraband through the desolate border area with Mexico. There were often Mexican convicts willing to do the same work for the chance of freedom.

There were caches of arms on the Mexican side miles south of the border. The laborers would take heavy wooden boxes and walk them across the unprotected border sometimes as much as fifty miles and hide them again as directed.

In one instance Chinese laborers carried two hundred boxes of 1903 Springfield 30-06 bolt action rifles over the border. They spread out to avoid making well-worn paths. There were additional laborers returning the landscape to its original condition after the boxes of rifles had passed through. The Springfield rifle was not a likely choice for smugglers as it was in short supply for US military use. However someone in high places must have had better connections than the US Army to obtain the weapons.

Well inside the US border laborers were told to dig a large trench to hold the boxes of small arms they had carried. The trench was about one hundred yards in front of an old barn. From the upper hay loft there were two manned machine guns. When it was thought the trench was large enough to hold the laborers, the gunners opened fire. Secrets were better kept with fewer loose ends.

• • •

A 1909 grey Ford Model T touring car rolled over a rough stretch of dirt road on the US side of the border between Mexico and the United States. It was the same road used by border agents as well as US Army personnel to ensure the fighting between Mexican rebels and Mexican federal forces remained on the Mexican side of the border.

The Model T had dual wheels on the rear giving it more traction. It was spotless. Not a scratch or speck of dust on its shiny exterior. It was driven by a middle-aged hatless man. Eyes sweeping back and forth, head never moving, and then a subtle nod.

Immediately thereafter a loud screeching sound much like a hawk came from the bushes. It was answered from some distance away.

At least one hundred twelve inch wide rough sawn boards were quickly hauled from the bushes and placed across the road and through the arid land on either side. They were put together by dozens of laborers forming a wooden road.

Soon after, two-wheeled carts with mounted artillery were guided and pushed by workers over the boards. When the artillery got to the end of the boards those boards at the rear were brought forward and the process started again. Any tracks remaining were soon wiped away by laborers.

The following day the same 1909 grey Ford Model T returned. The driver never stopped or got out. The Tin Lizzy remained spotless. There were fifty new artillery pieces stored near Alamogordo, New Mexico, north of the El Paso border crossing.

Chapter 74 – Little Darlings

Pete could tell her neighbor watched from afar but never entered her camp over the next week. Odd little Neighbor.

Ernesto was due to come up to check on things. She was wondering what she should tell him. He being the mother hen would probably make her have Juan as a bodyguard. Maybe worse, he'd leave Juan and Essie both to ruin a perfect setting. Just no telling.

• • •

The next time Neighbor entered Pete's camp he brought a friend. Sampson. He had his wide grin hanging over his folded arms on his chest. The dogs were going crazy lunging and barking. He unfolded his arms and showed a pistol. He pointed it at the nearest dog and shot him dead through the head.

The others dogs whined and whirled in disarray. Pete barked an order only the pups would understand. The Mexican pointed the pistol at Pete's head and confidently said, "bang". Then pulled it down. Her neighbor also produced a gun in hand and both backed out of the camp should dogs attack.

All dogs stayed put as Pete had commanded. The two men angered her beyond what she had ever felt. They were willing to kill an innocent working dog to make a point. Pure evil.

She heard them chuckle as they left her area. Pete's path was clear. The dog had every right to attack but only barked. The dog had given the two leggeds the benefit of the doubt. The dog made a mistake in judging the evil of the two men. She would not make the same mistake.

• • •

Pete's first impulse was to skin the hide off the two while they were alive to feel it. She was cultivating anger. It would only get in the way. *Take a deep breath.*

Best to stay happy about the prospects. First to determine how many would be involved. If her neighbor had one friend, maybe he had more. Who leads and who follows. Always something to notice.

. . .

Winter wasn't ready yet but at the higher altitudes it wasn't unusual to have a few flakes on the ground until early sun warmed the earth. Often a skiff of snow made it difficult for either to spy on the other and not leave prints in the early morning.

It was cat and mouse. If they wanted to kill her, they could have done it when they shot the dog. She wasn't leaving her sheep and she would react as needed. Maybe her neighbors would find it to their advantage to leave her and her sheep alone. Maybe not.

. . .

She started her search. First the habitat. Scanning large areas to find what was needed to support the little darlings. It was a little cool on the upper plateau which meant she had to look to lower elevations and trust the dogs to do their work. Some of the best would be hiding and past their prime this time of year. But old and dry would work. Looking, tilting her head, and then moving on. From the bottom of her throat came a low rumbling cackle. Her helpers just appeared.

She gathered three of the mushrooms. Quite poisonous. She needed to take care to wash up after she was done. The spores could make her ill as well.

She crushed them between two smooth rocks. She let them dry in the sun for a day. Then ground them again.

. . .

She waited until they were out of their camp. Maybe they left to watch her with her herd. This wouldn't take long in any event.

She put a little of the mushroom powder in their corn meal, some in wheat flour. She eyed the rice and put a little there as well. These were not the normal insiders who gobbled and talked incessantly. They were observers or at least one was. She left and scrubbed her hands several times.

She could slip only a little in their grains. Too bad. They deserved more. She needed to be stingy to keep it well hidden.

She went back two days later to do some spying and see the results of her previous efforts. Maybe add a little more death to their food. She could smell them in the area. It was dangerous but she was far fleeter afoot then they. She'd had no doubts they didn't want her dead. At least thus far.

She approached cautiously. She could smell metal around their camp and the odor of men close at hand. It made it difficult to know where they were with scent in all directions. She went to the food boxes as she had done previously. That was a mistake. Something moved. Pete moved. Too late.

. . .

A heavy woven steel mesh came harshly down upon her. It crippled her ability to move. The weight had forced her to all fours. When she tried to get up and out from under the weighty wire netting they pounced with sticks and beat her from all sides until she was lying on the ground, unconscious.

• • •

Ernesto left for Pete's camp bringing Juan and supplies. Juan was doing quite well after his success in schooling and getting drugs hopefully behind him. Ernesto and Señor thought Juan may be able to take over checking on Pete and delivering supplies.

Ernesto arrived at Pete's camp and smelled no fresh fire or ashes. No Pete. The first thing to go through his mind was she was gaming him. Which she might do. But not after he called out to her.

Without her, sheep were on their own to graze at will. All signs added up to Pete being gone for maybe a week. He heard bells ahead. Still no Pete. Nowhere. Not good.

Ernesto saw nothing but empty space where he thought Pete might be. He went to the obvious places to observe sheep and no fresh Pete tracks.

Plenty of feed in patches and not evenly grazed as when Pete was there. Dogs were on duty and recognized Ernesto as friend. They came running with ribs showing. Small rodents were not easy to catch for sheepdogs trained and bred for other purposes. Ernesto tried his best to have the sheepdogs give him a clue. Nothing.

This was no Pete joke. She would sooner starve than leave the dogs to fend for themselves. Never. Ever.

Chapter 75 – The Compound

There were seventy-eight men working, both Chinese and Mexican. They were building barracks, storage facilities or were providing support such as food or medical assistance. No women were present but promises were being made. None of the workers were given any days off but were to be paid handsomely at the end of the job.

They had started a month earlier with one hundred men total. There were now eighty-one working the day shift. Two had been killed in accidents. Eight had become ill or injured and were in sickbay. Four were sleeping and would be put on nightly guard duty. Five had tried to leave without fulfilling their contract. Four of those had been caught before reaching civilization and killed. The one possible leak was assumed lost and eaten by bears.

There were five assigned to the kitchen. Two of those were designated hunters that would bring in elk, deer, bear, bighorn, snowshoe hare, ptarmigan, grouse and trout. They also brought in what they could of local plant life to supplement their diets plus dynamite, rice, potatoes, coffee, flour and cornmeal by mule. What they brought in from outside they took care to acquire from out of state to avoid suspicions from locals below.

The compound being constructed covered approximately seventy acres. Small diameter trees were used for log structures. The cabins had pitched roofs, the tallest with peaks of less than seven feet. Some were much shorter with fireplace and flume in one corner.

The perimeters of the cabins were rectangles generally about seven by ten feet. Some had frames for windows but no glass. Although the logs were hewn sunlight peeked through in summer cabins. Nothing was needed for their construction other than the tools to cut and fit the eight to ten inch diameter logs.

A skeleton crew was to remain for the winter and they would use the shorter structures with fireplaces, well chinked to help keep the heat where it would do the most good. They were engineered for housing men, storing supplies, food, weaponry, and avoiding the need for deliveries during winter months.

There were occasional dynamite explosions and excavation of the debris.

Below-ground storage was being built. The miners in the nearby mountains were making similar noises with their hard rock mining. The explosions and rumblings raised no eyebrows.

There was good water to be had year around. The small winter crew had enough stored firewood to melt snow and ice for their needs if their water froze. An abundance of game until late fall provided the needed protein and could be easily stored in nature's icebox.

There was no plan for the winter crew to leave the compound when the snow was deepest. Stock would be taken down the mountain in the fall with the summer work crew unless the work crew met with accidents on the way. Mules keep secrets.

• • •

Pete awoke in a small cabin with a dirt floor. Her vision was blurred and her body bruised. The cabin was built with hewn interlocking logs like others in the compound. This place was not made to house large humans.

The entry was about four feet in height and two feet in width. It had no windows or openings on the sides other than the entry that had no hinges or door. There was a small round opening in the roof in one corner. Beneath the hole in the roof was a bucket right side up.

A large bucket of water was in a corner on the opposite end to the entry with a cup attached to one side. In the center an empty bucket. Maybe her privy. Her knife had been taken from her scabbard but her scabbard remained with the small knife sharpener in an adjoining pocket. Not much use at this point. *No knife.*

The entry was blocked with logs poking in from the outside. They were somehow attached, lashed or interlocked. They didn't wiggle or give the impression they were about to.

She heard plenty of activity from outside all around her. She waited in full Focused Attention gathering whatever Universe had to offer. And she waited.

A guard was on duty by her cabin. She had never more than two minutes every few hours when her guard left or changed places with another. She heard on occasion someone getting on her roof or getting down. She was unable to connect to whatever he was doing there.

• • •

Pete slowly went around to each upper log on the sides of the cabin, pushing and pulling when she felt she was alone. She did the same with the entry logs blocking her exit. If she lifted the logs at the entry they would move, but only a small amount. She lifted again and then rotated the upper log at the entry and the log became unlocked and she could push it out. She pulled it back in.

• • •

She noted activities around her cabin with her ears and the slim horizontal cracks between logs. A short mestizo with sharp features under a floppy brimmed straw hat seemed to be in charge. He wore no sign of his position but his eyes traveled constantly. He'd move to communicate with someone, then return to his central post. Different men came and went from his presence wherever he was. He seemed to be directing more than one project and was obviously the Bossman.

Dynamiting was done and all activity stopped when someone hollered and then blew a loud whistle. Men scrambled behind cover and a few moments later a blast shot rocks and debris in all directions. The dynamite blasts were clearly opening holes in granite for whatever the reason.

She heard mules approaching and then being unloaded. She counted more than sixty workers from her vantage point. She had no idea how far she had been brought from Neighbor's camp. She would need to escape to reconnoiter her location.

She saw the afternoon sun disappearing through the narrow horizontal cracks in her cabin jail. A cooked bird was dropped down from the small roof hole into the bucket in the corner. A large cup of rice was dropped through a few moments later. The small bird was a ptarmigan, fire roasted.

Pete tore off a drumstick and took a large hunk in her mouth. Not bad. She waved at the bucket and held the cooked bird up to give thanks.

• • •

Pete kept an eye peeled through the horizontal cracks between logs in her little cabin cell. After nearly a week of confinement Pete realized something different was happening. She saw a German Shepard trotting over to Bossman. It looked like one of the German Shepherds often at the side of the DA.

Bossman opened a small pouch on the dog's collar and took something out. He unfolded paper and concentrated on it. He turned it over and wrote or drew something on the reverse side. He folded the paper again and placed it back into the dog collar's pouch. He pointed, gave a command, and sent the dog away.

Pete linked to an old friend and mentor. A scruffy grubby looking sheepdog with one ear up and the other down. She connected to a time long past. And smiled.

The German Shepard still in the campground turned in her direction. The dog stopped and stared at her. He looked away and put his nose in the air. Turning back he pulled his lips up marginally to give a slight smile, then left the compound.

• • •

That night she laid waiting for the camp to quiet down. She had a lesson when she was quite young that had always stuck with her. Don't get caught sneaking out if you know the rule is not to leave.

• • •

Nearly five hours after sundown the camp energy quieted. She heard her guard walk away as sometimes happened. The same person generally was gone to the count of one hundred.

It was time. She would take the risk of someone on the roof. Being with humans had dulled her from knowing more.

She moved the top log by lifting and rotating and pushing it out about two feet. The next few logs were pushed out in the same way. She slithered out on her belly as easily as a lizard through an open door.

Chapter 76 – The Note

The DA's guard dog left the compound in the Colorado mountains with a note from Bossman in his collar pouch. His journey would take him down the mountain and back to Aztec. Before reaching Aztec the shepherd veered off toward Señor's Rancho. The dog had never been to the Rancho but his direction was clear.

He reached the ranch house and scratched on the front door. Señor came out and was taken aback. He tilted his head with a questioning look on his face. *What is it stranger?* The dog knew what he knew and turned away, leaving Señor running fingers through his thinning gray hair.

The German Shepard went to the bunkhouse and with the door open walked in. He had his nose in the air and quickly left. From there he went to the small barn next to the bunkhouse. There he found Ernesto, lightly pawed his pant leg and turned as if to leave. But did not.

Ernesto had no doubts about this messenger. He tried to connect as he would with Raven or any other messenger in Universe. It was up to Ernesto to take what he got. The dog took the same responsibility for his part in the communication. He wouldn't leave.

Ernesto bent down and held the dog's muzzle between his palms. The well trained guard dog pulled his head up and turned toward the large barn door. Then whirled back toward Ernesto. *This is no accident my four legged friend, is it?* Ernesto paused and connected. The dog pulled his lips back in a smile as he had done with Pete.

Ernesto trudged outside and the German Shepard stayed one step ahead. When Ernesto stopped, the dog did likewise. Ernesto viewed to the right. The dog turned and stared straight into Ernesto's face. Ernesto viewed left and the dog's focus never wandered from Ernesto's eyes. Ernesto gazed down and the dog whirled and showed him the back of his head and neck. Again.

Sorry for my blindness and taking this long. Ernesto pulled the pouch opening apart and saw a white paper folded tightly. He opened it and found gibberish written and a map of sorts. *And now what do I do with this my new friend?*

• • •

Ernesto wasted no time finding Señor. He knocked on the Rancho door puffing from the trot over from the barn. Señor opened the door and saw the dog at Ernesto's side. Señor tilted his head and a thought dawned. The dog needed a translator and found Ernesto.

Ernesto grinned at Señor as confusion was chased from Señor's expression. He handed over the paper and waited for some word from Señor.

Señor took some time with the note before handing it back to Ernesto. "I am guessing this is German? This note was brought by this dog? A German Shepard?" he realized how crazy his words must sound. "Pete does strange things Ernesto but I don't believe Pete got this dog to write."

"No doubt Señor this dog did the delivery at the least. Pete having something to do with this also makes sense. He looks like one of the dogs normally by the DA's side along with those absurd bodyguards. I was hoping you might translate it or know someone who could?"

After a pause and a deep breath Señor spoke. "I have no idea about the German, if it is German, this dog, or why the DA would want us to have this note. See how the map shows a sharp cut on the edge of a flat mountain? It could be Table Mountain by its shape here in the left corner. Since Pete is missing and was last known to be in that area let's assume for a moment this has something to do with her. But from the DA?"

"No Señor, no chance. I can't see the DA doing anything to help anyone but himself." And now it was Ernesto's turn to pull in a full load of air knowing the consequences if this involved Pete. "But why German? Has Essie been teaching German?"

"Maybe it was not written by Pete but she directed this dog to come to us somehow. She is capable of that for sure. But why German Ernesto? After the marshal's visit it does at least bring to mind the German war machine."

"Yes. There is at least a connection. But either way Essie may be able to help with the German. I didn't think Essie knew German but maybe she does."

"Yes, let's go find the little genius."

• • •

The two men found Essie reading in her room. "Ola Essie. Can you decipher any of this note?"

Essie studied the two pages and then returned it. "Looks like German and a man's writing. Looks like a map of sorts on the second page. I see three words I can translate and since they are not together it does you no good."

"Do you think Pete has anything to do with it from those three words? Did you teach her German?"

"I did not teach her German, no. And the only known about Pete is nothing is impossible. But this is not a writing style I recognize. Therefore I would guess it is not her hand. The three words are 'building', the verb, 'men', and 'completed' or 'made ready'."

"Any idea who could help with this translation?"

"Padre knows several languages and I believe one he studied was German or Russian. Not sure."

"Want to take a ride with Ernesto and see if you can round up Padre? While you're in town please pick up mail."

"I am ready. Anything to take my mind off Pete."

"Essie do you think Pete has the same abilities she once had when she first arrived?"

"An interesting question Señor that I have worried a lot about recently. I can only hope she can unlearn what she has learned and return to the natural flow she had when we first met."

"To me Pete has changed from those first days. We relate and communicate better which is my main concern."

"If anyone is to blame Señor it would be me. I did everything I could to get at least one of her feet clean, in shoes and within society. We talked and read and made a place in her mind for intellectual endeavors. It only makes sense it could have squeezed out attributes such as her natural intuitions she would need to protect herself."

As Essie and Ernesto were leaving the Rancho the German Shepard bounded in the back of the wagon. Ernesto beamed at the dog's knowing.

• • •

Padre wouldn't be easy to find as he didn't have set duties anymore. He spent most of his time with the poor helping to make their lives better and talk of voting and politics.

First stop was the little church in Aztec. The two piled down from the wagon and the dog stayed put.

They hustled out of the church moments later with no idea of where to look next. The dog was out in front of the horse. Waiting.

Ernesto looked at Essie and Essie gave a Pete shrug. They leapt back in the wagon and trailed the dog going south out of town. Where the road took a fork to a little farm the dog took the fork to the right. They followed.

Padre was in a small field with his shirt off behind a plow horse. A young boy of not more than ten years was watching from the side. When Padre finished his row, he put the plow on its side, gave a rub on the horse's neck, and approached the wagon. Essie had the German note in her hand waving it like a flag. The dog soared in the wagon as if he knew the next move.

Padre stared at the note's first page and then reread the first page again. Then the second page, taking his time. He gave the note back to Essie and put his index finger in the air as a sign to give him one second. He ran back to the overturned plow and waved the young boy over.

Padre tilted the plow upright and put the reins over the lad's shoulders. A gentle slap on the horse's rump sent the two down the next row. Padre jumped in the wagon, took the reins and they were off. "No time to waste Ernesto. I'll explain on the way. "

• • •

"How did you get this German message Essie?"

"Ernesto took it off the collar of our dog friend here."

"Where did the dog get the message?"

And they told him the story. When they were done he said, "It might be best to return the note to the dog's collar and send him on his way. I'd like to follow the dog if that were possible to see where he delivers the message. But that takes time and may alert the wrong people. Since Pete may be in danger, I think we should make the priority to locate this place shown on the map."

Ernesto neatly folded the message and put it in the dog's collar like he had found it. Padre stopped the wagon and gave the order in German. The dog jumped down from the wagon and without looking back, continued on his mission.

Chapter 77 – Jail Breaks

Pete wiggled clear of the opening from her little cabin jail. She moved headlong and a slip noose attached to the end of a pole dropped over her head. It quickly tightened around her neck. She dove forward while attempting to get her fingers under the rapidly shrinking loop. She grabbed at the cord noose and it was too tight to get a finger under it. She felt woozy. Her world went black.

• • •

Pete awoke slowly. She realized in her unsteady state she was back in her little cabin jail. It was the same cabin. Fresh water had been added to the water bucket. Small human tracks wearing sandals had come and gone. The person would weigh about one hundred pounds. The tracks showed slow methodical movements.

She reached up to her neck and felt an abrasion from the noose. The remainder of her body had a few aches and pains from her beating under the steel mesh. *How long ago was that?* Nothing else new except a thick metal ankle bracelet attached to a hefty iron chain. She could lift it but her running would be slowed.

There was a time she would have easily known her plight long before the noose slipped over her head. *Whatever happened to my naturalness?*

• • •

Three sunsets later a cougar looked down from a rock perch above the mountain compound. Then towards the little cabin jail. The cougar radiated a soft ruby glow from its fur. It intensified as did the luminescent yellow-green eyes.

The cat leapt down from his overlook about a thousand yards away. He smoothly loped down the hill toward the camp. He cautiously meandered in and out of cover and rocky outcrops until downwind of the camp. Then looking right and left, sauntered up to Pete's cabin.

There was a Chinese man standing on the roof of Pete's cabin holding a long pole with a slip noose tied at the end. The glowing ruby lion stood silently behind him flicking his tail. The man turned sensing something. Startled, he leapt down, stumbled, and never looked back. Pete turned and removed the log and scurried out as before.

The cat had done its job. It was Pete's turn. And run she did. But not long and not fast carrying the heavy chain. A man came up behind her riding horseback holding a tube to his lips. A quick blow and a dart hit her in the back. Her world went black. Again.

Chapter 78 - Rat

Pete drifted back to consciousness a third time and had no idea how long she'd been out. She was more than six feet off the ground inside a steel net enclosure. Maybe the same material that came crashing down on her when they originally caught her in their camp "salting" their food. *Had it been days or weeks since then?*

The holes in the mesh were barely large enough to push three fingers through. Larger than her knife width. But she had no knife. She felt naked.

The mesh had been drawn together at the top with steel cable making a wire mesh sack around Pete. The cable was attached to a rope out of the reach of her knife if she did have one. The rope then was thrown over a tree limb to hoist her up in her cage. If she had her knife she would need to cut steel net or steel cable to free herself. Not likely. And no knife.

• • •

Pete was strung up within hearing distance of three men. They sat around a small fire looking over at her now amused. One was Neighbor, a second was Sampson. The third had his back to her. Sampson spoke first to Pete. Hola amiga. Que tal.

They had somehow found the mushroom powder and avoided its toxic effects. *More mistakes.*

The third spoke German quite well and was the leader. As he turned she saw who he was. It was the District Attorney who intervened with Ernesto and the sheriff the day Essie put the deputy on his back. Neighbor showed no difficulty in understanding any of the languages. He never spoke but would nod in understanding. *What was his part in all this? And German seems to be connected. Again.*

She had underestimated their awareness and cunning. Three times she had been caught in their traps. What had happened to her ability to connect to Universe and know these things? Mistakes must be paid. No recriminations now.

She recognized Neighbor's camp and her present location. Her hands were not tied but with no knife she saw little use. Her steel mesh cage pulled up tight around her like a sack holding a melon. It squeezed her arms and legs together affording only restricted movement. They didn't know she spoke German which may eventually help but for now, it wouldn't cut steel. *Stay light and positive, go with the flow.*

The District Attorney Wagner spoke only German as he gave orders to Neighbor. "We do not want her dead if we can help it. You let Sampson know where she cannot hear. Do you understand? If she causes problems and must be killed we want it to look natural, her body to be easily found, and far downstream. It will keep inquisitive eyes from looking for her up here."

Neighbor nodded his understanding. Pete nodded to herself from her cage above.

"We may want to move the artillery without notice and by next year they will have another herder. Maybe one of our own if we are lucky. She seems to have some special power and abilities. If we can get her back to Germany maybe we can learn more of them. Ja?"

Again Neighbor nodding acknowledgment.

"We need her weak to control her if we decide to smuggle her out of this country. Feed her only a little after the third day. Just enough to keep her alive. Give her water three times a day. And do not under any circumstances let her down to the ground for any reason. She relieves herself from up there. Is all this understood?" The neighbor wagged his head in strong agreement. And again the DA repeated, "Verstehen Sie, was ich meine?"

• • •

The first day she could do little, close to their prying eyes. She slept and waited for an opportunity. But at night when she heard sleep, she worked her hand up from her side to the top of her metal cage. She measured the steel cable with her fingers that held it together.

• • •

Sampson gave her water through a straw three times per day still dangling in her mesh cage. He could easily reach her mouth but Neighbor could not.

She was hungry which diverted her attention. She made food her intention not focusing on hunger.

When darkness took control and stars lit the sky her captors retired for the evening. She gave them credit for double checking her wire cage and going to their bedrolls sober. Worthy adversaries.

Bird-E landed in the aspen tree next to where she was strung up. The bird sensed her predicament. Bird-E flew off and quickly returned with an offering. A freshly killed kangaroo rat. Pete stuck two fingers through the mesh and waited, wiggling her digits in a twisting teasing fashion.

The bird flew close by and grabbed the mesh with an iron grip of its own. The little owl waited until she had a good grasp between her thumb and forefinger on the rodent's hind quarter and then released the prize into Pete's two fingers. Pete worked the little fury carcass through the mesh carefully.

These little owls were not known to her for their generosity. She accepted it as pity food and acknowledged her friend's hunting abilities. The little guy gave a wink, a nod, and was gone.

The rat was a blessing. It was far better than nothing and might save her life once she got it down. She would prefer a few berries to go with the small morsel of meat as they were sweet this time of year. More like raisons.

Next Bird-E brought berries as if Pete's thoughts were on the menu. "What a good friend Bird-E. You share and ask nothing in return. Things unfold as they should."

Essie would call it good manners. Bird-E brought something Pete would like even if the bird didn't eat such things.

She needed the glucose from the berries as enough water was being provided by Sampson. Little wild strawberries, currants and gooseberries were on the menu. Some remained on the stems. Some a little dry but quite sweet. Back and forth, time and time again the little owl brought her berries knowing they were a favorite. She was engaged. Her feathered friend had the will to know her need and bring it. A divide was being crossed. One she hadn't fully experienced for some time.

She worked the hide off her main course while eating a few berries. She chewed the sinewy muscle off the hind leg. *Not bad actually.* It helped to be hungry. She washed it down with a few more berries.

She thought the guts were likely the best and easiest to digest. They were next. Bird-E brought only one rat. *Maybe this bird shares what he doesn't' like. I will have to ask Essie about those manners. Good. Stay light.*

Full of fresh food she saw the connection of her sharpening stone and the steel net. The stone shaved her knife. The stone would wear thin the wire holding the net together. *Now is the doing.*

She got her hands down to where the stone was kept in her belt. Just a little at a time, inch by inch until the sharpening stone was in her grasp. She had only to stay alive and strong. *One berry and stroke of her sharpening stone at a time. The stream flows and the stone cuts.*

She filed each night on the wire cable holding the top of the mesh cage together using the edge of the sharpening stone. It took five nights to cut nearly through and weaken the metal cable.

Chapter 79 - Map

"Ok, give us the translation Padre." Essie vibrated the words out.

"It's a message from someone with a work crew. A storage depot is nearing completion. The map included shows the location North and East of Table Mountain. Then, the terrifying part. The sheepherder is giving them trouble and could they eliminate the problem. We now know where to look for Pete."

They pulled into the telegraph office in town and Padre ran in. A few minutes later he was back in the wagon.

• • •

WESTERN UNION

MARSHAL MCCLEAN
UNITED STATES MARSHALS OFFICE
DEPARTMENT OF JUSTICE
WASHINGTON DC

NOTE INTERCEPTED STOP STORAGE DEPOT AND PETE LOCATED STOP SEND BACKUP ASAP STOP CANNOT TRUST ANYONE HERE STOP CONTACT SEÑOR FOR MORE INFORMATION STOP

FATHER GREGGORY
WESTERN UNION OFFICE
AZTEC NEW MEXICO

• • •

They stopped back at the Rancho and dropped off Essie. Padre gave Señor the news. "I telegraphed the marshal Señor, and gave him the message. I have been giving the marshal information over the last year but nothing this definitive. I have no idea how long it will be before help is on the way. This is all sensitive information according to the marshal."

"Padre, you're a spy?" Essie blurted.

"Spy may not be the correct term but yes, I've been gathering information behind the scenes for the marshal."

"Keep talking Father."

"I was given information from a parishioner that weapons may be hidden in southern Colorado somewhere. Until now I hadn't put that fact together with Pete's disappearance. But we now know there is a secret compound above Pete's camp. It is quite likely those responsible for the weapons took her prisoner. On our way to the compound we'll also look around her camp for any sign of weapon or personnel to guard them, time permitting."

"Don't you need to wait for the marshal?"

"We can't wait with Pete missing. Let's go full speed ahead and sensitive and secretive be hanged. I'll get the word out as we leave town. If it's ok I'll have them contact you Señor to coordinate timing. I have no idea what we'll confront, meaning everyone needs to know the risks."

Ernesto was his deliberate self. "Can you tell us more Padre?"

"I'm sworn to secrecy not only by the marshal but by the seal of the confessional. I want to protect those who have trusted me and my vows. But for now I think we have a time problem. All points to Pete being held captive or was. It may already be too late."

Señor stepped forward and looked first at Ernesto, then into Padre's eyes. "I don't like the idea of having you two in harm's way before we can get a small army to help. But that will take maybe a few days to get them gathered. If you two can stay out of trouble and do the scouting, it could be useful and save time. I will have men up to the rim of Dollar Lake in five days, this Saturday. You can meet them there. Be clear if Pete is gone, you can't bring her back."

Padre and Ernesto stood motionless. "OK you two, I know God will watch over but He may not waste His time if you do foolhardy things."

• • •

Señor was long past the nagging feeling in his gut. The message left little doubt. He knew Pete would be back by now if possible. He also had no idea what trouble may be waiting up the mountain. There could be a few men or a whole army. They may be trained and well-armed or only a construction crew. Padre and Ernesto would likely know within three days after leaving. But with Pete at risk he knew they would err on the side of endangering themselves.

Señor also sent an emergency telegram to anyone at the Federal Marshals Office in Washington DC.

WESTERN UNION

UNITED STATES MARSHALS OFFICE
DEPARTMENT OF JUSTICE
WASHINGTON DC

PLEASE SEND HELP AS SOON AS POSSIBLE STOP MARSHAL MC-CLEAN HAS NOT RESPONDED YET STOP

SEÑOR PEREZ
WESTERN UNION OFFICE
AZTEC NEW MEXICO

Chapter 80 – Pain

Sampson rode into Neighbor's camp with an two extra saddle horses and pack mule. A body was draped over the horse. The corpse was cut free and dropped to the ground. Sampson rolled him over. It was Marshal McClean. His pockets were searched and his credentials were taken.

Pete saw his face and felt a tear dampening her cheek. Then down her insides. A few soft sounds of sad music came from the same place. *Grubby, you help find his wife Frida.* He was dragged off out of sight. Determination started filling the sad void.

• • •

Sampson continued giving her water. This day all movement had stopped. The cold nights and lack of food may have made his daily chore of giving her water no longer necessary.

Maybe he'd get in trouble from the DA. He was to keep her alive unless she escaped and death was the only alternative. She was to be used in a German study to help in the war effort.

He could put her down the mountain without a scratch on her. He couldn't see the need to keep her alive as he was ordered. *What is there to study?*

He loosened the rope holding the cable and her cage and lowered her down. There was no movement whatsoever. He leaned closer to see or hear breathing. Nothing. He stuck his finger through the steel wire mesh to see if there was any life and poked her in the eye. She flinched.

He jumped back startled as if struck by a rattler. He was well out of her reach if she did try anything. He hauled her back up the tree in her swinging cage and thought himself lucky. This one had too many ways of breathing life into herself while sucking it from those around her. Maybe there was reason to find the source of her power.

Chapter 81 – Last Journey

Word was sent from the DA by a four legged courier. Pete had become too big a liability. Too many people were looking for her. She was clever and may escape. Her usefulness to the German war effort was not enough to take the risks.

• • •

This day the Neighbor came instead of Sampson. He looked up at her in her cage. He hitched a mule to a wagon. He drove the wagon under her and undid the rope and cable system keeping her aloft. He lowered her gently into the wagon. Sampson cautiously gazed from a distance around the morning campfire.

Neighbor tied her wire cage down in the wagon. When well secured he waved Sampson over. Sampson got up in the wagon, took the reins, and released the brake. The wagon rolled slowly away from camp.

• • •

The location of her release was by design. It was to be about a quarter mile above some older occupied cabins a long distance downstream. Someone would surely find her or some of her. That would put further searching in the territory upriver unnecessary.

The two traveled silently for most of the day. When she saw the river coming into view as the evening approached she knew this was her last chance. She had already overheard what was to happen if they didn't take her to Germany. This must be the spot in the river where it was to happen.

There was only Sampson without the others to back him up. Too many hands and eyes around their camp for her to make a safe break. The odds were looking better, one against one.

He was larger, at least in body. He still had the advantage of Pete's confinement within the heavy steel mesh.

Hers was one of surprise. And the obvious. Like all things wild, the wild is only a short breath away.

She did have a lot of experience of cold bathing in her youth. The frigid Vallecito River would affect her little. The big plus brought a smile to her lips; she would finally have plenty of water to drink.

• • •

Sampson went straight to the task at hand. He tied the end of the steel mesh cage to the wagon with good solid rope. He backed the wagon into the river with a few gentle jerks on the reigns. This could have been the end of the plan if the mule balked at the maneuver but he didn't. The mule continued backing the wagon until nearly half way across.

There was a long board in the wagon. Sampson wedged it under her cage and pried on it until it moved. With a large grunt he shoved her wire casket out the back.

Her cage easily weighted her down and rolled out of sight. It didn't travel far or fast rubbing across the bottom, stopping now and then against a heavy boulder only to find a way around the impediment to continue the journey down river. It soon reached the end of the rope still attached to the wagon.

He knew it might take some time to be sure Pete was no longer a threat. He sat back down in the wagon and rolled himself a cigarette. The weighty cage had gotten to the end of its tether and tried to go further.

Pete's executioner sat in the wagon smoking his cigarette. As the tension increased from Pete's cage in the current, the wagon slowly slid sideways and followed the rope downstream. The mule was forced to go backwards and follow the same path.

When the mule had had enough the animal tried to reverse the progress of the wagon in the current. It was a stout mule and could hold its own under normal circumstances. But not this day. The mule's footing on the slippery rocks on the bottom of the river was giving him the untenable feeling he might no longer be in control of the wagon with the river current acting on the steel mesh and on the wagon itself.

When the feeling reached the point of fear the draft animal reared with bowed neck and back and bolted toward safer dry ground. The wagon was torn in two pieces.

The wagon bed and rear wheels followed the wire mesh down the river. The remainder of the wagon, the tongue and front axle, was heading toward shore hitched to the mule. Sampson was dumped in the Vallecito River and had enough trouble keeping his head above the frigid water to worry about mule, wagon or Pete.

The mule pulling the front wheels reached shore and turned to watch the circus he'd left behind. What little of the wagon remained was quickly drifting out of sight down river.

• • •

Sampson dragged his soaked hulking frame to dry land cussing the mule every step. He grabbed the mule's halter and they both gazed downriver into the evening's dwindling light. No sign of the wire cage, Pete or wagon bed.

• • •

It was past dark and Sampson wasn't dry and warm enough to think straight. His orders were to drown Pete. Then release her to float downstream unencumbered in the mesh cage close to a summer cabin. When she was found it would be a simple drowning and nowhere near the hidden artillery.

As near as he could tell, he'd released her. The fact she was in her cage was not good. It was to look natural. He would have to go down stream and find her, pull her out, and set her free or on the river bank for others to find. Either way, it was her last journey in these mountains.

• • •

It was daylight the following morning when Sampson walked as best he could downstream keeping an eye along both edges of the river. It didn't take long to discover rope and wagon bed caught between a river boulder and a log not far from the river bank. As he approached he breathed a sigh of relief and worked his way into the river to haul it out. He was once again wet and cold but at least happy he'd was at the end of this unpleasant set of circumstances. He had to release Pete and then ride back up the mountain bareback on a mule. Hopefully a two hundred seventy pound rider wouldn't upset the draft mule.

• • •

He found the steel wire mesh at the end of the rope. To Sampson's surprise she had been torn free somewhere. Her last journey was underway.

Chapter 82 – Let Go and Let God

Padre rode a horse provided by the church out of Aztec heading toward the mountains. He led a pack mule and an extra saddle horse. He had close to 85 miles to travel and thought the extra horse insurance. Either his horse or Ernesto's may pull up lame. It may be useful to get Pete out if she was injured. He washed the thought from his mind but brought the extra horse nonetheless.

He was dressed like mountain people without the white collar. Ernesto was with him in the beginning but not for long. He was soon left behind by Padre's faster horse and athletic stamina. Ernesto's horse had the same size heart as the man who rode him. Neither knew how to quit.

The first evening Padre had the pack off his mule and a temporary camp set before Ernesto smelled the smoke from his fire. Few words were spoken as they downed their supper and retired early.

• • •

The following day they were both off before rays of light peered over the mountains. Breakfast was bread and jerky washed down with canteen water. Padre was soon a couple of miles ahead of Ernesto having switched mounts for the second day.

Padre pushed the stock but knew the limitations. Keeping close to Ernesto would also prove valuable with his knowledge of the area.

He was ready for what lay ahead but he must now let go and let God. He realized more than ever the strong feelings he had for Pete were not helping. He eased back and took a deep breath.

• • •

On the second evening Padre reached the summer pastures Pete knew well. The sheep had been driven down the mountain leaving the meadows an eerie quiet. But it was more than that. *Is Pete trying to tell me something? Is it here I should look for Pete?*

Padre's parishioner informant told him about artillery hidden in the forest with a security guard. After seeing the German map he connected the weapons to Pete's disappearance. With the compound being a few miles to the north it made sense they might have taken her prisoner if she got too close.

With the eerie feeling and empty pastures he heard voices again. Similar to the voices he heard at the exorcism. He couldn't make out any meaning but it was the same choir.

According to the German note Pete was more likely in the compound but the information now was several days old. He would look here while waiting for Ernesto.

He went off the west side of the plateau meadow toward the upper Vallecito River far below. Easy in the beginning but now the deadfall and trees were making it more difficult for the stock.

He loosely tied his horses and pack mule knowing he might not return. He wanted to give them a chance of survival if events went wrong.

He saw the sheer bare walls of Table Mountain distinguishing it from others in the distance. He stayed as quiet as he could but needed to scout the area for hidden artillery before daylight was lost. He guessed there was at least another hour of twilight and it gave Ernesto an opportunity to catch up.

He was closing in and could feel it. He saw more signs of humans. He felt certain a watchman wouldn't take kindly to his visit if this were the place. And maybe Pete would be here.

He moved ahead slowly. He found where stock and wagons had used a bench running north and south. He went north.

He came to a campsite with plenty of gear and signs of more than one human. No Pete. The fire had been recently doused as it was warm and wet.

Padre did a quick reconnoiter to get information that might help and hightailed it out of the area knowing he had already pushed his luck. He met Ernesto back up the trail still making his way down. Not a happy meeting.

No artillery. No Pete. Not yet.

• • •

Neighbor had plenty of notice of Padre's arrival signaled by the noise of stock hooves echoing from above. When Padre left, Neighbor followed him. Neighbor overheard part of the conversation between the two men.

There was no doubt what their visit was about. What they were looking for had been taken down the mountain that morning by Sampson. Maybe that would be the end of it. But there was the question in Neighbor's mind of how they knew about his camp and the sheepherder. And did they know about the compound being built further up the mountain?

Chapter 83 - Prisoners

The location of the military compound was such, it needed little protection from the outside world. There had been no minerals found that far up, hunters did not need to go that far to find excellent game, and pasture was poor.

The following morning after locating Neighbor's camp, Padre and Ernesto approached the compound area shown on the map. They approached slowly seeing more sign of humans. Since a dog had been used for messaging there may be more canines used to secure the site as well.

Neighbor had followed the two. They knew exactly where they were going. He learned what was needed and it was time to get them out of the way.

With the worry of Pete weighing on their shoulders they made plenty of mistakes and were quickly taken prisoners. They were stuffed in the same little jail that had once been used for Pete.

• • •

"Padre what did we do to deserve all this attention? I didn't think anyone would touch a priest and here you are next to me."

"Quiet in there or I'll pistol whip you and gag whatever's left of your face."

In a whisper, "Priests are supposed to stay neutral but in this case I didn't feel the people in my parish were safe."

"How so?"

"If the US enters the war in Europe, Germany wants Mexico to attack the US. The DA believes he would be in a good position to gain power if he were instrumental in a successful attack on the US."

"What's the DA's plan?"

"They've hidden armament to help Mexico invade this country by squeezing from both the north and the south on the old Territory boundaries."

The logs came tumbling out and their guard gave Ernesto a swat in the head with his gun. Then gagged them both.

Chapter 84 – Have Brothel Will Travel

The Madam, three of her best girls, and their hired muscle and driver were heading up the mountain an hour before the sun was ready to do the same. She felt fortunate to be this far along.

The ladies wore loose-fitting men's clothes with their more revealing apparel in the back. They'd gone all night taking their chances the big moon would be enough. There were several places where they had to double back to find a better route. Tied to the back of her wagon were saddle horses if needed in the rough terrain.

The best information Madam could get from a talkative client was Pete may be held up the mountain. She pulled the information from a man who had worked in a mysterious compound construction crew. The complex was some distance above but on the same mountain Señor's sheep had grazed for years. She was given rough directions and her driver thought he could find the way.

The Madam had no real expectations other than the ever present dangers, excitement and likelihood of servicing whatever workers might still be up the hill. A few gold coins might make it worth their while if Pete wasn't in the neighborhood.

• • •

Four ladies came riding horseback into the compound as if they owned the place. Not a single man questioned their arrival and most tipped their hats at the surprise.

A six-foot-five nice-looking young man in a red and black checkered wool cap gave a wave and the four ladies went in his direction. Madam started things off.

"Hi sweetheart. Can you tell us who runs this show?"

"Sure, the guy over there with the floppy straw hat is the boss."

"Could you do us a favor?"

"You betcha"

"Do you think you could keep the boss busy while we throw a little party around here?"

"Am I included in your party?"

"Actually honey you're the guest of honor."

"What have I got to do to earn your favor?"

"You take these toys over there and let the boss play with them. A little rope, some handcuffs, and maybe a rag to stuff in his mouth."

"But he's the boss and..."

"A lady likes to think she's the one and only boss and wouldn't you like to have Darlene here be your boss?"

"Yes ma'am I sure would. Do you want me to start keeping the boss busy right now?"

"The sooner you get started with him the sooner your party will start with Darlene. And we'll make it a freebee cause you are way beyond cute." The conversation came to abrupt conclusion. Soon after it ended Bossman was well occupied with Madam's toys securing him to a tree.

The young man put Darlene on his shoulders and carried her out of the compound. She waved to a few of the on-looking workman with powdered and perfumed bloomers on each side of his head like blinders on a milk wagon horse. Darlene's dress was piled near the edge of the compound and a line of well-mannered workers was forming behind it.

• • •

Men jumped at every little detail that might keep the Madam happy and her girls in the camp. It didn't take long and one of her new clients showed her to a cabin with logs blocking the doorway. The Madam pointed at the logs and they parted easier than the Red Sea had for Moses.

Madame had a dress and some scarves in a large purse. Not a perfect fit for Pete but could be used to sneak her out.

Madam swung her swing in a most provocative manner as she came around the corner and looked into the miniature entrance of the cabin. She bent down on all fours, put her purse through the doorway, and peered in. She let her eyes adjust to the darkened interior. She hoped upon hoping to see Pete. She continued to wag her rear for whatever entertainment value it might have for those outside.

She found Padre and Ernesto gagged. In a low breathy exaggerated tone, "Hello Padre. Oh, would you look at this. My Ex..eh, client and favorite dulce, Ernesto, now wishing he didn't know me. Hello Honey. I thought I might find Pete here but a girl's got to take what she can get." Muffled replies emanated through their gagged mouths.

"You don't say. I know we haven't always seen eye to eye in the past Padre but maybe it's time we bury the Bible and talk about your Exodus?" After heaving her ample breasts and giving an inflated sigh, "And you Ernesto were all cuddly until you found a lovely mate. Now you act as if we've never met. If I wasn't well adjusted, you may have hurt my feelings. What is the matter with you guys anyway? You have normal needs and you try to hide them or get all embarrassed?"

Having to remain on all fours she entered the low doorway as best she could with her fancy dress by her hips. They couldn't help but notice her bosoms being acted upon by the forces of gravity.

The Madam turned while still on all fours and had seven men gawking at her backside pointing their way through the doorway. "You boys go play somewhere else." They did not want to aggravate the Madam. They quickly did an about face and found other things to occupy themselves for the time being.

"You've got to fix those speech impediments boys. If there's ever anything my girls can do to help either of you, I hope you won't be bashful?" She had ample chest and wanted to get a little off while she had them compromised. "Look you two, I've made my choices. I'm ok with them. Some ladies get dinner for jumpin into bed with their date. I get money. I don't see either as wrong. I'm ok with the barter system but cash suits me better."

Padre wagged his head up and down making pleading noises. Ernesto hung his head knowing the punishment was well deserved.

"Any sign of Pete?"

Both shook their heads 'no' in unison.

"Damn, I was hoping to get Pete out of here. Instead I get stuck with you misfits. OK, then let's see about you two while I'm here."

The two men looked a little sheepish. "Ernesto, no need for shame. I fulfill a social need and those needs aren't always lifelong. Oh Padre, you've decided you need my services? They've only given me ten minutes and all new clients deserve more time. How would you like to hide a Bible in here?" Madam bent a little lower, showed Padre a cleavage that could easily hide a few hymnals, then looked him directly in the eyes. "Or maybe you prefer a different gender?"

"Let me loosen this a little and slip it down Padre." The Madam untied the gag and dropped it in his lap. Padre had his turn with the sagging head. "Yum, I can say no to everything but temptations, Padre. You are a handsome devil. Maybe under the circumstances 'devil' isn't politically correct." Madam was beaming with pure delight. "As I am sure you both would agree, we should all forgive and never forget these good times."

"Thank you," they both said in unison loosening their jawbones after the restrictions of a tight gag.

"Maybe we should figure a way to get you out of here because time is ticking. Save the fun for later?"

"You've gotten in here somehow," Padre suggested. Ernesto was still silent thinking it may be better to stay captive than being saved and return with the Madam.

"Well clearly I am here, yes. You do realize I rub elbows and maybe a few other body parts with people that get a little squeamish about killing a priest. However Padre you have created enemies in high places so it may only be a matter of time."

Turning to Ernesto and leaning in close. "Now you Ernesto are in an entirely different category. You are cute in a back woodsy way and I'll do what I can to see you safely out of here and back into Essie's arms." She gave him a little pat on the thigh.

"Any ideas?" questioned the two with a degree of harmony.

"If you could fill out my dress Padre ... we might pull it off," she giggled like a little girl at the quip.

"I'll try anything you want," returned Padre.

"Please Padre, some other time. Let's change clothes and you tie me up. I doubt you've had experience with bondage but give it your best shot."

Padre was nowhere near getting half of her witticisms. They both stripped their outer clothing and she said in her suggestive voice, "So tie me up, big boy."

"Don't you want to cover up with my clothes? And what about Ernesto?"

"I don't have your sense of shame Padre. Half the men in this town have seen my naked ass and the other half are outside waiting. And you're supposed to be in too much hurry to tidy me up. Can you imagine Aztec picturing you dressing me in your clothes? I ask for two things Father and we'll consider this a freebee. Don't make the knots too tight and second, when you leave here, show me your sexiest feminine walk. As for Ernesto, throw your arm around him and pretend he's your best gal pal."

Ernesto could see she wasn't kidding and hated to look this gift horse in the mouth. He therefore accepted the inevitable for the opportunity to literally sashay out of the mess he was in. Madam had to restrain a catcall watching their performance.

Padre made a ridiculous Madam. He swung the large purse over his shoulder that held the ladies clothes now on Ernesto. The scarf and shawl did a great job of hiding Ernesto's lack of feminine charm. With luck, the workers would be more interested in what other feminine treats were walking the compound than to pay much attention to the tall lady and her portly balding companion.

There was nothing that could prepare the Madam for Padre's stroll. He easily frolicked past the sentry with Ernesto under his arm, hiding in the Madam's dress as best he could.

• • •

At the far end was sharp-featured Bossman sitting under a tree. He remained tied to it with a frown on his face and rag in his mouth. He was being watched over by a young man wearing a red and black checkered wool cap, brim pulled sideways and a wide grin to match.

Madam was already planning how to make her entrance back in town. Oh how she would like to keep those two men in ladies' clothes as she waved to the crowds. What a parade that would make. But for now, she better focus on trading her way out of the compound and down the mountain. *All in a day's work.*

Chapter 85 – Holding Her Breath

Pete holding her breath tumbled and bumped along the bottom of the river trapped within the steel mesh. Her lungs were starting to burn. She would not breathe in the deadly water as long as she had consciousness. There was a sudden jerk on her cage as it came to the end of the rope attached to the wagon and mule. She lost precious air with the jolt.

She started moving again and a second jarring came when her cage struck a boulder. The weakened cable gave way and she felt the mesh grow larger and move away from her. The work on the steel cable with her knife sharpener finally did the trick with a little help from her friends, River and Rock. She was free of her confinement.

She rolled on her back with just her mouth and nose above water. Nothing would ever compare with the first breath of sweet fresh air entering her lungs. Her body brushed against several structures and the river current easily pusher her around them.

In the dwindling light and with Sampson occupied, she was free and no one was the wiser. It gave her the advantage of time and surprise if she saw fit to use either.

• • •

Pete had been interested in traps from a young age when Selina had showed her the first one. This time the lure would be her.

Neighbor knew she was to be held captive or killed. Sampson knew she had better not show up alive after it was his job to dispose of her corpse. All she had to do was dangle the bait.

The DA would be the most difficult to eliminate. She couldn't get within a hundred feet of the DA and penetrate the dervish bodyguards, particularly if she were the bait.

Chapter 86 – The New Girls

Madam's wagon and her girls were clear of the compound. Madam hadn't arrived yet. However she was in sight, on horseback, and catching up rapidly. Their driver had taken a horse and left earlier at Madam's request. She felt she could handle the working crew easier without chaperoning.

• • •

They were cheerfully riding down the mountain with a noticeable quiet coming from the new girls, Ernesto and Padre. They remained dressed in their ridiculous lady's clothes. The disappointment of not finding Pete was partly expunged by being a little giddy due to lack of sleep and the rescue of the misfit males.

The echo of giggling about the events of the day were merrily bouncing off the high country mountains. Madam chirped, "Days like this are worth more than money. Oh, guys, sorry. I couldn't reasonably explain why I needed your pants so I had to leave them back there. Is anyone for a homecoming parade back in Aztec?"

• • •

On the way down the mountain they met several cowboys sent from the Rancho. There was no use Padre and Ernesto hiding from the truth the way they were dressed. They made the best of it as they all set camp for the evening.

The conversation quickly turned to Pete and her whereabouts. The hands from the Rancho were disappointed Pete was not found. The information was shared the Federal Marshals were not coming anytime soon. The reality of the situation was there was no reason to confront those building the compound. If no Pete, why shoot the place up.

• • •

The following day Madam and her girls passed the word to others coming up from town. It always ended the same way. "Turn around and let the lawmen do their job. No sign of Pete." Ernesto and Padre were getting used to the ribbing.

"Oh, who's the new girls in the back Madam?"

. . .

Pete's Reflections

I showed Neighbor and Sampson my trail. They were surprised their job wasn't done. The path was easy to follow but not easy to find their way back. Simple as picking wild strawberries. They were lost and found a good place to camp for the night. Under a Shush Tree. They gathered wood for their fire. They liked the sweet smelling bark and the smoke from their fire drove them senseless. They laughed at their misdeeds. They were rewarded.

Flying insects, magpies and crows came a calling. Raven took the eyes. The others made their marks under the Shush Tree. Stinging lips and faces. Fate for needlessly killing an innocent dog plus a good man and my friend, Marshal McClean. And the Black Wolf followed.

Chapter 87 – Lobo Negro

Pete didn't know the word pheromones, nor did the Ancients. But they knew the effect.

Chemical pheromones emitted by some plants can be used in communicating reproduction or needed protection. A mechanism used to call helpers to do their part in a symbiotic relationship with the plant.

Bees, crows, magpies, wasps, hornets and Lobo Negro all did their part to protect the tree. A dizzying disorienting chemical for those disrespecting or harming the tree attracted those defending the tree. The substance was especially potent with the burning of the dried bark sometimes used in the Ancients' pipes and ceremonies. A balance was maintained.

• • •

The Walk of the Wolf was not uncommon. Those that disrespected the natural order of Universe were doggedly followed by a lone black wolf and his penetrating unnerving eyes. Lobo Negro would not attack unless asked, but would never be more than a few steps behind. Waiting.

His prey would eventually oblige with the needed request when their suffering could no longer be tolerated. After being asked, a ruby glow would flow from the black wolf's coat signifying the end was near.

Sampson and Neighbor gave thanks when the black reaper accommodated. The natural order was returned. And then there was one.

Chapter 88 – Lady in Red

The DA never gave up on his dream of owning Señor's Rancho and being El Patròn. It was too late now to make it part of the war effort but his desire for the place would not end with that defeat.

• • •

A woman in red walked in the Court House. This woman by her manner attracted a lot of attention from men. She walked like Madam and had an air like Madam. She wore makeup like Madam. She had long dark hair put up fancy with curls dangling down as did Madam. But anyone with one eye could see it was not the Madam.

The lady walked the hall inside the courthouse. <u>Court Room</u> was stenciled on the first door. She walked a little further. <u>District Attorney</u> was on the next door. She turned to the door behind her and saw <u>Recorder</u> written on the door. The lady knocked and entered.

The county recorder greeted her officiously. "Good morning. How may I help you?"

The lady replied in a similar fashion. "I want to know your procedures for recording a legal document?"

"You bring the document in and pay a fee of 3 cents per page. You also bring identification. I write the description of the document, your name and date in the Recorder's Book making it a public record with legal status. What kind of document is it? A marriage certificate?"

"No, my no. No, it establishes my ownership of all water on the Perez ranch and all the land it runs over." This information surprised the recorder. He swallowed moving his gulper in his throat up and down.

"I don't believe we know each other. Are you a relation to Señor Perez?"

"No, I'm an attorney and a relation to Pete. Are you acquainted with Pete?"

"Oh yes, most people in these parts know Pete." After a short pause. "Did Señor Perez somehow split off the water from the Rancho? And the land the water runs over is a new one on me. When irrigating that would mean a lot of land. Not sure how that could be done right off and it might make the rancho nearly worthless, if it could be done." The recorder couldn't make sense of what he had just been told.

"Will you have a complete legal description of this property, along with the water rights to be transferred and signatures of the principals involved?"

"Yes."

"Do you know when you will have these documents?"

"I will have them when I return."

The Lady in Red left before more questions could be asked leaving the recorder with mouth open and eyes empty. The recorder walked across the hall to the door marked <u>District Attorney</u>. On either side of the door were his two bodyguards as usual. The recorder tapped the door lightly as if afraid of it. "Enter."

The Lady in Red heard the knock and reply as she walked out of the Court House. She smiled at all the promptness.

District Attorney Wagner with his German Shepard shot out his office door. His two bodyguards whirled to follow close behind. He didn't turn but stuck his hand up and the two guards and their canine helper came to a grating halt. The dog gave a small whine as the guards' coats came to rest.

The lady stood beside her buggy pulling her black hooded cape over her fancy red dress. DA Wagner spurted and puffed down the Court House steps. "Allow me to introduce myself. My name is J. P. Wagner. I....."

She finished with her cape and turned to get into her buggy. He used his finger on her shoulder to keep her attention on him. Glancing at his finger the lady curtly stated, "Do you want to keep your finger Mr. J. P. Wagner?"

"I must apologize eh ah.. I wanted or eh ...wonder if you might assist me in my inquiries?"

She swung easily into the buggy. "No. Sorry. Maybe another time." The lady tapped the reins and departed. Her dust churned around Mr. J. P Wagner.

He made a quick motion as if holding reigns in front of his overhanging belly and a dervish rode to his side and leapt off his mount. He helped the DA into the saddle with some effort. Two more bodyguards came running to his side as he fit his oxford wingtip shoes into the stirrups. "No need. I'll take care of this little lady." He placed his hand in the air putting them on hold as he left bouncing hither and yon in the saddle.

Wagner followed as best his round body could sit the saddle attempting to make up the distance. However there was no need as the tracks were fresh and easy to follow.

He found the lady's buggy near a stream. He gathered his horse up and removed his rear end unceremoniously from the saddle after his rough ride. He pulled his rifle from its scabbard. Not that he needed an equalizer for her but for beasts that might inhabit the area. He raised the rifle to his right shoulder to get the feel and power it gave him. Then followed the only possible way she could have taken up a seldom-used trail.

The DA Wagner gained on her but not without puffing like a steam engine. He caught a glimpse several times only to see her disappear rounding a crook in the trail beyond him.

Wagner approached a bend in the trail. It narrowed to no more than eight inches across. A gigantic granite wall was on his right and a steep sixty foot cliff on the left. The lady made it. He could make it.

He swallowed hard and put his eyes on his shiny oxford street shoes. He held his rifle in front of his chest and kept his back tight to the wall as he inched around.

He looked out from the cliff and viewed two vulture witnesses perched on a dead snag. Where footing was nastiest he saw the lady sitting on a rock with her black cape towards him.

The woman raised off the rock and turned. As she did the black cape dropped from her shoulders. She had a taut bowstring with a blunt stone arrow nocked, aiming straight at his head. No sharpened point of steel or

flint but an oblong rock secured to the shaft with rawhide wrapping. The arrow could easily knock him off balance on the ledge, leaving no marks that his fall would not easily cover.

He struggled to get his rifle shouldered. The wall was too close to swing the rifle toward her. There were sounds of loose rocks going over the cliff as he made the attempt.

This Lady in Red could make herself appear as a rock or a pine or even another human if need be. With a little help from her friends. But here, there was no need.

She felt the bowstring start to slide. Soon the string would run out of fingers and no longer be under her control.

A few more rocks bounced down the cliff. He raised the rifle with his left hand alone. His back steadfastly against the cliff. Raven cut the afternoon sun aiming an ominous shadow across his face. His attention went to the bird, now hovering in the wind barely above him. Then across to the two buzzards.

The lady's arrow had a wasp peering over the feathers near her fingers. The wasp departed towards the DA a moment before the arrow started its jour-

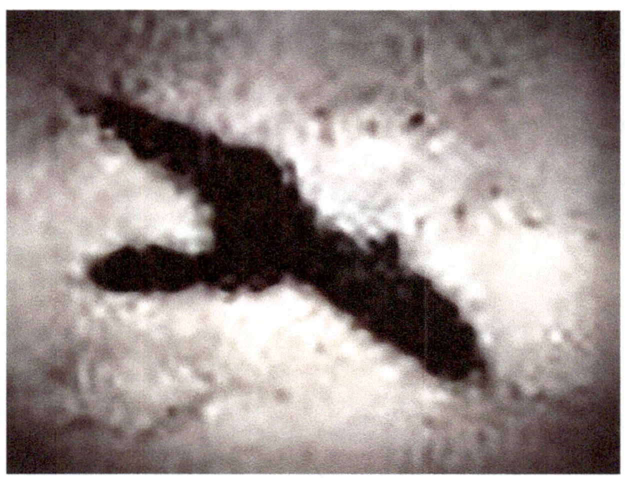

ney. The wasp buzzed past the rock head of the arrow towards the intended target. Wasp wanted the privilege. But the race needed to be won.

"Lady, you have me all wrong. I've done nothing … ."

Maybe you should have.

The silence was broken with a strident scream like a red-tailed hawk but with a human quality as well. The loud croak of Raven gave him a jolt along with the sound of the arrow.

There were more sounds of rocks cascading and the THUD THUD THUD of something softer and heavier journeying to the bottom of the cliff. The Lady walked to the edge and picked up Mr. J. P. Wagner's rifle in her red gloves. She looked down.

Sixty feet below at the bottom of the cliff were rocks and grass. To the right was DA Wagner. A gold pocket watch pulled from his suit lying beside him. Further to the right was a blue silk jacket with ties instead of buttons.

One vulture and one magpie were nearby. Two coyotes were quick to run. A few feet away from the scavenging birds were huge faded bib overalls with rusty buckles on the straps. A floppy brimmed hat rested beside them.

Raven looked over his shoulder at the Lady in Red with Wagner's rifle still in her hand. The Lady turned to leave and threw the rifle over the edge.

A CLANK was heard somewhere in the distance like a tin bowl striking a barn floor. The sound of a trap once set by Pete at a young age. She took two steps, picked up her arrow and checked the feathers.

Chapter 89 – Best Buddies

Pete now dressed in her common clothes had a red dress thrown in the back of Madam's buggy. She'd given the DA's riderless gelding a swat to send him back toward town, then headed toward Madam's.

• • •

She met Padre close to Aztec on the road back to town wearing a surprised look. "Well look at you. All smiles Padre."

"I can't believe what my eyes are telling me. You're here and alive!"

"You're too melodramatic. You didn't know where to look is all."

"Half the state was looking for you and they didn't know where to look either. Where were you and don't start that old shrug and bob routine. I want answers. Are you alright?"

A giddy high bowled through her body from surviving her capture, confinement in her cage, lack of food, her escape in the river's depths, and the pressures of allowing others to follow her. She started ramblingly incoherently. "Sure, I'm alright. I hope you're alright. And I don't mean from years back either. If I did torture you, I didn't mean to. I didn't even know what that was or how to do it." *Why am I doing this?* "If you can't take the heat, get off the stove Padre."

"This isn't making a lot of sense Pete."

"No, I'm probably not alright now that I take stock. I feel a little off-balance. Not your fault this time Padre. Don't try to take credit." Pete gave a big goofy grin waggling her head and Padre had to laugh.

Ernesto was told where he might find Padre. He came riding up hard trying to catch him and his breath. He wanted to give Padre the news about the new marshal coming. The marshal didn't expect to have much resistance from the construction workers.

"And look who tumbled down the mountain. Señor Sancho Turtle. My best buddy in this whole world."

Still wheezing and gulping needed air. "Oh you are a sight for these old

sore eyes Pete. And Padre I'd appreciate it if you don't rile her up none. She's hard enough to live with when she's happy."

Pete wasn't clear what had gone on but Sancho was there and that felt real good. She felt the camaraderie every time she put eyes on him.

"You fella's talk while I find something to take up space in my innards."

"We don't need to do the talking." Ernesto shot back. "You were the one taking a long vacation on Señor's wages. And you got a lot a tellin to get us caught up. And where did you get all that bruising? …and in the back of the wagon I see a red dress and whew, downwind, your buckskins smell kinda ripe."

"That last wiseacre wisecrack will be overlooked since I'm way past hungry."

Pete started rummaging through the things under the seat of the buggy. "You probably think the story about you getting caught with ladies' clothes on isn't worth telling. Shame and more shame to the both of you."

"Pete were you responsible for sending that German Shepard with the note in his collar and …."

And Pete had better things to do with her mouth than spit answers. She was literally starving when she spied a can. It was beans and no telling how old. She grabbed the beans and reached down for her knife in her scabbard. She looked over at Ernesto. He had his knife out, butt end pointing toward her, waiting. Ernesto just knew. Pete grinned at Ernesto's awareness.

She took his knife and opened the can by stabbing his knife clean through cutting the can in half. She turned each half upside down, one after the other, and her mouth caught most of the frijoles. No spoon, nothing else was needed. She loved acting like a cave woman in front of Padre. She thought he wanted her to be all refined, nice and ladylike. *What a great waste of a cave woman.*

Padre let out a slow questioning look. "How did you know we were up the mountain and got stuck in that little jail?"

"Let her go and I'll explain it to you. If I can Padre." Ernesto leaned over and pointed to the back of the buggy. "See that red dress in the back of the buggy? Looks like one of Madam's with some altering. Chances are her Madam highness has spilled more beans than Pete here."

"Listen to Sancho. He IS smarter than he looks, thank God. Oh, I gotta go but girls," and a long pause and a grin made both Padre and Ernesto aware it was a reference to them wearing lady things, "be VERY careful not to eat anything from my neighbor's camp up the hill. I'll tell you why later." She slapped the reins and made the patented Pete exit.

Chapter 90 - Pete's Date

Stories were being aired. Pete, Essie, Padre, Señor, Sancho, Juan and Ed were sitting around a fire at the Rancho just outside Essie's cabin. Padre opted for the kitchen table but was outvoted.

Juan and Ed each had smiles with the invitation. Juan sat by his grandpa, now the grandson was clearly a part of the team and traditions. Ed sat by Pete and displayed the strength of the strong silent type. All could feel his confidence by his warm beam and calm eyes willing to settle on anyone.

When Pete was done Essie couldn't sit still. "Are you having us believe your neighbor was spying on you and you didn't go down and cut his ear off?"

"That was the old Pete. I'm not sure who I am anymore. I'll have to give all this to Universe and see what I get. Either shed all this people stuff or hang up my knife and dirty feet. Just can't make it in both worlds if I straddle the fence. What do you think Sancho?"

"There is no way Pete you can make it in the insider world without some of your outside ways leaking a little. But I don't see any harm if a leaky bucket gets the job done." After a big smile he continued. "In case you go back to your old ways any time soon, Essie and I would like to invite you all to our wedding."

Madam showed up late. "What did I miss gang? Sorry, duty called. And here are my two favorite misfits with gender disabilities."

Pete piped in. "They're talking wedding Madam. Ernesto and Essie are talking wedding. Wedding! As in kids, house, laundry and the whole calamity."

"Yes, we hope so," Ernesto beamed. "And Padre if you could put your political stuff aside, we'd like a church wedding and then a reception outside. Up the mountain as close to God as possible would be perfect."

Pete wiped a big smile from her face. "No church wedding. I don't want to stand outside looking through the window."

Essie couldn't hold it in. "Pete, yes, inside with shoes, dress and powder on your nose. And with a DATE."

Señor was all grins. "I'm in. Got to see those toes in foot jail."

Juan broke in, "I vote Pete stays outside the church. She's no fun when she's mean."

Ed's shoulder touched Pete's. The energy was visibly there if anyone cared to read it. With Essie's demand for Pete to have a date Ed lightly touched her finger with his. She tapped his back in the same manner completing the message.

With the touch Pete pontificated to the group. "Very funny people. I got news for you. You can take feet to water but that's as far as they go with shoes on." It sounded to most like she might be there with dress, makeup and a date. And dirty feet.

Chapter 91 - Pete's Final Reflections

Piñon got me started down a path that introduced people. Those I met were outside what I thought was normal for humans but few were outsiders, outside in nature.

Madam wasn't average because she dealt in sex. Padre was too upwardly mobile in the church with an intellect and education beyond the common. Juan was left behind in school and separated by drugs. Essie had her scarred skin and a brilliant mind offending some. Señor was separated and embodied by times gone by. Muir wanted to be left outside but couldn't accomplish his goals without insiders. Ed had his stuttering. Ernesto chose to be outside the norms so he could cherry pick what he wanted from life. The Lost? Well, I guess that goes without saying. It looks like we all are a little or a lot abnormal. Few are able to accept it and call it home.

Friend, loyalty, and devotion was introduced by Essie. She was the gateway to words and education that opened so many doors. She had more sand and determination than I ever found in anyone else. Including me. Hardships make us stronger.

Ed brought unspoken words and feelings I knew were real. He brought himself, once he found the confidence to discover who that was.

Ernesto had a connection to me as he did with so much in Universe. He wore it easily like his bandana. He accepted me and gave me a space to be me. Sancho gave me direction to live in both worlds allowing me to travel a little closer to my own kind in the process. A worthwhile journey. There may never be another like him and like the little spring flowers, he gives me hope. What a human.

Muir was close to being a friend and I will keep trying as long as life is granted to us both. Friends never should be in complete agreement. Life may have to give him up and take him back before I can climb that hill. I am glad Muir and Roosevelt accomplished what they did. Yes, we have to get beyond man's roads and signs to feel the majesty. And I will always keep fighting for more. I know what exists and hopefully, now, you do too.

Padre, unknowingly, did me a great favor. He had incredible talents. He could easily fool any unwary human. Me in particular. It was a stirring beginning. But he let me peek behind the curtain to see how it was done.

Señor, like the rest of the people, was not like the rest of people. He didn't have history, but he was history, never to be found in any book. He carried it like Mountain. His manner won't die as long as I am on the earth.

Madam showed me to never try to be someone else. I could never play their game better than they could anyway. No matter how hard I tried. I am here to play me, better than anyone else ever could.

Federal Marshal McClean had his way of keeping distant and yet close. I will miss Marshal McClean. Life isn't fair and there isn't anything I can do about it. I wish I had longer with him. But like with four legged friends, some people don't live long enough either.

Mrs. Harding was someone who had a way I call friend. If I did take her up on her offer of higher education I might be able to find a few more people like her around my campfire someday.

Forest was something I was introduced to after leaving the plains. It was like bathing. Bathing isn't done with one or two drips. It's the same with Forest. Forest can clean the inside of a person. Some might say cleanse the spirit. I wanted Essie to forest bathe, to help quiet her mind. Feeling one tree might break the ice but it would take a forest to complete the job.

The Lost of the Ancients were natural and used paths. They saw I was coming by my path. I was humbled and honored by their welcome. They knew by Connecting, not learning or remembering. Not their words. It was not their way. With them I knew to keep an eye on every ending; it was always a beginning. They showed me my trail was the one in front of me, either way I turned. It had no beginning or end. Questions like how, why or when caused disconnection, and getting lost from answers. Not easy for two leggeds to grasp.

Piñon was my living oracle, Raven my guide. And Grub will always remain by my side. Whenever I connected to Universe, they were there. They directed me.

Pup never needed any more humans. When I wanted to connect to him, and I did on occasion, he was ready with a grin and a greet. Yes, four leggeds don't live as long as they should, except what we carry with us.

• • •

For those not cut out to be an outsider with armloads of naturalness I would like to emphatically state my beginning was not child abuse or cruelty. What's important is not what people think now but how it felt to me, then. I was happily free to flow in the great river of Universe unencumbered by the limitations of society, bringing exhilaration and enchantments. It brought the confidence to follow my own star. I was blessed with an upbringing few will ever know. Thank you Karl, Selina, Caroline, Raven and Grubby.

• • • • • • • • •

Book II

In the Beginning

Chapter 1 - Late 1800's

If you spoke to Karl or knew what he said you knew German. It aggravated Karl to hear any words but German in his presence. His wife, Selina, didn't speak often but when she did it was a mixture of German learned from Karl, Spanish Basque from her childhood, and some English. When angry she'd throw in a few Lakota words. English was spoken in schools and Selina wanted her children to learn a little English at home when possible to get them ready. But not around Karl.

Karl, a large pragmatic gruff man, had a small sheep ranch in South Dakota. He couldn't take his sheep far from the ranch for better pasturing and get the other ranch duties done without the additional help of a sheepherder. Selina had played the role full time until the birth of her first child.

Karl married Selina Wilhelmina before her sixteenth birthday. She knew better than he about frontier life and the raising of sheep. Although quite striking in appearance, her history made her scorned by suitors. However to Karl she would be a valued frontier wife. She was Basque by birth and was well equipped to handle sheep and the extremes of the South Dakota prairie.

Salina's parents had sheep and were killed by Indians before her 13th birthday. She was taken a slave by the marauding band of Lakota. Although she had been abused and traded several times over the following two years she gained good knowledge about flora and fauna from her captors. When she became pregnant, she was given an herbal mix causing her to miscarry. Her owners didn't want her mixing blood and wasting time caring for an infant. When she got headaches she learned ground willow tree bark made them disappear. When she wanted clothes for the winter months she had to make her own from hides she herself skinned and tanned.

After her two-year internship she had gained enough confidence and cunning to make her escape. She was taken in by a German couple and renamed Selina Wilhelmina near her fifteenth birthday. Not long after her arrival her guardians told her she would marry Karl Ostreich, a rancher in need of a good wife and who was willing to take her. She hadn't been particularly happy with the German couple and she had no choice anyway.

Karl had no interest in Selina's past, as their relationship was based on necessity. Selina's first pregnancy with Karl was not received well. Karl, like the Indians, saw her spending more time with a child which meant less time with his sheep. However, he had no knowledge of the alternatives. When their first born was a girl, Caroline, it made the matter worse. However it wasn't long before the big German's eyes sparkled. Karl loved Caroline and he often played and rolled on the floor, letting her ride him like a horse. Caroline was nearly three years of age when Selina was pregnant again.

Selina had prepared Karl's favorite meal of chopped cabbage and bacon with vinegar dressing when she told him of the new pregnancy. He looked up mid slurp with a big German smile. "This time it will be a boy and his name will be Pete. Pete will be happy on the prairie with my sheep. This family is two boys and two girls from now on."

But luck was not with him and his new daughter was born with a gravelly gurgle. Karl's face puckered up with the news like he'd swallowed a thistle. He recognized the reality with a wave of his hand and a quiet shake of his head. Pete would be the shepherd he needed.

Chapter 2 - Grubby

Karl's dugout home was made by digging into a hillside which made most of the home below ground. His ranch house faced south and the southern wall, sixteen inches thick, had been constructed of adobe sod. It was mostly a small subterranean home staying cool in summer and warmer in the severe winters. A sleeping loft was built for Caroline and the furnishings were kept simple. They consisted of a wood table and chairs, a wood chest for clothing, a feather bed and a wood stove. Utensils were hung on the walls as were heavier clothing, coats and hats. Meals were cooked outside in the summer to keep the home cooler.

A root cellar dugout was nearby for food storage. Corrals and a barn were thirty yards from the home. They were used during winter feeding and birthing of the lambs in the spring. There was a wire strung between the house and the barn held up by brushwood found nearby. It served as a clothes line and also a guide to be grabbed when traveling to and from the barn during the horrific blinding winter storms. The barn, feed loft, and corrals were a mix of sod and precious lumber.

Karl had a few other animals: four pigs, six ducks, and fourteen chickens all fed mostly from table scraps and overage from the garden. A horse was available for pulling the wagon and plowing the garden. A cow provided milk and cream for butter.

The most important animals on the ranch were the sheepdogs. The work dogs took their responsibilities quite seriously. Protecting and keeping the herd together meant the difference between success and failure on the ranch. In general they were between fifty and seventy pounds, wore long dirty shaggy mottled black, brown or gray coats shielding them from the elements and floppy ears to keep out burrs and debris. They were fast, aggressive with predators, obedient, and aware.

A favorite young pup less than a year old paid close attention to Karl's eyes and body language which made him good at predicting Karl's needs. The dog's name was Grub and he wasn't a handsome dog. He was especially ugly with gobs of thick multicolored fur patches protruding in clumps where it was not well matted down with burrs. Both ears hung low with the weight of rubble they had collected. In between the two ears was stiff fur standing up like renegade feathers. The most distinctive marking on this dog was its one brown eye unmatched by a spooky blue eye.

Recently Grub had spotted a coyote particularly bold in its attempt to watch the herd and wait for a straggler. It was always a little too far to make it worthy of a chase. However this morning it made a mistake and was not paying attention as Grub slithered up with belly to grass.

In a last minute dash by Grub the coyote whirled and tried to outrun the fast ranch dog. Grub was only gaining slightly but enough to give him hope of catching the trespasser. Grub outweighed the coyote by thirty pounds and was solid muscle with a longer stride. The coyote's advantage was it could cut back and forth more quickly causing some loss of balance to Grub's heavier frame.

Grub's attention was focused on the coyote and the chase. He did not sense the three other pack members rapidly approaching from the sides. White gleaming teeth tangled those first few seconds as they collided in combat.

Grub grabbed one by the throat and threw him to the ground tearing his neck and windpipe. This gave a second coyote the opportunity he needed. He gripped then ripped the tendon running down Grub's right hind leg. Without a whimper, Grub turned, but it was already too late as the damage had been done.

The three remaining coyotes now backed away a few feet. They surrounded Grub, feigning moves in and out. They kept him confused and turning on three legs.

"Boom" came the single rifle report sending one coyote in the air with a quick reflexive leap only to hit the ground with a hole torn through its side. A second shot only threw dust on the remaining coyotes zigzagging a rapid exit.

It was Karl's rifle ringing out in Grub's defense. He sputtered German down the hill towards Grub fearing the worst. Beside Grub lay the two dead coyotes. Grubby had been suckered by an old coyote trick.

Grub looked up at Karl with adrenalin still pumping. Grub started licking the injury. It was easy to see the extent of the injury when the dog's head was pulled to one side. The muscle was ripped and the ligament damaged. The white tendon visible didn't look severed and Karl thought it might mend. "You are lucky my friend, bullets aren't cheap" He turned and trudged toward the barn. Grub followed on three legs.

Inside the barn the big German built Grubby a place to restrict his movements by leaning two old gates forming a small triangle against a wall. He threw in some hay for bedding and walked heavy footed to the house.

Chapter 3 – Dolls and Dresses

Two little well-groomed girls in dresses and ribbons were squabbling at the supper table waiting for Karl to arrive. They were wrangling over a sock doll with a horse hair pony tail.

Pete was banging utensils creating a rhythm for her chant in German. "Mommy, Mama, dolly mine. Mommy, Mama, dolly MINE. Mommy Mama DOLLY MINE". Reluctantly Caroline returned the doll to the determined Pete.

Pete gave a gravelly victory giggle, "He He He ." Caroline started to reach for the doll back which started the two fighting again as Karl walked in the door.

Karl was not a patient man on a good day. He saw Pete, now three years of age, in dresses, bows and clutching a doll instead of a lamb. It was clear Salina could not or would not start Pete in a different direction from Caroline.

If he didn't act quickly it would be harder on Pete, if not truly impossible. Karl had his eyes opened when he saw Caroline, now six, being primed to help a future husband. He'd seen her helping Selina with laundry on the scrub board and caring for a make believe baby.

Karl knew they would all starve without the timely help of a sheepherder to tend his growing flock on the prairie away from the barn and corrals. The larger the herd, the further away they would need to graze. He could not attend the flock while putting up more winter feed and building larger corrals. Selina could not watch the sheep as she had once done because of the added work of a young family and a larger garden.

His course was clear. Pete didn't have to learn ranch work at age three but needed to be unhooked from the program Selina was providing. Pete needed to be prepared mentally and physically to tend sheep and to face the hardships and dangers alone on the prairie. A good sheepdog like Grub would guard and defend Pete in her early years as fiercely as he had protected his sheep. It had to be done and a warm summer evening was as good a time as any.

Karl bellowed, "Tough guys don't play with dolls and it's time you learned". He stood her on the kitchen table and tore Pete's dress off, buttons flying.

When he grabbed for the doll Pete turned quickly and he missed. Infuriated he reached and caught hold of the doll with one hand but she wouldn't let go. Pete was bobbing up and down over the table like a yoyo at the end of the doll. Her feet were not touching the kitchen table but she had a wide grin as long as she had hold of the doll. And she would never relinquish her doll. "Nein, nein."

"You have the grit of a good sheepherder, yes you do." With her success at hand she gave a wary smile.

He gently lowered her back down to the table and removed his knife from its scabbard. He pulled up Pete's auburn ponytail as she turned to show her victory trophy to Caroline. With one quick slash Karl cut her hair close to her scalp. He dropped her hair on the table with pink bow still attached. Pete looked down with eyes bugged disbelieving. She reached for her hair and ribbon with one hand which made it easy for Karl to jerk the doll from her tiny clutched fist. He grabbed a blanket off the back of the chair and took Pete, now in her underwear, out the door toward the barn.

Karl entered the barn and went straight to Grub's pen. He slid back the gate with his foot and placed her on the same hay that made a bed for Grub. He glared at Grub, one hand on his hip.

Grub knew a command was coming. Grubby understood communications best by body language. A body would move or position itself differently regardless of the verbal noises.

Already annoyed with Grub he yelled at him "Stay. Guard." He pointed an open palm first at Grub then an index finger at Pete now sitting inside the enclosure. He slid the gate closed and secured it with a wire. He left them both alone for the evening, Grub to lick his wound and Pete to cry herself to sleep … both without supper. He exited the barn door and latched it. **CLA Click.** Sounds to Pete soon became more significant than spoken words.

Grubby accepted his new responsibility as seriously as he did his old job with the sheep. He curled up next to the front entrance. Pete would have to go through him to leave. As Pete quieted for the night, Grub exhaled an extended breath to end an exceedingly long day.

• • •

The next morning Karl and Caroline sat at the table eating breakfast. Selina was clearly unhappy and slammed her plate on the table as she fumed. She feared without housewifery skills no man would care or provide for Pete.

Karl broke the silence first. "Pete will not live in our house or have dresses, ribbons or dolls. She will not woman talk or do women work. She will see Caroline sew, wash, clean, and be fed by a man. Pete will learn she is different, better off and earn her keep a different way. She will be liberated from woman's work."

"No man will have Pete without woman skills. No esposo. She will need you and your ranch to survive without a husband."

"I will have a good sheepherder and a good large herd, yes. All of this will provide a good living for all here, including Pete. You stay out of the barn and corral area until she learns her place."

They finished breakfast in silence. After breakfast Karl left the house with a plate of food and a small denim shirt over his arm. He let out the chickens from their overnight roosting pen and entered the barn.

Karl opened the lean-to confinement area to let Pete and Grub out. He put food and the denim shirt down in front of Pete. Grub limped out, glanced sideways at the plate knowing he had not been given permission to eat, and turned to watch.

Pete silently with large eyes looked up at Karl. "Put the shirt on. Stay in the barn or corral. This is your work area now. Yah?" Karl swept his hand to designate the corral and barn to both Pete and Grub.

Pete gave a wide-eyed slow nod and picked up the shirt. Karl walked out of the barn. Karl left the barn door open showing her she was free to leave the inside of the barn and roam the corral. Grub followed him out.

Pete peered around the corner of the barn door wearing her denim shirt, unbuttoned inside out over her underwear. Karl made eye contact with Grub and Grub pulled himself up on his three good legs. Karl pointed first towards Pete and then to the corral and barn area again designating the boundaries of Pete's confinement. "Grub, guard Pete … here."

Grub flopped back down to sun himself never wavering his attention from Pete. His head was on his front paws while he looked out the upper corner of his eyelids.

Pete warily searched for Karl and walked in the direction of the corral fence. Grub jumped to alert but stayed steady. Anticipating Pete's move, Karl appeared. He held his palm up to Grub, which put Grub on "whoa" as Pete neared the corral fence. Karl started to trot in her direction when Pete bent down to slide under the fence. She started to giggle with a victory so near but Karl's large hands scooped her up from behind.

Karl took Pete inside the barn screaming and her intensity hurt his ears. He left moments later with the ear-piercing sound muffled as the door latched. **CLA Click.** He shook his head to empty the blaring noise from his head.

Later the same evening after feeding Grubby, Karl brought him in the barn with his leg wound still oozing. Karl closed both in their lean-to pen without a sound being exchanged. Karl left and latched the door on the outside. **CLA Click.** Only the chirp of crickets and rustling of barn animals could be heard from the darkness inside.

• • •

The next morning, light and Karl entered the barn at the same time as the door opened. He put down a plate of food, slid the lean-to gate open and departed, propping the barn door open.

Pete didn't take long to down her breakfast and then looked around the corral area. She peered around corners, often turning quickly to look behind her. She tilted her head trying to sense where he was, but she did not leave the corral area.

• • •

The first week's food was brought by Karl twice per day; after breakfast on the way out to work and after supper, both without a word. She got more than enough to eat and drink including both milk and water. It was up to her how she allocated the food and if she saved any for snacks or lunch.

She found table scraps spread for barnyard animals in several tins placed on the ground as she foraged during the day with nothing better to do. Sometimes she would eat nearly everything on the plates leaving the chickens only what she had rejected.

She found a worm under a dish. She glanced toward the house. She dangled the worm over her mouth with head tilted back watching the house out of the corner of her eye. She dropped the worm in her mouth. Her action received no response from the house. She made a face at the taste and texture. The following week had no change to the routine and she did not challenge Karl again.

• • •

She had been potty trained in the house with her business generally done in the outhouse or in a chamber pot. However Selina generally accompanied Pete. Although a chamber pot was placed nearby in the barn, she would now relieve herself in her underpants and no one would either scold her or clean her up.

Karl would not be easily manipulated. He believed it would do her good to live in her own filth and learn she would not get treated like a baby because she acted like one.

She and Grub were soon fed together in the evening and then both were put into the lean-to enclosure. Pete remained barefoot, still in underwear and denim shirt and without pants. Her legs were crusted and soiled as Grub would often point out as he sniffed her backside.

• • •

One week to the day had passed. Karl brought out a bucket of kitchen scraps, clean blanket, towel, underwear, denim shirt and chamber pot. He put the chamber pot inside the barn. He took the old one out and put it by the corral gate. He put the new clothes by the watering trough. He spread the kitchen scraps in tin plates on the ground and dumped the rest in the pig trough. He walked to Pete and held out a finger for her to grab. She did and the two walked silently to the corral water trough.

He gently pulled off her soiled denim shirt and messy underwear. He gradually dipped her into the trough. She gave a gasp but did not fight the cool water. His large hands tenderly bathed her. He smiled making playful splashes but she did not respond. As the chunks of brown hay and filth melted away several strawberry colored rashes appeared.

She accepted a gentle toweling as the bath in the cool water felt good. He dressed her with new underwear and denim shirt. He brought her to the chamber pot and reminded her what she must do there. "Use this pot. Pull your pants down and it will keep you cleaner and your legs won't hurt." Karl left.

The third week Karl brought out the same clothing as before but pants were added to the mix. "You can have pants like a big boy if you keep them clean."

Pete promptly looked up with big green eyes and gave a somber nod. She did a perfect job the following week keeping her new pants unsoiled except for her rough and tumble play.

Her days continued to acquire structure. Karl gave Pete chores like gathering eggs and putting them in the basket or putting her dinner plate and glass next to the door. She was expected to be his gopher and get tools or nails in his repair jobs. She also was to accompany him when he would inspect the farm animals within the corrals.

Grub was the perfect nursemaid during this critical time. He permitted obstacles in Pete's life and allowed her the space to work them out generally unaided. However if he sensed real danger he herded her in a different direction or physically stood between her and trouble.

When he sensed she was getting bored he invented play. He brought her numerous light hearted moments licking her face until she fell over. Once on the ground he alternated tickling her sides with his snout and licking her face until she could stand no more. When done with this rough play, Grub laid flat on the ground and let Pete straddle his back. Grabbing a tuft of his fur to stay aboard Pete was hoisted up for a show off ride around the corral. His gait had a hitch that gave Pete a bump jarring ride making her spasm in cute gravelly cackles. Grub would never regain full use of his lame hind leg.

Chapter 4 – The Fundamentals

Pete had several important elements to her character making her a good candidate for the family shepherd. The first was she was born with a large helping of grit. Karl had that right. A second was an abundant sense of humor, finding hilarity, absurdity and fun in every day. And if something wasn't ludicrous enough, she would twist things a little harder. A third component was Focused Attention. Her awareness developed further in the "outside" world. Lastly she learned easily in her outside environment. One such lesson was life, under some rare circumstances, could only be governed by the excessive use of force.

• • •

Pete had three events early on having a lasting effect beyond living with Grub as her mentor. They were a driving force to obtain the character needed for success in her life.

The first involved a raccoon. Pete was taken by the raccoon's cute little masks and manual dexterity but she never was able to get close to one. The dogs knew better and would run them off, often causing a huge brawl. Coons would weigh easily over thirty pounds and put up quite a fight with a dog twice their size.

Pete's first meeting up close was a nasty encounter and she experienced firsthand their true nature. A coon brazenly ambled past the dogs busily eating and into the barn. He found Pete with a plate of food, alone, sitting on an overturned bucket. He looked both right and left, then put his nose to the air. Without further hesitation he lunged straight at her with a loud coughing snarl showing lips curled and plenty of glossy sharp teeth.

Pete screamed and shoved her plate of food at the coon in self-defense. Grub was there on his three good legs before the plate hit the ground. He jumped between the coon and Pete tumbling Pete backward off the bucket. If a fight to the death ensued, it would put Pete in the middle of a tangled mess of claws and teeth.

Grub glared at the coon eye to eye; first the brown eye, then the eerie deviant blue eye. This was accompanied by a low rumble from the deeps within. The coon blinked and leaned a little toward a possible exit, never moving his eyes from Grub's focused blue eye.

At the same time Pete whimpered from behind the bucket. The coon whirled in a blur and left only unsettled dust and some of his fur wedged between Grub's front teeth.

Grub returned to Pete's side. He put his muzzle under her hand and led her to bed in the lean-to pen now always open. Pete lay down and Grub pressed tightly beside her. Grub gave her a few extra swipes of his tongue and felt her snuggle close as he turned to guard the entrance. She squeezed his fur. Grub's eyes didn't close as darkness took over. Not this night.

• • •

The next incident had even a larger effect on Pete's life. It eventually led to the skills taught by Selina that gave her confidence and freedoms most women of the times did not enjoy.

One evening, long after Pete had fallen asleep, Karl came out to the barn stumbling drunk. He had some German rancher buddies over for a beer drinking evening. He thought Pete would mix well and put on a show. Karl boomed in drunken German, "Pete, wake up…my friends and I need some entertainment. Come to the house and do us a little dance." He slid the sleeping blankets toward him and scooped her up in her underwear and shirt.

Pete was not fully awake. He slung her over his shoulder and carried her to the house. Karl put her feet down on the table but she remained half-asleep. Pete stood not moving. All clapped a lively rhythm. Karl reached over to the stove, got a thin stick of kindling, and switched her legs. "Now dance you little son of a bitch."

Pete's eyes opened wide when she felt the sting on her bare legs. She danced with the tempo of the pain provided. The loud drunks around the table all clapped their hands to the rhythm. Pete was then given beer until it made her dizzy. She kept falling and the men roared with laughter.

Karl put her on the floor before she fell off the table. He looked up and saw Selina above on the sleeping loft. Selina remained silent and quickly pulled back from sight. Any interference now would make the matter worse.

• • •

Pete awoke the next morning back in her hay bed and tangled in blankets. Selina, beside her, reached over and gave her a hug. Pete spoke first. "Karl es malo".

"Talk English."

"No goot Karl."

"Men do bad, yes."

Pete was red in the face and pointed a finger several inches from Selina's face. "No goot Karl and no goot you!"

"Very very sorry. Karl's rules or he kick me out. I make it up to you. I teach you easy things to make you free. Free of fear, free of husband and free of woman's work. But no talk near Karl. No talk where Karl hears. No English, no Spanish around Karl. Yes?"

Pete paused and then spoke slowly. "You, Caroline en casa, in howz."

"Me and Caroline inside with Karl. You outside with Grub. You learn good, you own sheep, you boss. You not slave to any man. Easy choosing. You choose Karl … or choose Grub? Choose inside with Karl or outside with Grub?"

"Grubby. Grubby …."

"Don't talk to Karl about teachings?"

Pete agreed with large eyes and a nod of her head.

Selina had stayed from Pete's view and made the separation as pain free as possible. However after the previous evening and Pete's subsequent positive attitude, it was time to break the rule.

• • •

Pete was dressed and sitting quietly with Grub when Selina returned for Pete's first lesson or "teaching". Selina entered watching over her shoulder to be sure she had escaped Karl's notice. She had a soup bowl about eight inches in diameter and a twig with a small spur branch near the bottom end.

Salina took her thumb and forefinger and made quite a show of prying open her eyelids. Learning began by paying attention. Seeing could only be accomplished by carefully looking. No words were spoken during the first lesson.

Selina took the small-branched twig about four inches long and squeezed some cheese on the shorter spur branch. She propped the inverted bowl up on the longer branch of the twig and the shorter spur was near ground level with the cheese pressed on the end.

Selina scampered her hand and fingers back and forth as if it were a mouse. She lightly tapped the cheese as if her finger was the mouse, which

toppled the branch trapping her hand under the bowl. Pete nodded and wanted to try by herself by grabbing the bowl and twig. Selina got up and left the barn.

Pete continued to work with the twig, bait and bowl. Her young hands did not make the proper setting for a couple of tries and it toppled on her wrist. She got up frustrated, walked around with her hands on her hips, and took several deep breaths. Then back she went to the bowl and twig. She tried several more times before she got the bowl propped up and balanced on the twig.

Pete moved back and patiently sat. She nibbled from the cheese hunk in her hand not used on the trap. Her eyes grew large as a chubby mouse came near the bowl. The mouse sniffed, then nibbled on the cheese. The bowl dropped. <u>CLANK.</u> Pete had successfully set her first trap and caught a mouse.

• • •

Using two fingers in a walking motion with a nasty scowl on her face Pete spit words at Selina. "Two leggeds nasty",

"Not all people nasty."

"ALL."

"You mean drinking men?"

Pete nods, "and duck".

"Mean with beer Pete."

Pete's palms turn up. "Why?"

"Beer makes crazy."

Delivering a mime Pete pointing to herself first, then shook her head no, then rubbed her stomach and wiggled her head around her shoulders. *Not crazy but sick and dizzy.*

Chapter 5 – Whitey

Pete's run in with Whitey the duck was the last incident that starting turning things around. In the beginning the chickens and ducks didn't know what to make of Pete. She was exempt from establishing herself within the literal pecking order. But she was eventually challenged. Near the top of the pecking order was a large white duck clearly not afraid of anything including the head rooster with his two-inch long spurs.

Whitey had successfully chased Pete away from freshly scattered food until he had his fill. He menacingly charged her with wings and neck outstretched and beak clacking. CLACK CLACK CLACK. His beak grabbed her clothes and underlying skin. When she tried to straight arm the barnyard bully he pinched both her hand and arm.

She ran to Grub crying. Grub did nothing but console her by licking the fresh wound. Whitey looked on from afar a little apprehensive as to what Grub might do.

The next day it happened again. However this time Pete came back at Whitey yelling and arms waving wildly. The duck hesitated but Pete didn't press her advantage. Whitey regained control and charged back. CLACK CLACK CLACK while Grub stoically observed from a distance.

The third day Pete had a different look about her. She had her nose picking up scents and her ear attuned to every little rustle. She showed this "Focused Attention" many times afterwards when the situation called for it.

Pete kept a watchful eye for Whitey but continued to pick at newly-spread scraps. Pete's rear was tantalizingly in the air swaying like a metronome. Whitey methodically made his way toward her picking up speed as he approached the interloper. The large white duck with neck outstretched was about to extract some measure of pain. Pete amplified the sound of duck feet coming toward her with Focused Attention; pit.............pat.............pit..........pat...........
pit..........pat......**PIT..... PAT**

She reached for a stick positioned inches from the food. The duck's head came into her peripheral view. **WHACK.** Little Pete swung the stick with a bulbous end connecting perfectly with the duck's head rendering him a pile of feathers and fluttering eyes. Whitey, dazed, wove his way into the barn.

Pete brushed her hands together, held her head high, and strutted in a gesture of victory and freedom. Grub observing from a distance gave away his reaction to her use of force with a small waggle of his tail. Nothing more.

• • •

Play consisted of anything in her imagination, with Grubby or with barnyard friends. She appeared to have developed relationships with birds, animals, and even insects as well. It was difficult to know, however, whether she was communicating with these creatures or simply had an active imagination.

• • •

There was no shortage of crows and ravens in the area. She not only distinguished ravens from crows but between the individual personalities. She gravitated more toward the older more mature ravens and their subdued thoughtful personalities. They were quite smart and had the ability to make relationships. The adolescent ravens were more like crows and easily as troublesome.

A mature raven seemed to take a liking to her early on. The raven would croak and flit to a perch in her sight. Pete would raise her arm and he would swoop down and land nearby. Pete would spread her arms and glide around the corral and the bird would follow her bouncing on two legs with wings outstretched. It wasn't unusual for Pete to invite the raven for a few scraps from her plate in the evening.

Raven was to become the wayward sibling. Grubby was both mother and father to Pete providing the warmth and caring of a mom with the discipline and hard knocks of a dad. Raven was more of the court jester teaching her things Grubby would not, like taunting and stealing. One time Raven rode on Grubb's back pecking at his tangles and burs. The first time Pete saw Raven tormenting Grub in this manner it started the long standing struggle with the curry brush.

• • •

Pete spied the horse's curry hung in the barn and got it down using a long stick. She chased Grub most of the day trying to comb the tangles out. Every time Grub lay down she snuck up on him and worked on the tangles, mats, and messes wound tight in his shaggy fur. If Grub tried to avoid the torture, Pete waved the brush in the air and demanded his attention by yelling, And whooping. Grub's body language stated he clearly wanted to leave the corral area but he had a commitment and Karl to answer to.

Several hours after Pete crawled into her bed Grub approached carefully with his nose up and ears perched to verify the depth of her sleep. When he had assured himself of his safety, he slinked back to his post at the entrance of her hay bed. As he snuggled down to enjoy a quiet night of deserved dog slumber he heard a soft evil gravelly giggle, followed by the torture of the currycomb.

Although uncomfortable he let it go on until she fell asleep exhausted. He retrieved the curry from her clutched fist and made his way out of the corrals to the ranch house porch. He dropped it close to the front door and quickly returned to the barn. Grub never fully adjusted to Pete's preening but it came with the job. The curry found its way back to the barn.

• • •

When Pete happily accepted her new environment Selina was given permission to load kitchen scraps into her bucket and return to the corrals. It was a fun day for both.

When Pete saw her entering the corrals without looking back for Karl, Pete gasped and ran to her. They were meeting where Karl could see. Selina knelt down and soaked in Pete's hug. When Selina felt Pete's grip loosen a little she stood and handed Pete the bucket without a word.

Pete took the bucket hesitantly and followed Selina to a tin plate on the ground. Selina knelt, reached in the bucket and put a handful of scraps in the plate for the animals. She took Pete's hand and stuck it in the bucket. Pete withdrew it with scraps in hand but her eyes never left Selina's. Selina looked to the plate on the ground and nodded to it. Pete followed her eyes and complied, putting scraps on the plate.

Selina gestured for Pete to move to other plates and then the pig trough with finger and hand motions. Pete left Selina's side and dropped food on a plate. She turned and showed Selina a long skinny carrot and stuck it in her mouth, crunched it, and then returned to filling the plates.

Selina turned to home through the corral's gate when Pete was busy at the pig trough. Pete looked up, dropped the bucket, and churned toward the departing Selina already outside the corrals.

One moment Pete was on her feet and the next, THUD, she was lying on her back looking up in a daze at the bottom rail of the corral fence. And Grub's face. Grub's muzzle pushed her back toward the barn. She took a deep breath. She stared into Grub's dirty fury muzzle and a little grin grew on her face.

Pete righted herself and walked away from the fence. She started playing with a stick scratching the dirt. Quickly she spun again toward the corral fence. THUD. Pete gazed into Grub's deviant blue eye and gave her most evil gravelly cackle. *Next time Grubby.*

• • •

A dirty-faced Pete tramped to the watering trough and removed her clothes. She climbed in and took a bath without help. She started making duck sounds and it wasn't long before she had an audience of barnyard animals.

She scrubbed herself without soap as she had none, and dunked her head under to complete the task. She didn't have a towel but she first shook like a dog. Next she ran her hands over her legs, arms, and head as if she had a towel. Lastly she spun in circles arms out under the warm sun. When done she gave her dirty clothes a shake and put them back on.

• • •

Pete watched Selina milk the cow. She was entranced with the squirting of milk from the cow's teat to the bottom of the bucket. Pete got her head in the way. Selina gave a little squirt down the back of Pete's neck as a way of getting Pete to back up.

Pete turned in surprise. Selina opened her mouth in an exaggerated gesture. Pete accepted the signal and exposed the largest target she could like a baby bird in the nest. Selina squirted a little milk at Pete's gaping mouth. Some hit the mark and the rest dribbled down Pete's face and chin.

Immediately after Selina left with the bucket of milk, Pete got under the cow and tried pulling and squeezing the teat. It produced nothing. Pete left thinking only Selina could get milk.

Early the next morning the cow was up and standing but still not awake. Her udder was larger and the teats fuller and hanging lower. Pete thought maybe she could fool the cow while it was still asleep. She snuck up on the cow to get some creamy rich warm milk.

Pete crawled across the barn floor and slid under the cow. She pulled on the teat gaining nothing for her efforts. She tried sucking on the teat and still zero. She pushed and pulled as if the teat were a pump handle. Nothing happened except the cow slowly moved her head to see what was going on back there. Pete glared at the cow, pointing her index finger at the cow's head, and the cow obeyed, turning her head back around.

Pete grabbed the teat in more earnest. Again and again she pulled it to no benefit. Pete gave a sharp disgruntled slug to the utter. *Ok, don't give me any milk*, and the milk let down. The cow looked around with large loving tolerant brown eyes and gave an approving nod.

Pete gave a last grab and squeezed. It was a forceful final rebellious crush making a strong fist around the teat. The teat, defeated, relinquished a small squirt of milk. She did it again and got the same result. The third time she crawled beneath the teat and aimed at her wide open mouth. It wasn't a lot, or a direct hit, but Pete was enthusiastic with her new skill.

She was in hysterics and started victorious squealing and dancing. She hoisted her hands high above her head and ran in place raising her knees higher and higher with each step. She danced, skipped and grabbed the swinging cow's tail lifting her feet off the floor. Pete was ruler of the cow.

It didn't take her long to learn sneaking and war whooping wasn't as necessary as a full udder and letting down the milk. The efficient technique of squeezing down the teat didn't come easy to tiny hands but when it did Selina knew. The cow afforded Pete many a good meal and a great deal of entertainment.

Selina knew from the varying amount of milk received each day Pete was having success with the cow. She saw Pete was being far better prepared for hardships than Caroline. But this did not relieve her fears Pete would pay the price of being "peculiar" the rest of her life. Pete had launched but where would the miniature arrow land?

Chapter 6 – Home is Where You Are

As days grew shorter and colder in the Dakotas, Selina made Pete a heavy bulky sheep skin fur coat for cooler mornings and evenings. It made her look like an unsteady fat rollie pollie lamb. It was difficult to get it hooked in front by herself but that was another hurdle to overcome.

By late October of the first year in the barn Selina would watch her daughter play on the other side of the corral fence in the evenings. Selina sometimes howled like a coyote with a slow mournful yodeling melody. "yo-hoyohouloohyoohoo"

This song was not like the morning sharp tones "HARK HARK YIP YIP YIP WEHOWEE gathering a pack during a morning greet before setting off on the hunt. It was the howl of a bitch to a distant pup to see if all was ok. Pete answered the call as she too was familiar with the song, and then both mother and daughter settled silently into the sunset.

• • •

Pete had turned the corner. She easily preferred living and working with animals instead of doing house chores and interacting with the two leggeds across the way.

Karl had given up the practice of giving her a bath when he recognized she had taken up the duty herself. He put out soap and towel and was pleased with the independence she showed. An important trait for his young sheepherder.

In the fall when the trough showed a layer of ice he considered bringing heated water from the house. However that very day Pete showed more gravel than grit. Pete broke and removed the pieces of thin ice on the surface of the trough. Then having her bath ready, she climbed in squealing like a pint-sized piglet. The show far surpassed Karl's wildest expectations knowing he would not put his stubborn German body into the icy water.

When done, which included a dunking of her head, she bolted from the icy water, purple skinned and gulping air. She increased the number of baths per week apparently enjoying the freedom of choice and the exhilaration of the adrenalin rush the ice water provided.

• • •

The leaves showed signs of fall colors and Karl made stacks of sod bricks about twenty inches square. He formed a room outside next to the barn. He used the barn wall for one side of the room about six feet square with a roof sloping away from the barn. The only entry to the sod room was a hole he cut in the barn wall he could barely squeeze through. He put a stove inside the sod room with a vent stack out the roof. Lastly he nailed a sheepskin from the top of the entrance to cover the opening keeping in the heat.

Karl called for his helper. "Here Pete".

Pete came to the small opening and pulled back the sheepskin far enough to gander in. Karl had a few pieces of split firewood stacked inside. "Firewood goes here. Stack it like this. Bedding goes over here." Karl drew a line in the dirt with kindling to show the bed area and firewood location.

Karl squeezed out through the little opening. Pete left and returned with one piece of firewood. She stacked it near Karl's and turned to find Grub with another stick in his mouth. He released it into her hands and left for yet another. She turned and neatly stacked it.

Karl entered with supper, warmer winter clothes, woven mat and furs for bedding. He handed the dinner plate to Pete. Reaching through the opening he dropped the clothing at her feet. He crawled inside with Pete through the small sheepskin covered opening. He reached outside and drug the mat and bedding through the opening. The clothing included heavy sheepskin pants to go with her sheepskin coat, long johns, mittens and a fur hat.

"Try these on. My hired hand needs warm clothes for winter." Karl helped her with the coat and pants and then left. She looked quite proud of her new work clothes.

Pete went outside her sleeping quarters, turned over a bucket and ate with Grub at her side. Raven joined them for supper. She gave a small piece of bread to Grub and heard the objection from Raven. "YAK-YAK." She smiled and teased him with a small piece of bread before letting him take it from her hand. Afterward she strutted around banging on her chest shouting nonsense orders to no one in particular. She was a short round teetering snowman in her bulky awkward sheepskin clothing. She spun and fell, giggles filled the barn.

• • •

A week later a slight skiff of snow was on the ground. Karl departed the corrals on horseback. Selina left the front porch with a cloth sack in her hand. Even with Karl gone she only gave Pete a slight head movement toward the open prairie beyond.

When Pete caught up to her, Selina placed the loose cloth bag over Pete's head. Without sight there were no more visual gestures only slight hand pressures directing Pete. The bag was open at the bottom providing air and visibility down.

"Deer never lost. Fear comes if you can't find home. Make all earth home ... like deer."

Pete was sandwiched between Selina and Grub as she left the corral area. Selina's forefinger was in Pete's left hand and a tuft of Grub's fur was squeezed tightly in her right. She could watch her feet... leaving the corrals.

After an hour walk, turning several times in different directions, then spinning Pete around, Selina took the bag off and put her palms up. The skiff of snow had melted that would have shown their tracks and way home. "Take me back."

Chapter 7 - Blizzard

Winter mornings were normally black in the barn until someone came out and lit the lantern high over Pete's head. There was fencing keeping the sheep and other animals away from Pete's area but the darkness was normally filled with a chorus of comforting barn sounds of bleating, grunting and crowing.

This morning however was not normal. The worst storm of the winter was blowing. Karl had used the clothesline to guide himself to the barn through the blizzard and brought Pete breakfast.

The usual barn noises could not be heard over the howling gale force winds. Pete sat on the floor with her breakfast plate and a mouse on her shoulder. The mouse peevishly waiting for a scrap.

• • •

Karl squeezed past the sheep-skinned door to tend her stove in her adobe sleeping quarters. A few moments later Karl warmed his hands in front of the fire. Pete intently watched from the entrance, having pulled the sheep skin aside.

Karl barked in German, "You bring in here more wood today. Remember, fire and stove is dangerous. I touch stove. You don't touch. Yah?"

Pete nodded and Karl squeezed back out past Pete. She watched him cross to the sheep on the other side of the barn. She turned and entered the adobe room toward the stove. She reached out touching it with her index finger, and quickly jerked it back in pain. She stuck it in her mouth. The only sound came from the crackling freshly-lit fire in the stove. The hot stove had blistered her finger. A teaching.

Pete also learned nature gave teachings frequently. Winter ears and fingers could easily get frostbitten without the proper care. Nature's punishment was swift and consistent, making learning a simple matter.

• • •

An hour after Karl left for the morning, heavy winds still screeched, clawing at the barn siding and door. Pete had shut the narrow entry barn door and kept it from blowing in by placing several heavy rocks at the base.

Pete in her heavy fur clothing ran at a rope attached to the loft and grabbed it, swinging her feet off the ground. She dropped from the rope and looked for something else to do. She walked to the door and moved the rocks at the bottom. The door swung open with snow blowing in. Grub lifted his head in her direction. Pete shut the door pushing hard with her back to keep it closed. Grub put his head back down.

Pete stepped aside, the door flew open, and she plunged outside. She tried to orient but the seventy mile an hour gust tore at her eyelids. She staggered then righted herself. The next blast blew her off her feet propelling her like a tumbleweed. She rolled and bounced in her bulky sheepskin clothes picking up speed. Fear shot through her with the disorientation. She came to a jarring halt face up at the lower rail of the corral fence. She lay on her back like a fat beetle having no traction of feet or hands. Blowing horizontal snow chipped at her face. She looked to the side only to find Grub's muzzle enforcing the corral fence rule.

He got behind and pushed her in the direction of the barn but she was nailed to the fence by the storm. He pulled her by her sheepskin clothes but the clutching fingers of the wind did not let her go. He turned around several times laying down beside her partially blocking the force of the winds. She seized a tuft of his fur and righted herself off her back. She enthusiastically grabbed a second handful of fur and slithered onto Grub. She gripped even tighter by squeezing arms and legs to his torso. He struggled up on his three good legs with Pete clutching tightly.

He weaved his way toward the barn nearly losing her twice. He staggered into the barn and collapsed. Pete scrambled off. She put her back to the door and moved rocks in place with her feet to hold it shut. Breathing heavily she looked at Grub. She grinned and nodded her head as if she hadn't had enough.

Grub got to his feet and limped straight at her. He pushed her away from the door and on to the floor with his snout. When she tried to get up in her bulky clothes he easily tipped her over again using his muzzle like a battering ram.

He growled. Pete grinned pointing her little finger in his face. His stern posture showed he meant business and this was no game. She laughed. He showed teeth.

"GRRrrr"

"No goot Grubby. No talk."

Grubby moved back to the door and flopped down in front of it. He exhaled a deep breath of pure exasperation. He lowered his head daring her to challenge him. Maybe some other day when he wasn't so grouchy.

Chapter 8 – Spring

It was a relief when the plants released the life they held. The first buds of spring were fat and starting to burst. The birds enjoyed the sun's warmth right along with Pete. She found a patch of dirt and ran around arms outstretched. She twisted and spun until she fell with dizziness. A little Junco swooped down beside Pete on a pile of old snow and gave a chirp. Pete grinned and chirped back.

• • •

Karl was finishing the plowing in the garden and tipped the plow over on edge. He unhitched the horse as Caroline and Selina, both wearing dresses, left the porch. They headed toward the garden to break clods in the newly-turned soil as Pete watched from the corrals in overalls.

Karl, with the help of two dogs, drove a few sheep into pens in the corral area. Pete knew to stay out of the way but remain close. Karl made a quick trip inside the barn and returned with shears. It wasn't long and the sheep were relieved of their fleece and more were driven into the shearing pen. A small pile of fleece was growing under the protection of a shed roof.

Karl motioned for Pete to follow him into the barn where there were several ewes and newborn lambs. Once inside Karl signaled Pete to come closer. "Here Pete, take this knife and put it on like this. It's sharp. Be careful." He wrapped a scabbard and knife hanging from a thin rope around her waist and tied it on. Pete caressed the knife on her hip.

Karl turned and showed her how to keep a baby lamb close to the ewe. The lamb wandered off and Karl pulled it back and put its nose right on the ewe's teat. Each ewe was earmarked with a notch.

"This is what you do. Make sure the lamb feeds or you'll have to feed him by hand." Karl left Pete with the ewe and lamb. Pete's nose went deep into the lamb's side. She inhaled the sweet smell of newborn lamb.

Karl had a bottle in his hand and waved to Pete to come to him. Karl put the bottle in the lamb's mouth and gave it to Pete. "Here, grab this bottle. This is what happens if you don't keep the pair close after birth. The ewe rejects the lamb. We call them 'bum lambs' when we hand feed."

Pete's demeanor was always distrustful of Karl but when she got near the baby lamb all that vanished. The lamb jerked and pushed while Pete giggled herself silly. Karl shook his head and left. Pete reached down to be sure the knife and scabbard were still at her side. Back to the baby lamb.

• • •

By the age of five Pete was loving her life. She stoked her own stove in the barn, helped with the gathering of the wood, and felt quite self-sufficient. She was learning more and more from Selina on the sly, which put a little swagger in her walk. Except if Karl was around.

After shearing and lambing the summer months afforded Pete and Grub the luxury of sleeping under the stars. After chores around the corrals she could go to her camp next to a nearby creek. Her living area was expanded to be anything south away from the house without boundary.

Pete loved being on her own and Karl was ecstatic seeing her doing well without constant human companionship. Pete didn't know lonely, she knew it as freedom.

The bad incident with Karl and the drunks laughing and making her dance was all done inside the house which reinforced the idea being an "insider" was not for her. When she felt the independence of her creek camp she connected and was an undivided part of Universe. Even the prairie dog town nearby got a kick out of her whooping and giggling. Many would crawl out of their holes, stand on their back legs, and listen intently to the new neighbor.

• • •

"Mama, me with man?" pointing to herself connecting two fingers.

"Your story not told, Pete"

Pete's palms pointed up to question. *"Marry?"*

"Woman must obey man and he provide. You are different if you choose. You can provide for yourself."

"Me, choose?" Pointing to herself then picking something from the air.

"Yes."

"Caroline?" Miming long hair being combed and palms went up again.

"She needs man to provide food and shelter. You don't. You take sheep as pay. Start your own herd. No need to find man."

"No man."

"Lucky you."

Chapter 9 – Teachings

Selina had been studying Pete playing with Raven. She thought Pete was in a make believe world. As she came out to the corral area with garden scraps Pete approached her wanting some answers. However Selina never did figure out the questions.

Pete used the words "talk-talk-talk" mixed in with other sounds and gestures including mimes of Raven, croaking, and fingers from each hand wiggling. First her fingers pointed toward each other, then outward. At the end she turned her palms up signifying a question.

When Selina stood there flabbergasted, Pete repeated the question getting frustrated. Selina could only give a lame reply mainly in hand gestures. *Raven is the messenger, not me.* Selina seemed to know less than Raven about Pete's questions. Pete walked over to Raven and the questions began again leaving Selina out of the conversation.

• • •

Later that afternoon Pete and Raven were playing more aggressively. When Pete was not looking Raven dove close to her head, startling her with a loud flap of wings or tap on the head with his claws. Raven would claim victory by gliding to a nearby perch and give a generous croaking noise and then glare first with one eye, then tilt his head and use the other. Pete was determined not to let Raven catch her off guard but her mind would soon wander. Raven would sense her lack of awareness and the game would start again.

In the weeks to come, Pete's developing Focused Attention could sense the bird's approach. She would swiftly make a grab for the bird, forcing Raven to adjust quickly to avoid her grasp. This made her the winner of the game. The triumphant corral croaking noises were being replaced by gravely teasing snickers.

• • •

Pete wanted to fly like a bird and especially tumble in the sky like Raven. After a successful game of tag with Raven she sat cross legged with arms knotted across her chest on the ground in the corrals. She had a determined expression on her face melting into a smile.

She spent the remainder of the day developing wings by tying hay on her arms. Dissatisfied with the results of flapping around the corrals like a scarecrow she went to the loft and soared off.

She found her hay "wings" more of a handicap than an advantage when they caught air in an unpredictable manner. Flying with Raven would take more practice.

• • •

Raven was not well liked around the corrals which didn't bother Pete. She wasn't always liked either. Raven stole and ruined many nests full of baby birds but that was how he ate. He stole scraps of food right from the mouths or beaks of barnyard residents which distressed them. She voluntarily gave Raven scraps which avoided the thievery from her.

She had witnessed the exchange of goods or barter at the ranch and the system worked well. If she traded something of value like leaving food for chickens and taking their eggs then thievery was acceptable. However those that stole without some exchange from her would absorb the worst Pete had to offer if she could catch them in the act.

One evening Raven hit a little closer to home when he absconded with the last piece of sweetbread Pete had saved for an evening treat. He didn't leave anything in return but he did something far worse. He flew to a rafter and put the piece of sweetbread down without eating it. She sat steaming mad glaring at him.

Stealing without using or eating had some other meaning or teaching from Pete's perspective. He stared down at her watching her reaction closely. He tilted his head one way then another. When she looked away he croaked to get her attention back on him and what he'd done.

She had learned to closely watch everything for teachings. She noticed the unjust teaching from Raven had a blinding effect. She took a deep breath. Taking and using was natural. Raven had given Pete a first lesson on cussed or maybe evil. It would be a time before she learned the words.

• • •

One day Raven returned after two weeks of being gone. He didn't fly in and land but waddled in stiff-legged and dragging his right wing. Pete watched the bird and gave him a scolding for not being more careful.

She fed Raven and encouraged him to stay in the barn with her for more than a month. At the end of that time she put the bird on the fence rail and pointed telling him to fly. He glided down but did not flap his wings. He had been seriously injured but would one day fly again. He retained the droopy wing.

Chapter 10 – Fire

Pete made quick finger gestures like flames licking the air, then hands out warming in front of a fire, then turning palms up while looking at Selina. She was quite mesmerized watching the fire dance, licking and cavorting with the burning wood.

"A long time ago, fire hide in wood. Two leggeds learned to rub sticks together and coax it out into dry leaves." Selina brought her hands together and had Pete do the same. She then moved them back and forth in a rubbing motion first slowly then more rapidly until Pete felt the heat being generated on her own hands.

Fire was started with matches always well protected from the elements. However Selina showed Pete how to make a bow drill or fire bow as well. It had a string looped around a shaft making the shaft rotate rapidly as the bow was drawn back and forth. When the tip of the shaft was placed in a small hole in a board with tinder added for fuel it burst into flame after enough friction had been done with the fire bow.

Fire and matches were introduced to Pete by Selina as magical forces and were always handled with care. Fire was given great reverence as it had the power to help or destroy life while having a mesmerizing effect on unwary souls. Fire would be used in tanning, making a brittle needle bend without breaking, and food preparation, making unusable grains or beans into something she easily chewed and digested. Most importantly there was no reason to be cold again with a fire.

Selina showed fear if fire was brought into the barn and made a large show of dousing it with water immediately causing some smoke where it had been. Salina then used the smoke to kill a mouse in a bucket by simply putting it to sleep. She left the mouse in the bucket as a lesson showing the mouse would never wake up. Death like fire was taught as an important aspect of life.

Chapter 11 – Curriculum

The teachings from Selina had a broad cultural background merging Basque, Native American and Prairie traditions with some science of the time. They began at age three and continued until Pete left. Each lesson built upon an earlier one.

There were many practical lessons on hunting, gathering, tanning, medicine, and tool making. As Pete practiced and improved her skills, she didn't need parental or peer encouragement supplied by Selina, Raven or Grubby. She would be the judge of her own success and she did not give approval easily.

• • •

Selina took care never to have chatty sessions or teach indoor skills, getting them both in trouble with Karl. The nearest thing to normal schooling on the ranch was to learn to count and multiply by fives. Pete visualized fingers on a hand covering sheep on the range and multiplied by the number of fives she could see. There were five fingers on a hand and five hands were twenty five sheep. If there were seventeen hands and two fingers she had eighty seven sheep. An important aspect of sheep herding was to lose no sheep which meant keeping an accurate count. If an animal was lost it was of utmost importance to get a handle on it.

Selina didn't instruct in gardening as it was considered woman's work. But hunting and gathering could be used on the range for a well-balanced diet as well as a diversion from the desolation and boredom of sheepherding. It gave a sense of calm when connecting or being one with nature.

She took Pete to explore the countryside and gathered edibles including roots, fruits, nuts, grains, mushrooms and berries as she had been taught by her parents and her Indian captors. Pete saw the importance of remembering where plants were located. They could be easily found the next year or returned to later when the edible portion was ready to collect.

Pete was taught how to thresh wild grains and seeds and separate the palatable portion from the chaff. She could distinguish poisonous and medicinal plants, paying particular attention to the leaves with colors and shapes for identification. An entire lesson was given to testing plants edibility as safely as possible when there was no alternative to starvation. Some plants like mushrooms were never tested and only eaten if absolutely positive. Pete discovered the hard way about look-alikes but Selina never let her get worse than a case of diarrhea.

Pete learned to weave. It was woman's work but useful with herding sheep. Tightly-woven baskets held water and loosely woven baskets were good for carrying things. Sleeping mats protected her from dirt and moisture. She also wove bonnets or visors. There was no end to the weaving materials with the many grasses and plants in the area. Along with the practical, Pete had a flare for the aesthetics of design.

• • •

Selina had started Pete in observing and predicting the weather. The color of sky, clouds, winds and their subtle changes were all observed. Some skies looked like a sea of ice and others had dark warriors marching over the countryside.

The weather was not looked upon as a rival or an opposing force but a constant companion. It was generally a silent partner but there were times it would want to be heard or seen. It would flash, yowl and boom. The fury in a storm wasn't to be feared but respected. It was best to give weather the space required to unfold. If Pete fought the weather and got wet clothes on cold days, the winds would punish her body to teach her more respect. She had no idea of the concept of wind chill factor, but she knew well the effects of wet clothes on a windy day.

• • •

Pete loved life and was totally enchanted by all living things. She saw all things as living and more importantly, connected.

She saw herself fitting into the larger scheme of things. She knew she was

a part of this living organism which included all things from rocks to the majestic eagle.

The key to every problem was always within Pete's grasp. The answer was ever-present; it was only a matter of making the connection. It was taught by Raven, Grubby and Selina to take responsibility for its discovery whether she looked within or at the world around her.

Remaining composed was an important factor in problem solving. When Raven stole her sweetbread and didn't eat it was an emotion repeated several times over. Anger and fear disturbed the calm. Lost was the best lesson. "Lost makes crazy mind, runs feet. No good."

• • •

The first teaching with a cloth bag over Pete's head was to show her what a challenge being lost was and to experience the fear accompanying it. Then came the lessons that would give the solutions.

Navigation was important both by day and by night. Tracking the sun's path from morning till evening was important. It gave not only east and west but the seasons as the track was further north in the summer and further south in the winter. Selecting prominent landmarks on the horizon was an easy method to keep from walking in large circles. Drainages like creeks could be followed up or down to return to a starting point such as an evening's camp. Their sound was also a navigational tool.

Selina took walks with Pete until she was sure Pete was well familiar with the sounds of nature. Then she put a hand to her ear and moved her head to a cocked position to record the sounds and make use of them.

As Pete moved the sounds gave her relative positioning. A creek behind her would let her know she was traveling away from the creek as the sound decreased. If paralleling it the sound was constant and off her shoulder. Animals like squirrels were used to tattle on those who walk near and the racket could be used to locate others in the woods whether they be two leggeds or four. Some birds were also good gossips like magpies, jays and crows.

Pete was curious about the stars and it set her imagination in a swirl when

Selina taught her primitive celestial navigation as a potential tool. The heavens were not random and chaotic but like everything else they had order, whether she could recognize it or not. The fact the stars were not random but actually had formations and locations fascinated Pete. She learned the shape and orientation of the dippers. It took Pete some time to find the Big Dipper and Little Dipper. Many star groups could be made by the mind to form a similar pattern or "dipper". However there was only one Big Dipper with the right size and shape. From the big dipper she located the Little Dipper's tail and the North Star down at the tip toward the horizon. It structured and defined the night sky in the mind of the little outsider.

• • •

Pete learned how to avoid being stalked. She practiced vigilance. She also would turn back on her own trail to find tracks of others on top of her own. She would pay attention to her scent cone direction, the ground cover on which she walked, and movement. The eye picks up motion better than shape in a dense environment. Pete was a quick and eager learner.

• • •

Her sense of hearing and smell grew to be nothing short of astonishing. Whether it was genetic or because she had underutilized other parts of her brain, Pete located by sense of smell better than any human Selina had ever known. She could smell things far better than Selina, therefore Selina was also learning during these teachings.

Selina started a program of hiding things which Pete found by using scent instead of the normal human custom of sight or thought or logic. This further developed the skill within Pete, making it her go-to method of locating objects or directions in many situations. Hiding a bucket filled with water was particularly easy for Pete to find.

Scent had also become a large factor in the relationship between Selina and Pete. Upon greeting, Selina took both of Pete's hands and kissed them lightly across the knuckles. In turn Pete would pull Selina's hands close to her nose and mouth. She inhaled in a series of short sniffs to 'see'; bacon and cabbage for dinner last night, biscuits and ham and eggs for breakfast, laundry done that morning and the oil lamps had been filled. A story told by aromas.

Chapter 12 – Pete's Classroom

It was early morning when Selina, now pregnant again, looked out the window and saw Pete age six put her finger to the sky. Noticing the odd posture she stopped to watch. A few moments latter a monarch flitted to the end of her finger. Pete gave the butterfly head tilts, eye glances and hand gestures.

That afternoon Selina wanted to know more seeing Pete had an understanding beyond her own. Selina asked Pete about the butterfly by her own hand gestures.

It was the language they had developed using posture, hands and darting eyes to show, tell and otherwise exchange ideas from the time when the spoken word was forbidden. In this case the use of words couldn't cover the concepts anyway.

Pete's eyes went vacant as they appeared to travel to a place for her eyes only. She placed her right hand in the air for several minutes as if it were a lightning rod to summon some energy and then brought it slowly back to the ground in front of them. A jay swooped down a few seconds later, tilted its head back and let out a greeting at their feet. "yah yah yah." The arrival of the jay brought tears of joy and wonder to Selina's eyes.

• • •

Pete's sight could detect subtle differences in body language, movement, or when something was out of place in her surroundings. She coupled this ability with her constant awareness. Pete was eerily vigilant.

Pete's gaze was like being searched. She would frisk and give a patting down both inside and out. Whoever or whatever looked in her direction always found a pair of watchful green eyes ready to return a stare.

• • •

Pete's camp on the creek near the corrals was filled with brook trout. Selina brought a line and hook and tied them onto a stick five feet long from the stream bank. Next they found bait which was in abundance. She showed Pete worms under rocks away from the creek bank, hellgrammites under rocks touching the water, and grasshoppers offering a challenge to catch. Pete had a great time grabbing the grasshoppers. She was reluctant to give up the chase and start the next lesson and game of fishing.

Selina hooked a grasshopper through the wing and back plate and gave Pete the pole to let the hopper set easily on the water and drift in the current. It had barely hit the surface when the line and grasshopper in a quick splash jerked below. Pete pulled up the prize and was now hooked herself on the game of fishing.

Next Selina unwound a piece of twine to obtain several small grayish brown threads. She cut two pieces of feather brought from the chicken house similar in color to the grasshoppers. She wound and tied the feathers with the thread near the eye of the hook making a head. The remainder of the feathers formed a body of the imitation grasshopper. She handed Pete the feathered hook and had her tie it on the end of the line which was learned from a previous lesson. After an hour they had colorful spotted brook trout cleaned and ready to cook and smoke.

The next lesson was on making a shortened sewing needle into a hook. Fire helped bend the needle and two rocks were used to pound the end to add a barb. The barb made it more difficult for the fish to slip free from the end of the hook. She used a small smooth river stone as a whetstone to shape the sharp end as desired. She gave all the hooks to Pete and returned to the house.

• • •

Pete gained knowledge of tanning skins brought back from a time Selina would have rather forgotten when she was a slave. Selina brought out a freshly-skinned lamb hide and a finished hide she had worked on herself to show the end result made into a hat to keep ears and head warm. The tanning process involved the cleaning of the hide and removal of flesh and fat. Then stretching and drying the hide until a proper time for tanning. Several techniques were learned including soaking in urine or crushed tree bark, or squishing brains on the flesh side. Boiling the skins a great deal loosened and allowed fur to be scraped off to make rawhide or furless leather for summer moccasins.

Chapter 13 – Birthing Time

Pete always worked with Karl at birthing time. At age eight she was in charge of birthing without Karl's help. It had her up all night and day with only small naps. She was responsible for isolating the ewe and her lamb until the ewe recognized the lamb by smell. If successful the ewes were turned back to the flock always able to find the smell of the newborn. Pete was able to use her own sense of smell and remember which lamb belonged to which ewe without the aid of markings.

Lambs before they were put on summer range had tails docked for cleanliness, ears notched for identification, and males were castrated. Pete could take a lamb's front and hind feet in hand and dump them on their rump accomplishing these tasks with a few quick moves of her knife. Her hands and eyes were like a twinkling star.

• • •

Pete had acquired a great deal of quickness. She saw the strength of her opponents could not affect her if she could not be caught or touched.

In the beginning Pete chased Grub and tried to grab his bobbed tail squealing in delight when he let her win the game. By the time she was six Grub learned these games were best played by the younger dogs not plagued by injury. He sat on his tail until she gave up the game. By the age of eight she'd corner, tag or tackle any dog on the ranch. When they attempted to return the favor she would bob, weave and backpedal to stay clear of their grasps.

• • •

Selina had taught her to use a whetstone to sharpen the knife Karl had given her. Pete learned the angle of the blade to the stone was to be exact if it were to hold an edge yet be sharp as a razor. If done correctly she could shave the hair off her arm with one quick stroke.

Her skills with the skinning knife evolved. She started using her skinning knife as a toy. The risk and danger of catching the rotating razor sharp knife kept her engaged. She put it in the air with one slow revolution, catching the bone handle on the way down. She increased the speed of rotation over the months until she was comfortable at two revolutions. She progressed until she calmly reached into the spinning mixture of handle and blade and grabbed bone avoiding the lethal flashing steel.

Chapter 14 - Weapons

Pete was naturally attracted to weapons. They were her toys. The sport of rock throwing made a stone a toy if thrown at a target until she could consistently hit her mark.

A sling, if used properly, would add distance and force to the stone as it was an extension of the arm. The sling was made by Selina to fit Pete's size from one long piece of supple leather with a pouch in the middle looking like an eye patch. The pouch was made by slightly dampening the leather and pressing and working a small round stone into the pocket to stretch and make a place for the stone as the area dried.

The sling was the most difficult weapon for Pete to master. It may not have been an accident Selina chose this weapon as her first. Grub sat like the dutiful parent and watched the practice sessions generally turning his back and ears as the screaming commenced. The lesson on patience and work ethic was as useful in Pete's life as the sling itself. Pete, like Grub, was no friend to defeat.

In the beginning it was a large source of frustration. It was tricky to learn the motion to get the sling started without dropping the stone to the ground. Then a moment later, to release only one end of the leather at the exact right moment to send the stone on a successful journey to hit a target. The easy part was finding projectiles or sling stones nature readily provided.

Eventually Pete learned it was not the sling needing work but how she handled it. She knew she couldn't be beaten unless she first admitted defeat. She had no words to describe the feeling but she knew it just the same. And there was also need for the calm she learned from Raven after the stolen sweetbread incident. Several deep breaths were required during each practice day. Sometimes more.

She eventually got some improvement after months of practice. Maybe it was luck but she hit a post with a stone. It wasn't exactly where she wanted to hit on the post and it was only once but she did hit it. And with that success a war whoop was heard around the corral. The practicing continued until she was proficient at not only hitting a post but an object placed on top of the post. She always kept the sling with her wrapped around her head holding her hair from distracting her.

The throwing knife was different from her skinning knife as it had to be more durable. The handle on her skinning knife if used for throwing would crack apart from the steel if hit broadside or hit handle first. The throwing knife was a solid piece of steel with rawhide wrapped on the handle. It was well balanced making it rotate evenly when thrown correctly. She started practicing with the throwing knife after the sling.

Pete played with the throwing knife like her sister had with dolls. At first she threw it at a corral post until it penetrated blade first at two paces every time. Then she moved back to four paces until she had the rotation just right. She continued until she was proficient at eight paces and if she ever missed she would start over again at two paces until she never missed. Once proficient at hitting the post within eight paces she placed a mark on the post and started the game over again making it necessary to not only stick the post but slice the mark as well.

Pete's last toy was a bow and arrow. She started with a bow later the same year as her throwing knife. The skill of making a bow and arrow was not learned well by Selina during her time with the Lacota but she nonetheless gave Pete the idea of shooting the slender piece of wood with feathers on one end. Selina knew the selection of wood for the bow was important but she didn't know which wood or tree to select. She decided to let Pete take the lead and only give Pete the idea of the bow by making a small replica that shot less than ten feet. Pete took to the idea right away and practiced with the small bow until the bow broke when it became too dry.

• • •

Pete set upon the task of finding better stouter wood for her bow-making. She not only wanted it to pull harder so as to shoot the arrow further but she didn't want it to break when fully pulled to her cheek. She knew she needed good bow wood but what tree would help her?

She went to the creek and stood by a cottonwood. She looked up and down the trunk wondering if he could help. The tree gave an odd shake with the help of a gentle breeze. Pete took two steps back and held her hands out as if they were limbs and gave a questioning look.

Cottonwood knowing she would not be satisfied with its softwood, gave her directions to Oak. It was there she learned about hard wood and how proud Oak was of his strength. *Cut and shape in the direction of growth.* She needed to have the grain run the length of the bow and not across it to keep it from splitting when fully dry.

It was not a trial and error process. It was sit first with the trees and second become one with their way of life. Listen but not with her ears. She learned about tree rings of growth and the grain of a tree that follows those rings. She inspected fallen branches and trunks to find the truth of the matter.

The oak branch was too thick and not the correct profile requiring carving to get the needed shape. It would be whittled top and bottom with the thickest portion in the middle and thinner with notches to hold a bow string at both the ends. It also would take more strength to pull but in turn, would send the slender arrow further with more power behind it.

The bow was "strung" by placing one end on the ground with string loop in a notch near the end of the bow. Then placing a knee in the middle bending it while pulling the upper end toward her, allowing a string loop to be slid up the bow and held in place by a second notch. Arrows were made by finding very straight sticks and placing a groove at one end of the arrow to hold onto the string of the bow. Often they needed some whittling to make them smooth and fly straight.

Duck feathers left by the large white duck were shaved and glued to the grooved end creating an arrow that would fly true. The white feathers made the arrow easier to find in the brush. No sharp point was initially made on the arrow nor was an arrow head utilized. Selina thought it might keep the barnyard safer. Eventually when Pete got proficient she used sharpened bones tied firmly to the end of the arrow to make hunting arrows.

It was one of Pete's favorite pastimes for many months requiring numerous replacement strings as they wore and broke. Eventually Pete's strength increased and she needed a new stouter bow and the bow making process started again.

She found a use for blunt arrows when taking grouse. A sharpened point would often deflect off their wing feathers allowing the bird to escape. They also could tear a hole in otherwise good breast meat. The blunt end dazed them until she could gather them and quickly dispatch them with her knife. Later she found binding a blunt rock to the arrow tip would more surely stun them. In all cases she was respectful of the life she had taken and acknowledged their importance and sacrifice. The intent of the unspoken message done with hand gestures was always similar. *When you see our Creator, give thanks.*

Chapter 15 - Summer Camp

The old scabbard at Pete's side was weathered but held her new bone-handled knife well. She had sharpened the steel blade nearly out of existence on her old knife. Pete, now nine years, continued wearing the leather sling around her head. It held her short dark sun-bleached brown hair in place and away from her eyes. She had a lean build, wearing coveralls and sporting bare feet. Grub, now with a greying muzzle was limping at her side as she delivered supper dishes to the corral fence post.

Her focus went to the porch where Caroline, in a dress and ribbons, was darning socks. Her brother Karl Jr., in coveralls and age three, was playing in the dirt out front.

Pete took her skinning knife, not her throwing knife, and threw it at a corral fencepost. She no longer was concerned about ever missing and ruining the bone handle. The post showed the marks and wear of many hits. It stuck blade-first in the post. WHISH THUD.

She wiggled it out and gently threw the knife up in the air several times, rotating it slowly as she moved back five paces. She grabbed it, turned quickly, and flicked the knife sticking the post where she intended.

She moved to the watering trough where a sharpening stone sat nearby. She dipped the stone in the water and worked on the edge of the knife.

• • •

It was early in the evening with the first stars starting to show. Selina, displaying a little grey in her hair, strolled toward the corrals with a small cloth bag in her hand. Pete nodded. Selina returned the nod and joined her. Selina put her palms up in a questioning gesture. "Summer Camp"?

Pete pointed to the North Star, a bright twinkling speck near the horizon. She put her back to it and pointed with both arms to the south as if she was directing traffic.

In the dwindling light Selina pointed to weeds on the ground. She rubbed her stomach and put palms up. Pete selected a few leaves of Lamb's Quarter from the weeds at their feet having a triangular shape and rough edge.

Selina raised her eyes toward Pete's head. Pete took off her sling and Selina felt the softness and inspected the cup that would hold the stone. Selina gave an approving nod.

Selina gave a bow pulling gesture bringing the imaginary bowstring to her cheek.

Pete gave a quick negative shake to her head.

Selina gave a questioning look with palms up.

Pete made a gesture with her two forefingers touching each other. Then pulled them apart as if they were broken. She shook her head with a negative facial expression.

Selina nodded with a soft grunt understanding the problem. The twine Selina had was not strong enough.

"You go with Karl to summer camp."

Pete wasn't happy sharing the prairie with Karl.

Selina handed Pete the small cloth sack. Selina put her fingers to her mouth and made a sick gesture with her hand touching her stomach. "Dried inky cap mushroom. Put this in his food. If he has alcohol he gets sick."

Pete nodded as they walked. She stroked imaginary long hair down her shoulder. Selina shook her head no.

"Caroline get lost, frightened, and animals eat her."

Pete rolled her shoulders and dangled her arms miming a four legged animal. Then she touched her stomach and opened her mouth like she was heaving. Pete smiled at her own joke of making an animal sick if they ate her sister.

Chapter 16 – Greener Grass

Living out of the wagon with Karl was to be an improvement for Pete. She would have plenty of groceries to choose from including Selina's chocolate baked goods. Her favorite.

It was Karl's intention to make sheepherding at Summer Camp something she enjoyed and looked forward to. However his plan had flaws. First she had to share the space with Karl at least some of the time. She also had to cook what he preferred to eat. No amount of his yelling would improve the chef.

• • •

Pete herded the sheep towards Summer Camp with the help of four dogs at a slower pace than Karl's wagon. Grub stayed by Pete's side never involved with the herding of sheep. Pete saw a rabbit sniffing the air, nose twitching. Pete did the same to pick up the scent.

Pete was clearly confident and took the responsibility of the herd. The dogs kept stragglers within the herd with little effort. She stepped into the herd and gently helped young lambs stuck or having difficulties.

Her hearing distinguished the clatter of dragonfly wings, then the buzz of a bumblebees, ending with the whir of quail wings. Her hearing and sense of smell were keener than her sight.

By the time she danced into camp, Karl had the wagon unhooked. He'd set up camp, grained and hobbled his horse, and was awaiting her arrival with a smile on his face. The music of freedom and wide open spaces kept her dancing and working the sheep all day. The melody quickly subsided as she saw Karl.

"What's for supper?"

Pete shrugged an answer of unknowing. Karl went up into the sheep wagon and called for her. Pete dragged herself into the wagon.

Karl pointed to different cupboards and drawers. "Potato, cabbage and bacon. Supper tonight. We store food in here and down there. Here's salt, pepper, matches. You can look around and find things. Put the bacon in the pan and fry it crisp. Cut these vegetables and put them in the pot."

She was clearly distracted with Karl's presence. She put bacon in the fry pan looking at him rather than the bacon.

"You have to build a fire in the stove. It won't get hot by itself."

She put kindling in and lit it with a match. Karl grabbed a liquor bottle from a cupboard, opened it and took a swallow. He left Pete to cook as he stepped down from the wagon.

Pete cut potatoes and cabbage and dumped them in with salt into the pot. She located the sack of dried crushed inky cap mushrooms as a precaution against alcohol abuse and added them. Satisfied she stepped down out of the wagon while supper cooked.

"Did you have any trouble today?"

Pete shrugged and wagged her head no. She wandered over to check on the sheep and dogs nearby.

About thirty minutes later Karl drew his nose up and sniffed the air.

"Pete, come here. Did you put water in the pot?"

Pete gave a quick shake "no" with her head.

"Pete, quick, dump water in the pot."

Pete flew up the steps into the smoking wagon. She grabbed a water jug and dumped it into the smoking charred mess and then jumped down from the wagon.

"What's my dinner look like?"

She rolled her eyes.

Karl scowled and muttered to himself as he climbed the steps into the wagon. Smoke billowed as he entered. Starving he stared into the drowned blackened murky mess in the pot. With some reservation and a deep breath he grabbed a spoon and started shoveling it down. It tasted worse than it looked. He hollered, "I can't eat any more of this garbage." He picked up his whisky bottle and took another swig.

• • •

Pete was outside studying a few trout feeding on the surface of the stream when Karl came down from the wagon. He opened his mouth to say something when an odd pale look washed down his face. Without a single word, he closed his mouth and hurried by Pete. A loud retching sound was heard across the prairie. Maybe the mushrooms didn't agree with him.

• • •

Later the same evening loud snores came from inside the sheep wagon. Pete was nurturing a fire by gently feeding it with skinny morsels of wood. It was an art to keep the temperature so as to brown, not burn, her dinner. She rolled freshly-cooked trout meat from the bone.

Chapter 17 - Solitude

The next morning Karl stood over Pete with his rifle in hand. "You learn to cook or I'm not coming back any time soon. You'll be here miles from home, all alone, for at least FIVE months. Understand?"

Pete nodded, stifling the joy the German words brought to her ears. All she had to do was be a terrible cook. Easy. She was off to a great start.

"I hope you shoot better than you cook. It's important to have coyotes afraid of you or they kill my sheep. And NEVER point a rifle at anything unless you mean to kill it."

He moved the action back and inserted a shell. He put the butt to his right shoulder and balanced the rifle in his left hand with this right hand around the stock and trigger guard.

"Put it up to your shoulder like this. Now you try it."

Karl handed the rifle to Pete and pointed to the forward site and then the rear site. "Line up the top of this forward site with the rear V site and put them on your target. Aim at that rock out there by the bush. Squeeze the trigger, don't jerk it."

The rifle was awkward and unsteady in Pete's hands. The stock was too long for her size, forcing the trigger too far from her shoulder. It was end heavy and waved all around. BANG.

Dirt flew fifteen feet to the left of the target rock on the ground. After reloading the single shot rifle, she shot far right and low of the target. Karl shook his head in disgust.

"You wave the rifle all around. Maybe you could steady your elbow on the ground if you lie on your stomach. When I get back, I want to see dead coyotes, not dead sheep."

Pete nodded but with no heart in it.

"It's the only way out here."

The rifle was a noisy business making her ears ring for hours. She didn't like the rifle kicking her shoulder either but Karl was firm on its use.

"I'll leave gear for a tent camp with an extra tarp. I'll be back by horseback in a few days. Do you think you'll be ok without me?"

Pete nodded more enthusiastically.

• • •

Karl left with the horse and wagon. He was proud of his hired hand at age nine and what he had been able to teach her. It brought a smile to his face to see his plan working.

There were wagon tracks and the smell of gun powder as a reminder of Karl. She took her bare foot and started erasing his wagon tracks by her camp. As she finished tidying up, the air filled with more pleasant scents. Sounds became clearer like the prairie dog bark in the distance and the songbird from the nearby bush.

When she turned back to the pile of gear dumped on the ground, exasperation showed on her face. The heap had a heavy fry pan, small pan and lid, coffee pot, bowls, water tote bucket, plates, cups, cooking utensils, two safe food storage camp boxes with lockable sides holding the smell of bread and sweet chocolate cakes which did not escape her notice, rifle, ammunition, a large bedroll wrapped in a heavy tarp, and a spare tarp with tools of the sheepherder's trade like pliers and sheep hook. To the side were her tent, her clothes and mat, and bow with quiver. Maybe she could find a way of putting her tent in Karl's pile in trade for the sweet cakes.

Pete left camp with her handmade bow, quiver and arrows. She turned back for a quick glance at the pile of gear and saw Grub guarding the pile. She raised her hand as a signal for Grub to come to her side.

• • •

Every few days she moved her camp to accommodate better pasture and keep a good vantage point to the sheep. It required numerous trips between the previous camp and the new one to carry all the heavy bulky camp gear. She would have preferred to have less gear with fewer luxuries along with fewer trips. She didn't want the wagon even if Karl did offer it. Rigging the horse and wagon would only add to the workload if she was tall enough. She would also have to keep the horse in sight or hobbled.

Her ability to keep her flock under control with little use of dogs was nothing short of remarkable. She knew before the sheep did where they wanted to go for the better pasture, water and a place to bed down.

She sensed trouble before it could reach the herd. So did Grub by displaying more alertness. Raven also helped, more often than not, by pacing back and forth in a nervous manner.

Pete looked forward to the vast expanse of range and the freedom she felt when left alone. She had always liked choices and this was the perfect place for it. In all directions the solitude made her feel welcome.

There was no trepidation with getting lost as she had been practicing for years with Selina even after blindfolding and dizzily spinning which was fun in itself. Panic shuts down everything. To her the open prairie was the same as walking around the barn.

There was no anxiety about being attacked by wild animals although she had a great respect for the power of the larger carnivores. She knew she had a place in nature and felt comfortable within the natural cycle of birth and death. Fear only existed around Karl and breaking his rules.

Chapter 18 – Predators

She hiked confidently, eyes up and alert, circling the sheep. She stared intently at a bird's nest with woven strands of grass and twigs. She thought she could build structures for herself someday and not need the tent in her pile.

She passed by a swampy cattail area then on to a hill overlooking the sheep. She squatted over tracks of several coyotes. Pete moved to Focused Attention looking at coyote tracks and scat. She measured the tracks with her fingers. She bent down and sniffed the scat without knowing why. The sniff gave her the coyotes activities, where it hunted, the location of the den, gender and preferred diet. When she looked up she saw a grouse. She pulled out an arrow with a blunt rock firmly attached by rawhide to the end. She nocked the arrow and looked down past the rock at her prey.

She shot well and stunned the bird. She walked over arms outstretched as if they were wings of a hawk and swooped down on her quarry. She quickly dispatched her dinner with a slash of her knife. She inspected both ends of the arrow before returning it to her quiver.

Pete picked up the grouse in both hands and motioned, arms outstretched to the sky, then slowly down past herself to the earth, then back to the sky. She laid the bird down and stroked its feathers. No words were spoken but acknowledgement and appreciation was given. She accepted her part in making the cycle come full circle.

She put the bird breast down on the ground, stood on the wings outspread, and pulled up on the feet. The bird easily came apart exposing the breast meat and wings under foot. The internal organs dangled from the back that was attached to the feet in her hands. She threw the nutritious guts to Grub. She took a few feathers from the wing and tail and stuck them in her leather sling headband.

She returned to camp and built her customary small fire. She sat close to the flames with Grub at her side. Coyotes howled in the distance as dusk closed in. Stars began poking holes and filling the sky with twinkles.

• • •

The next morning Grub sat overlooking the sheep near the tent. He had a slight waggle to his tail. Raven paced back and forth by his side. The sound of coyotes were in the distance.

Two coyotes peered over a ridge. The four dogs guarding the herd chased them out of sight. Three other coyotes came from the opposite direction, skulking close to the herd. Grub gave a low soft rumbling growl deep in his throat. Raven continued pacing.

The three coyotes continued their slinking and weaving toward the sheep. A few sheep got up and moved away from the approaching coyotes except for one ewe still lying on the ground facing away. A coyote made his run toward the remaining ewe. The other two positioned themselves so there could be no escape.

The ewe started to stand but clearly too late. The predator was focused on his attack. As she stood, the sheepskin dropped to the ground. With bow and arrow nocked and steady in her hands Pete turned and pulled the bowstring all in one motion. The arrow had a sharpened cutting bone attached by rawhide to the end. Shewsht.

The arrow flew hitting bone and flesh as the coyote charged. CHUP A second arrow coasted into position nocked and ready should she get the chance. And she did. Shewshsht CHUP. The last coyote zigzagged leaving a crooked trail.

• • •

Pete scraped the underside of a coyote hide. She put the hide aside with a satisfied look. She checked her arrows. One of the feathers was missing. She pulled one of the grouse feathers from her headband. She measured it against the other two feathers and trimmed it to match with her knife.

• • •

Pete returned to the swampy cattail area seen the previous day and dug roots with a sharp digging stick. She put them into her woven collection sack. On her way back to camp she checked on her herd.

• • •

The next morning Pete was up early looking over her sheep at first light. Crows and magpies squabbled in the distance. She walked toward the clamor.

A doe was dead and partially eaten. Pete bent down finding coyote tracks. Something moved off to her side. A new born fawn blinked in the bushes. Nothing escaped her awareness including the well-camouflaged eyelid of the fawn.

She rubbed a hand on the doe's fur and stretched it toward the fawn. The fawn moved its head closer to the ground as Pete approached with her scented hand stretched out. Pete gave a soothing high pitched lullaby sound. "Uhmm.. emmmum… ummm"

The wet nose of the fawn wiggled as it picked up the scent from her hand. Pete slowly pulled away a few inches and the little fawn stretched its neck to take in the smell, being careful not to move his front cloven hooves any closer to Pete.

Pete backed up a little further and made the sound again. "Uhmm..emmmum… ummma"

The fawn gave up the fear and came toward her making a pathetic sound similar to a baby lamb. MEHAAA MEHAAA. Pete slowly rose to her feet and returned to camp with the fawn following, legs gyrating.

• • •

Pete slowly brought a bottle of ewe milk to the fawn's lips. She bumped her nose against the bottle, responding more to smell than sight. Licking her nose and lips the fawn came at the bottle more aggressively. Pete gave a low pitched giggle together with a soothing sound for the little orphan.

• • •

Karl rode up to an empty camp easily located by sheep sign and his gear. A gunny sack with provisions hung from his saddle horn. He dropped the bag in the camp. Dogs barked continuously.

He went on where sheep grazed and mumbled. "No Pete." He dismounted and tied the reins around the saddle horn but loose enough for the horse to graze. He walked toward the sheep and hollered. "Pe… eete. Pete!"

Pete silently inched behind Karl. "Yuh."

Karl's shoulders lept up. His feet followed. "Heh! Don't do that. Make some noise first or something. Everything ok? Coyotes should be a problem this time of year. Any losses?"

Pete nodded, agreeing to anything he said.

"You've lost sheep?"

Pete quickly shook her head 'no' to satisfy Karl's quick temper.

"Nine, all goot, all goot." Pete pointed to skinned carcasses on the ground nearby.

"No problems?"

Pete gave another quick shake of her head 'no'.

"I've been riding since 4 AM. Feed me and I'll get back to my ranch work."

Pete showed a happy face. She whirled with light steps and jogged back to camp. Karl took long fast strides but soon walked alone.

Pete went to the nearby creek. Near the water's edge, there were rocks with cold water slowly moving through them. Her cooking pot was wedged between rocks with the lid above water. A flat rock weighed down the lid and pot to keep the food inside cool and secure.

Pete put a few thin dry sticks on her smoldering morning fire. The sticks come to life with fire when she blew a couple of long steady breaths. She placed the pot near the fire happily stirring.

Karl broke the silence. "Got coffee?"

Pete shook her head no.

"No coffee? You better be careful."

Pete looked up with some confusion.

"I'm not kidding Pete. I am important to your survival. Emm… what's in this?"

Pete made hand gestures for the long ears of a rabbit.

"I'd rather not know I'm eating a long eared rodent. Next time I ask what's on the menu, ignore it."

• • •

Karl left summer camp towards the ranch. Pete took out a coyote hide to do some more scraping. She had several more beside it.

The young fawn slept in the bushes behind her. A yearling doe bounced out of hiding to her side. Grub came to her on the other side. Pete stroked Grub's head gently. The doe put her head on Pete's lap for a nap.

Raven flew in and strutted around the fire pit, with one wing down. It approached Karl's lunch plate with spoon and several morsels of food. Raven ate the food and Pete gave a "you're welcome" nod to the bird. Raven gave a quick look of acknowledgement and flew off with the spoon. Pete leapt up stroking her knife at her side. The thief took a scolding. Grunk Gerunk! All good fun for Raven. He flew back over her head dropping the spoon nearly hitting her.

Chapter 19 – Doors Open and Close

Pete's facial features, now scarcely thirteen, weren't cute but exotically beautiful with an olive complexion, high cheekbones, straight nose completing an angular face, and full lips. Pete kept the physique of a young slender good-looking boy as she edged into her teens. She had thin bones, square shoulders and sinewy well-defined muscles.

Her short dark brown hair was slightly sun bleached and barely covered her ears. She kept her hair trimmed with her knife, cutting it by feel when it got too long and catching debris. It was held in place with her sling.

Her green-eyed gaze was one not easily forgotten by man or beast. She stared with total abandon giving her entire attention to the tiniest detail like any successful predator. Her movements were always smooth, balanced and graceful, never fitful.

Pete was confident in her use of weapons and in her environment which generally was not inhabited with people. She found humans untrustworthy like coyotes or coons too close to the henhouse. She was comfortable with her place in nature, no less than the trees and stars. And no better.

She had no problems or fears associated with the starting of her period the year before. As instructed by Selina she placed dry leaves or soft rabbit fur in her underpants and changed or washed them several times a day as needed. She had recognized the difference between male and female farm animals and when dogs were in estrus. She assumed her period was similar to a bitch spotting blood. The thought gave her another feeling of belonging and fitting into the grand scheme of things.

• • •

Pete stood near the corral fence watching Karl and a young Karl Junior, now age seven, helping with sheep. She walked to the barn and smelled the flora revealing the fragrance of spring.

Pete had a woven mat and summer bedding in the corner of the barn and Grub laid on it. A thin Grub was showing his age with a totally grey muzzle and had difficulty getting up. There was a dish of food uneaten in front of him on the floor. She got him up but only for a few strides and he stopped. She returned to her sleeping area and motioned with her hand palm down on her bedding. Grub complied. Pete gently stroked his head, then left.

Pete returned a couple hours later to find a raccoon facing Grub and eating his food. Shaking, Grub looked up at her and back to the coon. Pete pulled her knife. As silently as the moon moves behind a cloud she approached the coon from behind and cut the throat of the intruder. Pete threw the carcass to the side with the same emotion as having removed a sliver from her foot. She had not killed the coon with anger for she had learned anger and fear were not her friend.

She laid down beside Grub with her arm over her longtime friend and mentor. She gently put her hand in his fur as she had for many years. Their relationship had come full circle. Grubby had protected her from a coon in her first year in the barn. She had the opportunity to return the favor.

• • •

It had been a particularly hard winter and Grub, now in his teens, showed increased arthritic pain. He was considered quite old for a sheep dog. His diet was supplemented from Pete's hunting and gathering keeping him well fed. He remained at his post over the years near her head while she slept. The previous winter she started throwing a doubled blanket over him to help shed the winter's cold.

This morning however he did not start licking and grooming as was his customary exercise. Pete reached up to feel the comfort of his warm body under the thick tufted fur. She sensed only cold. She grabbed a little deeper in the fur and found more of the same. There was no movement with his breathing and a deep hollow place started growing within her chest. Tears developed from her eyes and cut a path down her cheek.

Pete felt Grub wouldn't leave regardless of his pain unless he knew she was ready. She was pleased his pain had ended but the crater remained. It was Grub who had licked away a thousand tears and gave her support in that first hard year in the barn. Pete had another tear forming in the corner of her eye. It didn't drop and she didn't wipe it away. All natural for a longtime friend and mentor.

Pete rose from her mat next to Grub and dressed slowly. She walked to the dead coon, picked it up by the hind leg, and exited the barn.

At the far end of the pasture, there was a dead pile. It was a pile of decimated carcasses of dead sheep, coyotes and ranch garbage. Raven, two coyotes, one vulture and one magpie were in the area. The two coyotes were quick to run. Raven looked up and studied Pete. Nothing disturbed the magpie and buzzard. She flung the coon onto the pile and returned to the barn.

She left with Grub's body in her arms and walked toward the dead pile. Only Raven remained at the dump. Pete continued past and walked toward the open prairie and a rock outcrop.

She placed him gently down. She removed rocks and dirt with a stick and her hands for several hours. She placed him in the tomb and covered him first with leaves and spring flowers. Eventually she returned the earth. Then she piled and rolled large rocks on all sides until she felt his body was safe from the coyotes he hated.

She sat remembering their adventures and what he had given of himself to her. A vulture drifted in on the light breeze to land on the top of the rock outcrop. Pete was attuned to the signs connected to everything natural. The vulture's arrival was a reminder of the abstract. The earth's soil was a birthing place. Life is a cycle, without end.

• • •

The sun was heading toward the horizon pulling down the dusky shade. Raven gently floated in not wanting to intrude. They both surveyed a common scene at the end of an uncommon day through a thin spotty cloud layer.

Pete looked back to the sky. She saw a translucent Grubby with a bounce to his step trotting away without the limp. He turned back in her direction. His ears were held with full attention and excitement on what lay ahead. His figure was in the wispy clouds near the horizon and he gave a slow wag of his stubby tail. She knew to her core Grubby was free.

She felt a vast sense of purpose with the new adventure before her. She had no inkling as to what it was. She would leave and without doubt find the next door open and waiting. All she had to do was to look.

Raven looked intently into her face. Having her attention he gave a couple of croaks. He bounced twice with both wings out to the south and west toward the setting sun. The sounds and sign were crisp and clear. WHOOP WHOOP WHOOP. He returned to her side. Pete nodded and rose from Grub's headstone.

Chapter 20 – The End and Beginning

The following morning in the barn she took inventory. She had two choices. Travel slower, with greater effort and more luxury, or go with less baggage and have freedom and speed. The latter would have her more dependent upon what she found on her way connecting her to Universe. She decided upon the second alternative, knowing the possible hazards. She could mitigate most by stopping early enough each day to gather what she might need and set up a good camp and bed.

She left behind warm bedding and many items used for meal preparation. They would have saved her work each evening making her bedding and meals.

A last and most important possession would make the trip regardless. She had room for the life-force of Grubby. A smile came as it always had with Grub's presence.

Pete never had any close human companionship except Selina which had been strained by Karl's intervention. Loosing Grub was like losing a tooth. He couldn't stay anymore but probing the hole felt funny for the rest of her life.

The barnyard animals were more like work friends. Beside Grubby and Raven she had only short-term acquaintances with the local mice, ground squirrels and the many feathered friends she found along her childhood path. She would do the same as she traveled. She would pass the evenings finding out the local gossip and would be eager to pass it on at her next stop.

Pete's general direction was set by Raven. She would first travel more south than west and then when the time and place looked and felt right, she would start her journey over the Great Divide. Her exact direction was chosen to accommodate the signs and smell of people, the best traveling terrain, swollen rivers, and keeping a good stream to her side whenever possible.

Pete's curiosity was always on the prowl and one might think her speed would be slowed substantially by her many new encounters. But her curiosity was even more compelling and it kept her moving to see what was over the next hill. Selina had described the Great Divide running like a backbone mostly north and south. She wanted to see this wall of mountains and experience the creatures that lived like she did.

• • •

The possessions were laid out. She looked twice at her warm bedroll and her bow again, but decided against both. Her sling made it easy to take small game like rabbits, frogs or her favorite evening meal, grouse. If she were to use her bow it would ruin an arrow most days whether she hit her prey or not. Her hands would also be full and not free for other uses.

After viewing the pile she set out to cut a purse or pack from leather to contain the possessions. She tied the purse together using strips she cut from scrap leather. Lastly she cut two wide straps. One strap went over her shoulder and the other around her waist to keep the purse from flopping as she jogged.

She took a long last walk around. She found nothing left behind worth the space. She said goodbye to Rooster, the chickens, pigs and their horse. She thought of Whitey who had lived a long healthy life after their clash, as a nicer duck. She got a special sentiment for lessons learned.

• • •

The next morning, Pete dried herself from her early morning bath and put on her jogging clothes. She wore rawhide pants cut at the knees, a sleeveless rawhide shirt and her headband.

She strolled around the corrals and gave a last nod, smile or pat to the animals. Selina was on the porch watching the goodbyes in the corrals.

Pete put on her packed purse and walked outside the barn.

She faced Selina and put her arms out from her sides. She mimed an eagle's smooth and powerful flight using shoulders and arms. She turned to the south and west and mimed the launching of an arrow from an imaginary bow.

She turned back to Selina now joined by Caroline. Selina nodded and clasped her hands together sending Pete a prayer of good journey. Looking to the heavens, spreading her arms as if she too could feel favorable winds: *"Daughter, go with Him and listen. Everything will have His voice. Walk in His beauty and respect all things He's made. Look for wisdom hidden in every leaf and rock. Find compassion for what we have done."*

Caroline waved a small goodbye with only raised fingers. Pete gave her a smile and a nod. An acknowledgement of them going their separate ways.

The End and Beginning

Epilogue

Pete was my grandmother. None in the immediate family called her by the name my great grandfather Karl had given her. She was a quiet woman offering few words of either discipline or encouragement. She had a gentle smile I can easily see through the clouds of time. I do wish I could pepper her with questions after learning of her beginnings from my mother. But of course I would probably get the same reception as did Essie.

Pete's written words "I was happily free to flow in the great river of Universe unencumbered by the limitations of society bringing exhilaration and enchantments…" brings to mind Abraham Maslow's "Peak Experiences" developed decades later. His self-actualized person combined focused attention, lack of self-consciousness, flawless performance and elation. Pete consciously knew Piñon guided her travels but did she know Universe had a hand on her pen?

I was around ten years of age when she died of a malignant brain tumor. The last few days before she passed she spoke nothing but German. My mom said she had never heard her speak a word of German until that time. The doctor said it wasn't too unusual. When the brain receives pressure from a tumor, long forgotten or repressed events and abilities can be remembered.

John Muir was the great grand uncle of my spouse. His father was quite strict with his Bible teachings and kept John busy working long hours on the farm in Wisconsin. He eventually walked those many miles through the US, South America, Canada and Alaska. Both Pete and Muir had covered great distances on foot. John's handwritten letters include pressed leaves and radiate his exceptional energy and love of nature. A letter and his father's Bible sit on special spots in our home. Yes, we never get to go back but oh if we could someday all sit around the same campfire.

"The clearest way into the Universe is through a forest wilderness." John Muir

He capitalized the 'U' in Universe.

About the authors

The authors are outside people searching for nature's splendor and a road connecting to lesser-known places. Summers are spent in the high Rocky Mountains. How they grapple, write, and understand life may be better illustrated than described. Above is their modern day sheepherder's wagon designed and built by them for their winter travels in the southwest.

Some cabins still standing in 1981 around the compound.

The evidence has since been torn down.

Inside a shorter chinked cabin with a fireplace built for winter.

Authors showing height of a taller cabin in 1981